CW01082149

Uncharted Therapy

Tiffany Killoren

For Dominique.
I see you in every butterfly. Fly high.

Prologue

You had to look past it, the peeling paint and front porch railing that was slightly slanted; you had to see beyond the neglected shrubs that had been taken over by weeds and the shingles that had fallen from the roof and now lay homeless in the front yard. You had to look past all of it to see the house for what it was—a whitewashed relic with decorative trim along its front porch that made it look like a gingerbread house, a house that was sure to have a doily or two covering any space not already claimed by some black-and-white image of seemingly unhappy relatives on their wedding day.

Julia looked past it all; she loved the way the railing felt as she walked up the front steps, the wood worn smooth by all the hands before hers gliding up its inviting arch toward the wrap-around porch and protective gingerbread trim.

Her mother wouldn't approve, a fact that played no small role in Julia's decision to rent the house. Even in this day and age, her mother would never understand her want – her *need* – to embrace the countryside and live alone among its undisturbed wildflowers for a while. For reasons her daughter couldn't understand, she still clung proudly to the traditions of

1

the south, complete with nostalgia for Southern Belle etiquette and chilled juleps with just the right amount of mint. Julia was pretty sure the year's events had dropped her from *belle* consideration, by today's standards or those in effect when women were actually called such things. No; she was no belle and had always disliked the taste of mint. The wildflowers, with their colorful whimsy, were calling to her.

Even before she stepped inside, Julia knew. She stood on the front porch, listening to the wonderful sound of nothingness engulf the house and embrace it in a state of calm. With no wind to be seen or felt, the wooden chair a few feet away from her began to rock like someone was there, sitting and patiently watching as Julia pretended to ponder the decision that she knew she would ultimately make.

Yes, she would stay.

Chapter 1

Back in the Day

It simply wasn't Christmas without Annie McGallagher's cherries jubilee, the flambéed medley of cherries and kirschwasser like warm drops of heaven sitting atop ice cream. She brought it every year, balancing the bowl carefully on her legs during the twenty-second drive from their house to the Blackwells'. The joyful concoction made an appearance of its own each Christmas Eve as their neighbors Hank and Clara clapped with childlike excitement as if the jubilee was a guest itself. The cherry goodness was a staple at the Blackwells' post church service dinner, the white porcelain bowl as much a fixture on the table as the pink, floral-detailed depression glass goblets that Clara brought out once a year from their front row position in the china hutch.

Christmas was a time to indulge—in sweet and savory delights and turning a blind eye to bedtimes, although the Blackwell and McGallagher children were always eager to go to bed this particular night of the year.

While Clara and Annie busied themselves putting the final touches on Christmas Eve dinner, Hank and Burt would sink into the old leather sofa and catch up as if they didn't see each other on average five times a day.

There was talk of the upcoming election, the name of some newcomer, Jimmy Carter, was tossed around as a potential ticket rival to Ford the next year. The Watergate scandal remained front and center news, the cast of characters involved falling like dominoes throughout the year. But the men were much more interested in discussing Bobby Fischer's refusal to play Anatoly Karpov for the world chess championship.

The little ones were constantly shushed by adults as they ran around the house. But any ability they had to remain calm all but expired during the forty-five-minute Christmas Eve church service.

The top of the tree—a Douglas fir—was bent over at the ceiling and caused the entire tree to lean slightly to the left. Clara had told Hank it was too tall. Hank hadn't listened.

The multi-colored Christmas lights had been a challenge that year, the hunt for the single burned-out bulb eliciting a few curse words from Hank and tears from the children. All of which were quickly extinguished when the culprit was found and the living room was once again filled with green, red, blue and white lights that danced among the shadows on the walls.

The turkey was a little dry, but it wasn't anything that gravy couldn't solve. Clara and Annie indulged in a few glasses of white wine as they warned the children that Santa was still being sent behavior reports en route to houses that evening. Bored with talk of chess and politics, the women talked in hushed tones about a new show, *Saturday Night Live*, that was said to be pushing boundaries, and a movie about a killer shark that gave them nightmares based on the description alone. There was laughter and flushed cheeks from the wine, anxious children and after-dinner coffee that paired perfectly with the cherries jubilee. There was much unsettled in the world at that time, but one thing was certain; In that sweet old house just outside Friendly, Georgia, with an inviting front porch and tire swing, there was love.

That Christmas in 1975 was magical. Two families gathered together in tradition, embracing all that life had to offer and blissfully unaware of any challenges, heartbreak or pain that life inevitably had in store. Back in the day, good neighbors were treated like family; moments of silence were embraced as opportunities to pray and reflect, not something to run from or avoid. There was a time that bikes were ridden on gravel roads without care or worry of the resulting dust on clothes or the time it took to reach your destination. Back in the day, if an orange fell from your grasp, you simply let it roll.

Chapter 2

When Life Gives You Oranges

Lemons.

They say when handed them in life, you should make lemonade. They don't say that about oranges.

The stupid thing rolled faster than she could walk in her heels, disappearing beneath a car that had just pulled into a parking space. Trying to cover the hole in the bag with her left hand, Julia bent over to see where the orange had landed, tilting the bag just enough for six more oranges to escape from the hole in the bottom and rush to join their friend, who had a head start rolling back toward the entrance of the Shop N' Save.

"Shit!" Julia said, readjusting the useless paper shopping bag in her left arm, trying to save the rest of the groceries from falling into the puddles.

A gray-haired man exiting a car shot her a look of disapproval, his billowy eyebrows creating a giant gray caterpillar across his eyes. He didn't bother to lean over and catch the few remaining oranges before they disappeared beneath his car. Slamming the door, he opened his umbrella and shook his head.

"Oh, for the love of Pete," Julia said a little more loudly, the bag now tearing along its seam, sending a container of sour cream to the ground where it crashed dramatically and sprayed creamy whiteness across the man's car hood, and onto a black cashmere sweater coat and bag of a woman too busy pushing a full cart and trying to get her car to automatically unlock to notice.

A half-gallon of orange juice broke free next, its paper carton not strong enough to sustain the blow as it joined the sour cream molding itself into a gooey film as it mixed with rainwater.

Julia dropped the bag completely. Staring up at the sky, she let the misty air cover her face and took in a deep breath. Her latest self-help book purchase, *Discovering the Better You*, claimed that a cleansing breath was key to lowering her heart rate and maintaining a sense of calm during stressful situations. Julia took another breath, careful to "draw from the belly" as the book had instructed, letting the air out of her mouth in small, calculated bursts. She didn't let herself stray in mind or thought, a point that the book emphasized repeatedly.

Julia looked down at what remained from her quick run into the Shop N' Save: the box of tampons completely submerged in a pothole, and a four-pack of toilet paper covered in tiny water droplets.

Deciding that the toilet paper was the only thing salvageable, Julia waved without looking at a car slowly driving by, and bent down to pick up the package of two-ply that had somehow been spared.

Her shoulder-length hair had come out of its elastic tie, a few chunky split-end strands plastered to her face from the rain, while the rest lay at unnatural angles from hair spray that was now just sticky residue.

Julia clung to the toilet paper and just stood there, unmoved by a cart boy from the Shop N' Save staring in disgust, first at the mess that he would have to clean up in the parking lot and then at the woman who was responsible for it.

Julia's black dress pants clung to her legs. The rain was now picking up and soaking the apple green cardigan that she had bought the day before on clearance at Ann Taylor. It wasn't until after her PowerPoint presentation at an afternoon status meeting that a colleague had pointed out that the tags were still attached and dangling from her armpits. Her shoes, open-toed black pumps that she had always hated because they required pretty toes, were tightening around her feet and filling with water under her freshly painted pink nails.

She breathed again, desperate for a sign that there was still potential for her to find the *better* Julia like the book had promised. She had found the book buried in a clearance bin at her local drug store, and considered it a sign. A sign of *what*, she was now not so sure.

Julia then did something that she had wanted to do all day. She did something that she had wanted to do for weeks and months, but had not felt brave enough.

Julia screamed.

She clutched the toilet paper against her chest like it was a two-ply, plastic-covered life preserver and let out a scream that started in her belly and built strength in her windpipe, a scream that flew through the air and echoed off each droplet of rain. She bent over to draw in more air and arched her back to let the sound rip from her lungs.

Her head throbbing from the exhilaration of it all, Julia could feel the small hairs on her arms stand at attention, more from shock than from the cold rain that dripped down the back of her sweater and soaked the skin beneath.

With her fingers burrowing small holes in the plastic, Julia filled her lungs again, readying herself for an energy that filled every cell, tissue and organ of her body before escaping into a dizzying release.

"God damn, motherfucker!" Julia screamed, now wide-eyed and staring at passersby as if challenging someone to comment.

"Damn, shit-covered day!" she screamed again, tearing the plastic around the toilet paper and throwing rolls as far as she could toward the exit of the parking lot, coming close to hitting a shopper who dodged the flying two-ply just in time. Julia tossed the last roll into a water-filled pothole. It landed on top of the box of tampons that had started to disintegrate, so that individually-wrapped tampons shot to the top of the puddle like torpedoes.

"Fuck!" Julia shouted, arching her back and clenching her fists at her sides, feeling a surge of adrenaline with every profane word released into the universe.

She finished with a long scream that took every ounce of breath left in her lungs, leaving her lightheaded and staring at the sky.

Julia closed her eyes against the steady rain falling on her face and dislodging strands of hair that had become stuck to her cheeks. She covered both ears with her hands, trying to shut out the sound of car doors and horns.

Her eyes still closed, Julia didn't expect the hand on her elbow, a gentle squeeze of her arm that brought her back to the scene of floating tampons and melting paper cartons. She jumped when touched, startled and immediately embarrassed by what the scene must have looked like to a stranger, to someone who didn't know her or understand that she was just having a really bad day. This screaming figure in the parking lot really wasn't her. She didn't know who this person was.

"Ma'am, you okay?" the older man asked. The amount of pomade in his hair shone like a skating rink in the rain, the tiny droplets bouncing off the sleek surface and falling onto the straps of his deli apron. An engraved name tag that said *Hank* hung crookedly along the top of the apron's front pocket, a few food stains splattered across the navy-blue cotton and a few more marking the rolled sleeves of his white shirt.

"Ma'am?" he whispered again, trying to spare her more attention from the small crowd that had started to circle them. "Let's go on into the store and we'll get you a cup of coffee."

Not letting go of her elbow, Hank listened politely to Julia's attempts at explanation as he guided her toward the store's entrance and away from those who were speaking in hushed tones to one another, friendships instantly formed in the parking lot by circumstances that provided fellow shoppers a morsel of great gossip in common.

"There, there," Hank said gently, walking through the automatic doors and nodding as Julia told him about the forgotten sweater tag and an afternoon meeting that started to go downhill when she lost her internet connection and her brand-new pin-light pointer went dark, leaving her to wave it around the room like a powerless magic wand.

He guided Julia toward the deli, its red faux-leather booths and a few stand-alone tables starting to fill up with families catching a quick dinner before tackling their weekly grocery shopping.

"I'm seriously okay," Julia said, pulling her arm free and grasping her elbow with her other hand to keep Hank from taking it back. "I just had a bad day, that's all."

Hank's eyes looked intently into hers, but she saw nothing in them except sympathy and doubt. He gestured to the counter that held five tall carafes of brewed coffee and towers of disposable cups, but Julia stopped him before he could offer her a cup of something that claimed to capture the aroma of a mountain morning or a setting sun.

She grabbed hold of Hank's hand and shook it aggressively,

hoping that her now lucid demeanor and strong handshake would be enough to convince him that the Shop N' Save had simply caught her during a bad moment, on a bad day, in what was already a very bad year.

"Thank you, kind sir," Julia said cheekily, hoping to convince Hank that he had simply misjudged her eccentricities as signs of a more serious disorder. "Note to self, bring my durable recyclable bags next time!" She laughed a bit too loudly, still pumping Hank's hand like it was on hinges.

"Dear, can I call someone for you?" Hank asked, taking his hand back. "The rain's probably coming down pretty hard now and maybe you'd like a ride." He seemed desperate to get her to stay, his concerned look breaking into a panicked expression at her attempt to leave.

Oh shit, he's stalling. Julia adjusted her purse strap on her shoulder and gathered her hair into a wet bun at the nape of her neck, securing it with the black elastic tie. *Someone's called 911 and I'm going to get hauled out of here in an ambulance and carted off for a psych evaluation.*

"Seriously, I gotta run," Julia said. "Thanks again for all of your help and I apologize for any trouble." Turning her back to Hank and starting her way through the produce section, Julia shouted lightheartedly over her shoulder. "Apologize to the young man who had to clean up my groceries outside!"

She blindly searched for the car keys in her purse, rummaging through the bottom of the bag with one hand without breaking stride on her way to the automatic double doors at the front of the store.

She was desperate to feel the sleek turquoise and silver pendant key chain that her friend had given her for Christmas, a gift that had made her both cry appreciatively and laugh with a twinge of embarrassment. During an after-work happy hour that involved too many of the bar's signature pineapple martinis and extended into the early morning hours, Julia had joked with Genevieve that some girls were simply not destined to open a little blue box from Tiffany & Co.

Genevieve had then spent more money than she should have on the gift and, in a story revealed at the next happy hour, had threatened the salesperson with a discrimination claim if he didn't throw in the signature blue box with the purchase, citing fabricated legal precedent that prohibited the disparate treatment of consumers based on sales total.

That box now sat on Julia's bathroom shelf, a daily reminder that little blue boxes had always been available to her; there was no need to wait for a man to find her worthy.

Dammit, where the hell is it!? Julia was now out in the rain, forgetting to look before crossing the grocery pick-up lane because she was searching frantically for the keys with both hands. A white minivan slammed on its brakes and honked loudly, Julia pausing in her efforts only long enough to flip the irate woman behind the wheel her middle finger before resuming her search into the black hole of her Michael Kors tote. The minivan driver honked again and Julia waved her middle finger over her head to acknowledge receipt of the message.

Hank had been right, the rain was now coming down in heavy sheets that made it hard to see more than ten feet in front of her. Julia approached her small silver SUV, still unable to find her keys and hoping that she had left it unlocked so she could at least sit inside and regroup. When she was about twenty feet from her vehicle, she was relieved to see that the pothole was now clear of sanitary supplies, and the toilet paper, orange juice carton, and sour cream container had been removed, their absence making Julia feel one step closer to washing away the entire experience.

Noticing a small shiny object nearby, she raced over to a

shallow puddle and pulled out her car keys, only then remembering that she had taken them out her purse before the grocery bag broke and embarrassment ensued.

Thankful for this one small token of good luck in her day, Julia jumped into her SUV and slammed the door behind her, resting her wet head against the black leather headrest and sinking into the seat. Normally, she would have watched the weather channel and brought a bathroom towel to place on the seat to protect its leather if she got caught in the rain, but the thought of such a thing seemed ridiculous to her now.

She used her sleeve to wipe off her forehead and smoothed her hair back with both hands, finding some small comfort in the fact that the rain had tamed her split-end strands.

Julia put the keys into the ignition and the soothing voice of an evening talk show host came through the speakers, tenderly informing listeners that the phone lines were open and she was interested in hearing everyone's thoughts about the once highly respected high school teacher who had just been arrested for fathering a child with a fifteen-year-old student.

Julia hit the radio power button and sat in silence, not quite ready to start the windshield wipers and become seen by the world again. The rain created an opaque blanket over her vehicle that made her feel as invisible as she was numb inside.

She sat that way for a few minutes, following the path of the raindrops from where they fell until they disappeared into the window seams.

Buckling her seat belt, Julia finally turned on the wipers and put the SUV into reverse, just in time to see the blue and red spinning lights of an ambulance come to an abrupt stop at the Shop N' Save entrance.

Maybe things would have been different had she bought lemons.

Chapter 3

Kinda Like a Spa

"Oh, honey." She put a tissue to her nose and patted it a few times, first on the left and then a few times on the right, before crumpling it into a ball until it disappeared in her hand.

"Honey, oh dear." She lowered her head and spoke in a whisper. "Oh, oh, dear."

Evelyn Marsh sat on the edge of Julia's couch in a way that made her look like she would be infected with a terrible illness if more than a quarter of each butt cheek touched the light blue fabric. She had never liked the couch and had tried desperately to talk her youngest daughter out of the purchase, sending her links to mocha-colored options with emails that described them as "more reflective of the design taste of successful thirty-somethings," "colors that you won't someday regret," and "couches that will go with any furniture that might be added at some point in the future."

After thirty-four years of being her mother's daughter, Julia had become skilled at reading between the lines. So she assumed that her mom believed that mocha-colored couches attracted eligible men and robin egg blue couches repelled them. Evelyn always seemed so confident in her observations that Julia sometimes wondered if she was copying language that she had read in a *Help Your Daughter Avoid Being an Old Maid* handbook.

Julia pulled her throw blanket tightly around her shoulders and brought her knees up so they would be covered. She repositioned herself in the chair, a vintage piece that she had found at a flea market. She had fallen love with the chair's ornate wooden arms and silver nail heads and had carried it ten blocks through the streets of Atlanta and up the stairs to her fourth-floor loft. Then she had paid a small fortune to have it reupholstered in dark gray velvet.

Evelyn thought the chair belonged in Good Will, along with veneer furniture and last year's large-collared jacket trend that no respectable person would still have in their homes.

"It's not a big deal, Mom," Julia said, pulling on the blanket's edges that had fallen from her shoulders. "Seriously, don't worry about it."

Evelyn leaned back as if she had been hit with an invisible force, as if the absurdity of her daughter's words carried as much sting as a slap to the face.

"Not. A. Big. Deal?" she repeated. "Why, yes, it *is*." Evelyn raised her palms toward the ceiling to ask for God's intervention, a signature move of hers that she liked to whip out from time to time. She waved her palms back and forth and shook her head to signal that her pot of motherly love had been emptied and there was nothing else she could do.

Julia tried to discreetly remove a piece of lettuce from her teeth that had bothered her since lunch and waited for her mom to finish.

Finally, Evelyn brought her hands back down into her lap and stared intently at her daughter. "Are you aware that Helen Wainsfield saw you?" she asked, her lips pursed so tightly that they almost completely disappeared. "*Helen Wainsfield.*"

Helen Wainsfield was the church secretary at First Presbyterian, a beautiful white stone church on the corner of Hayfield and 22nd Street in the Peach Hill suburb of Atlanta. Helen Wainsfield had been church secretary for over thirty-five years and made it her business to identify the sinners from the saints among the congregation and, if need be, extend judgment to their next of kin if circumstances warranted. She sat behind her oak desk in the office as if protecting God himself, jumping out of her chair at the mere suggestion that someone see the pastor without an appointment and stated reason for the visit, the latter of which she required to satisfy her own curiosity.

The thought that her daughter and, by default Evelyn *herself*, would be the subject of one of Helen Wainsfield's gossip-filled phone calls was almost unbearable for a woman who put on mascara and at least a tinted lip balm just to walk to the mailbox.

"Evie, leave her alone." Nathaniel Marsh had been sitting in a rocking chair on the other side of the room leafing through one of Julia's college textbooks that he had plucked from her bookcase. He flipped through the book, which was about human sexuality, and stopped to go back to a particular page, adjusting his reading glasses to get a closer look at something that had caught his interest. Shaking his head and raising his eyebrows in a questioning manner, Nathaniel shut the book's cover and rested it on his lap.

"Maybe Jules doesn't care what some bleach blonde bitty thinks of her," he offered to the room, looking up to stare directly at his daughter in a showing of support, but choosing not to look at his wife.

"Thanks, Dad," Julia said, rolling her eyes at the situation. "Besides, wasn't Helen Wainsfield caught with her hand in the church coffers recently to help finance her latest round of Botox?" Julia exchanged smirks with her dad before looking back at her mom. "Sorry, but I don't think that I should be judged for a few choice words in a parking lot by someone who steals from a church because she's not comfortable with a few crow's feet."

Evelyn looked up toward the ceiling again in exasperation, throwing her hands up in another attempt to convince God to leave whatever emergency may be taking up his time so he could talk some sense into her daughter. Just then, the front door of Julia's apartment flew open and bounced loudly off the spring that stopped it from hitting the wall.

"What have I missed?" Liv shouted, moving her two-year-old from one hip onto the other as she walked in wide steps down the hallway toward the living room. Dropping her Burberry diaper bag onto the floor, Julia's oldest sister didn't acknowledge anyone in the room except for her mother, looking to Evelyn for a down-and-dirty update as to the status of the discussion.

Liv was five years older than Julia and a virtual clone of their mother, except for her thick dark hair that refused to shape itself into any respectable style and was kept instead in a sleek ponytail at all times. She had married an up-and-coming lawyer at twenty-three years old, which was old enough to have earned a college degree, but young enough to avoid anyone thinking that she didn't have a line of respectable suitors ready and willing to pop the question.

Charles and Liv's first child, Meredith, was born a year later, followed by twin sons, Henry and Thomas, two years later. Her youngest, Samuel, was a late-thirties' surprise and quite the scandal within Liv's life of Bunko gatherings and PTA fundraisers.

Evelyn hadn't taken the news of another grandchild well, concerned about the conclusions that some people could jump to given the unexpected age gap between Liv's youngest children. After Samuel was born, Julia could have sworn that she caught her mom studying his little face for any sign that he didn't share the same paternal DNA as his siblings. When confronted, Evelyn had simply claimed that she couldn't tell his eye color and had to study his face long and hard to figure it out.

Liv was still waiting for her mother to say something and was growing frustrated by the silence. She put Samuel down and adjusted her ponytail, watching as her son ran full-speed into her sister's arms and wrapped his chubby arms around her neck. His soft blond curls tickled her cheeks as Julia hugged him tightly. She brought him onto her lap and tucked him snugly under the blanket so just his tiny forehead and blue eyes peeked out into the room.

"So...?" Liv asked. Getting no response from her mother, she looked over to her dad who had resumed his freestyle studying method through the outdated edition of *Human Sexuality*.

Hands on her hips, Liv looked annoyed that she had made the trip from her gated community twenty-five minutes away. She looked exhausted and stressed, the result of balancing both teenage mood swings and toddler antics, her refrigerator covered in sports schedules and charts with smiley face stickers to document successful poops in the potty. Liv often claimed that she was surviving on lattes and prayers to get through each day.

"Listen, Julia, this has *got* to stop." Clasping her hands in a signature Evelyn-move, Liv pumped them in front of her like she was praying for Julia to cooperate. She stood that way, waiting for someone to say something, and she looked less than amused when Samuel started to giggle from under the blanket.

"Listen, I appreciate the concern, but I don't think this little intervention is really necessary," Julia said, trying to look less annoyed than she really was. "It's not like I make a habit of losing my cool in public and I'm not the first person in the world who dropped the F-bomb when she had a bad day. Get a little perspective."

"You dropped the *F-bomb*?!" Evelyn and Liv both yelled at the same time, as if the word alone escalated the situation. Their mouths hung limply, waiting for some indication that Julia's rendition of events had been exaggerated. She didn't give them any because they hadn't been. She had dropped the F-bomb more than once during her therapeutic vent in the parking lot three days before. Julia didn't subscribe to her mom and sister's Southern manners handbook; to her, some situations called for chewing out the universe and she wasn't about to apologize for it.

"What kind of emotional baggage are they packing today, Jules?"

Julia hadn't seen Georgia walk in. Her other sister was a welcome sight among the waves of dissension that had been hitting her from two directions with the combined force of a gale wind that smelled of her mother's Yves Saint Laurent perfume and the hand sanitizer that Liv practically bathed in.

Georgia had her strawberry blonde curls pulled back into a low tight bun, the ends of the original ponytail creating a fan of hair across her neck. She was still wearing her scrubs, so Julia assumed that their mother had called her at the hospital and ordered her to attend the emergency family meeting before she even went home and changed.

"Hey, Georgie," Julia said, taking one of Samuel's chubby hands and waving it in the air at his aunt. "Sorry you've been summoned to discuss my latest tarnish to the family name."

Georgia walked over to their dad and kissed him on the cheek, looking at the page of the textbook that he was reading and sitting on the arm of his chair.

"I'll explain that picture to you later, Dad," Georgia said jokingly, grabbing hold of one of her ankles and pulling it up under her. "So, Jules, how's it going?" she asked, a more serious expression taking over her face and her voice a bit softer. Georgia was always the voice of reason in the family, the practical child who had gotten all three sisters' shares of rational thought, leaving the other two with a surplus of dramatic and unfiltered tendencies.

"I'm fine." Julia felt no need to offer anything more and didn't, choosing instead to take her nephew's hand and make him slap himself softly on the cheek, the result of which was booming two-year-old laughter that filled the room and provided a distraction from words yet unsaid.

"Honey, we're just all worried about you," Evelyn began, turning on the talking-to-a-scared-animal tone that she liked to use when trying to convince people to see things her way or, when she was really desperate, "God's way."

"Everybody needs a break sometimes and we think that this might be a good time for you to take a little vaycay," Evelyn continued, now a bit more animated to show her excitement at the idea of a vacation. She smiled widely, her red lips perfectly lined and ready to launch into as many details as Julia would allow.

Evelyn reached into her purse and pulled out a glossy brochure. She handed it to Julia, but little Samuel grabbed it from his grandmother before his aunt even had the chance to take her hands out from under the blanket. Truth be told, she probably wouldn't have reached for it anyway.

"Samuel, give it to Aunt Jules," Liv said sternly, gesturing for him to hand it over. Emboldened by his aunt's firm hug around him, Samuel made no move to do so.

"Enlighten me," Julia said. "What's the exciting *vaycay* that you want me to go on?" The thought of a white sand beach was not that objectionable to her, especially if the resort was all-inclusive and had a liberal happy hour.

"Well, honey, it's kinda like a spa," Evelyn continued, trying to pry the brochure away from her grandson. Thinking it was a game, he howled with delight at the tug-o-war match and grasped his fingers tighter. Julia whispered something into Samuel's ear and his grip immediately loosened, a look of toddler defiance and pride shot at Evelyn, the loser in their battle of strength.

"Southern Sunset Center," Julia read aloud, flipping open the front page of the brochure that had an image of a setting sun among mountains on its cover. "At Southern Sunset Center, we're committed to helping you achieve your potential. Sometimes, dealing with your past in a supportive environment is the best way to focus on your future. Our professional staff help residents explore the life issues that are preventing them from living the life that God has planned for them."

"What the hell is this?" Julia asked, waving the brochure. "Are you suggesting that I need fucking rehab?!"

"Language!" Liv yelled, covering the living room in three large steps and ripping Samuel from Julia's arm. Unfazed, he grabbed a-hold of his mom's ponytail and yanked it as hard as he could while he laughed, kicked his legs, and said, "Mommy funny, Mommy funny, Mommy funny!"

Liv freed her hair from Samuel's hands and put him back on the floor where he ran directly into his Aunt Georgia's arms.

"It's not *rehab*," Liv said, taking her ponytail out and starting all over. "There's spa services there and even yoga classes. Hell, I wish I could go there for a month." Any intention that Liv had to appear understanding and sympathetic had gone out the window when the F-bomb was dropped and her son ran across the room with strands of hair that he had ripped from her head still firmly clasped in his hands.

"A *month?!*" Julia laughed. "Sure, no problem, I'll take a

month off work and spend it in counseling group sessions with meth addicts and kleptomaniacs."

"We've already taken care of that," Liv said without thinking, rubbing the spot on her scalp that had suffered the brunt of the damage. She was too busy focusing on herself that she didn't notice her sister and parents staring holes into the side of her head, a scene that had played repeatedly in their family over the years.

"What are you talking about? *What* is she talking about?" Julia looked around the room for answers, avoiding eye contact with Liv, who was suddenly aware that she had spilled a bit too much information too soon.

Julia let the blanket drop onto the floor as she stood and made her way into her kitchen, its tiny galley design providing little room to escape. She opened the refrigerator, using the door as a protective shield, and let the cold air wash over her. She stared at the half-empty bottle of Pinot Grigio on the shelf, its screw-on cap still sitting on the counter from the night before. At that moment, she wanted nothing more than to chug it, losing herself in the dulling effects of grape juice gone bad in the most wonderful way.

"Jules, I'm really sorry that you got ambushed like this." Georgia's voice wrapped itself around the refrigerator door in an informed whisper, a tone that Julia imagined she talked to her patients in at the hospital when she was telling them particularly bad news. "I wanted to talk to you alone about this, but Mom insisted on everyone being here."

Julia stepped out of the refrigerator and shut its door. Georgia, the shortest of the three girls, stood barely five-foot-three and looked particularly small standing there in the kitchen.

"Wait, *you* think this is a good idea?" Julia whispered, not because she thought there was any chance the rest of her family couldn't hear the conversation, but simply to signal that she didn't want them to. "Georgie, this is ridiculous and I can't believe you guys told work." Julia covered her eyes with her hands, her stomach now in knots at the idea of T. West Publishing thinking that she had to get sent away to therapy. She had only been in her sales manager position there for six months, but she had hoped to be given the chance to write copy for the magazine as she worked her way up.

The thought that the editor of one of the most popular couture and lifestyle magazines in the city would now want to open a door for her to show her writing skills seemed a long shot. That door had effectively been slammed shut when Cecily Jones, editor-in-chief, received a call about her mentally unstable staffer. Julia could only hope that her mom hadn't been the one who dialed.

"Jules, you've been through a lot. A *lot*." Georgia, the tough as nails surgeon who could lose patients on the table and still keep her happy hour plans, was now starting to cry. "You've been handed a lot this past year and I think it might be good to get away for a little while." She couldn't look directly at Julia when she spoke; the events of the last year were never considered a topic of suitable Southern conversation, but their effects had taken their toll on Julia and aged her in both spirit and body.

Julia felt her shoulders relax, unaware until that moment that they had been clenched. She could argue otherwise, but in her heart she knew that this little intervention had nothing to do with her parking lot tantrum or the embarrassing aftermath among the church-going circuit.

Julia put her hand out, palm up, and stared directly at her sister without speaking. Georgia gave her the glossy brochure and squeezed her sister's hand, both of them choosing to ignore the onlookers who now stood in a line a few feet away.

"I gotta pee!" Samuel's voice bellowed from somewhere in the apartment, breaking the awkward silence and causing Liv to dart quickly from the room.

Julia opened the refrigerator door and grabbed the open bottle of Pinot Grigio, raising it in the air in silent toast before bringing it to her lips and chugging what remained.

Chapter 4

Heavy on the Pink

"Is it at least co-ed?" Genevieve scanned the back of the brochure and studied it for any signs of male life.

"Does it matter?" Julia responded, taking a sip of her rum and Diet Coke then stirring it with the thin cocktail straw. She took another sip, thankful to taste slightly less of the rum and more of the sweet aspartame.

"I can't believe you had an intervention." Genevieve laughed, tossing the brochure across the table and snapping to get the waiter's attention.

A dark-haired waiter who looked barely old enough to serve alcohol was quick to respond, Genevieve's Greta Garbo looks more than enough to make up for any offense that her snap may have caused.

"Get you another one?" he asked, taking Genevieve's empty martini glass and placing it on a tray of dirty appetizer dishes from another table. One plate contained a virtually untouched serving of buffalo wings and Julia was tempted to grab a few, just to see what he would do.

"Yeah, but can you ask him to go a bit heavy on the pink this time?"

The waiter smirked and nodded, looking at Julia to see if she needed another drink.

"I'm good," she said, trying to wait until he was out of earshot before laughing. Genevieve always included nonsensical instructions with her cocktail orders, just to see how many people would question her on them or call her out. Very few did. She recently ordered a margarita at a local Mexican place and told the waiter to "make sure the worm is warm." He brought her margarita, along with a worm from the bottle of tequila and a match.

"So, you're seriously going to this place?" she asked, shaking her head in disbelief. "So you had a shit year, who hasn't? You don't need rehab, I mean, we make fun of celebrities who go to rehab for anxiety. Anxiety is just a part of life."

Genevieve piled her dark—almost hay-colored—blonde hair on top of her head and secured it with a single bobby pin, a few loose waves falling down the side of her face like it had been perfectly planned. She stared at Julia with one eyebrow raised slightly, waiting for her to confess that this was all just a big joke and she wouldn't be piling into her SUV the next day to drive to the middle of nowhere to get help that she didn't need.

Genevieve was actually called "Garbo" by some of their friends, her porcelain skin and naturally arched eyebrows an obvious nod toward the siren of early films. Although Julia agreed, she thought their similarities extended far beyond looks; Genevieve's sharp wit and cutting humor made it seem like she was always on the verge of lighting up a tipped cigarette and putting someone in their place. At that moment, with Genevieve's eyebrow raised liked a gun cocked for fire, Julia felt like she was about to be on the receiving end of a plume of smoke and lecture about life.

"I mean, seriously," Genevieve continued. "The psychic fair's next week. Who's going to go with me?"

For the last four years, the girls had spent an evening in the shabby ballroom of a rundown hotel in a questionable part of town to experience all that there is to see at the city's annual psychic fair. What started out as a fun girls' night out, was now a firm calendar entry, text messages exchanged to coordinate schedules as soon as the lime green billboard that advertised the event rose like a beacon of psychic glory off the highway.

They had tried a bit of everything that the vendors had to offer over the years, including tarot cards, energy healing, and a rather disturbing step into past life regression that placed Genevieve in a log cabin slinging oats to cows that she had to milk daily. Although a clairvoyant hinted that she would die at a young age, Genevieve was more disturbed at the thought that she had spent any lifetime doing manual labor. She preferred to think that she spent her past lives rubbing elbows with European aristocracy.

"Go and ask them how I'm doing," Julia offered. "It will save you a text message."

"You know I can't go by myself," Genevieve said. "If we go together, it's a girls' night out. If I go alone, it's kind of, I don't know, *sad*."

Julia knew what she meant. They didn't take the fair seriously; the girls took from the psychics what they wanted, leaving what they didn't want to hear behind. For them, the fair was an opportunity to explore the unknown in a safe and controlled way, dismissing any prediction that didn't suit them or their immediate plans for the future.

They always ended the evening with a cocktail as they rehashed the night's events and looked jokingly for the handsome stranger that one particular psychic always claimed was waiting "for the right time" to make his appearance.

"Maybe you should take Evelyn," Julia offered, giggling like a schoolgirl at the thought of her mother attending such an event. "She'd probably end up telling the psychics what the future holds for them if they continue such sacrilegious practices."

"Lord," Genevieve said, visibly disturbed by the thought. "The church ladies would probably picket the hotel entrance if they knew about this. But, maybe I should ask *my* mom," Genevieve said, looking amused by the idea. "I bet she'd go."

Genevieve's mom, Lily, was only seventeen years older than them and, for all practical purposes, was considered one of the girls. Genevieve grew up in a house with primary-colored walls, the Beatles blaring on the record player, and limited rules from a mom who was trying to figure out motherhood when she still needed a mom herself. Lily was funny, easy to talk to, and seemed to lack the ability to express surprise or judgment. Julia felt a small pang of jealousy, not only because Lily might take her place at the psychic fair, but also because she didn't have a mom who would ever want to go.

As the waiter placed a bright pink martini in front of Genevieve, another man appeared to her left, dressed in a tailored black suit and Burberry tie. With one hand raised in silent apology for disturbing, he looked first at Genevieve, and then at Julia. "I was going to offer to buy you lovely ladies a drink, but it looks like you've already ordered your next round."

Genevieve looked at Julia and winked, sipping her heavy-on-the-pink cocktail before responding.

"You don't want to get involved with her," she said, nodding toward Julia. "She's heading to rehab tomorrow." Julia smiled innocently, locking eyes with the stranger. It took everything in her to play along and not laugh. To keep her composure, she raised her glass in silent toast and took a long sip from the straw.

"Alrighty then," he said with his hands raised in surrender, turning around and returning to his seat at the bar. He looked annoyed, most likely not used to the feeling of someone having a laugh at his expense, even if the laugh obviously had nothing to do with him.

Genevieve always did that. Her Garbo-ish energy the obvious reason for a steady stream of drink offers, she always made it seem like Julia was the one that men were vying for. Julia was attractive, but few were going to approach the two of them and single her out as the prize at the table, especially today because she hadn't bothered with makeup and was halfway to the bar before she realized that she had forgotten to put on a bra. The drinks before you go to rehab aren't the ones that you dress up for.

"I think you hurt his feelings," Julia said, readjusting the orange cotton headband that kept sliding off the base of her neck. With makeup, Julia looked like she was a professional in her thirties, complete with shoulder-length side bob and cotton-blend cardigans. Without makeup, she looked like she was in her mid-twenties and on her way to a spin class—the only casual clothes that she owned were shorts, T-shirts, and yoga pants.

Julia had woken up with a painful pimple in the corner of her right nostril and she touched it softly to see if it was still there. Although she blamed the pus-filled pore on the stress of the situation, she knew that it was more likely the result of running out of makeup remover cloths last week and being too lazy to buy more.

"I bet that zit will help you make new friends," Genevieve teased. "Especially if you keep playing with it and it grows from your love and affection."

"You know what I think," Julia responded, choosing to ignore her friend's comments and continuing to touch the pimple that now throbbed from being disturbed. "I think maybe I do need to get away for a while. I would have preferred a beach somewhere and list of must-reads, but maybe it won't be so bad to unplug for a while."

Genevieve put an elbow on the table and tried to rest her chin in her hand nonchalantly, unable to mask the fact that she was about to say something that might be taken the wrong way. "So," she finally said. "Have you talked to him recently?"

Julia rolled her eyes in mock disgust, but she could feel her neck and cheeks warming with the flush of embarrassment. She shook her head a bit too violently, failing in her attempt to act offended that such a question was even asked. "No, of course not."

Genevieve tried to meet Julia's eyes, but they were darting around the room too quickly for her to keep up.

"No," Julia said again to bring home the point. "I wouldn't do that."

Genevieve rolled her shoulders and stretched her back, swinging one arm over the back of the bar stool and grabbing her wrist with her other hand. She sat that way, perched sideways and staring suspiciously at her friend until she accidentally made eye contact with the waiter and he came back to their table.

"All good here, or do you need another?" His question was directed to Julia, who had taken the straw out of her drink and was tipping it toward the ceiling to release one of the ice cubes stuck to the bottom of the glass into her mouth. She shook her head and crunched loudly, enjoying the numbing cold of ice that still tasted slightly of rum.

"Maybe he'd go to the psychic fair with you," Julia joked, tipping the glass again to get another cube. Usually one for comic relief, Genevieve didn't look like she was having any of it this time. She tilted her head to one side, a curl escaping from the bobby pin and falling into her face. She tucked it behind her ear and started playing with the small charm attached to the bottom of her martini glass.

"I saw him the other day." Genevieve didn't look at her

friend, choosing instead to pry open the ring of the small charm and take it off the glass stem completely.

"What? Where?" Julia asked, immediately aware that she sounded too excited to now try to play coy.

"I had to run into that new ritzy grocery store on the corner of Bluff and Elm a few days ago," Genevieve explained. "I never go in there, but I was completely out of toilet paper and had no choice but to pay top dollar unless I wanted to shake it off every time I peed." She smiled, trying to lighten the mood, but Julia was sitting wide-eyed across from her, ready to pounce if her friend didn't get to the details quickly.

"Anyway, I ran into him at the check-out. He was one lane over and it would have been pretty obvious if we pretended we didn't see each other." She shrugged, acting like the story was barely worth mentioning. "That's it. He waved awkwardly, I gave him the finger, and then I grabbed my two-ply and left. I figured you might want to know."

Julia said nothing. There was really nothing to say because the story really wasn't one, it was just a description of two people who shared the same airspace at the same moment in a grocery store. To Julia, however, that run-in was a reminder that the film strip that played over and over in her mind was based on a true story.

It was a reminder that a man walked freely in this world, going about his day and routine unscarred by the same events that had kept Julia from leaving her bed for weeks. That run-in reminded Julia that, while she packed for a thirty-day trip to a facility that wanted to cure her with love and light, the co-star of her drama was buying organic pasta and wine without any sign of dysfunction or residual damage.

"I feel like a complete shit, but I'm supposed to meet Sean in ten minutes and we're twenty minutes from the restaurant,"

Genevieve said, looking at the clock on her phone. "Want me to cancel? I totally will."

"No, no," Julia said, waving off the suggestion. She tried to appear as normal as possible, but the three rum and Cokes combined with Genevieve's story about buying toilet paper made her a bit woozy, her head filling with fog.

"What happened to Trey?" Julia asked, trying to appear casual. "I thought you decided he was a better fit." Trey was a personal trainer who had recently convinced Genevieve to go out with him after months of not-so-subtle flirting between the two.

"He never paid when we went out," Genevieve explained, tossing some money onto the table for her drinks and putting the phone into a side pocket of her black clutch. She applied lip gloss without a mirror and rubbed her lips together, drawing a finger along her lip line to remove any excess. "I mean, seriously, I'm a tattoo artist. I don't have any money and he's not good-looking enough for me to spend money that I don't have."

Genevieve may look like Greta Garbo from the neck up, but from the neck down, she was all Kat Von D. A black and white image of scales, a tribute to her Libra sign, covered her left arm from shoulder to a few inches above her elbow. Her right arm was home to more colorful images, including a miniature solar system with planets dancing around a sun with fiery rays. Genevieve had no real reason for getting a tattoo of the solar system. Like most decisions in her life, she got the tattoo first and tried to figure out why later.

"You sure you don't want me to cancel and stay here with you?" Genevieve offered again. "I wouldn't be heartbroken. We're meeting at that new sushi place and I'm not really in the mood for raw fish. I'm never really in the mood for raw fish, but especially not after pink cocktails."

"No, go and have fun," Julia said, reaching into her bag. "I have to go home and mentally prepare for tomorrow," she added, throwing a few bills onto the table. "And, I still have to do a load of laundry. I read that step one of any recovery process is to face problems head-on in clean underwear."

The girls waved to the waiter and pointed to the table so he knew they had left money. Genevieve looped her arm through Julia's, locking elbows and walking out of the bar as friends united. Once outside, Genevieve removed the bobby pin and combed through her hair with her fingers, the only effort that she was willing to make for a date that she wasn't that excited about going on anyway.

"Call me whenever you get settled, earn phone privileges, or they let you out of the padded room," Genevieve said with a laugh. She grabbed Julia and hugged her tightly, squeezing her in silence for a minute because neither of them knew what to say. Without letting go, Genevieve whispered something into Julia's ear. "In all seriousness, you've been given this time, so take it. Get back to that spunky girl that we all love."

Genevieve released her grip and wiped away the tiniest of tears. She started walking down the opposite direction that Julia had to take, turning around and walking backwards, waving and winking before turning again and disappearing around a corner.

Julia stared after her friend, long after she was out of sight. She didn't want to go home, but didn't want to stay here either. Standing in front of the bar at that moment, Julia felt on a smaller scale the same way that she felt about her life as a whole —she didn't want to stay, but didn't know where to go.

Chapter 5

Billboards

How does one get here? Julia didn't smoke, but might have considered starting if she had a pack. The scene seemed to call for it. *How does one get here*—both figuratively in life and on this road, seemingly a million miles from the life she left behind. Yes, she certainly would have smoked if she had them.

The road that had brought Julia here was so narrow at points that the line in the middle seemed more of a technicality than anything. Since leaving Interstate 75 an hour before, Julia felt like she had been driving further into the center of the Earth rather than into the most southwest portion of the state, the towns and other signs of life growing further apart as she ventured into the nothingness under the night's sky.

The one radio station that she was able to get was home to a particularly excitable preacher who was determined to convince all listeners that the heat of the southern noonday sun in summer was nothing compared to the heat of damnation that was awaiting all sinners in hell—of that he was certain. He was only more sure of the fact that a fair share of the listening audience was going to end up there if they didn't change their ways.

Her phone battery dead and the charger packed somewhere out of reach, Julia chose to drive the last fifty miles in silence. The trees that lined the rural highway only added to the blanket of darkness that seemed to have swallowed her car, small yellow highway markers the only thing that periodically let her know that she was still on some identifiable road and not in the centrifuge of some mystical black hole that had no exit.

Her tank less than one third full, Julia started to feel the rise of panic at the thought that she had missed her turn and was driving into true no-man's land. Leaning forward nervously, she clutched the steering wheel and peered into the darkness for any sign that told her where to turn or, for that matter, any divine sign to turn back.

"Evie, leave her be, this isn't a trip to Club Med." Julia's dad was standing on the sidewalk in front of her Locust Street apartment building, gesturing for her to hand him the bag that she was holding so he could add it to the rest in the trunk. Julia tossed the small toiletry bag to him and he caught it by its strap, placing it snugly in between her suitcase and a few green recyclable bags packed with snacks and last-minute items that she had bought at the drug store that afternoon.

"I wish you would have gotten on the road earlier," Evelyn said, shaking her head at something invisible in the air. "I really hate the thought of you driving on unfamiliar roads after dark."

"I'll be fine, Mom," Julia reassured her. Truth be told, Julia hadn't intended on leaving the city this late. She had managed to avoid starting the four-hour drive until her parents showed up and pushed her out the door with her belongings. "I like driving at night," she lied.

"Nathaniel, maybe you should take her," Evelyn said,

turning to her husband who was checking one more time to make sure the door of the small SUV was tightly shut. Nathaniel sighed and looked at Julia for some sign either way as to her preference, but she knew that he was silently hoping that she would insist on going alone because he was really looking forward to pouring a healthy glass of Dewar's scotch and finishing his cigar when he got home.

"No, no, no," Julia said, letting her dad off the hook because it was the only way her mother would drop the idea. "The drive's mainly interstate, and I have a few audio books that I want to listen to," Julia said, lying again.

"I just worry that you haven't packed enough," Evelyn said, trying to peer into the back of the SUV. "There may be little get-togethers, you never know."

"Hopeful that I'll meet my soul mate in rehab?" Julia asked sarcastically, tossing her keys into the air and then swinging the silver ring of the key chain around her finger, trying to appear blasé. She wasn't actually feeling blasé about any of this, worried both about finding the place and then what awaited her there once she arrived.

"Of course not." Had she ever wished for such a thing, Evelyn now looked like she was re-thinking the idea. The likelihood of finding a suitable mate with some rehab-worthy addiction who was still accepted by the church ladies seemed remote. "Of course not," she said again, this time looking like she was trying to erase any evidence of prior thoughts that could be used against her.

Julia gave each of her parents a side hug and avoided eye contact as she got into the driver's seat, glancing out of the passenger side window only once briefly to wave before she cranked the steering wheel to maneuver her way out from between two poor parallel park jobs.

Then she made her way down Locust Street heading for the interstate. Although the calendar claimed it was officially fall, late summer was still clinging to life and temperatures fluctuated greatly based on the season's mood and time of day. Julia turned off the air conditioning and lowered all four windows, feeling an odd comfort in the whirlwind of hair that both hid her face and the road while she was driving. She was on her way to the Southern Sunset Center, some cream-colored building with a bad faux finish on the cover of a glossy brochure that now peeked out from the pocket of her purse.

Traffic was light and Julia had to find ways to not make good time. She figured the later she arrived, the better the odds of the staff leaving her alone for a good night's sleep and delaying the inevitable until morning or, if she was lucky, until after the "buffet lunch of fresh greens, farm-to-table vegetables, and delectable delights that refuel and energize the body while reinvigorating the mind."

Julia's diet often consisted of coffee and chocolate so, as long as this place has a fair share of both, she figured she could bypass the farm-to-table line and go right for the delectable delights. The thought of it now made her blindly reach into her purse and grab the one-pound bag of M&Ms that she had thrown in at the last minute. Tearing it open with her teeth, she grabbed a handful and threw them into her mouth, a few making their way down her shirt and into her bra where she decided to leave them for the time being.

The sun was growing sleepy, falling steadily toward the horizon for its evening rest. Its red and orange glow now softened, Julia thought of Georgia, both the colors and comforting feel of the setting sun a reminder of her sister's berry-hued hair and calming presence. Julia never would have agreed to this trip had it not been for Georgia. She was used to her mother and oldest sister's dramatic ways, but Julia could always count on Georgia to see things from her perspective and give a supportive wink during family skirmishes to let her know that she wasn't alone.

Georgia was the smart one; she had been valedictorian, graduated from college with honors and on a full scholarship, and breezed through medical school while holding down two jobs and volunteering at an animal shelter on weekends. She was only two years older than Julia, but had accomplished more in her thirty-six years than most people do in a lifetime and still found time to take out burrs from homeless animals' fur along the way.

Although the latest in her daughter's professional accomplishments was always the focus of Evelyn's ladies-who-lunch conversations, everyone knew that she was silently distraught that only one daughter had blessed her with grandchildren and the other two were closing in on poor-egg-quality age.

And, ever since Julia walked in on Georgia with another woman in her shower a few years ago, she knew that her mother's dream of a son-in-law for her second daughter was highly unlikely.

You've been through a lot. Georgia was right, she had been. If she had a dollar for the number of times that she had been told over the past year, "That which doesn't kill us makes us stronger," she would be on a beach vacation at some all-inclusive resort in the Caribbean right now instead of on her way to a cream-colored, faux-finished building with people who promise to help patients find their true selves because, apparently, those selves are hiding somewhere in its seven acres of "untouched Southern land."

Although the setting sun danced along her passenger

window, Julia didn't put down her visor to keep the glare at bay. She liked the feeling of the bright light shining onto her face, the road before her now appearing like a small slit in a screen as she drove with squinting eyes. She really didn't think that old adage was true. Sometimes, "that which doesn't kill us" turns us inside out and leaves our soul to weather like a Georgia peach left in the noonday sun. Sometimes, life experiences are merely survived and leave us fractured at our core, the slightest wind enough to shake our foundation and make us question all that we know. Sometimes, "that which doesn't kill us" makes us wish that it had.

Julia did what she always did when thoughts of the past year started creeping onto her mental screen. She changed the channel. Diversion seemed just as healthy an approach as addressing issues head-on, perhaps even more so because it wasn't accompanied by the headaches or stomach pains that came with confronting her demons. If demons can be contained behind locked doors, Julia really saw no reason to let them out; and, if it was true that humans only use ten percent of our brains, she was sure that they could find a comfortable place to hide.

Turning toward the billboards that lined the lonely two-way highway, Julia focused her attention on their faded colors and peeling corners, signs that billboards in the area probably changed advertisements no more than once every ten years. An approaching billboard had a pink background with a triple XXX displayed boldly in black, alerting drivers to the sex shop that was three miles ahead and offered peep show discounts for lonely truckers. The fact that the original scarlet of the background was still visible in a few areas suggested that this particular sign had been there since well before Julia was even old enough to enter such a store. This was confirmed when, three miles down the road, she noticed an abandoned building in the distance with two XXs still standing on its roof, the third hanging off the side, dangling by its corner.

The next billboard had all but given up on the state of Georgia, advertising a resort in Florida that was hundreds of miles away and in the opposite direction. Julia imagined a family of four driving along the highway and becoming so excited by this billboard that they turned around and drove straight to Florida, only to find the resort hadn't been open since the late 1990s and was now a retirement village. The thought was silly, but silly helped her change the mental channel.

Still thinking about the pretend family of four and their reactions to vacationing with the senior circuit, Julia almost overlooked the next billboard entirely. Its location on the opposite side of the road was an easy miss. What had started out as sky blue was now a sickly pale background for a group of three people smiling into the distance with their arms around one another. One was mid-laugh, the look an unfortunate one when blown-up to billboard size because, rather than happy, the woman looked like she was laughing crazily at something that only she could see. In faded orange letters, *Southern Sunset Center* was written across the top, and Exit 210 was barely legible at the bottom of the sign. Julia was energized by the prospect that the facility had suffered the same fate as the sex shop. But the feeling was short-lived; the glossy brochure with this year's date quashed any hope that the Southern Sunset Center now stood abandoned on its seven acres of true selves waiting to be found.

Julia stared at the gas gauge, willing it to stay above the tiny line that would officially alert her to a fuel problem. As long as the vehicle was silent on the issue, she felt safe. If the tiny orange gas-pump shaped light came on with its *ding*, there would be nothing left to do but panic.

Orange lights that *ding* with warning are hard to ignore; it's like a vehicle losing patience with its driver and standing up to take back control.

Julia had taken Exit 210 almost an hour ago and, even if she turned back now and drove to the interstate, she couldn't remember the last time she saw a gas station. Her dad had told her to get gas in a particular small town because it was going to be her last opportunity for a while, but Julia hadn't been paying attention because she was still on the sidewalk in front of her Locust Street apartment and she could no more imagine running out of gas at that moment than she could picture the desolate road that she would be driving down.

Tree branches hung at such odd angles over the road that Julia was sure one would break as she was driving under it, either pinning her inside the SUV or killing her immediately. She wasn't sure which would be worse. Over the last half hour or so, Julia had also convinced herself that this is exactly the type of place reclusive groups of mountain people would choose to build their alternative civilizations, lying in wait for naive city girls like her so they could eat them and use their teeth in jewelry. Julia kept one eye on the trees above and the other on the dense woods lining each side of the road, holding her breath in wait for something either to fall or peer back at her from the belly of the darkness.

Ding.

"Well, that's just wonderful," Julia said, staring at the orange light on the dash. Grabbing another handful of M&Ms from the bag on the passenger seat, she started pouring them into her mouth, stopping only when she realized that she might need food if she ran out of gas and was trapped here for days.

Dropping the remaining M&Ms from her hand back into the bag, Julia bit off the few that stuck to her palm and licked off the red and green dye left behind. Even given the circumstances, she couldn't help but smile at the thought that her mother would be appalled.

Just then, two yellow eyes appeared and stopped on the road just ahead of her, forcing Julia to slam on her brakes and brace herself for impact. Feeling nothing, she sat and waited for whatever had appeared to make itself known, eventually seeing a fluffy black and white tail attached to a fat raccoon waddle across the road and disappear into the brush. Julia leaned her head against the seat and closed her eyes, too tired to be as scared as she should have been. Blinking a few times to adjust her eyes to the darkness, she caught a glimpse of a shimmery light reflecting off her headlights about twenty yards away. Leaning across the seat to make sure the road was raccoon-free, she crept forward. Partially covered by a branch that hung particularly low to the ground, was a yellow sign in the shape of an arrow pointing toward a paved driveway.

This can't be it. If the driveway led to her destination, first impressions were as abysmal as the landscaping.

Pulling into the driveway at an angle, Julia put the SUV into park and jumped out, looking around for any signs of raccoons or reclusive cannibals.

Noticing a wrought-iron gate with rusted security speaker a few feet down the drive to her right, she parted the waist-high grass like she was wading through water and walked carefully along the path illuminated by the SUV's lights. She reached up and tore a few leaves from the sign. Squinting to read the silver reflective letters hidden underneath, she slowly made out the words that arched around the image of sun.

Welcome to the Southern Sunset Center.

A pile of cigarette butts lay on the ground from ghosts who

have gone before her, final drags enjoyed before being tossed into the grass and extinguished for what lay beyond. It was there, standing at the entrance of a rehabilitation center that was supposed to help her make better choices in life, that Julia wished she had taken up smoking.

Chapter 6

Intake

"We've been waiting for you."

The woman who had greeted Julia wasn't dressed like a doctor or nurse, but she had a stethoscope around her neck and was holding onto a brown clipboard covered with pharmaceutical stickers. She had leathery skin from too much sun and bleach blonde hair that was frayed at its tips, both of which made her look older than her true age, which Julia guessed was around forty-five. The small wrinkles that intersected her top lip suggested that she was a smoker and had been for quite some time.

"We were expecting you a bit earlier in the day," she said, repeating the message in case Julia had missed it the first time. The woman wasn't cold, but she didn't come across as warm either; a steady lukewarm was about all that Julia could gauge of her reception. She stared at the clock above the woman's head. It was eleven fifty-five.

"Oh," Julia said, not sure of what else to say. She watched the woman write something down on the clipboard and couldn't help but feel like she had failed some early assessment, her late arrival some mark against her on the checklist of functional adult behavior.

"You can leave all of your bags here," the woman said, gesturing with her head toward the sitting area in the lobby. The green and mauve love seat, gold winged-back chair, and brown leather sofa were arranged in living room formation, complete with a honey oak coffee table that held fanned copies of *Good Housekeeping* and *Psychology Today*. The reception desk that greeted incoming patients had a green vinyl countertop and held at least fifteen plastic display cases for information sheets on disorders and addictions, a virtual all-you-can read smorgasbord of *The Diagnostic and Statistical Manual of Mental Disorders*.

"I'm exhausted," Julia said. "Let me just get my saline solution so I can take my contacts out before I go to bed." She started walking toward her bags that were piled near the door, but the woman grabbed her elbow and stopped her as she walked by.

"Afraid not, honey," she said unsympathetically. "You still have to meet with Dr. Rayborn. All patients have to go through full intake as soon as they get here." The woman wrote something else on the clipboard and Julia assumed that it was another mark against her.

The woman left Julia standing there as she returned to her perch behind the desk and started typing something into the computer while reading what she had written on the clipboard.

This is it, Julia thought. *As soon as that woman hits* enter, *I officially have a rehab file.*

The woman's gaze moved between the clipboard and the screen and she hit backspace once or twice to make corrections. After taking a few seconds to read what she had typed, the woman sat back in the chair and hit the *enter* key with one loud tap of her pointer finger.

And there you have it.

Julia had been driving for four hours and wanted nothing more than a soft pillow and clean sheets. Her teeth felt fuzzy from the film of chocolate and she knew without conducting a sniff test that her armpits smelled about as fresh as they felt, her T-shirt damp from the heat and stress-induced sweat. Just as she was starting to wonder how long she would be left standing there, a wooden door marked *Patients and Personnel Only* swung open and a petite brunette appeared wearing an AC/DC T-shirt and ripped jeans. A tiny diamond shone on the side of her nose and a ring of keys hung from one of her belt loops.

"Ms. Marsh, I presume?" she asked, extending a hand. She had a beautiful smile that warmed Julia from the inside out. "I'm Samantha Rayborn, one of Southern Sunset's physicians."

Julia took her hand and shook it firmly, surprised that the tiny young woman who looked like she belonged in a chic underground bar scene was actually the doctor in charge. Unlike Julia's, Dr. Rayborn's bright green eyes were alert and didn't reflect the late hour in any way. Even her handshake was more energetic than Julia could muster at the moment.

"Come on back," she waved, turning toward the wooden door and gesturing for Julia to follow. She looked over her shoulder to address the woman behind the counter. "Would you check with housekeeping to make sure that Ms. Marsh's room is ready. I'm sure she's exhausted."

Julia shot the woman a look, but she already had the phone to her ear, presumably trying to call up housekeeping. Dr. Rayborn was holding the door open for her, and Julia was happy to leave the lobby of mismatched furniture and follow her.

The temperature was noticeably cooler as soon as she crossed the threshold and entered a green-tiled hallway. Plastic sheets of florescent lighting covered the ceiling and hummed softly, the only other sounds coming from the squeak of Julia's sandals and the pings of Dr. Rayborn's keys knocking into one another. Julia followed her around a corner and down a yellow-tiled hallway along which were wooden doors with brass name plates under frosted glass windows.

Dr. Rayborn opened her office door and gestured for Julia to take a seat on the visitor-side of the desk, plopping herself down into a worn black leather chair that swiveled from the momentum. On her desk, piles of file folders, notepads, and medical journals vied for the limited space.

Bookshelves covered the wall to Julia's left and the wall behind Dr. Rayborn's desk. They were packed so tightly with periodicals and textbooks that some were crammed in sideways. Others teetered in piles on the floor. A familiar orange and blue binding caught Julia's eye—the same human sexuality textbook that she had at home was one of the dusty books on the bottom shelf. It was leaning against colorful textbooks on psychology and addictive behavior, a few of which still had the college bookstore stickers on their binding.

Julia wondered when Dr. Rayborn had graduated from medical school, guessing that it was probably recent enough for her to still get together with past roommates to discuss her crazy patients over martinis.

"How on Earth did you end up out here?" Julia asked, realizing that it came out a bit ruder than she had intended. "I mean, this was quite a drive. Where's the nearest restaurant? Target? Gas station?" The last question brought renewed life to the panic that she had felt earlier and again made her wonder how she would ever fill up her tank to get home.

Dr. Rayborn smiled as she scanned through a pile of manila folders, plucking one with Marsh, J. typed in bold black font on its label. She opened the file and smoothed down the single page that filled it.

"I grew up less than twenty miles from here," Dr. Rayborn explained. "I lost my older brother to drug addiction when I was a teenager." Trying out a few pens on a notepad before finding one that worked, Dr. Rayborn looked into her coffee cup and wrinkled her nose at what she found. "It's not for everyone, but I always knew that I'd come back to help people closer to home."

Julia looked up at the framed diploma that hung crookedly on one wall—New York University School of Medicine. Dr. Rayborn was a Georgia girl, but Julia admired that she found a way to bring a bit of New York back with her: the diamond stud in her nose the only sparkle in an office that smelled of musty paper and stagnant coffee.

"So, what's going on here?" The question really wasn't a question, just a statement thrown out into the room by Dr. Rayborn as she began to read the page in Julia's file. Julia wondered what it said and who'd filled it out, inching her way closer to the desk by pretending that she just needed a place to rest her arm. She was only able to read a single line entry at the top of the page because it was bolded and in larger font than the rest. It said "SEA."

Dr. Rayborn's face softened as she skimmed the paragraphs, tapping the end of her pen on the paper and then flipping it with one hand to tap it on the other end. She crossed her hands in front of her and caught Julia's eyes darting quickly from the paper.

"Do you want to read it?" Dr. Rayborn asked, tapping the file again with her pen. "I'm not going to hide anything from you. This is your journey."

Up until that point, Julia had really liked Dr. Rayborn. Her use of the term "journey" to describe this experience, however, rubbed her the wrong way. It made it sound like she was going to eat granola bars, learn a few yoga stretches, and undergo some spiritual awakening. Julia didn't consider life so far to be a journey. She considered it more a series of pit stops and U-turns, with miles re-traveled that she should have left in the dust years ago. That single word had suddenly changed her perception of Dr. Rayborn, as judgmental and close-minded as that might be.

Julia had driven four hours into a largely uninhabited part of the state to a place that greeted you with photocopied cheat sheets about your condition and unfriendly staff. At that moment, she felt entitled to close her mind and pass as much judgment as she wanted.

"No thanks," she responded to Dr. Rayborn's offer, her interest in the file suddenly gone.

"Okay," Dr. Rayborn said, offering a smile that seemed more sympathetic than friendly. "I'd like to just read a few lines from your file, if that's okay." But she offered no opportunity for Julia to respond that it was.

"Julia is strong. She is intelligent, funny, and kind. She is also sad, judgmental, and bitter from the challenges that life has handed her. Julia is not broken, but I'm concerned that she thinks she is."

Julia felt a warm wave of guilt wash over her from the judgment that she had just passed onto Dr. Rayborn for a perceived poor word choice. And, from Dr. Rayborn's knowing grin, Julia was pretty sure that the judgment was evident. She wished that she felt ashamed, but instead, she simply felt exposed.

If Dr. Rayborn noticed any change in Julia, she didn't let on. She continued reading. "Also, I'm not sure what the 'curriculum' is there, but don't try to pull any new-age stuff on Julia. A good cup of coffee and quiet place to land at the end of the day is a better fit for her than forcing her to learn about star alignment and her astrological propensities."

Both women laughed.

Julia realized that Georgia had been the family member to fill out her paperwork and, for that, she was thankful. Even if her sister felt like she needed this place, Julia took comfort in the fact that she still knew who she was and what she needed. That the sister who knew her best considered her bitter and judgmental, however, was something that Julia chose not to focus on.

"So, what does SEA stand for?" Julia asked, feeling a bit more comfortable now that the energy in the room had been lightened.

"Everyone who enters the facility has to be given an initial diagnosis based on their file for us to determine where best to put them and the help they might need," Dr. Rayborn explained. "SEA stands for 'Stress, Exhaustion, and Anxiety.' We classify guests this way who aren't suffering from something catastrophic or life-threatening, but who simply need some help finding their way.

"Let me ask you something," Dr. Rayborn said, folding her hands again on the desk and leaning closer to Julia. "Do *you* think you need to be here?"

Julia sat in silence. An hour ago, she didn't think that she needed professional help, but she hadn't considered herself overly judgmental or bitter either.

"I don't think I *need* to be here," Julia finally said softly. "Do I think I can get *something* out of this place? I guess we'll have to wait and see."

"Fair enough," Dr. Rayborn said, closing the cover to the file and placing it on top of a pile that looked dangerously close to sliding off the edge. "Let's get you to your room. It's after midnight and you must be exhausted."

Julia followed Dr. Rayborn back into the hall and down the corridor that they had passed on their way to her office. They stopped in front of dark wooden double doors with *B-Wing* painted on their face in white block lettering.

Dr. Rayborn took a small plastic card from the back pocket of her jeans and held it in front of a box on the wall until its tiny light turned green and the locks clicked open. "Everyone wants to know why the wings are locked if you're here voluntarily," Dr. Rayborn said as they walked through the doors and down a hall of tiny pink tiles. "The locks aren't to keep anyone in. We want to make sure your personal belongings are safe; and we don't want any of our guests dealing with more physically and emotionally intense issues in other wings of the facility to have full access to your accommodations."

Physically and emotionally intense issues. Julia couldn't help but wonder what was covered under this cloak of political correctness.

"Okay, here we are," Dr. Rayborn said, stopping in front of a wooden door marked with two number stickers that didn't match. "You'll be in room number fifteen."

Julia walked into the room and was relieved to see her luggage piled in the corner. The familiar Laura Ashley overnight bag and worn gray suitcase were small comforting reminders of home in a room that lacked much of anything else.

She hadn't slept on a single-sized mattress in decades, but there it was, pushed against the wall and covered in white hospital-style linens and a fleece blanket in burnt yellow.

A desk and chair that could have been plucked from her college dorm room were on one wall and a particle board wardrobe stood on the other. A lamp was lit on the small college dorm desk, painting the room's cream walls a pale yellow by its soft glow. A tiny bathroom was hidden behind the open door to the room and Julia breathed a sigh of relief that she wouldn't be expected to use a communal bathroom.

"Get some sleep and we'll talk again tomorrow," Dr. Rayborn said, patting her lightly on the arm and shutting the door.

"Goodnight," Julia said after the door had already closed. She turned the dead bolt and leaned against the wall, hitting her head on a metal coat hook that was too close to the door frame to serve any useful purpose. Julia had bypassed the level of exhaustion that actually allowed sleep and was now functioning on auto-pilot, her body moving by muscle memory rather than conscious brain command. She felt slightly buzzed, the kind that you feel from a few margaritas; the kind of buzz where you're aware of what you're doing, but have lost all ability to care if any of it is right or wrong. If this buzz had been caused by cheap tequila and a rim of salt, Julia could have curled up in her own bed and nursed any hangover with coffee and an HGTV marathon. But this exhausted-in-your-bones-anxiety-buzz was not going to go away with a good night's sleep. This buzz was going to stay awhile.

Julia zipped her overnight bag open, pulling out less-than-neatly folded T-shirts and shorts in various shades of khaki. Essentially, she had packed ten versions of the same outfit that she had on, each varying only in their neutral pallet shade and placement of cargo pockets. She eventually found the pink tank top and yoga pants that she wore as pajamas and sat down on the bed, kicking off her sandals and flicking them toward the far wall.

As she pulled her T-shirt over her head, the body odor that had been trapped in the cotton blend was set free and released into the room, mixing like a potpourri with the lingering scent of industrial-strength cleaning supplies that had been used to sanitize the space before she arrived.

Hearing something fall onto the floor, Julia noticed a few M&Ms roll toward the desk and disappear under a piece of linoleum that had come partially unglued. Finding another candy stuck in her bra, she pulled the green M&M from her cleavage and ate it to celebrate her arrival.

Chapter 7

The B Wing

Julia pulled the limp pillow over her head, but all it did was muffle the voices that were streaming like radio static under her door. She blindly felt for the travel alarm clock on the nightstand — 6:13 a.m.

Feeling heavy from the bags' weight under her eyes, Julia swung her legs out from under the blanket and sat there for a minute as her mind replayed the events of the last twenty-four hours.

She was in rehab. Even if she left now, she would never be able to erase the blip on her invisible life record. She had been admitted; it was official. Like a red stamp staining a manila file folder, REHAB was now part of who Julia was.

She felt ashamed. A two-week stay at a Sandals resort so much more respectable in terms of getaways. At least she could have returned with a tan and stories of umbrella drink bars. The thought of drowning her sorrows so much more appealing at six in the morning than the thought of actually facing them.

Stretching toward the ceiling, Julia could smell herself. The body odor that had grown from anxiety-induced sweat and a hot car ride had apparently fermented overnight and did little to help her self-esteem as she prepared to face her first day. Her first day in REHAB.

Julia looked for a wall calendar and black sharpie, supplies that she would have expected to see in any place built on finite stays and countdowns until release. Seeing nothing except a blank journal on the desk, Julia picked out clean underwear, shorts, T-shirt, and a purple polka-dot bra that she had expected to wear somewhere a bit more fun.

Shadows of walking feet emerged from the gap under her door, hushed tones growing louder as daybreak turned into daylight. She decided to stay in her room as long as possible, assuming that her late-night arrival would buy her a bit more time before she had to join whatever schedule grounded life at the Southern Sunset Center.

She wasn't in any hurry; if her first day could be spent in avoidance, she would welcome the opportunity to put a giant X through day one without having to do anything at all.

With limited warm water, the shower didn't take up as much time as Julia had hoped. She jumped out of the shower stall with still-soapy hair when the water cooled suddenly, afraid that it would turn ice cold without warning.

Bundling her hair in a towel, Julia looked at herself in the mirror and lost any ounce of hope she had left. The mascara smears were nothing compared to the cystic pimple that had continued to grow next to her nose. Julia's thirty-four years looked like they had pulled double duty and the aged image looking back was like a fast-forward screenshot of her older self.

Hot, Julia thought.

She touched the pimple, but it showed no signs of being pick-able. Typically, she would have gone for it anyway, totally incapable of resisting the urge to dig a small crater whenever a blemish surfaced.

Today, however, she thought it best to rely on her overpriced concealer and a heavily-lined eye to draw attention upward. Searching her suitcase for her makeup kit, Julia sifted through its contents and found no sign of it. Her makeup kit, plastic bag of disposable razors, and can of hairspray that she had grabbed from her apartment bathroom at the last minute were all gone.

"No, no," Julia said in disbelief, dumping the toiletry bag onto the bed to make sure her concealer wasn't hiding itself a bit too well among the cotton balls and small packages of Q-tips.

"You've got to be kidding me," Julia whispered, standing back and looking at the small pile of clothes on her bed, none of which could help camouflage a pimple or create a heavily-lined eye. "Son of a Sunset Center..."

Pissed, Julia wasn't about to sit back while her makeup products and cheap razors were filling some freebie box that staff were dipping into. She quickly brushed her teeth and got dressed, her hair dripping onto her shoulders as she turned the door lock and entered the brightly lit hallway. Too fired up to take notice, Julia didn't look as she flew out of the room and collided with a woman walking by. The book that the woman was carrying flew from her hands and landed with a loud thud on the linoleum floor.

"What the hell?!' she said, looking at Julia for explanation. "Maybe look where you're going."

"God, I'm sorry," Julia said, beating the woman to the book and picking it up for her. "Seriously, I'm sorry," she said again, handing over the book.

The woman looked her up and down slowly. "I'm Gwen," she said, staring skeptically at Julia while extending her free hand to shake. Gwen was stunning; she looked a little older than Julia and stood about five-foot-nine, with flawless black skin and light blue eyes. Her hair was pulled back tightly and secured with a pinstriped head scarf, an effortless look that Julia would have never been able to pull off. Most people couldn't. Julia couldn't help touching her pimple again, aware that she was now drawing even more attention to it.

"I'm Julia," she said, taking Gwen's hand and shaking it. "I'm new here and was a little ticked to find half my stuff missing this morning. Sorry, again. I wasn't looking."

Gwen smiled, revealing a row of perfect white teeth.

Ridiculously white, Julia thought. *She must not drink coffee.*

"Yeah, that's the first little surprise in this place," Gwen said. "We're not allowed to have any personal grooming items other than toothpaste and basic stuff like that. They don't bother telling anyone that we should make sure to get a wax before coming here." Gwen smiled sympathetically at Julia. "We get to keep our deodorant, so that's a plus."

Julia smiled, but wondered if the comment was directed toward any lingering hints of her sweaty body odor. She made a mental note to smell her armpits as soon as Gwen turned around, now concerned that the tiny bar of soap hadn't been up for the hefty task that morning in the shower.

"Are you heading to breakfast?" Gwen asked, gesturing further down the hall. "It's not much, but there's coffee."

"Coffee, yes," Julia said. "Yes, yes."

The women walked with others toward the end of the hallway, the opposite direction from which she had come the night before. She followed Gwen's lead as they turned left and approached a single-file line of women that spilled out into the hallway from double doors. Julia felt like she was in high school again. She thought she had left behind the cattle-call feel of mass meals with her Trapper Keeper and copies of *Teen Vogue.* Her life was coming full circle; the universe had now decided to send her back to learn lessons that she should have learned the first time, lessons that she didn't learn because she was too busy siphoning liquor from her parents' crystal decanters and making copies of Liv's diary entries to even notice.

"The first few days kind of suck," Gwen offered, peering around the line of women to check out the breakfast menu. "There's a lot of hand holding and getting in touch with your feelings," she said, making air quotation marks with one hand as she stood on tiptoe to look over the other women's heads at the breakfast bar.

Julia wondered what Gwen was here for; she wondered what *everyone* was here for. The women around her looked no more dysfunctional than the average thirty- or forty-somethings trying to make their way through life, except without lip gloss and styled hair.

The line moved quickly, but Julia realized that wasn't necessarily a good thing. The first item coming into view in the help-yourself buffet was a sad cluster of bruised bananas hanging from a hook over a bowl of apples and pale oranges. Julia passed on the fruit and was surprised to see Gwen twisting off a particularly bruised banana, which she put on her plate next to a bowl of flesh-colored oatmeal. Julia had never been a fan of the mushy stuff and was pretty sure that, even if she had been, the color of this particular batch would be enough to quash it.

Gwen spooned brown sugar into her bowl—Julia counted four heaping spoonfuls before she finally stopped—and added a handful of blueberries into the mix.

Blueberries too? Julia thought, now convinced that Gwen must have some sort of stain-resistant coating on her teeth. Not wanting to appear snobbish about the menu, Julia grabbed a dry bagel and a container of strawberry cream cheese before filling a ceramic coffee mug at a side table. She dumped three containers of creamer into the mug and watched the coffee rise dangerously close to the top, the comforting white swirl of cream and familiar smell temporarily lowering her heart rate before she launched it upward again with caffeine.

Following Gwen to a round table by a window, Julia sat down and ignored the bagel, focusing solely on the coffee. She took tiny sips, studying Gwen from behind the mug. If she noticed, she pretended not to, mixing the bowl of sugar, berries, and oatmeal into a pasty blue concoction that looked no more appealing than it had before.

Julia wanted to ask Gwen why she was there, but wasn't quite sure of rehab etiquette. She had no problem sharing her stress, anxiety, and exhaustion diagnosis, but didn't want to assume that others felt the same, especially if they had an acronym stamped on their folder that was more sensitive than one that described just about every woman Julia knew.

Just then, a woman burst into the room and started gesturing wildly. Julia couldn't hear what she was saying, but she was obviously upset about something and was appealing to the crowd for support.

Gwen noticed Julia staring and glanced at what had caught her attention. She smiled. "Oh, that's Bebe. Don't worry about her; she launches into a rant every day about something or other."

Julia couldn't look away, both concerned and intrigued at the blonde woman with dark roots who was making her way from table to table talking to women who looked like they wished she would let them eat their bruised fruit in peace. She had an interesting look: her wrinkle-free skin so smooth that it actually aged her. It was impossible to tell how old she was; Julia guessed early fifties, but wouldn't have been surprised to learn that she was a full decade younger.

Rather than youthful, Bebe was an imitation of what a real person is supposed to look like. Julia couldn't help but stare. Her face looked *off*, like she was wearing some synthetic cover that was trying to protect the real thing.

"She's a character," Gwen said, eating a giant spoonful of oatmeal. "She's here for selfie addiction."

Julia laughed and waited for Gwen to do the same. She never did. Gwen spooned another mound of oatmeal into her mouth and raised her eyebrows at Julia with a smirk.

"Not kidding," she said. "She's apparently here for some narcissistic tendencies and an addiction to taking hundreds of selfies. We call them 'asses' here—the Addicted to Selfies crowd." Gwen laughed, but Julia looked at her in disbelief, as the dark-roots woman with plastic skin moved closer to their table.

Addicted to selfies crowd. There's more than one? Julia thought. The idea of more than one woman who had to seek professional help because they couldn't stop posting pictures of themselves to social media seemed too absurd to be true. Their self-absorption would have risen to life-impairing levels in order to qualify for any type of addictive behavior. Julia couldn't get her head around the thought of group therapy for women who tossed reality aside for one they created with photo filters. Psychology courses must have changed a lot since she took them in college.

"It's actually pretty sad," Gwen said. "She has a couple of kids and things spiraled out of control. I heard that she was brought up on child endangerment charges for trying to teach her sixteen-year-old how to inject her lips with stuff she bought in bulk from Mexico. She's here as part of some sort of diversion deal."

Gwen turned to the brown banana and showed no hesitation as she peeled it back and broke off the top half. "If you ever talk to her, don't get freaked out if it looks like a spider's crawling on her face. She has fake eyelashes and the glue's coming undone on them. She loses about one a day."

Everything in Julia was telling her to run. She didn't belong here: a place where bananas were brown and selfie addiction was real. A place where eyelashes were mistaken for spiders and deodorant was a luxury item. She could leave now and still spend a few solid weeks at a Sandals resort that offered complimentary razors instead of confiscating them. The coffee was helping Julia wake up in more ways than one and she was one sip away from asking for a to-go cup and taking it on the road. She was willing to test her luck with the empty gas tank.

With a blueprint for her getaway fast taking form, Julia was startled when a curly-haired woman in a purple yoga top jumped into the seat beside her and perched herself halfway over the table on her elbows.

"Bebe's in fine form today," she said, looking first at Gwen and then at Julia, apparently not bothered by the fact that she and Julia had never met. "I didn't do the writing assignment that Farkle assigned." She said this with a shameful grimace, like a schoolgirl confessing that she didn't do her homework and was worried about what the teacher might say.

"Cate, this is Julia," Gwen said, taking a big bite out of the second half of the bruised banana. "Julia, this is Cate. Resident rebel."

"Oh, whatever," Cate said, sending a small wave in Julia's direction. "*The Sound of Music* was on last night and I decided that singing along was more important than writing a journal entry about my love of Oreos."

Love of Oreos. Julia didn't even want to ask, although she got the impression that Cate would be happy to share just about anything.

"So, do people call you, Jules?" Cate asked, glancing at Julia's still untouched bagel.

"Sometimes," Julia answered. "Close friends and family."

"Well, we're just one big happy family here." Cate smiled, tucking a few loose curls behind her ear. She looked around Julia's age, but maybe a little younger. Cate's arms were ripped, the tiny veins that lived along her muscles protruding from the tanned skin that tried to provide enough coverage but had somehow failed. She looked in incredible shape, but there was a hollowness around her eyes that suggested good health extended only so far.

"Did you want my bagel?" Julia asked after noticing Cate glance at it again. "I haven't touched it."

Cate shook her head silently and looked away, her eyes now fixed on Bebe who was bouncing her way over to their table.

"Ladies, I don't know what I'm going to do," Bebe started, looking like she was about to bubble over. "This has just gotten to be too much. They've taken away everything. *Everything*." If she was hoping for a reaction from the table, nobody obliged. Bebe stared at Julia for a moment, perhaps waiting for an introduction, but then launched into her complaint after realizing that she wasn't going to get one.

"Dr. Barkle now wants me to go without a mirror," she said. "He actually wants to take the mirror out of my room, like I'm not worthy of my reflection anymore or something." Although big tears were now streaming down Bebe's face, Julia sensed that she was pretty good at creating them, having seen her wipe away a few at every table that she visited that morning. Julia also noted the name Dr. Barkle and assumed that Cate's "Farkle" reference had something to do with him. Her mental note file was growing by the minute and she wished she had a pad with her to write it all down.

"There's only so much I can take," Bebe said. A close-up view of her face made it no easier to tell her age, which Julia now guessed was somewhere around forty-four going on fifty.

Bebe's lips were inconsistently puffy, the right side of her top lip looking a lot fuller than the left.

Good grief, Julia thought. *The top lip literally looks like it cannibalized the bottom one.* She then touched the pimple pulsating on her face and realized she shouldn't be so quick to judge someone's appearance that morning.

"They say that I have body dysmorphic disorder," Bebe said, putting a hand on Julia's shoulder and talking directly to her. "They say that I don't realize how beautiful I really am."

"No, actually, that's not what they say," Gwen interjected, rolling her eyes. "You won't stop messing with your face and taking pictures of yourself."

Bebe looked mortified. "That's not true! That's not true!" she said, shaking a long finger at Gwen. "I don't know how beautiful I am!"

"Well, maybe they mean that you don't know how beautiful you are on the *inside*," Julia offered, trying to neutralize the situation. She smiled at Bebe, who now looked even more frenzied than when she had approached the table. Noticing a small black wispy thing stuck to her cheek, Julia was relieved that Gwen had given her the heads-up as to falling eyelashes.

Bebe left the table, but not before giving Gwen a look from hell. She approached a table full of women about twenty feet away and started gesturing, wiping away a few tears that had somehow started to fall again.

"So, are you in Farkle's morning session?" Cate asked, tearing off a small piece of the bagel that she said she hadn't wanted.

"I got in late last night and don't really know what I'm supposed to do," Julia answered, pushing the bagel further in front of Cate. "Am I supposed to go somewhere this morning?"

Gwen wiped her hands off with a paper napkin and pushed her plate aside. She had finished every last drop of oatmeal and the banana peel lay on the plate like an octopus with its tentacles spread out in all directions.

"They'll find you," Gwen said. "Someone will make sure you go where you're supposed to."

Before Julia could respond, static came over the intercom system followed by a high-pitched beeping sound and a woman's gravelly voice. "Julia Marsh, please report to the front desk."

"Let the healing begin," Julia said, grabbing her empty coffee mug and waving shyly at Gwen and Cate. "Guess I'll see you later."

"Good luck," they responded at the same time. Cate grabbed the bagel that she insisted she didn't want, tore off a piece and squeezed the entire container of strawberry cream cheese onto it before shoving the pink-covered bite into her mouth.

Julia walked past Bebe, who had moved on to another table and audience, this one looking no more interested in her story than any of the others. She tossed her hair back and wrapped a small section around her finger like a curling iron.

"*Beautiful*," was the only word that Julia caught as she walked by.

Chapter 8

The Barking Farkle

"Dr. Rayborn's gone home for the day." Dr. Barkle skimmed the contents of the same manila folder that Julia had discussed with Dr. Rayborn the night before, raising his eyebrows slightly and chewing on his bottom lip as he read.

"I guess I thought I'd be meeting with her," Julia continued, pretty sure that the man across the desk wasn't even listening. Dr. Barkle's office looked nothing like Dr. Rayborn's.

The heavy walnut desk with elaborately carved legs looked out of place next to industrial metal shelving that held neatly stacked piles of papers alongside ten years' worth of issues of *Psychology Today*.

The winged-back chair that Dr. Barkle was sitting on was in stark contrast to Julia's vinyl-covered and ribbed pea-green seat that looked like it had been torn from the wall of a subway station.

His entire office had been furnished out of the pieces left over from an old person's garage sale, the worst of the worst that remained from decades of accumulated crap that wouldn't sell.

A heavily framed oak clock ticked the seconds loudly away, its small pendulum swinging like a hypnotist's charm to lull visitors to sleep. Julia did feel sleepy, the stuffy windowless office sucking away the energy that her morning caffeine had falsely granted her.

"I just got off the phone with your mother," Dr. Barkle began, closing the file and crossing his hands on his chest. He looked like a pregnant woman with his arms resting across his large belly, a thin short-sleeved work shirt with pit stains and unkempt mustache doing nothing to help the look.

Skillful minds might sometimes take an unexpected form, but there was something *off* about Dr. Barkle. He seemed like the kind of guy who would grab a six-pack and drive his wood-paneled station wagon to a peep show over his lunch hour—there was an ick-factor about him. Something gross.

Julia was suddenly awake. A series of possibilities flashed across her mind at the mention of a phone call from her mother, but Dr. Barkle was quick to provide context. "She wanted to make sure that you arrived okay," he said. "She mentioned something about your poor sense of direction."

"Oh, that's lovely." Julia smiled, trying to sound playfully annoyed, but really just relieved that it was nothing more. Evelyn Marsh wasn't known for minding her own business and Julia fully expected her to be overly involved in this process because she was footing the bill. If she couldn't be a mother-of-the-bride, she was going to be mother-of-the-emotionally-in-need, a title change that would cost her a sparkly new dress but pay her in loads of sympathy.

"It says you got in pretty late last night," Dr. Barkle continued, sticking a finger in his ear and twisting it multiple times before flicking something onto the floor. "Did you get breakfast?"

Gross.

Julia nodded, a bad coffee film still coating her tongue.

"So, here's what's going to happen," Dr. Barkle said, pulling his chair closer to the desk so he could rest his arms on it.

Julia thought he must have something against letting his arms hang freely; they had to be supported at all times.

"You'll have private counseling sessions every day, as well as group therapy sessions. We make every effort to place residents in groups that best fit their individual needs and pathway for improved health."

Julia was pretty sure that the last sentence came directly from the center's brochure.

He continued, "Here at Southern Sunset, we believe in taking a step back and making things simple. We don't allow various personal items, not because we think you'll use them to hurt yourself or anything, but because we like to focus our work on the inside out." Although he was looking her directly in the eyes, Julia was pretty sure that Dr. Barkle didn't believe a thing he was saying. His big belly and outline of a tank top undershirt were out of place in a sales pitch for inner wellness.

As Dr. Barkle scratched his head and looked around like he was trying to remember where he was, Julia tried to make sense of the cluster of papers and knickknacks that covered his desk.

At the base of his computer screen, a small family of four cacti wearing tiny sunglasses sat at attention in a terracotta bowl with a sign reading "Welcome to Tucson" stuck in the soil. A picture frame sat on the corner of the desk with its back facing Julia. She was tempted to twirl it around to see the people who earned such a spot, finding it hard to imagine a wife waiting for the likes of Dr. Barkle to return home and resume his position on the couch. Maybe there were kids, too; the ones who like to go around school and tell everyone that their dad is a doctor because it makes them feel important.

Stop judging, girl, Julia scolded herself. *He's sitting on one side of the desk and you on the other.*

"You'll be seeing Dr. Rayborn for your one-on-one session," Dr. Barkle finally said, as if remembering the checklist that he was supposed to go over with new patients.

Julia tried to hide her relief, but let a small smile escape. She felt oddly comfortable with Dr. Rayborn; if she was going to get anything out of this experience, it wasn't going to be sitting across from someone who publicly mined for ear wax and didn't understand the importance of sleeves in undershirts.

Stop it, Julia thought again, smiling a bit wider to hide the judgment.

If Dr. Barkle noticed the smile or look of relief on Julia's face, he pretended not to. "For residents like you, we strongly suggest that you participate in our meditative activities, like." Dr. Barkle rummaged around on his desk for a moment before finding a piece of paper with a bullet-point list. "Meditative activities, like," he continued, not even trying to pretend like he knew what they were. "Yoga, Pilates, meditation, and..." he flipped the paper over. "...nature walks."

Residents like you. Whatever reputation a "stress, exhaustion, and anxiety" diagnosis may carry in this place, Julia was pretty sure that Dr. Barkle wasn't buying into its clinical legitimacy. That made two of them, so she was actually fine with that.

"Personally, I do a lot of yoga," Dr. Barkle said, patting his large belly and laughing. His laugh caught Julia completely off guard; it sounded like an injured seal calling for help. An injured seal with hiccups.

Barking Farkle.

Dr. Barkle wasn't exactly what she pictured when she thought of psychiatrists. He didn't wear reading glasses or a beige cardigan. There wasn't a couch in his office or a box of tissues in easy reach for patients to blot their tears when they relived tough memories.

Julia had yet to see a thoughtful or pensive look cross Dr. Barkle's face. She bet he had a retirement countdown clock somewhere so he could watch the minutes tick away until he could leave this place and *residents like her* behind and spend his days in Key West wearing tank tops that he got free from some beach bar.

Julia managed a polite smile and pushed her chair back to signal that she was done with the conversation. Dr. Barkle handed her a piece of thin yellow paper, its pink and white copies left on the clipboard in front of him.

"You'll need to head on down to the medical office for your check-up," he said. "All residents get a physical after admission." Dr. Barkle sat there for a moment before realizing that proper etiquette dictated that he should probably stand up and see Julia out.

She didn't give him the chance, however, instead heading for the door and pointing down the hall in silent request for guidance as to the direction of the medical office.

"Walk toward the mess hall," Dr. Barkle said. "Last room on your left."

Mess hall. Julia wondered if Dr. Barkle had a military background or if his army reference was just par for the course from someone wildly unqualified to work somewhere that boasted "sensitivity from professionals who can relate." She walked down the empty hallway slower than necessary, relieved to have a moment to herself.

She heard muffled voices in the distance and the humming of fluorescent lights overhead echoed off the tiled walls, sounding like a beehive. Julia wondered if she had time to get another coffee before heading into the medical office, but thought better of it when she burped suddenly and could taste the leftovers of her last cup.

She found the frosted glass door etched with the word

"Medical" and pushed it opened, peeking inside to make sure she wasn't walking in on someone mid-exam.

"Come on in, love." An elderly black woman gestured from behind a desk. "No need to be shy."

"I think I'm supposed to give you this," Julia said, handing her the yellow paper.

"Oh yes, thank you," the woman responded without looking at it, placing it on an impressive pile of papers of the same color. The pile next to it was blue and fewer in number. Out of curiosity and an indifference toward others' privacy at the moment, Julia tried to read the tests required by the blue sheet. She saw the words barbiturates and cocaine on a long list of other drugs.

"I'm Mona," the nurse said, busily pulling gauze and other supplies from a drawer. "This won't take but a little minute of your time," she said with a thick Southern accent, patting Julia on the arm and motioning for her to sit on an exam table. Based on her short gray hair and wrinkles that carved deep valleys across her skin, Mona looked around seventy years old. She may have very well been younger, but her heavy weight made it difficult to walk and aged her with each painful step that it took for her to shuffle from one drawer over to the next.

"We just need to make sure your clock's tickin' and your pipes are clean," Mona said, trying to separate two rubber gloves that had become stuck together when she pulled them from their cardboard box.

"No worries," Julia said with a smile and shrug. "I don't really have anywhere to be."

As Mona battled with the rubber gloves, Julia looked around the room. It had been painted a cheery yellow and, unlike many of the other rooms in the building, had a large window that let in an abundance of natural light. Julia felt a shift in her energy level just sitting there, the bright yellow combined with sunlight a natural remedy for the lethargy that had almost made her catatonic sitting in Dr. Barkle's office. A string that spanned from one end of the wall to the other was used as a clothesline for children's paintings, brightly colored rainbows and a two-headed green monster with orange eyes doing more than anything else to lighten the energy in the room.

"Those are my grandbabies," Mona said with a proud grin, nodding at the artwork after seeing Julia's stare. "Henry is three years old and a little Picasso, that little one. Penelope, I call her Penny even though her mama doesn't like it, she's five years old and just the smartest little thing." Mona stopped what she was doing and stared at the artwork, smiling the broad smile of grandmothers everywhere who get the opportunity to enlighten strangers on the many gifts of their grandkids.

"Yes, ma'am, those grandbabies are my world," Mona said, turning her attention back to Julia. Her smile remained, revealing a few missing teeth on the bottom right side.

"Let's go ahead and start with this not so fun part," Mona said, inspecting the veins on both of Julia's arms to see which one was best fit to give up a little blood. "Look at those pretty arms," she said, tying the rubber band around Julia's upper arm and swabbing an area with cool antiseptic. "Lord knows, I don't always see such pretty arms," she said, gliding the needle into Julia's arm. Even done perfectly, the resulting sting was always enough to make Julia wince and look away.

"No, I've seen me some arms that have so many track marks you could play connect the dots," Mona said, drawing the blood needed and then smoothly removing the needle. "That's the work of the devil, that stuff," she said, putting a cotton swab onto the site and placing Julia's hand over it to apply pressure. "Drugs are the devil's work. He takes so much more than he gives, that one."

"I'm sure you see some interesting stuff," Julia responded,

not sure of what to say. Genevieve had battled drug addiction during a particularly dark time in her life, so Julia had witnessed the hopelessness that followed a high and felt helpless during her friend's descent. In typical Genevieve fashion, she had managed to kick the habit without professional help, her only nod to her past a black "H" that she had incorporated into one of her tattoos as a daily reminder of the drug that enticed her over to the dark side for a while. She hadn't thought of her since arriving, but now Julia was overwhelmed by a need to talk to her friend, a friend who would encourage Julia to embrace long leg hair and have the perfect words to describe the women that she's met here so far.

"Okay now, we just need to go over some background and then you'll be free to go after you pee in a cup."

"Awesome," Julia said, sounding more irritated than she had intended.

Mona settled herself back into her desk chair, letting out a huge sigh as if standing for ten minutes had completely wiped her out. She pulled out a clipboard and pen and started running down a list of medical questions that were standard in any check-up: family histories and past diagnoses the launch pad for assessing current health.

"Diabetes, stroke, heart disease."

"No, no, no."

"Diagnosis of schizophrenia, suicidal ideations, bipolar, or depression."

"No, no, no, and no," Julia answered without really listening, her relatively clean lifestyle and simple medical history making it easy to answer "No" to just about everything.

Mona flipped the page over and started on a second list, starting to check "No" to each before Julia even answered.

"Normal menstruation?"

"No," Julia answered. "I mean yes," feeling like she had

been caught not listening when a curveball question was thrown her way.

"Caught ya," Mona said, laughing, leaning back in her chair so far the hinges were stretched to their maximum and the chair's legs were ready to come off the ground.

"Currently pregnant or pregnant within the last twelve months?"

Mona marked "No," but then looked at Julia when she failed to answer.

"Honey?" Mona asked. "You okay?"

Julia hadn't seen it during her first office go-around, the finger painting that was taped to the side of the metal file cabinet. Tiny little fingers had painted stick figures surrounded by flowers and a sun high overhead. The word "family" was written in blue marker across the bottom.

Maybe it was Mona and her grandmotherly nature, or the comfort of the yellow room and the warmth of the sun. Maybe it was exhaustion and feeling homesick for all things familiar. Maybe it was the painting of a family by tiny hands that reminded Julia that, although she had come close, she had no stick figures of her own. Whatever the cause or combination, Julia felt her shoulders slump and a heavy weariness seep into her body. She couldn't keep the tears from coming. For the first time in as long as she could remember, she didn't even try.

Chapter 9

It's a Wonderful Life

The black Mercedes was in perfect condition, except for a small dent in its back left bumper from misjudging the distance of a parking lot light pole, resulting in a minor imperfection to the gold-plated license plate frame. The frame was a bit gaudy, but it had been a gift from his mother when he bought the car and he didn't want to offend her.

The dent bothered him, but he hadn't gotten around to fixing it. Julia caught him checking it out every time he walked around the car, inspecting it to see if it had somehow morphed or grown while he was away. Guys were weird about their cars, so Julia considered his preoccupation with a barely noticeable dent an endearing trait to be added alongside his love for his mom and his secret fondness for Neil Diamond tunes, the latter of which he never would have admitted had Julia not caught him singing "Heartlight" in the shower.

Yes, Matthew Harris was a Neil Diamond-loving mama's boy who had walked into Julia's life with a smile and drink in hand. Genevieve and Julia had been settled in at their usual table for about a half an hour at the time, just long enough to finish their stuffed mushroom appetizer and order another round of drinks. The bar, which catered to young professionals, was known for its happy hour scene, so that they were approached really wasn't unusual; but that *Julia* was the object of the attention was.

Matthew Harris had approached their table without giving Genevieve a second glance, sitting the white wine sangria in front of Julia and giving her the best opening line that she had ever heard.

"I've had a really shitty day, but I've been sitting over there smiling every time you laugh," he said. "You've got the best laugh in this place and I thought it deserved a drink."

Julia didn't know what to say, catching a tiny flicker of jealousy in Genevieve's eyes as she, too, struggled to make sense of what was happening. It wasn't that Julia was unattractive, but whatever dazzle she brought to a room was always overshadowed by the *je ne sais quoi* that surrounded Genevieve.

Julia typically wore her shoulder-length chestnut hair tied back because it was too fine to actually work into any style, but the look suited her. With big brown eyes, chiseled cheekbones, and full lips, she had often been told that she looked like a dancer—perhaps a retired ballerina on her way to the show. She wore minimal makeup, just enough to play up her long lashes and pouty lips, but her understated beauty was always in the shadow of Genevieve's glamorous style. They were now both somewhat stunned to have stumbled upon the one person who seemed entirely unaffected by Genevieve's cosmic power; not only unaffected, but oblivious.

Flattered, Julia blushed slightly at the attention that her childish giggle had brought to their table. Her laugh had always made her feel self-conscious, and she had struggled over the years to shake its schoolgirl pitch, but genuine laughs are the one thing you can't relearn. It's not like learning to walk a different way or use table manners; laughing comes from that innermost part of the soul that makes imitation impossible. It is like eye color. You can put in fake lenses, but everyone knows that the real you is hiding somewhere underneath.

"Well, thank you," Julia said, pushing her empty wine glass toward the middle of the table and reaching for the full glass. "Are you here alone?" she asked, gesturing toward the empty chair beside her.

He accepted and the three of them spent the next two hours ordering round after round of drinks, playing a surprisingly competitive game of darts, and being the one table in the place that everyone wished they were at because they were having so much fun.

Not much substantive conversation was had, but Julia learned a few facts about Matthew. He was thirty-nine years old, a rising star in a public relations firm, and relatively new to the area after relocating to Atlanta from Chicago.

He was horrible at darts, but his careful attention toward the dart board gave Julia the time to study him without being noticed. He was over six feet tall, had light brown hair that was worn long enough to curl slightly behind his ears, and he had a faint scar next to his left ear.

Dressed in a button-down and khakis, he looked the part of an up-and-comer in the corporate world, but he was far from the metrosexual that Julia tried to avoid. His nails didn't look manicured and his stubble not intentional; the dark shadow on his neck and jawline more a didn't-have-time-to-shave look than anything else.

His thin lips and the slight bump on his nose added to a package of visual imperfections, every one of which fell into the positive category on the checklist that Julia was creating.

By the time they had finished their third dart match, Julia had come to a conclusion. She was wildly attracted to this guy who thought her giggle was endearing and who had the nerve to approach her and tell her so. In terms of chemistry, Julia was pretty sure that their test tube would be bubbling over right about now.

That first night at the bar turned into another, and another after that. Julia, Genevieve, and Matthew met for drinks after work and spent each evening sitting at the same table, drinking the same drinks, but telling different stories. By the third night, Genevieve had tried to bow out, but Julia wouldn't let her. She didn't want the dynamic to change. There's nothing worse than putting your own hypothesis to the test and finding out that you had made a fatal miscalculation. Perhaps she had; perhaps she and Matthew wouldn't work if it was just the two of them. If she could have three nights of hopeful contemplation, she saw no need to give up a fourth, or a fifth and sixth if Genevieve could be talked into it.

If all went well, Julia might be able to build a serious relationship with the guy without ever having to leave her best friend at home, backed up by the comfort that comes with knowing that someone has your back and is there to fill in any awkward gaps in conversation. Genevieve knew everyone, knew about everyone, and knew the latest news that only those in-the-know knew. Next to cab money and pressed powder, Genevieve was the best possible thing to bring on a date.

If Julia had hopes to continue with the festive threesome, Matthew had other ideas. After a few weeks of meeting up somewhat regularly for a dart match showdown, he texted Julia one night and asked if just the two of them could go out.

It didn't even bother Julia that he had texted instead of calling. Sure, calling to ask her out officially would have been nice, but Julia didn't mind the impersonal nature of a text message. It gave her more time to think of witty responses and allowed her to wait the appropriate ten minutes before responding. Julia caved in after three and happily accepted his offer. She decided that mind games were for twenty-somethings; big girls needed to act like it and accept a date when a cute guy asks her for one.

Matthew looked as relieved as Julia did when, sometime during their first official date, they realized that they were laughing just as much as when Genevieve had been with them. They ate sushi and talked about their families, places they've traveled and wanted to, and any regrets that they were still trying to remedy in life. Their first date blended into a second, a third, and many more after that, seeing each other as much as work schedules allowed. Sometimes it was twice a week; and sometimes travel schedules meant text messages and phone calls were going to have to do, and conversations were resumed over room service on one end and take-out on the other.

Julia waited two months to sleep with him. She was actually proud of herself for waiting that long, intentionally not shaving and wearing unattractive cotton underwear to curb her urge to tear it all off at the end of the night.

The grown-up part of her brain wanted to leave sex out of the relationship until they had built something for it to grow on.

The teenage part of her brain was enjoying the heated anticipation that each make-out session brought, the heavy kisses and groping on her couch making her feel like they were about to get caught by a set of parents who would gasp in horror at the sight of unzipped pants and a bra lying lifeless on the floor.

Julia was enjoying the sexual tension, the groan that Matthew made when she pulled his hands away to stop him from going too far. She was a lovesick teenager basking in the anticipation of it all, especially the dramatic goodbye kiss at the door that filled her with enough fantasy material to get her to their next liaison.

She was in her own romantic comedy, complete with

moments of erotic breathlessness and giggles over their fortunes told by the stale cookies that came with their boxed chow mein. She was Meg Ryan, but without the perfect mouth and blonde hair.

Genevieve was horrified. She couldn't imagine waiting more than a few dates to sleep with a guy who she found as irresistible as Julia did Matthew, but Genevieve had never seen *Sleepless in Seattle*, so what did she know.

Sex came after a few months and it didn't disappoint, the hands that she had turned away during so many breathless moments now free to explore wherever desire took them. Matthew was great in bed—a perfect combination of youthful giddiness and master craftsman when it came to technique and willingness to please.

Julia had read about a post-sex glow when you finally experienced the good stuff and was pretty sure she had it, examining her face in the mirror after particularly raucous romps and marveling at how her skin looked better than after any facial. She was more than happy to add this particular item to her skincare regime: sex was better than extractions for clean and healthy pores.

Sex came first, followed closely by their first lover's spat. Julia was actually relieved when they argued for the first time, considering it yet another sign of a healthy relationship between two people who weren't interested in playing games. Nobody's flawless, so she considered minor disagreements the product of a perfectly imperfect relationship and she was quite proud of how they had talked this one through.

Julia had tickets to the opening night for an exhibit in her favorite art museum, but Matthew had canceled at the last minute because he was taking clients to dinner. Even when she was acting the role of disappointed girlfriend, Julia hadn't really been that upset with Matthew. They both understood that work obligations came first sometimes and her reaction stemmed more from her love of a little drama than from any genuine pangs of frustration.

For the first time in as long as she could remember, Julia felt like she was in a functional relationship. The early stages of relationships are full of butterflies and sexual excitement, but they make way for something even better.

She felt comfortable walking around her apartment in underwear and bra-less under a tank top when Matthew was around, his love of her body adding to the confidence that she felt displaying it in ways that she normally wouldn't have. She felt sexy and uninhibited in the bedroom—while effortlessly poised outside of it—a combination that she felt should be on a billboard, advertising what it felt like to be a *woman*. A *natural* woman. It had taken Julia thirty-four years and her share of kissed toads, but she finally understood what that song was all about.

Matthew had clients all over the country, so Julia didn't see him as often as she would have liked. But she saved up little tidbits of news to share with him in whirlwind fashion when they did get an evening together to just put their feet up and catch up. If he stopped by the gas station on his way to her apartment, Matthew would bring her a gossip magazine and her favorite pink lemonade. They would then talk about their weeks as Julia educated him as to the salacious celebrity cover story or the latest guy that Genevieve was dating and whether they should try to schedule a double-date.

Julia would pick up Matthew's dry cleaning and hang it in her closet, which she claimed was for convenience, but was really because she liked to open her closet door and see his perfectly pressed work shirts greeting her. They got to the comfort level where they ordered each other's coffee and didn't have to ask what the other one wanted on their half of the pizza.

They would pee with the bathroom door open, and they would have sex post-gym and pre-shower.

Matthew sat through *It's a Wonderful Life*, despite admitting that he had always hated it, and Julia went to an Atlanta Braves baseball game instead of attending a one-day art exhibit that she had been waiting for since its announcement the past summer. They were in a grown-up relationship that was full of compromises and tiffs, compliments and words of encouragement, and lemon drop shots during dart marathons with high fives and celebratory kisses in the middle of the bar.

The word "love" had been thrown around a few times, but Julia didn't need anything more than what she had at that moment—a good guy who made her feel like everything she thought, felt, and did mattered in a world when so few things actually did.

After almost seven months together, their relationship had something else. It had a lime green sticky note with a woman's handwriting that Julia didn't recognize tucked inside Matthew's wallet. A note the color of fluorescent jello that was enough to undo all that had been built on surprise pink lemonades, tuna rolls, and hour-long phone calls.

A tiny piece of paper that was strong enough to viciously snatch Julia from her romantic comedy and remind her that life wasn't always what it seemed. Life wasn't so wonderful after all.

Chapter 10

Story Time

"I'm fine, really."

"Rose, you're *not* okay and that's okay," Dr. Rayborn said, leaning forward as if they were the only two there, and not sitting in a circle of twelve nestled in the corner of the center's community room. "It's okay to grieve the death of your mother and acknowledge the pain that you feel with her loss."

Rose didn't look convinced. She pushed a few of the curls out of her face and tucked them safely behind her ear, eager to establish control. The curl rebelled and sprang back to its spot over her left eye. She blew upward, sending the curl into a freestyle spin before landing right back where it started.

"Yes, I realize that and I'm perfectly fine." She smiled sweetly and looked around the room like she was embarrassed by the attention. "I'd like to talk about how everyone else is doing," Rose said. "After our last session, it seemed like there were some issues left unresolved that people probably want a chance to discuss." She sat with her hands folded on her lap, smiling at every face around the circle that was now studying hers for some hint as to her true state of mind.

Julia had seen Rose a few times. The methodical way that

she poured milk onto every spoonful of cereal was hard to miss in the small dining room. She usually saw her sitting alone, but never felt a please-invite-me-to-sit-with-you energy coming from her table.

Rose seemed to be one of those people who liked the time to herself, usually reading while eating, coordinating a page turn with each bite. Julia wondered about her. She wondered why she chose to read instead of interact, and whether her sweatshirts embroidered with kittens and flowers reminded her of a beloved pet or sunflower garden back home. Rose was quiet and withdrawn, sometimes sporting wire-framed glasses and other times not. Her exposed gray roots were in contrast to skin that looked like it had never gone without sunscreen or moisturizer, a battle between middle age and youth fought at her hairline.

Julia had only been at the Southern Sunset Center two full days, but she already wondered about this woman who now sat with her ankles crossed and hands folded on her lap like a rule-abiding church goer. Julia didn't know much about Rose, but she was sure of one thing. Somewhere behind her sweet smile and concern for other people, Rose was one thing. Sad.

"Wait, are we Facebook friends?"

Rose suddenly turned to Julia and stared back. It wasn't until she noticed everyone staring at her that Julia realized the question had been directed to her.

"Yes, I'm pretty sure we're Facebook friends," Bebe said, clapping her hands as if she had just solved a challenging riddle. "I mean, I have thousands, but I thought I recognized you and that would explain it." She sat perched on the edge of her plastic chair and waited for Julia to confirm that they were, in fact, connected socially.

Julia hated that she felt embarrassed; she felt guilty, but she didn't want anyone to think that she and Bebe ran in the same circles, concerned that her credibility among the other women would be damaged by any insinuation that she, too, was part of the selfie circuit.

Julia caught Gwen's eyes as she rolled them, the focus of the room shifting in less than fifteen seconds from talk of someone's dead mother to popularity on social media. Bebe was still staring at her and waiting for an answer, the smile on her lopsided lips suggesting that she was confident there was a connection between her and the new girl.

"No, we're not friends on Facebook," Julia said, hoping the absurdity that she felt at the suggestion didn't come across in her tone. "Pretty sure, no."

Bebe sunk into her chair, defeated, waiting for a moment to see if Julia would realize her mistake. It didn't surprise Julia that Bebe had thousands of Facebook friends, the quantity somehow validating her in a way that quality never would. Julia felt a little sorry for Bebe, her attempt at connecting with the new girl shot down in a public way that was probably mortifying for someone who put such a great deal of emphasis on perception. Bebe now looked sad, too. Everyone in the room was sad; Julia already didn't like these group sessions.

"Gwen, would you like to get us back on track?" Dr. Rayborn asked with a sigh.

Julia had been pleasantly surprised to see her when she walked into the room that afternoon, fully expecting to see Dr. Barkle in all of his pit-stained glory wielding a clipboard and earwax. Apparently, he had to leave early and Dr. Rayborn was filling in for him. Julia couldn't even imagine the Facebook friend dialogue with Dr. Barkle in the room, although she bet he wouldn't find Bebe as off-putting as everyone else, her perky fake boobs enough to make most men forgive her internal flaws.

Gwen sat directly across from Julia in the circle of chairs. She unfolded her arms and put them on her knees, leaning forward and clasping her hands like she was watching an intense football game. "Well, let's see, where did I leave off?" Gwen said.

"I'm not sure where you left off in group session with Dr. Barkle, but you can start wherever you feel comfortable," Dr. Rayborn responded, clicking the end of her pen and flipping over a page on her small writing pad.

Gwen bit her lower lip and looked up at the clock on the wall, perhaps trying to estimate how much sharing she'd have to do until time was up.

"Alright, well, I guess I'll talk a little bit about what we did during private session this morning," Gwen said, looking at Dr. Rayborn for approval. Getting a nod in return, she leaned back and clasped her hands behind her neck, stretching like an athlete before a race.

"So, I worked at a pretty high-profile law firm downtown Atlanta," she started, relaxing her shoulders and looking at the ceiling. "Demanding work, long hours, and intense people. I was there for six years and worked on really complicated cases with make-it-or-break-it results for our clients." She paused to inspect one of her fingernails and bite her lower lip again. "Long story short, we got a pretty bad result for one of our clients. The client was mad and the firm looked pretty bad because we were confident that things would go our way. In hindsight, maybe a bit too confident."

"I simply can't imagine going to school that long," Bebe whispered loud enough for everyone to hear. Although she was leaning toward Rose, she clearly intended for the entire room to hear her thoughts on higher education. Rose looked straight ahead and didn't make eye contact with Bebe.

"As everyone knows, we don't comment during others' sharing time in group sessions," Dr. Rayborn said, looking straight at Bebe.

Bebe sat back up straight and twirled her hair, completely unfazed by the fact that she was a middle-aged woman who had been scolded during circle time.

Gwen shot Bebe an irritated look, but looked like she didn't care enough to make an issue of it. She glanced at the clock again. "So, basically, my boss threw me under the bus," she continued. "He told the client that my work hadn't been up to par, arguments should have been made that weren't, and that my filings with the court weren't what he would have expected 'from an attorney of my experience.'" She said the last part with air quotes.

"That must have been frustrating after you gave so much to your firm," Dr. Rayborn said, stating the obvious.

Julia hadn't known that Gwen was a lawyer, but it didn't surprise her. She seemed like she could handle her own with the best of them and Julia made a mental note never to get into an argument with her.

"Well, yeah, it pissed me off," Gwen said. "Every single thing that I did on that case had been reviewed and approved by my boss. He complimented me throughout the case, told me that he was going to recommend that I get a huge bonus at the end of it and said that I had pretty much paved my way toward partnership." She was getting fired up talking it and Julia could see her hands trembling. She couldn't imagine sitting here telling her own story: something about the echo from the cinder block walls and cheap coffee in disposable cups made her feel vulnerable.

"How did you handle it?" Dr. Rayborn asked. She clearly knew the answer, tilting her head as if to ask if Gwen was willing to go all the way with the story.

"Not well."

"Can you elaborate?"

"I was pissed."

"Yes, you've said that, but can you talk about what exactly you did?"

Gwen took a deep breath in and stretched her legs out in front of her, reaching for her toes and giving Dr. Rayborn her own version of a tilted-head look.

"I retaliated."

Everyone in the room looked riveted, eyes wide and sitting at attention, waiting for the next morsel of the story. Julia felt like a voyeur; she listened to Gwen's story unfold and just wanted to know what happened next, nothing to contribute to all of this except shameful curiosity and an interest in the details of someone else's imperfect life. She felt kind of bad, but not really, her participation in group session one of the requirements listed on the welcome materials that she had skimmed a few lines of and then tossed in the trash.

Dr. Rayborn didn't look like she was enjoying Gwen's coy responses. She sat in silence twirling the pen around her finger instead of asking her to elaborate one more time.

Gwen looked uncomfortable. She was still stunning in her classy pulled-back hair and stylish yoga outfit, but she looked uncomfortable with sharing more details.

Julia looked at Dr. Rayborn, and then around the room, wondering if there were group rules for what to do in the event of a therapy stand-off.

Rose seemed as uncomfortable as Gwen, taking a tissue out of the sleeve of her sweater and twisting it until it broke in two. It wasn't hard to conclude that Rose didn't like confrontation, even if she was just a witness to it.

Bebe was busy smoothing down her eyebrows and trying to pull a few stray ones with her fingers.

"I'm not proud of what I did," Gwen finally said.

Dr. Rayborn didn't say anything.

"I had been under a lot of stress and I guess I just snapped."

Snapped. Julia wondered if Gwen had murdered her boss, her shameless curiosity now at a feverish peak. Assuming she wouldn't be in the B-Wing of some self-help treatment facility if she had killed the guy, Julia looked at the clock to see how much time they had before the session ended. If Gwen didn't finish her story in time, Julia was going to feel like she did when her favorite show was interrupted for breaking news.

"I had a really sharp letter opener in my office," Gwen continued, measuring with her hands how long the opener was.

Holy shit, she did it. She stabbed him. Julia couldn't believe this. The woman she had hung out with the most since arriving was a murderer. She wondered if she had read about this in the news. She wished that she had spent more time reading the actual news instead of just the entertainment and fashion sections.

The women in the circle looked a bit on-edge as to what they might hear. Everyone that is, except for Bebe, who either already knew the story or who was so intrigued by the cuticle that she was trying to pull loose that she found dealing with its imperfection far more important than the story being told.

Julia was pretty sure the brunette sitting next to Gwen leaned a bit away from her. In contrast, Dr. Rayborn looked calm and sympathetic, like she was proud of Gwen for having the courage to stand up for their dysfunctional version of show-and-tell.

"I'm not really sure what came over me, but I took my letter opener. And..." Gwen gestured a stabbing motion with her hand raised, bringing her clenched wrist down again, and again, like she was reliving it. "And, I stabbed his tires." Gwen dropped her raised hand and shook her head in embarrassment.

Julia leaned back and let out a breath, not realizing until that moment that she had been on the edge of her seat and holding it in. Her new friend wasn't a murderer, not of anything alive, at least.

"It was only strong enough to puncture the tire one time and then it bent, so I took it and scratched the outside of his car, every car door, mirror, hood, everything." Gwen rubbed her eyes and didn't make eye contact with anyone. "I wrote *asshole* on the side of his car. It was a bright red Porsche, so it showed up pretty good."

The room was quiet and even Bebe's attention had been momentarily turned away from self-grooming to Gwen's story. Julia was pretty sure she saw another spider eyelash on her cheek.

"It was horrible, obviously," Gwen continued. "Another attorney saw me do it. I got fired the next day and hauled out by security. There was a school bus full of kids parked out front for some sort of field trip, so that was really awesome," she said sarcastically. "I also got arrested and my bar license revoked." For the first time since starting her story, Gwen looked up and made eye contact with the women around her. There were tears, small tears that she didn't bother to wipe away.

"I'm here because I agreed to get some in-patient help with my 'anger issues' as part of my plea deal." With that, Gwen threw her hands in the air to signal that her story was done and there was nothing else to share.

"I know that was really hard for you," Dr. Rayborn said, with a supportive smile. "You feel regret for what you've done and now need to find a way to move forward from all of this. Sharing your story is an important first step in that process."

"Sounds like the asshole deserved it," a petite woman with a tattoo sleeve said, giving Gwen a thumbs-up.

"Kara, that's not productive," Dr. Rayborn said. "We all know that retaliating with violence is not the best solution to any problem. It just makes you feel better in the moment."

"Yeah, yeah, I know," Kara responded. "But it's done, so I'm just saying it sounds like he got what was coming to him. Karma's a bitch, baby." She gave Gwen another thumbs-up, but this one was down by her side so Dr. Rayborn couldn't see it.

Rose was crying and Bebe looked at her like she would catch something if she got too close. "Why on Earth are you crying?" she asked harshly.

"Bebe!" Dr. Rayborn scolded. "We all handle things differently and Rose's reaction is completely fine. We don't judge here."

With the attention now back on her, Rose seemed to cry even harder, the broken tissue doing little to dry her wet cheeks and blot the stream of tears.

Gwen looked exhausted, but somehow lighter. She gave Julia a small smile and shoulder shrug from across the circle. Julia winked and smiled in return.

"So, we have a little time left today," Dr. Rayborn continued. "Julia, this is your first session. I don't expect you to share today and please feel no pressure to do so, but you are welcome to talk if you want to."

Julia didn't want to, but she didn't want to appear uncooperative either. She figured saying something was better than not saying anything at all. "I actually have a question," Julia said.

"Of course, feel free to ask anything you want," Dr. Rayborn said. "We're an open and supportive group here." She gestured around the room, stopping briefly when she came to Bebe as if realizing that the description might not fully apply to her.

"Thanks," Julia said, realizing that she was leading the group on by making them think she was actually going to ask something substantive.

"Just curious," she said, feeling a bit guilty. "When's yoga?"

Chapter 11

Sincerely Yours

It should have been her birthday. On the outside, it would have been. People would have been extra nice to her. Maybe the super friendly receptionist at work with the uneven bangs would have brought in a plate of chocolate chip cookies, an email circulated to co-workers to let them know that it was Julia's special day.

Genevieve would have insisted on a happy hour and her mom would have called her—exactly at 4:25 p.m.—to remind her about the twenty hours of labor that she went through before finally welcoming a nine-pound baby girl who, even at birth, hadn't been petite.

It would have been her birthday on the outside, but inside it was just another day that would start with a toasted bagel and end with scentless soap in a lukewarm shower.

When she reached Dr. Rayborn's door, she was relieved to see that it was cracked open. During her first few visits, Julia hadn't realized that she would crack open the door to let the next person know that the prior session had ended and it was okay to enter. Clueless, even after doing it a few times, Julia had barged into ongoing sessions and interrupted rather sensitive discussions.

The first time, she had walked in and caught the tail end of a discussion that had something to do with a purple vibrator and margaritas. The second time, Julia had walked in on a woman simulating snorting cocaine off the desk. The women had both seemed nice enough, but she hadn't been able to look at them the same way again.

Knocking softly as she opened the door, Julia saw the back of Dr. Rayborn's chair. It smelled like incense, a thick combination of orange and lavender curled itself around the door and hugged Julia before she stepped foot into the office.

"Come on in." Dr. Rayborn waved with one hand without looking behind her. "I'm just finishing up." On the corner of her desk lay an incense stick in a ceramic holder, inches of ash defying gravity as the tiny ember burned its way to the end.

Julia sunk into the upholstered chair with a broken spring, preparing herself for the squeak that it made each time she sat down. It had wooden arms and a heavy plaid fabric, the smell of smoke still trapped in its weave from a previous owner. She wondered if the incense was supposed to mask the chair's odor or if Dr. Rayborn just liked smelly things. The latter gave Julia more joy.

The chair seemed dirty and worn, a thousand butts probably easing themselves onto its frame during its lifetime, the collective weight of dust mites outweighing the chair as a whole. The thought of dust mites, butts from days gone by, and a few unidentifiable stains weren't enough to keep Julia from loving the chair. She rested her head on its cushioned back and imagined stealing this ugly chair and taking it back to her apartment so it could join the others.

"So," Dr. Rayborn said with a smile, twirling around in her own chair. "Happy birthday." She handed Julia a few colorful envelopes. "I took the liberty of picking up your mail early since I figured you'd have some cards in there. Looks like I was right." She swiveled back toward her computer again. "Go ahead and read them now. I have to finish up something quick and will be a few minutes."

Julia looked at the two envelopes, the lavender one in her mom's handwriting and the white one clearly from Genevieve based on the swooping initials that were in place of a return address. She tore open her mom's first and pulled the glossy card from the envelope. A photo of a kitten hanging from a tree that looked remarkably like the one that was embroidered on Rose's sweatshirt stared back at her.

Good Lord, Julia thought. *This is going to say something about hanging in there.*

The inside of the card didn't disappoint. In bold block letters, it read, "Sometimes, it takes almost falling to know our own strength." Beneath the text was a handwritten note from Evelyn that she probably penned sitting at the tiny writing desk that she had bought for the front hallway for "correspondence." Julia had thought it ridiculous, the notion that a letter written at a kitchen table somehow less meaningful than one written at desk with tiny cubby holes that kept a year's supply of envelopes, stamps, and monogrammed stationery. She was sure that her mother bought this card and designated a time to write in it, a cup of tea accompanying her to her tiny desk that held a tiny lamp, to draft "correspondence" to the daughter who had "gone away for a while."

> Dearest Julia,
> Daddy and I think of you daily and hope you are well. Please take this time to sort things out so you can return to us as the woman we know you can be. We all face dark times in life, but the important thing is to rise above them

and hold our heads high. Happiest of birthdays to you, my
love.

    Sincerely yours,
    Mother

Julia looked again at the card's cover, the fuzzy kitten trying desperately to hang on. It wasn't even a birthday card. Her birthday came second in priority; it followed the more important reminder to pull herself together and make them proud. As the kitten refused to fall, so should she.

She tore open the second envelope and smiled, expecting nothing less from her best friend. A gorgeous man with greased-up muscles graced the card's cover, a fireman's hat in one hand the only thing covering his private parts. The inside read, "Happy Birthday. Thought you might like a stiff one (drink, of course)." Typical Genevieve. Underneath, she had written a short note.

    Hey Hotstuff,
    Happy birthday and all that jazz. Look at it this way—
you'll always remember turning 35! We'll celebrate when
you get home and see if we can't find us this fireman. :-)
Love you lots. You'll get through this and we'll laugh about
it later.
    Xoxo
    Genevieve

Julia put the cards back into their envelopes just as Dr. Rayborn turned back around.

"Did you get some nice cards from home?" she asked. "Being out of touch can sometimes be the most difficult part of this process, but having a birthday while you're here is really tough."

"It's fine," Julia lied. "It's just another day. I don't like to make a big deal about my birthday anyway."

There seemed no point in telling Dr. Rayborn the truth, in sharing that she wished that someone could bring her a plate of chocolate chip cookies and a little tiara that she could pretend was ridiculous, but then wear all day.

She was thirty-five years old; her thirties were halfway over and the number of acceptable justifications for her still-single status seemed to be slashed in half with each passing year. The fabulous single ladies in their thirties with Hermes handbags and demanding careers were credible in their claim that they simply didn't have the time to settle down, the price tag alone of some of their designer shoes enough to warrant one-hundred-hour work weeks and late nights in the office. That wasn't Julia, though; she still got excited with a Michael Kors find at Marshall's and left her job promptly at five o'clock each day. She had the time to settle down, was running out of excuses, and had no fabulous shoes. Julia was turning thirty-five in rehab and there was no way around it. It really sucked.

Dr. Rayborn looked at Julia like she saw right through her, but she knew better than to push it. Psychiatrists probably know that line well; there might even be a class in medical school dedicated to knowing when to call a patient on a known lie and when to back off.

"So, what would you like to talk about today?" Dr. Rayborn asked. "We've talked quite a bit about your family dynamic and work, but I thought maybe we could explore a bit more the reason why you're here."

Julia had spent her first few sessions talking about anything she could to fill the sixty-minute session until the tiny alarm clock on Dr. Rayborn's desk beeped and signaled that it was time to go. They had talked about her parents and their opposite personalities that made it easy to play them off one another.

Julia had told her about Liv's role as perfect child and Georgia's ability to slide under the radar with lesbianism and other curveballs, any of which would have been enough to send Evelyn to rehab herself had she known about them.

Dr. Rayborn had asked a lot of questions about her relationship with her mother. She apparently found it hard to believe that Julia didn't suffer from some serious issues from a lifetime of being forced into a proper Southern girl box.

"Yoga was pretty interesting today," Julia said. She was aware that Dr. Rayborn was losing patience with her diversion tactics by the sound of her heavy sigh and drop of her shoulders. "Yeah, Bebe needs to learn the benefits of a sports bra."

Julia had been going to yoga for five days now, ever since her first group session ended with a discussion of class schedules, instructors to avoid, and a critique of outdoor versus indoor sessions. None of the other ladies in her group went, except for Bebe, who always spread her pink yoga mat out in the middle of the front row even if it meant forcing the person who had already claimed the spot to move over.

Bebe only attended indoor classes in the small gym, which Julia assumed was because she didn't consider it worth her time if there weren't full-length mirrors to watch herself in, so Julia quickly decided that outdoor classes were the best ones to attend.

For whatever reason, Bebe showed up in the small outdoor courtyard that morning and laid her yoga mat directly in front of the instructor who Julia was pretty sure said something under her breath when Bebe stretched toward the sky and one of her boobs flew out from the top of her sports bra. Her boobs were like water balloons that couldn't be contained and she spent much of the class trying to corral them back into place.

Dr. Rayborn just smiled, taking a few notes that Julia assumed had nothing to do with bra-less Bebe or yoga. She tossed the small notepad onto the desk with the pen and crossed her arms in front of her. "Julia, I can't make you talk," she said. "We both know that. I want you to get as much out of your experience here as possible, though, and we can't accomplish anything if you aren't willing to share here or in group session."

Julia knew that she had overplayed her "new resident" card, a thirty-day-stay short in comparison to the more extended stays for some of the women. The seven days that she had already managed to stay silent about anything not related to food, exercise, or celebrity gossip was a healthy chunk of her total program that she was wasting. Or, so she assumed the argument would go.

"I know," Julia said, feeling a bit guilty about the song-and-dance that she had made Dr. Rayborn play during these sessions.

She hadn't written in the journal that she was given on her first day and instead used it to play tic-tac-toe with Gwen over lunch.

She hadn't shared a single thing during group therapy sessions, unless you count her DIY recipe for salt scrub and the package of gum that she passed around the room.

Even during the sunset meditation practice that she had signed up for, Julia spent the hour mentally rearranging the furniture in her living room back home instead of clearing out the "busy thoughts" that could apparently be collected and swept from the mind like dust bunnies off the floor.

She was far from the ideal resident and was still convinced that self-improvement could be found at the bottom of a strawberry-flavored cocktail or on a receipt for pretty items that she didn't need and would probably never wear. Better yet, Julia would love nothing more than a hot bath and good book right now, convinced that even the most stubborn layers of life's filth could be soaked off and sent down the drain if she disappeared into the bubbles long enough.

"I don't mean any disrespect, but none of this is going to help," she finally said. "The yoga, group therapy, *this*," Julia said, gesturing around the room. "None of this is going to fix me. Life sucks sometimes, that's it. My life is more messed up than some, and less than others, and that's just the way it goes. I'm not suicidal. I'm not considering moving to the desert or joining some spiritual cult that promises to guide me to the meaning of life." Julia looked for some sign that Dr. Rayborn understood, that she realized that Julia wasn't maladjusted or in danger of succumbing to her sadness, but she didn't see any. Dr. Rayborn sat there stone-faced.

"I get it," Julia said. "This is just a part of my life, not the whole thing. It will get better, things have a way of figuring themselves out." It felt good to get her feelings about this experience off her chest, even if it meant offending Dr. Rayborn or undermining the work they were trying to do here. She felt lighter with each word, her opinions somehow legitimatized by their introduction into the shared space.

"Maybe, we talk *too* much. Maybe, being forced to rehash the stuff that we want to forget is the worst thing that we can do to move on." She was on a roll and couldn't talk fast enough to keep up with the thoughts racing across her mind. "I just don't know why it's so wrong to let yourself feel sad," Julia said. "What happened to just letting ourselves feel what we're feeling and not labeling it as anything other than *life?*"

The women sat there and silently stared at one another, Julia weighing whether any of her comments had crossed a line. She hoped not; Dr. Rayborn had been one of the few professionals there that she had genuinely liked and she didn't mean any of what she said as a personal attack against her profession. Like so many things in life, it depended on the person. Some people could benefit from a place like this, and others couldn't. Julia could only speak for herself, but she doubted that Gwen was a high-risk repeat-offender for destruction of personal property and, from what she could tell, Rose just wanted to be left alone to mourn the loss of her mother in her own way.

She still didn't know what Cate was here for, but had little hope that Bebe's self-absorption would somehow transform into sincere modesty during the course of her treatment plan. The flying boob at yoga class that morning was proof of that.

"Well, it seems like you have it all figured out," Dr. Rayborn said with a sly smile. Julia couldn't tell if she was annoyed or proud that her troublesome pupil had finally talked. Dr. Rayborn turned the small clock to face her and slid a button on the top over to shut off the alarm.

"I think we can end a bit early today," Dr. Rayborn said, crossing her arms on the desk and leaning toward Julia. "You might think that we didn't accomplish anything today, but we did, and I'm incredibly pleased. You were honest and quite correct. There's no formula for how this works, but I feel like I understand you a bit better now." She smiled again, but this time it was easy to see that she felt strides had been made, even though Julia felt exactly the same as she had when she walked in.

Julia played along, smiling as if she was also pleased with her "progress" and giving Dr. Rayborn a small wave as the door shut behind her. A man was mopping the floor right outside the office, walking slowly behind the wide sweeps of a mop that had seen better days. He stepped aside to let Julia pass, lifting the mop and wringing it out in the yellow bucket on wheels. He smiled, revealing a silver front tooth next to a hole where its neighbor once sat. Julia tiptoed around the wet spots and hurried down the corridor toward the cafeteria. Because she had been let out early, there would be no line for afternoon coffee and donuts. There wouldn't be a plate of chocolate chip cookies or birthday tiara, but a fresh cup of coffee and boxed donuts would have to do.

As she walked past the door to the medical exam room, Julia wondered if Mona was there. She stopped by from time to time to say hello, the cheeriness of the office and Mona herself were like little pockets of sunshine, stories of grandchildren and colorful artwork a welcome addition to any day.

"Knock, knock," Julia said, easing the door open and peeking inside. Mona wasn't behind her desk and the overhead lights and computer had been turned off; either she was gone for the day or planned on taking a pretty lengthy afternoon break. Julia looked down the hallway to make sure nobody was watching and slipped inside the office, closing the door quietly behind her. Two large wooden cabinets stood along one wall with pill bottles and equipment displayed behind their glass doors, their old key locks reinforced by black and silver padlocks that dangled awkwardly from the vintage medicine chests.

Might also want to consider locking the door to the actual office, Mona, Julia thought.

Julia wasn't here for pills, although the thought of a little synthetic help to sleep at night wasn't unappealing.

What she wanted was behind the striped blue and white curtain, a one-hundred percent natural remedy for even the bluest of blues and heaviest of days. Julia pulled back the privacy curtain and hopped up onto the exam table, drawing the curtain shut behind her. She tried to ease her way into a lying position, but the white paper lining the table made it impossible to be quiet, the loud crinkle-crackle of each wrinkle under her weight made her feel like a burglar waiting to get caught.

Resting her head against the padded headrest, Julia found what she was looking for. The afternoon sun shone brightly through the office window, casting a bright beam of light across her face. Laying there, she let herself soak up the warmth of the sun, trying to imagine the vitamin D seeping into her skin and filling her body with the energy from its God-given source. The sun's rays felt like the warm bath that she had been longing for, the layers of life's filth soaked up and sent spiraling down the drain. The coffee and donuts would have to wait; Julia needed this moment of nothingness to escape, relax, and dream about what her birthday would have been like on the outside.

Chapter 12

Extra Cheese

On the *outside*, streaming services offered a revolving selection of new releases and documentaries to choose from. *Inside* these walls, an old DVD player and dusty collection tested residents' patience and willingness to negotiate.

"I can't do it!" Cate jumped up and started pacing the room.

She looked thin; thinner than Julia remembered seeing her at breakfast that morning. Truth be told, she never really saw Cate eat. She usually just stole nibbles of food off people's plates that had been offered to her and declined, as if official acceptance would have counted toward something. Or against it. Julia wasn't quite sure.

"I will seriously lose my mind if we watch *Pretty Woman* again," Cate said, the veins from her sculpted arms bulging from the tension of being hooked together above her head in an impressive yoga stretch as she walked. "I didn't like the movie the first fifteen times and I'm not going to like it now," she said, pointing a warning finger toward a middle-aged brunette in the front row who was clutching the DVD to her chest like Richard Gere was about to make an appearance.

"Sylvia, put it away," Cate warned. "It's my turn to pick and I want to watch *Alien*."

"Absolutely not, I'll have nightmares," Sylvia said, recrossing her legs and shaking her head. Julia knew this little routine by heart, Richard Gere's biggest fan staging a protest against any movie that didn't involve him saving some beautiful girl from a life of prostitution or the same girl from running away from another wedding. Julia wasn't a huge horror movie fan, but at this point, she'd prefer to see an alien escaping through someone's rib cage than Sylvia recite an entire screenplay and tear up at the end like she was seeing it for the first time as she repeated "I just *love* him" over and over.

"Sylvia, that's only fair," Gwen said, standing up and making her way over to the coffee station. "You've picked Richard Gere movies every night for a week. Not everyone feels the same way about the silver fox that you do."

Sylvia sat back in her folding chair, but didn't let go of the movie, crossing her arms to keep Richard Gere from escaping his plastic case.

Cate tried not to look smug, but failed miserably, a wide smile forming as she sifted through the box of DVDs for the movie she was looking for. While the audience of twenty or so adjusted their expectations from romantic comedy to space-horror film, Julia saw a pretty blonde sitting by herself in the back of the room. She didn't know everyone in the place, but she was pretty sure this girl was new, the way she was trying to shrink within herself the telltale sign of a new recruit.

Julia walked over to the coffee station, passing Gwen on the way back and giving her a high-five in appreciation of her intervention in the movie dispute. The women had become close friends over the ten days that Julia had been there, seeking each other out whenever program schedules provided them the opportunity for some free time.

Julia really didn't want any coffee, but filled her paper cup halfway and poured in an equal amount of powdered creamer. She stirred it with a plastic straw, debating whether to approach the new girl and invite her to sit with them. Taking her chances, Julia turned and walked toward the back of the room and sat down beside the blonde uninvited.

"Hi, I'm Julia," she said with a smile. "Not sure, but I think you might be new?"

"Is it that obvious?" she responded, trying to smile, but looking like a terrified child on the first day of school. "I just got here about an hour ago. I'm not sure what to do. They really didn't tell me what to expect or where to go."

The conversation now started, Julia felt comfortable leaning back in the chair and settling in for a minute. Gwen was looking around the room for her, but Julia gave her a wink and head nod to let her know that she'd be back in a minute.

"It's hard," Julia said. "These first few days. I've only been here for about a week and a half myself, but it does get a little better. Everyone's pretty nice. Coffee's not great, though." Julia held up the cup and grimaced a little bit, making the blonde smile.

"I'm Vivian," she said, extending her hand to shake. Julia was struck by her piercing blue eyes—they didn't need a lick of mascara, eye liner, or the sparkly shadow that Bebe had somehow smuggled into the place.

Vivian was petite, probably five-foot-three at most, and wore her hair back in a slick blonde ponytail. Her nails were perfectly manicured, but not overdone, a simple nude gel polish making them appear as effortless as the rest of her look. Even in yoga pants and a simple gray T-shirt, some women exude style that can't be bought or manufactured. These are the women who you can just tell have clean cars that smell like lavender, no expired medications in their hall closet, and underwear without any holes. Julia had a feeling that Vivian was one of those girls. Despite such perceived perfection, she liked her immediately.

"Is it always like this?" Vivian asked, turning her attention to the DVD stand-off that had escalated to include "sides," a few women now standing behind Sylvia to show their rom-com allegiance and a few others moving their chairs closer to Cate.

"Only when it comes to movie night," Julia said. "Or game night. Or craft night."

Vivian gave her a small smile and rubbed her arms like she was cold.

"Why don't you get a cup of coffee and join me and Gwen?" Julia said, nodding at her friend. "Gwen's drama-free, which is kind of hard to find here." The image of Gwen using a letter opener to key her boss's luxury car then flashed across Julia's mind and she realized that "drama-free" might not be entirely accurate. When surrounded by narcissists and kleptomaniacs—the latter of which was rather shockingly disclosed by a particularly quiet brunette during group that afternoon—Julia figured it was all relative.

Vivian stood first and looked lost until Julia turned her toward the table in the far corner with the coffee-stained tablecloth and economy box of artificial sweetener.

Julia had yet to take a sip of her coffee, so she topped it off and poured in another creamer just to have something to do.

Vivian took one of the tea bags from a small clear plastic holder and poured a cup of hot water. Julia had never seen anyone drink tea in here, but it seemed like a more respectable kind of a drink than coffee. Vivian opened one of the little bags and dunked it politely two or three times before wrapping the tiny string around her finger so the end wouldn't fall in. Julia wondered if she would like tea and decided right then and there that she would try it, if for no other reason than to have a tea bag to play with when she got bored during therapy.

They stood there for a moment side by side, watching the drama unfold. The copy of *Pretty Woman* was now being waved like a flag of freedom.

Julia was pretty sure she knew why movie night caused so many problems, basic psychology principles are a hard thing not to soak up when surrounded by therapy sessions and textbooks that preach them daily. Many of the women here had been dealt a personal blow—infidelity, extinguished flames, and emotional betrayal all top contenders as trigger points for stress-related conditions.

Romantic comedies and family-based dramas, therefore, were the last thing these women wanted to watch. Harry and Sally didn't live happily ever after in their life story and Meg Ryan's furrowed brow and witty retorts were enough to push them a few solid steps back on their road to recovery. On the flip side, only a few in the group actually enjoyed scary movies, leaving the rest of the women to claim that they would suffer immeasurable harm if forced to watch any story involving an abandoned house or doll whose eyes shifted when you weren't looking. That really left little else, a small selection of animated features and Best of Saturday Night Live skits the entire universe of unobjectionable material.

"Okay, guys, this is a little embarrassing," Gwen suddenly said, standing up and rolling her eyes at Julia across the room. "I'm going to make an executive decision and veto both of your movie choices."

Everyone always seemed to listen to Gwen; watching her effortlessly take control back from the fractioned movie-goers made Julia think that she must have been amazing in the courtroom. Surely, even the most skilled litigators couldn't compete with the energy and momentum that came from one woman's determination to spread rom-com love everywhere. The fact that Gwen had silenced the room by simply standing and announcing that the ridiculousness was over was impressive. If there was ever any doubt, Julia now knew that Gwen was someone you wanted on your side—be it in a rumble or debate.

Gwen walked over to the box of selections and fingered through them before coming to a pink DVD cover, which she raised over her head in triumph.

"*Bridesmaids*!" she yelled, plastering a fake smile on her face to keep anyone from objecting.

"There's so much horrible language in that movie," Sylvia said, shaking her head. "I don't understand why saying *fudge* every other word qualifies as comedy."

"Saying *fudge* doesn't make this movie funny," Gwen quipped back. "Explosive diarrhea in bridesmaid dresses and an odd love of Wilson Phillips does." Without waiting for further objection, she walked over to the ancient DVD player and put in the movie, grabbing *Alien* from Cate's hands as she walked by.

Julia and Vivian settled into two seats beside Gwen's empty one and drank from their cups in silence. Gwen came back to her seat with the remote control in hand, gesturing for Sylvia to sit back down.

"Holy ridiculousness," Gwen whispered to Julia, pointing the control at the television and ordering it to play the movie. When the previews started, she seemed to relax in her chair, shaking her head and smiling. "I taught fifth grade summer school during college and just had a flashback."

"This is Vivian," Julia responded, trying to include her in the conversation. "She's new and this is her first night."

Gwen reached across Julia and shook Vivian's hand, giving her a wink in silent solidarity.

"Lucky you. You got to see a little drama before the movie even began."

Vivian smiled in return, but didn't say anything. Julia couldn't help but feel bad for her, sensing that her skin wasn't as thick as it should be. *A thin skin won't get you very far here*, Julia worried.

"Pizza's here!" someone yelled. The squeak of twenty chairs filled the room as women rushed to be first in line for the perfect slice of pepperoni with extra cheese.

"It's like a cattle-call," Gwen remarked, the three of them the only ones still sitting as paper plates were passed down a line of eager pizza-eaters. "It's like they've never seen pizza before."

"No, like everything else, it's all relative," Julia observed. "Take something away and you appreciate it more." She could sense Gwen staring at her, but pretended not to notice, grabbing the remote control and increasing the volume to drown out the sound of cardboard pizza boxes being opened.

As the movie began, someone shut the lights off and, with them, all need for small talk. A pizza box made its rounds and Julia grabbed a greasy slice before handing it to Vivian, who passed with a polite head shake and gave it to a woman sitting behind her.

Drinks tea and doesn't eat pizza. Julia thought back to the boxes of Chinese take-out in her refrigerator back home that she didn't bother to throw away before leaving. Vivian probably didn't eat anything with MSG. Julia shouldn't care, but did for some reason. One of her worst habits was the endless need to compare her life to others to see how she measured up. Wiping some grease off her chin with a paper towel, she made the conscious decision to start low and compare herself only to selfie addicts for the time being before working her way up.

Her mind on other things, Julia hadn't paid attention to the first few scenes of the movie, and was surprised to see that it was already at the over-the-top engagement party that used to be one of her favorite parts. *Used to be.* She now focused on the movie and its talk of wedding planning and bridesmaids—a movie that Gwen considered a safe choice for everyone in the room.

Julia gnawed on the pizza crust, secretly wishing that Cate had won her battle and aliens bursting from people's chests were on the small screen rather than bridal showers and the story of a woman's life that wasn't going according to plan.

Chapter 13

Inbox

The pizza pieces were like cardboard: any bend that they might have had now lost to time and exposure. Genevieve had brought it over, hoping that a pineapple and Canadian bacon pizza from her favorite place would entice her to eat. It hadn't.

Julia had taken a bite out of one piece and left the rest, the mummified remains sitting in the box adorned with a cartoon chef wearing a pizza hat.

Without getting up from the couch, Julia lifted one edge of the box to peek inside. The Canadian bacon pieces were shriveled into half moons.

Pushing the box further from the couch, Julia pulled up the blanket that had been balled up by her feet and covered her shoulders with it, pulling it tightly under her chin. She was now used to the sweat under her arms, the natural stickiness of her skin somehow more comforting than any perfumed deodorant. The thought of getting up and in the shower was too much; she was content to stay on the couch that probably now had a permanent sweat stain from where her body had been for the last three days.

Genevieve wanted her to go the doctor, but she refused. In time, Julia knew that she would regret putting her friend in this position; leaving her to pick up blood-stained towels from the floor of the bathroom and wipe droplets of blood that had leaked from her body. She didn't need a doctor to tell her what she already knew. Blood flow wasn't a good thing. It was supposed to be lining her uterus and protecting something small and wonderful growing there.

Julia had called Genevieve curled up on the floor of the bathroom. She didn't know where the bloody towels had gone. All she knew was that they had disappeared and shriveled Canadian bacon had shown up to take their place.

Julia reached for the prescription bottle on the coffee table. Her instructions were to take one of the pills once every four hours as needed for pain, typed neatly above the name of the prescribing physician—Dr. G. Marsh. *Georgia.*

If Julia had realized that her older sister had been brought into this, she had closed the lid on that memory, pushing it away with the hope that it would mummify and disappear into dust.

Genevieve had obviously made the call to loop in Julia's sister, but she could only hope that the news had stopped there: the thought of Evelyn bursting through the door at any moment gave Julia enough energy to peek over the back of the couch to make sure it was locked.

The shades were drawn on her living room windows, but the clock on the end table claimed it was 2:35p.m. On what day, Julia wasn't sure. She grabbed a greeting card with a picture of bright flowers on its front that had been left standing on the coffee table for her to see, the inside wishing her a speedy recovery and signed by her team at work.

Georgia might have contacted work, but Julia somehow sensed it was Genevieve; and, knowing her friend, she probably came up with some exotic disease that can only be contracted by drinking unfiltered water in the Amazon.

Julia fell back onto the pillow and pulled the blanket over half of her face, leaving one eye out to survey the room.

She felt like she had brought this on herself because she didn't have to look. She could have easily thought up fifty reasonable explanations for the lime green sticky note and left it where it lay, a small piece of paper inside her boyfriend's wallet with handwriting that she didn't recognize.

Or, it could have just been forgotten, its memory overshadowed by dinner cocktails and the movie that he promised to take her to. Julia had considered the approach of people who choose not to find out if they're at an increased risk for medical conditions. She could have done the same and spared herself the equivalent of a devastating diagnosis that, once known, is impossible to forget.

But when opportunity presented itself, Julia couldn't pass on the chance to flip through her life's pages and read the last page so she could feel good about how it ended. Like all of the endings that she read too soon, Julia had been lulled by false expectations and immediately regretted listening to the whispering voice that assured her that everything was fine. That it all would end well.

Of course, she needed to know the truth, but *need* and *want* are at different ends of the emotional spectrum. She had considered Matthew's open laptop that night a sign from above, an opportunity handed her to click on that tiny icon and explore his virtual mailbox without fear of being caught while he ran to the liquor store down the street for another bottle of wine.

First taking a mental snapshot of the computer's position on the coffee table so she could make sure to put it back correctly, Julia had grabbed the laptop and positioned it flatly on her crossed legs.

Tapping the mouse pad lightly, she was surprised at how easily it opened, his personal world of electronic communication appearing on the screen in less than a second. Careful not to click on any messages that were still bold and unread, Julia scanned his inbox for names that she didn't recognize or for subject lines that hinted of a personal nature.

It felt strange seeing her own email messages on his computer, like seeing a gift that you have given someone on display in their home—evidence that a piece of you has been incorporated into their life.

She had come close to stopping herself, but the personal violation had been committed as soon as she had opened his email and closing it now wouldn't absolve her of that. Julia scanned the email, breathing easier with every work-related message and spam advertising she saw in the long list of read and unread messages. She became distracted from her purpose, intrigued that Matthew apparently got regular massages at Lotus Spa, subscribed to news alerts from the BBC, and had earned preferred customer status at an online cigar store that also sold hookah accessories.

Just as she was about to open an email from a hair club for men to see if Matthew's follicles were getting a little help, Julia spotted an email with a subject line that simply read "Saturday." She double-clicked, expecting to see online marketing for a live band at a local restaurant or an announcement that tickets were now on sale for an upcoming show.

Hi babe,

I made reservations at the place you suggested for Saturday at 8:30. Later than I would have liked, but they don't have anything earlier. You've been working so hard lately—I'm really looking forward to a relaxing night out.

xoxo

There it was. The font might as well have been written with the same pen stroke as the sticky note, the author undoubtedly the same. And, there were more. Many more. Daily emails from HarrisFamily@yahoo.com had been read and responded to, a loving "xoxo" always the signature in messages that ranged from restaurant reservations to plumber appointments and items inadvertently left off grocery lists. Like floating above an accident where she was the casualty, Julia had a hard time looking away, clicking on emails faster than she could actually read them. They became a blur of x's and o's, a sentence starting with "kiddo sends hugs" the final kick in Julia's stomach that had caused her to slam the lid of the laptop shut and put it back on the coffee table.

Even then, she made sure to put it back where it was, like returning it to its exact position was going to turn back time and erase the smiling emojis that accompanied virtual hugs sent from people who had stolen her life and used it like a credit card to buy the things that she could never have.

Julia left. Before Matthew had returned with the bottle of wine that he insisted on running out to buy, Julia had grabbed her purse and left her own apartment. She didn't want to be sitting on the couch when he came back, the look of triumph on his face as he raised the bottle like a trophy won in battle.

She had walked down to the corner diner that was open twenty-four hours a day and parked herself in a booth near the window, watching Matthew jog back into her building's front door. He called her a few minutes later when he discovered she wasn't there.

Julia had waited, ordering a bottomless cup of coffee and sipping it slowly, studying activity in her apartment like she was on surveillance for a crime about to go down.

She wasn't ready for a confrontation, the dim lights of the

diner helping to make her invisible as urgent text messages were received and ignored. An hour passed before Matthew finally left with a final text begging her to call.

She didn't call, not until a few days later. Even then, she only got out the words "you're a liar" and "I know *everything*" before hitting "end call" on her phone five times and throwing it into the sink of dirty dishwater in Genevieve's tiny kitchen.

Her friend gave the phone the middle finger as if Matthew could see her and feel the sting of the words that she hurled at the phone mid-air.

The emails came to light on a Monday night, and the faint blue lines appeared the following Saturday morning. Julia was all but convinced that stress had caused her cycle to take a U-turn and delay its arrival for a while.

She had laid the pregnancy test on the bathroom counter while she brushed her teeth, assuming that she had a solid three minutes before any need to check the results, spitting soapy saliva into the sink as the lines magically appeared well before their designated arrival time.

Julia had grabbed the empty box from the trash can and read the instructions again, trying to find where she had misinterpreted the results. The instructions weren't vague, however. The picture of one versus two lines wasn't subject to interpretation.

Julia had brewed another cup of coffee and sat down at the kitchen table with the test in hand, in such a daze that she caught herself about to put the pee-stained plastic stick in the cup like a spoon to stir its contents.

Before her cup was empty, she had told Matthew via text, a simple "baby makes 3" message all that she felt he had deserved and as much as she had wanted to share. She ignored his replies and tried to delete them as they came in, catching "call me" and "please" among the words that disappeared with her steady command of the delete function. Julia sat at her kitchen table for the better part of the day, trying to come to grips with a reality that kept shifting and making her reassess everything she knew or had expected from life.

As her coffee cup was filled again and emptied, and petals needlessly plucked from the flowers that she had bought from a street vendor the day before, Julia's new world began to take shape next to the remnants of yellow daffodils and two bright blue lines that stared at her from a small plastic window.

Public opinion mandated that Julia immediately stop loving Matthew, but it simply didn't work that way. Aware that he didn't feel the same—that she had been some pawn in a life built on deception—Julia was both devastated and ashamed that her feelings for him remained.

Halfway through a pint of melting chocolate, chocolate chip ice cream, she had decided that unrequited love is the worst kind of all, rejection woven so tightly into its core that you're willing to shed layers of self-worth with every prayer that promises to give up *everything* if they simply love you again.

Julia knew in her heart that he never would, if he ever *did*, but the thought of keeping a piece of him made her feel less that this part of her life was a fraud—that she had been vindicated in some way. As shocking as the baby news was, it had given her something different to focus on, the hole dug by deception somehow filled by the revelation that she wasn't alone. That such validation came at the expense of other, faceless people wasn't something that she could allow herself to focus on. Julia's time with Matthew had been legitimized by a faint blue line on a plastic stick with color photos in the Instructions for Use that said *Congratulations* like this was the happiest news in the world.

Genevieve knew better than to try to spin this like a positive. Julia had lived with the idea of pregnancy for eleven days before the blood came, eleven days on a roller coaster of plunging panic attacks followed by a slow and steady rise to the top again with funny blogs posted on single-mom websites and more than a minute or two spent browsing IKEA's baby furniture options.

The idea of a baby had shone brighter than the light that Matthew had stolen from her, the need to take care of someone else stronger than any desire she felt to collapse into a blubbering pile for someone else to find.

She had felt like a grown-up, a single woman about to venture down a path that many had taken before her, armed with blog posts and informative websites, all of which assured her that she could do this alone. Julia felt like she had a purpose, if not a plan, and it was the only thing keeping her from letting Matthew's betrayal define her as the naive woman who looked for rainbows on a sunless day.

And then the blood came. It was a small amount at first and Julia tracked down the internet article that talked about normal early bleeding as "no cause for concern," which made her feel better for a while. And, then, more came. When the *spotting* turned to *flow*, Julia watched the scene unfold like still shots from a movie, all hope lost when the towels became heavy and her stomach started seizing, Genevieve's voice echoing through her phone even though she didn't remember calling her.

As her friend consoled her and promised that she'd be right over, Julia folded into herself and climbed into the empty bathtub, spreading the last clean towel across her stomach and legs to cover the red that she didn't want to see.

Before this, Julia had barely been hanging on; any inner strength that remained after discovering Matthew's other life had been focused on this one thing that demanded maturity and required her to hold it together. The thought of a baby was like a single weight keeping Julia's hot air balloon from flying away. With that weight's rope now cut, she had been sent drifting, flying without a plan, or answers, or anything that she needed to navigate her way safely back to the ground.

Chapter 14

Cityscape

The Southern Sunset Center must have bought them in bulk. The eleven-by-fourteen white gallery canvasses being handed out by the art instructor from a giant cardboard box under the tree were wrapped in plastic and bundled together. Everyone was handed one.

Julia reached down and tried to wedge one corner of the flimsy easel at her painting station into the soft ground to balance it and make it sturdy. Positioning her canvas onto her easel, she watched as Gwen fought with the legs of her easel and Cate caught her finger in the hinge of hers.

"Why am I doing this again?" Gwen asked, looking at Julia's easel legs for guidance as to how to balance hers. "I'm no painter."

"It'll be good for us," Julia said. "At least, that's what the flyer said on the bulletin board." The Artistic Expression class was targeted toward beginners and those without any artistic talent, or so Julia had interpreted its description on the purple paper that promised "a forum for creative expression—all skill levels welcome."

"Dammit!" Cate said, trying to pull the rusty hinges of her

119

easel apart. "Dammit, Julia, for talking me into this. I'm going to make you watch *Alien* for the next week." With a final firm tug, Cate's easel came loose and stood on its own. She readjusted the curly mess piled on top of her head and, although fighting the effort, Julia thought she looked very much the part of beautiful and tortured artist.

It was a gorgeous afternoon, not too hot now that the sun was setting slowly in the west behind the trees. The art class was well attended by Southern Sunset Center standards. At least twenty women now standing behind their easels and waiting for further instruction. Julia didn't recognize many of them, and assumed that they had come from one of the other wings; she considered these women outsiders, although, she realized, her feelings were unfounded given that she was just as much an outsider to them and for all she knew they had participated in this art class ten times before.

"Okay, okay!" The gray-haired woman who had been handing out canvasses clapped, summoning everyone's attention although nobody was really talking. "My name is Patrice Bonnet and I will be walking you through your artistic journey this afternoon." She wore a white poncho and long turquoise necklace, and had flowing gray hair that needed a trim. Despite her French name, Julia detected no accent and wondered if the name was real. Writers have pen names, so why not artists.

"I like to call this exercise *soul flow*," Patrice said, gesturing to illustrate waves moving from her chest outward. "We spend a few minutes at the beginning of the class in silent meditation and then use the deepest feelings that we've tapped into to paint from the inside out. There is no right or wrong, there is no official technique. If you paint from in here," she said, making a praying motion with her hands to her heart, "you have painted successfully."

Cate, whose easel was in front of Julia's, shot her a hostile glance and middle finger. Meditation wasn't her thing and Julia had led her to believe that they'd be painting Van Gogh knock-offs rather than getting in touch with their inner selves. Julia just winked at her and smiled. She could feel the same look coming from Gwen a few feet away, but chose to ignore it.

"Okay, ladies," Patrice began, putting her hands together and raising them toward the sky before taking in a deep breath and bringing them to her chest. With her eyes closed, she did the same movement again, a few of the women following her lead and reaching their extended arms upward.

Julia closed her eyes and rested her hands at her sides, trying to focus on the sound of the birds instead of the swooshing sound that Bebe's polyester athletic top made every time she brought her hands above her head and back down again. Opening one eye to make sure she wasn't the only one with them closed, Julia saw Cate and Gwen engaged in some sort of charade as they laughed at nothing in particular.

Kara, the brooding brunette with the tattoo sleeve from group therapy, had already started on her canvas, apparently foregoing the need for meditation and going directly for black paint, which she was slathering onto the canvas in thick layers. After Patrice finally opened her eyes and encouraged everyone to take in one final cleansing breath, Julia surveyed the paint colors that she had been given in small paper cups and felt completely devoid of ideas.

Paint from within provided about as much inspiration as the one-dimensional tornado that was beginning to form on Kara's canvas. Turning around, she was surprised to see Vivian at the easel behind her.

"I thought you weren't coming," she said with a smile, happy to see the pretty blonde was trying to get more involved.

Vivian shrugged her shoulders and rolled her eyes in feigned drama. She looked effortlessly cute as always, dressed in a gray tank top and jean shorts with her hair held back neatly in a green headband.

"I got here a little late," she said to Julia and Gwen. "What are we supposed to be doing?"

"Paint from within, child," Gwen instructed mockingly, gesturing wildly with her hands and looking toward the sky. "Listen to your soul and paint its colors," she continued in a whispered French accent.

"If I knew what my soul was trying to say, I doubt I'd be here," Vivian whispered back. Julia was proud of the retort; her new friend's wittiness revealing itself more and more with each passing day.

"Excuse me! I need more pink, I don't have enough pink." Bebe was studying her neighbors' paint supplies like she was on the verge of stealing them, her paintbrush held in the air like a pinky on a tea cup. "What colors do I have to mix to make pink?" Bebe asked the woman next to her, who pretended not to hear.

"If you run out of a particular paint, maybe tap into your energy to find a different color," Patrice suggested, trying not to target Bebe with the instruction. "This is all about fluidity, and flow, and unintentional cohesiveness."

"But," Bebe said. "I need pink. *Pink.*" She looked around, waiting for someone to appreciate the urgency of being left with only orange when bubblegum pink colors your world.

"Nice cat," Gwen said, commenting on Cate's painting of a brown animal with green eyes.

"It's a horse," Cate responded, taking a step back to examine her painting.

Julia tapped her brush into a cup of grass green paint and made wide strokes across the canvas with wispy motions. She decided to try to let go of deliberation and paint without intent, mixing colors without thinking and covering the canvas with bursts of color that formed nothing identifiable. Each stroke was like an individual painting to her, the depth and colors dictating themselves and Julia just along for the ride. That this wasn't a canvas worthy of hanging on display didn't bother her, its chaos reflective of a life that she sometimes tried too hard to tame. With a final stroke of green dipped into purple, Julia swiped the canvas with a wide finishing brush stroke and stood back to take in her creation.

"You need to relax, darling," Patrice instructed as she rubbed Gwen's shoulders and tried to work out a particularly harsh knot.

Gwen kept her head facing forward, but glanced at Julia out of the corner of her eye in a silent plea for help.

"Your tension is what's keeping you from painting from the inside," Patrice continued, turning Gwen around and poking her in the chest with her forefingers.

"You don't like my tree?" Gwen asked, pretending to be hurt and gesturing toward the brown and green blob of paint that probably wouldn't have even earned a gold star from a panel of kindergartners. Sensing her sarcasm, Patrice patted her gently on the back and made her way over to Julia.

"Ah, look at this color," she said, drawing an invisible circle around Julia's painting. "Look at the vibrancy and energy with which you made your strokes. This was a helpful exercise, no?"

"I enjoyed it, thank you," Julia said, ignoring Gwen's smirk in the background. Patrice touched her softly on the arm before continuing down her row, quick to take a sharp left so she could avoid Bebe and her sad attempt at pink flowers in a pink vase that sat on some sort of pink table.

Rinsing her brushes out in the small cup of water, Julia took note of how everyone was doing around her. Kara's storm had grown surprisingly impressive, its deep mix of black and gray oddly refined in the swirl of storm movement that she managed to capture and bring to life. A tall blonde with a tightly knit braid over her shoulder stood next to Kara and was using the edge of a piece of cardboard to form sharp color lines that reminded Julia of a Mark Rothko with bright yellow, green, and black color blocking that had made an impression on her during a trip to New York years ago. She had bought the museum book for this painting alone. That book now sat on her end table back home, a lemongrass candle resting on it. Buying that museum book had made her feel like a grown-up, like someone who could appreciate fine art and needed to have coffee table books supporting decorative candles in their home.

She had always wanted to go back to that museum, curious if the passing years would affect how she felt about the paintings. A trip to New York had been on her and Matthew's list of future plans, but she had buried it along with his promise to teach her to ice skate and wrap sushi. No longer seeing the colors on the canvas, Julia still continued to stare at the woman's painting and grew annoyed that such a simple image could bring back so many memories.

She hadn't noticed her earlier, but Julia now saw that Sylvia was standing before an easel in the front row. She wasn't surprised to see a beach with a bright umbrella taking form on Sylvia's canvas, the scene most likely ripped from one of her favorite movies that was set by the ocean and focused on long-lost lovers. Sylvia dipped her brush into a cup and started painting thin red stripes along the umbrella, dropping her head in defeat when a few red drops fell onto her pale-yellow beach. Julia didn't know the brunette standing next to Sylvia, but was impressed with her Warhol-ish painting of a can of Coca-Cola, made all the better by her announcement to the group that she was suddenly thirsty.

Her brushes soaking in the cup of water, Julia stretched toward the sky and started to wander away from her canvas.

Tempted to walk over to Gwen and start rubbing her shoulders, Julia thought better of it and walked toward the back of the group and out of everyone's way. Gwen hadn't been in the best of moods lately and she didn't want to push it. Ever since Gwen had shared in group therapy, her mood had plummeted along with her tolerance for ill-timed jokes or stupid comments. Truth be told, Julia was lucky that Gwen had agreed to the art class, the only extracurricular things that she typically participated in were Scrabble tournaments and an occasional jog around the grounds.

Julia felt sorry for Patrice, who apparently hadn't been able to avoid Bebe and was now engaged in some intense conversation about the arrangement of pretend flowers in a painted vase, and Cate was making her horse look worse by giving it a heavy black mane. It now looked like a cat wearing an overcoat.

Vivian blocked Julia from seeing the painting on her canvas, but then she knelt down to swat a bug off her leg and revealed what she had been silently working on since arriving just twenty minutes before. Julia couldn't believe what she saw—it was exquisite in its simplicity, much like Vivian herself.

Using the most basic of paint colors, Vivian had somehow mixed them to create a city landscape, its skyline and canal a three-dimensional photo that was expertly blurred to perfection. Julia hadn't realized how close she was standing, now just a few feet away from Vivian and impossible not to notice.

"Do you like it?" Vivian asked, glancing at Julia and then back to her painting, her head cocked slightly to the side.

"I can't believe you were able to paint this with what they gave us," Julia said. "And so quickly. This is truly unbelievable."

"I took a few painting classes," Vivian said, her head now cocked to the other side. "Years ago." The way she said the last two words suggested that those years might as well have been in another life.

Vivian had painted a shadowy figure on the city's streets, a lone person on a sidewalk in an otherwise empty city. Even the water in the canal, a realistic shade of gray and blue, had been painted to reflect the details of a bridge crossing over it and the mirror image of buildings looking downward. It was the shadowy figure that Julia kept coming back to and she noticed that Vivian was staring at it, as well. Julia wondered what she was thinking, if she had painted the figure as a way to remember something or a means to forget.

Vivian seemed a bit lost in what she had created, her hand still clinging to a paintbrush dropped to her side. Julia assumed, based on the intensity with which Vivian was studying her own work, that she truly drew from within to paint this particular scene, that it wasn't a pretend street in a make-believe town like the fake flowers that decorated a life filtered with pink-colored glasses. Julia's heart broke for Vivian at that moment; she looked like she was disappointed that the scene hadn't come to life, like she had hoped for the chance to disappear into the canvas and run down the city streets, alone and away from it all.

There was a familiarity to Vivian that Julia couldn't quite place, a quiet understanding between them, like a secret shared or common experience that nobody else would understand. *How sad*, Julia thought. *Kindred lost souls.*

If only she had known then just how sad and how lost they really were. And how kindred.

Chapter 15

Digging

The cool stone felt good under her thighs and Julia relaxed as she leaned against the bench's high back. The others were working in the garden on the opposite side of the yard, digging with tools as if they were searching for gold.

The sun's rays were just out of reach, the bench sitting in a part of the yard that was protected by the building's roof line this time of day and Julia felt comfort in the isolation of the shade. She sipped her lemonade, a cloudy solution that got the whole mix-water ratio thing wrong, but which nonetheless made her feel like it was a normal autumn day, if only for a moment.

"What, you don't like digging around in the dirt?" a voice came from behind.

Julia whipped around. A woman was walking toward her, an incredibly skinny woman with jet-black hair pulled into a loose ponytail and bangs cut too short.

"I'm sorry, what?" Julia asked, immediately realizing how annoyed she sounded.

"Your friends over there look pretty excited about a garden that I have yet to see grow anything," the woman said, taking a puff on her cigarette and pulling up the waistband of pants at least two sizes too big. She shifted her weight from one foot to the other, fidgeting the way school kids do right before recess. "Which one of the beekeepers is out here?"

Julia looked with curiosity at the bruised injection sites lining the inside of the stranger's arm. "I'm sorry, but I don't know what you're asking."

"Beekeepers. You know. The people in charge of you gals all tired and stressed out in the B-Wing."

Julia struggled to hide her shock. *Beekeepers.* What an offensive and juvenile way of describing the center's staff. She found herself embarrassed that she was among the group monitored by beekeepers, but then became angry that she was embarrassed. Who did this woman think she was?

The disdain for B-Wing residents had been evident in the stranger's voice and she was studying Julia's face for a reaction. Getting none, she continued.

"I just don't understand all of you over there, spending all of this time and money with the hope that someone with a degree from whatever school gives you the secret to a stress-free life. Here's a news flash: there isn't one." She inhaled the cigarette so deeply this time that Julia wondered if she was going to swallow it whole. "Meanwhile, those of us over here in the A-Wing have *actual* problems."

Julia felt a warmth rise to her cheeks and took a deep breath to calm herself. As much as this woman was out of line, there was something about her that told Julia to tread carefully.

"Well, one thing that I've learned during my time here is to never judge anyone else's battles," Julia said, returning her gaze to the group in the garden who were digging holes much too deep for any seed. She felt a sharp pang of shame upon saying it, however. As open-minded as she tried to be, she still judged Bebe almost daily. Seeing past her constant need for attention was going to take time. "I'm sorry for any issues that you are dealing with, but the women who I've met here are all doing their best. If our presence irritates you for some reason, maybe you should just leave." Turning to face the garden, Julia hoped her body language would signal that the conversation was over.

Sensing the woman slowly approach the back of the bench, Julia could smell the staleness of her cigarette breath as she leaned down and whispered, "I can't leave. I'm court-ordered to stay."

Julia jumped off the bench and faced the woman who was now exposing a grin of yellow teeth, a few missing on each side.

"Settle down, there," she said, gesturing to Julia like she was a scared animal. "Just trying to have a conversation, and one that I always wish I could have with you gals when I see you outside. It's so frustrating to see you all here. You're never going to find it, whatever it is you're looking for. This is just a distraction, a hiding place that makes you feel better about not putting the hard work in yourself."

She turned and pointed toward a window about thirty feet from the bench on the A-Wing side. "That's Becky's room. She's here because she got so high one night that she lit her Christmas tree on fire and almost killed her kids. She thought the tree had come alive. And that window next to hers? That's Naomi's room. She drank so much one day that she forgot to pick her kids up from school. They slept on the playground. She hasn't seen them in six months, but that doesn't stop her from wanting another drink. And Sam? She got a bad batch of cocaine and held up a grocery store before almost dying in the parking lot. From how she tells it, it was like a scene from *The Exorcist.*"

Julia felt her eyes start to fill with tears, but kept them at bay, not willing to let this woman sense how much she had shaken her.

"I hear there are women on your side there for stress." She

chuckled and shook her head at the thought, her loose ponytail sliding down the back of her head. "Stress? Welcome to life. Stop waiting for someone to figure it out for you. You're not going to grow because the calendar says you've been here for twenty, thirty or eighty days. Get on with it. Live your life and figure it the fuck out."

"Tina!" A woman appeared from around the corner, arms gesturing in an *are you kidding me* way.

"Settle down, Sue. I just needed a smoke break." As she turned to leave, she pulled up the waist of her pants one more time and gestured toward Julia. "I made a new friend."

"Get inside." Clearly, Sue wasn't having any of it.

Tina walked toward the A-Wing yard entrance and took one last long drag on her cigarette, looking back at Julia before flicking the end of it at her and disappearing around the corner.

Julia stared at the now-empty part of the yard for a moment before resuming her seat on the bench. She looked again at the women digging with shovels, hoes and a few on their knees with hand-held tools, moving the dirt from one side to the other. She watched and wondered—what were they really searching for?

Chapter 16

Nobody Likes to Share

"Leave her alone."

"Everybody else has to share," Kara said. "Don't you wish that I could have sat here day-after-day and avoided telling everyone that I can't stop taking a razor to my arms and legs to cut them until they bleed?" Her dark brown hair had been secured loosely on top of her head, a few strands covering her face and falling onto the black T-shirt that listed the complete concert schedule for a band that Julia had never heard of. The colorful tattoos that covered Kara's arms made it difficult to see any razor marks and Julia was slightly ashamed that she was even looking for them; she was slightly ashamed, but not enough to stop glancing at Kara's arms as she moved them, trying to distinguish blood-letting cuts from the detailed outline of a geisha tattoo.

"Leave her alone," Gwen said again, throwing her best shade at Kara. Gwen's mood hadn't improved these last few days, her patience now a thin line that nobody dared cross, except maybe for tattoo-wearing cutters who didn't seem to notice.

Rose twisted uncomfortably in her chair. She was wearing a

gray and black University of Illinois sweatshirt three sizes too big. She buried her hands in the sleeves, pulling the cuffs until they swallowed her limbs completely. Julia suspected that attention was the last thing that Rose wanted and the one thing that made her the most uncomfortable. Kara's harsh delivery enough to make her want to curl up further. Much to Julia's surprise, she didn't this time.

"Kara, is your mother still alive?" Rose asked, looking directly at her.

"Yeah," Kara said, looking surprised that Rose had actually responded.

"Then maybe you don't understand completely what I'm going through," Rose said, sitting up a little straighter in her chair. "My mother lived with me and my family for the last twelve years. We spent almost every minute that we were awake together, trying new flavors of coffee, working on projects that we saw on Pinterest, or shopping when we told everyone that we were going to the gym."

She took her hands out of the sweatshirt and rolled the cuffs up so they fit better. "My mother sat on the sidelines of every one of my children's soccer games. She went to school conferences, not because she had to, but because she liked to look at the artwork from all of the students on display in the hallways. She baked chocolate chip cookies when my kids didn't feel well, and took care of me when *I* got a cold, because nobody else noticed."

By now, Rose was crying, but not in an uncontrolled way. Her tears seemed to be coming from a place of frustration, rather than sadness. "I don't understand what would ever prompt someone to take a razor blade to their arms and legs and cut them til they bleed, so please don't assume to know how I should best handle losing someone whose presence I miss every single second of every single day." With that, Rose sat back in her chair and fumbled with the sweatshirt sleeves again, looking startled by her own words.

"Okay, okay," Kara whispered, raising her hands in mock surrender. "Sorry, Rose."

Dr. Barkle looked bored, writing something on his clipboard that Julia guessed was entirely unrelated to the exchange that just took place and Rose's minor breakthrough in terms of sharing her feelings. Based on his lack of eye contact and focused attention on the paper in front of him, Julia wouldn't have been surprised if he was doodling or working on his bucket list of activities for when he grabbed his last paycheck from this place and made his final escape.

Kara looked at him for guidance as to what to do now that she had apologized and Rose had stopped talking.

"Very good," he finally said, flipping over a page like his extensive notes had made him run out of room. "Very good sharing, Kara."

Julia rolled her eyes at Gwen, who took two fingers and rubbed her eyes furiously. Kara looked up at the ceiling in disgust and Rose continued to sit there, pulling herself back into the sweatshirt so the two sleeves hung limply like she didn't have arms to fill them.

"So, how's everyone doing on their journals?" Dr. Barkle asked, looking around the room for the first time. "As you recall, I've asked that each of you write at least one journal entry daily, and more if you like."

Julia and Gwen exchanged guilty glances, the last of their journal pages used that morning during a particularly competitive battle of tic-tac-toe and hangman. To keep from laughing, Julia stood up and headed over to the coffee and snack station, which could always be relied upon to supply lukewarm coffee left over from lunch and a wicker basket of individually-wrapped Oreos, Fig Newtons, and pretzels.

"Yes, yes!" Julia knew the voice without turning around, the eagerness with which Bebe approached all center activities either the product of genuine team spirit or cleverly faked to earn her an early parole. "I've brought mine today," she said, holding the small notebook up for the room to see.

"I'd like to share mine today," Bebe said, obviously pleased with herself.

"Well, Bebe, we typically don't share our journal entries," Dr. Barkle said. "They're supposed to be private, so you're encouraged to write about the things that you have trouble sharing with the entire room."

"Oh." Bebe looked defeated, her moment in the spotlight dimmed. "Well, can I show you later in our one-on-one session?"

Dr. Barkle noticeably sighed, his shoulders falling with the release of a deep breath that shrunk him a few inches in his chair. "We'll see, okay?" he managed to say, the sentence a statement rather than question. "We have some time left, so would anyone else like to talk?" Dr. Barkle glanced at the wall clock like he was disappointed that the minute hand wasn't moving faster. He took the end of his pen and scratched his scalp with it, without realizing that he was leaving blue ink marks on his balding head.

"Well, I guess it's my turn."

Everyone turned to Vivian, who had been all but forgotten. She hadn't talked during the first few group sessions and Julia wondered if she thought her grace period had run out. There was really no such thing in here, however; the only penalty that accompanied failure-to-share was having to sit and listen to everyone else talk. Some people, like Rose, preferred the wallflower approach. Others, like Bebe, shared more than they needed to, like the painfully detailed description of her hysterectomy during the last session.

"Oh, sure," Dr. Barkle said, glancing at something on his clipboard. "Vivian," he continued, trying to act like he hadn't forgotten her name. "Yes, Vivian, of course you can share. You're welcome to." He itched his scalp with the pen again and Julia thought she saw a few dandruff flakes fly into the air.

"Okay," Vivian said with a small smile. "Let's see, I'm not really sure where to begin."

"Wherever you like," Dr. Barkle said. "There aren't any hard and fast rules in here. If you just want to start by telling us something about you, that's perfectly fine."

You're really earning your paycheck today, Julia thought with irritation as Dr. Barkle glanced at the clock again and tried to act interested.

"Well, I'm pretty new here," Vivian started. "*Obviously,*" she continued with a laugh. "I grew up in a small river town in Illinois. It's along the Mississippi, but most people haven't ever heard of Glennway. It's pretty there. Lots of big old homes and history, well, as much history as you can imagine in small-town Illinois." She looked uncomfortable and Julia wanted to tell her it was okay, that there was no need to talk if she wasn't ready, but Vivian took a deep breath and kept talking.

"I always thought I was meant for something more than a small town," Vivian continued, shrugging her shoulders slightly. "Not that I thought I'd be famous or anything, but I knew that I'd leave someday for the 'big city,'" she said, the last two words in air quotes. "I married my high-school sweetheart right after we graduated from college, and then we headed off to Chicago, which seemed like the best 'big city' option." Vivian used air quotes around the words again, which made Julia wonder if people from small towns thought the words "big city" weren't enough of a characterization without them.

"Gosh, I guess you can say the years flew by," Vivian continued.

Gosh. Julia bit her lip to keep from smiling.

"Everything was really good. We settled into a pretty nice suburb that was close enough to the city to make getting around easy, but far enough away that we could have an actual yard." She looked around the room like she was searching their faces for understanding, but she hadn't really said anything worthy of a response quite yet. With the exception of Bebe, who looked ready to pounce on any reference to a topic that she could somehow infiltrate, the rest of the women were simply listening and smiling to show their support.

"Jay came first," Vivian said with a wide smile. "He was the most beautiful baby. Big blue eyes and a full head of dark hair. Such a sweetheart."

"Oh my," Bebe interrupted, waving her hands in the air. "That sounds just like my Andrew. He was a dark-haired stunner when he was born. Everyone said so, even the nurses."

Bingo, Julia thought. *There it is.*

Vivian just smiled politely at Bebe. "Yes, they're little miracles," she said, acting more polite toward Bebe's interruption than Julia could have managed. "Iris came two years later," she continued. "We were prepared to see the same dark hair, but she surprised us and came out super blonde, with almost white hair at birth. It never faded, either. She had the most beautiful color hair. Complete strangers would come up to us and comment on it." She stopped for a moment to let a memory settle, its unwelcome presence drawing the corners of her mouth down, one side of her bottom lip disappearing completely as she chewed it nervously.

"Iris was six years old," she said, passing a balled-up tissue between her hands, wadding it up and then making it smooth again over and over. "Everyone called it a freak accident, but it doesn't really matter what kind it is, does it? I mean, losing someone doesn't hurt any less if you know that they were a statistical anomaly."

Julia looked around the room and everyone, even Bebe, was staring intently at Vivian. Whether they admit it or not, everyone tries to imagine everyone else's story before they share it. The story that Vivian was now telling didn't fit the mold; it wasn't a story about cuts that heal or car scratches that can be buffed out. Julia didn't want to hear this story; she didn't want to think about her friend going through something for which she wouldn't have the words to help. Julia's heart was pounding and she looked over at Vivian, who had placed one of her hands to her chest to stop her own heart from leaping from her body.

"We were at the fair," Vivian said. "It was a county fair that we took the kids to every year, a small-town operation that made me feel like I was back home again." She shook her head and looked down, like she was disappointed in herself for ever thinking that going home again was possible. "I always insisted. I wanted the kids to grow up knowing the taste of funnel cakes and what it felt like to win a prize when you popped a balloon with a dart." Now tearing the tissue into small pieces, Vivian cradled them in her hands and tried to keep them from falling to the floor.

"They just didn't do what they were supposed to do," she said. "There were so many wires and cables running everywhere, from tents, in between the rides, you had to step on them and over them to get anywhere." Vivian was shaking her head and looking around at the other faces staring back at her. Julia's heart broke for her, the story clearly moving in a horrific direction that she wished she could turn somehow.

"I don't even know where the exposed wires came from," Vivian continued. "The police told us that it was only a matter of time before a child stumbled upon them, like my little girl had somehow saved others' lives or something." Tissue pieces falling onto the floor like snowflakes, she looked down at them and her empty hands, caressing her palms like she was trying to read her own fortune. "She died instantly. They said the wattage would have killed a grown man. She wasn't even fifty pounds."

Julia wasn't aware that she was crying until she felt a tear drop onto her arm. She looked around the room and saw that she wasn't alone; nobody was even trying to hide it.

"I guess that was the beginning of the end for me," Vivian said, wiping the tears from her cheeks and avoiding eye contact. "They say that losing a child can tear a marriage to pieces, but ours wasn't destroyed that way. It was more like a steady and methodical process where layers were dissolved daily. I tried, we both did, but it was just too hard. It took everything in me to give my son the attention that he needed. I didn't have anything left for my marriage. After everything, it seemed like such an irrelevant luxury in life that I didn't know what to do with anymore."

"Splitting up seemed so selfish, though, because of Jay, so we tried our best to pull it together. We decided to move and get a fresh start, but had to live apart for a while so I could stay and get the house sold as he started a new job. It was nice, the separation, because we could both enjoy being alone without the guilt of separating formally."

Julia noticed that they were ten minutes past the end of the session, but everybody remained fixated on Vivian, even Dr. Barkle, who had put down the clipboard and actually looked engaged for the first time since Julia had met him.

"It was our fifteen-year anniversary this year," Vivian continued. "We were getting settled in our new place and, for the first time since losing Iris four years ago, I felt hope. All of those years of couples counseling didn't do as much as a move to a new place for a fresh start.

"Anyway, I've never been the type to give gift ideas, it's just not me," Vivian said. "Even when friends and family beg me for ideas, I have just always felt it rude to actually tell them what I'd really like. For our anniversary this year, though, I had a special night planned just for us and wanted to look nice. I wanted to look pretty."

Vivian tucked a loose strand of hair behind her ear and Julia couldn't imagine her looking anything but, even with puffy eyes and a clean face, she looked like one of those celebrities who are caught without makeup and look even better than they do on-camera.

"I fell in love with a dress in a store window. It wasn't the type of dress that I usually buy, a bit more revealing, but I knew that he'd like it and I wanted to show him that I was making an effort." Vivian touched the collar of her T-shirt, the thought of a sexy dress even now making her a bit uncomfortable.

"He had asked me what I wanted and I thought it would be fun to have him pick it up, the thought of a big white box on the bed waiting for me kind of romantic." Vivian's cheeks flushed suddenly and Julia thought how innocent she was, blushing at the thought of a romantic gesture, She would probably have a heart attack if she knew some of the topics that Julia and Genevieve had discussed over happy hour cocktails. The anonymous letters in *Cosmopolitan* were nothing compared to the sexual deviancy that Genevieve had a knack for.

Vivian continued, "The more I thought about the dress, the more excited I became at the thought of getting dressed up and going out on the town. Those thoughts felt *normal*, which was such a nice feeling after spending years of feeling like a broken version of myself."

Broken. Julia thought back to her admission form and Georgia's assertion that she wasn't *broken*, but thought she might be. Julia didn't agree with her sister; everybody was broken in some way, but the shards of a cracked spirit appeared differently depending on how you looked at them and how splintered the pieces were. Julia suddenly felt like she had been broken in giant jigsaw pieces that could be put back together again; she looked at Vivian and was afraid that, based on everything she'd gone through, she was like a fractured stained-glass window that could be patched, but never fully repaired. For the first time since coming here, Julia felt fortunate that her story wasn't the kind that could keep an entire group of people riveted, long after the school bell rang.

"I thought I was being cute," Vivian said. "He kept asking me for anniversary ideas and I told him that I left him a hint, but he would have to find it. It was so silly, really." Rose had gotten up to get Vivian a new tissue and handed it to her, the snowflake remnants of its fallen neighbors still covering Vivian's shoes.

"Thanks," she said, dabbing her eyes and blinking a few times.

"I wrote down the store, dress size, and color, with a little heart around '15th Anniversary' and hoped that he would get it for me." Vivian smiled now, shaking her head at some thought that had taken over. "I wrote it on a little green sticky note and put it in his wallet."

Chapter 17

Chunks

Its reach was impressive, tiny pieces of bagel from her morning's breakfast forcefully expelled before they could be fully digested.

Everyone jumped up and moved as far away from Julia as they could, except for Vivian, who rubbed her back like a mother does to console a child. "Oh my gosh, you poor thing," Vivian said, a few pieces of bagel stuck to her outer right leg. "Can I get you something? Do you want a bottle of water?" She gestured for Bebe to toss her one and handed it to Julia.

Julia was frozen, stuck in a bent-over position as a wave of shock washed over her. She took the bottle of water without any intent to drink it, her quivering fingers barely able to hold on to the slick plastic.

The first wave of nausea had come with Vivian's description of a sticky note; the second wave had risen when she talked about checking their bank account to see if he had purchased the dress and found suspicious charges; and the third—a tsunami—had swallowed Julia completely when Vivian recounted emails, reciting Julia's own words back to her.

The weight of Vivian's hand on her back, moving in a gentle

circular motion, made the nausea rise once again, but Julia clasped a hand over her mouth to keep it from escaping. She just wanted to leave, get out of this room with its stories of children dying, ruined anniversaries, and sympathetic back rubs.

A filmstrip of her time with Matthew was playing like a movie in her mind. The reality that his wife was now wearing remnants of Julia's breakfast and consoling her after rehashing the death of her own child just minutes before added a layer of absurdity that was too surreal to fully process.

"I've got to go," Julia whispered, standing up and stepping into the pool of watery vomit. Not standing fully upright, Julia kept her eyes lowered and tried to block out the sickening sound that her vomit-covered shoes made as she walked toward the door.

"I'll go with you," Gwen said, but Julia raised her hand to tell her to stay where she was. Her room seemed like a world away, but she had to get there alone. The only thought getting her through was that she would soon be able to shut that door and lock herself inside the one space here that she could truly call her own.

Someone held the heavy door to the group therapy room open for her—she didn't know who—and she was only able to take in a deep breath when she entered the hallway and rounded the corner to leave everyone behind. Her mouth was dry and she opened the bottle of water, chugging half of it as she walked as quickly as she could toward her corridor and room number fifteen.

Fifteen. Fifteenth wedding anniversary. Julia stood outside her room and stared at the mismatched numbers, the bold number one and italicized number five looking back at her. She hated them; the sloppy room numbers and poor water pressure, the weak coffee and day-old bagels that she could now never eat again.

Her past had somehow found her here, in a place tucked away in a remote corner of the state that had promised to help her get back to where she needed to be. Julia had never bought into any of the self-help and therapy, but she felt betrayed anyway; her moral compass so drastically off-course that God found it necessary to blindside her with a windstorm that would tear off her sails and send her drifting out to sea. She hated these mismatched numbers; their sloppy merger just another reminder that some things aren't meant to go together. Making them sit there side by side wasn't fooling anyone.

Julia opened the door just enough to squeeze inside and then locked it behind her. The Hollywood gossip magazine that she had taken from the community room still lay open on her bed, an article about a vicious custody battle between two A-listers featured alongside advertisements for bust enhancers and ten-carat cubic zirconia rings. She swept the magazine off the bed and curled up on her crumpled comforter, pulling her knees up to her chest and trying to steady herself.

There was a soft knock on the door and Julia held her breath to keep from being detected.

After a few seconds of silence, the knock came again, this time louder. "Girl, are you in there?" Gwen asked. "I just want to make sure you're okay. If you want to rest, I get it, but I can't leave until you at least answer so I know you haven't choked on your own vomit."

For the most fleeting of seconds, Julia thought about telling Gwen everything. She thought about inviting her inside, locking the door again, and telling her absolutely everything from the first moment Matthew Harris entered her life. The thought left as quickly as it came, the energy that it would take to unload such heavy baggage more than she had. She knew Gwen enough to know, however, that she wouldn't leave the door without a response. Had the roles been reversed, she would have done the same, and couldn't fault her friend for her persistence and concern.

"I'm okay," she said, her voice cracking. "Seriously, I'm fine. I just need a little time."

The silence on the other side of the door suggested that Gwen was weighing her response, assessing whether her friend could be believed.

"Okay," Gwen finally said. "Let me know if you need anything. I'm going to that book discussion this afternoon and will be in the library."

"Have fun," she said, somewhat convincingly. "I'll talk to you later."

Moving her head over to the side of the bed, Julia watched until the shadow under the door shifted slightly and then walked away. She lay there for another minute, studying the sliver of light under the door and figuring out her next move. She actually knew what she had to do, but post-vomit lethargy had set in and her muscles felt like they were glued to the mattress. One cheek squished against the scratchy cotton sheet, Julia felt drool drop from her bottom lip and slide down her chin.

I'm gross, she thought. *I'm a thirty-five-year-old drooler who throws up in public and has affairs with married men. With men who should have been there for their wives, who were going through hell alone. I'm as gross, and vile, and disgusting as they come.*

Today marked Julia's eighteenth day at the center, but she was a shell of the already-fractured person that she had been when she arrived. She had felt sorry for herself, but she hadn't loathed herself.

Propping herself up on her elbows, Julia spun herself around and jumped off the bed. There was no point lying here any longer. There were things to do. First, she needed to get out of these clothes.

She rummaged through her suitcase. It was hidden by a heap of laundry that made it impossible to tell which clothing smelled of lavender dryer sheets and which stunk of stale sweat from her mid-afternoon jog and yoga class. She chose a few items that looked clean and tossed her vomit-stained clothes into the corner. They wouldn't be coming with her.

It didn't take her long to bring it all together. She checked once under the bed to make sure nothing important was left, and sat down, leafing through the pages of her journal to find a blank page. She tore it out and started writing, steadying her hand to make sure her writing remained legible.

> *Gwen,*
> *Sorry to bolt like this. I wish I could explain. I'm not sure how I feel about my time here, but I'm happy that we met. Without you, I don't think that I could have even made it this long. Don't worry about me; I'm fine. I'll be in touch. Please tell others goodbye for me and that I'm sorry that I couldn't say it myself.*
> *Jules*

She folded the note and wrote GWEN on the outside, sitting it like a paper tent on the desk. Grabbing her suitcase and balancing her purse and toiletry bag under her arm, Julia peeked outside her door and waited until a small group of women passed before heading toward the front lobby. There was no need to be so secretive—she was voluntarily there and she could voluntarily leave—but she didn't feel up to providing explanation or engaging in long goodbyes.

As she pushed open the double doors into the lobby Julia thought it felt like years since she had been in the room. The informational pamphlets on the front desk seemed like a morsel in her memory bank from a different life.

The same woman who had checked her in sat behind the desk, surprise shooting across her face when they made eye contact. "Going somewhere?" she asked, glancing at the suitcase and the toiletry bag that Julia had set down on the counter.

"Yes, I am," Julia responded. "I'm checking myself out. Where do I sign?"

The woman looked panicked, reaching for the phone like she was about to press a security button and summon men in white coats to carry Julia back to her room.

"I'm a voluntary admission," Julia said. "I can check myself out at any time and today's the day, so I'd appreciate it if we can make this quick."

The woman whispered something into the phone and smiled politely at Julia, as if doing so would buy her some time. She put the phone back on its receiver and turned toward the computer. "Name?"

"Julia Marsh."

"Date of birth?"

"Not relevant."

The woman looked nervous, clicking frantically and scrolling down the screen with her mouse. "Okay, then," she said, breathing a small sigh of relief. "You're correct. You are a voluntary admission."

Julia smiled, suddenly feeling sympathy for the woman who probably had to thwart regular escape attempts by women who claimed to be there voluntarily, but who were really there under court-order.

"Yep, like I said," Julia said. "Where do I sign?"

The printer started to rev-up, her discharge papers making their appearance just as Dr. Rayborn made hers through the double doors. "Julia, what's going on?" she asked, having a hard time hiding her concern. "Where did this come from? I thought we were making some progress."

"Hey," Julia said, trying to act as normal as possible. "Thank you for everything. I've gained a lot from my time here, but it's just time for me to go." The lie didn't fall easily from her tongue, so she turned away from Dr. Rayborn and pretended to read the papers that she had just been handed.

"Can we sit down and talk about this?" Dr. Rayborn asked.

"You know, that's really not necessary," Julia responded, scribbling her name at the bottom of the pages marked with a red SIGN HERE sticker.

The woman behind the desk looked at Dr. Rayborn for guidance, but her gaze was firmly fixed on Julia, searching for some explanation as to this sudden decision.

"Did something happen?"

Julia took the manila envelope that was handed to her, its contents—cell phone, keys, and disposable razors, and makeup—immediately making her feel like a missing piece of her identity had been restored.

"Oh, a lot's happened," Julia said, peeking inside the envelope and handing the signed paperwork back. "But that's the point, right? We're supposed to face a lot of stuff here and, you know, I have. *Tons.*" Julia knew that she was close to tipping her hand, the sarcasm that accompanied her last statement too obvious to miss.

Dr. Rayborn took a step toward Julia and leaned against the counter. "I just want what's best for you, Julia," she said. "I never like to see someone leave before they're really done diving into their issues fully. We've made a great start, but I think there's more work to be done."

"I totally respect that," Julia said, extending her hand for Dr. Rayborn to shake. "I really do. I'm not saying that I'm done diving into those issues, but I think there are some things that I need to do on my own, that's all."

Dr. Rayborn reluctantly shook her hand and clasped it with her other, patting it gently before letting go.

"I respect that," she said. "Can I at least give you my cell phone number if you decide at any point that you'd like to talk?"

"Sure, that'd be nice."

Dr. Rayborn scribbled her number onto a lime green sticky note and handed it to Julia, who quickly put it into her purse so she wouldn't have to think of its irony.

"Thank you." Julia started toward the door, balancing her belongings and a suitcase that felt fifty pounds heavier than when she had walked in weeks ago.

"Favor," Julia said, turning around. "I'm not sure what your protocol is, but I'd appreciate it if you don't go back to your office and call my parents. I don't want them to worry and I'll let them know myself."

"Aren't you going home?" Dr. Rayborn asked, looking increasingly worried.

"I don't think so," Julia said. "At least not right away." With one hand on the door, another thought struck Julia that caused her to turn back one more time. "Uh, is there any chance you guys have some extra gas lying around?" Julia asked sheepishly. "My car was on fumes when I got here."

Dr. Rayborn nodded and followed Julia outside. "I'll get the grounds crew to help you out," she said.

It was hot. Autumn was still being held at bay and the afternoon sun shone brightly, not a cloud in the sky to shield them from its harsh rays. The air smelled differently out front than it did in the courtyard, life inside was a more subdued mix of nature's potpourri. She stopped for a minute to remember where she had parked her SUV, and then spotted it. Since she had arrived at night, Julia hadn't seen the effects of the dusty roads on its silver paint finish. The vehicle chosen for what Evelyn considered its "timeless and age-appropriate appeal" now looking aged and weathered. She could relate.

Dr. Rayborn touched her on the shoulder and opened her arms to see if Julia would go for a hug. She obliged, appreciating the fact that it was probably not a routine send-off.

"Take care of yourself," Dr. Rayborn said. "You're a strong woman, Julia. I don't know if I helped you at all, but I really don't think that I can offer you anything that you aren't smart enough to figure out yourself." She gave her a go-get-'em type punch on the arm, which Julia found both awkward and sweet.

Dr. Rayborn walked off toward a shed that housed lawn equipment and a worker or two who always seemed to be on a smoke break.

Julia was glad that she remembered to ask about gas now, because it would have been more than a little embarrassing to make a grand departure and then walk back half an hour later to beg for help after stalling on the side of the road.

As Dr. Rayborn disappeared into the shed in search of a red gas can and someone to fill it, Julia hit the unlock function on her key chain and heard the familiar sound of her SUV's hatchback magically opening.

She was ten feet from her vehicle before she noticed the one parked next to it, a black Mercedes with a dent in its bumper, the gold license plate frame blinding Julia in the afternoon sun. She turned around expecting to see him, expecting to come face to face with the unassuming man who managed to destroy two women's lives, but saw no one other than a resident staring at her from behind the wrought-iron fence.

Raising one hand to bring the cigarette to her lips, Tina raised the other to say goodbye and nodded to Julia in approval.

Chapter 18

Friendly

You've Got a Friend in Friendly

The rectangular welcome sign looked like it had seen better days, its green background a milky sea foam color and the picture of smiling people so faded that they looked like ghosts.

Julia drove past the sign and into its town limits. Milkweed grew so high along the road that they formed their own soft brown skyline. The sun was setting quickly and she was already in need of gas; the center only had enough to fill her tank a little more than halfway. The fuel light wasn't on yet and she had already found a town to stop in, so Julia felt somewhat ahead of the game compared to the last time she was behind the wheel.

Friendly

Pop: 1432

The number on the second sign seemed so precise, like the births and deaths in town always found a way to cancel each other out. She slowed down to the posted twenty-five mile per hour speed limit and coasted through town, assuming that the decorative streetlights and designated parking spaces in front of the dime store meant that she was on Main Street.

No buildings on the street were taller than two stories and, despite the town's small size, she had a hard time taking it all in at once. A narrow brick building with bright blue awning caught her eye, yellow letters spelling out *CAFE* in a semi-circle displayed crisply on its large picture window. There were two old men sitting on a bench outside, one smoking a pipe. She spotted a red, white, and blue barber pole outside a door one block further down, its stripes still spinning despite the CLOSED sign in its front window.

A blue pick-up truck passed her slowly on the street, the driver giving her a one-finger wave and nod of his head like they were old friends. She raised her finger in return wave, but was too late, the truck turning a corner before she caught on to small-town greeting protocol.

Julia pulled into one of the angled parking spaces and got out of her SUV, stretching toward the sky to release the shoulder knots. She caught a few women watching her from the window of a shoe store, their whispers about the stranger in town evident despite the thick glass between them. When they saw that Julia had spotted them, both women spun around and leaned their heads closer together, resuming their conversation and glancing back to see if she was still watching.

The humidity had made her khaki shorts stick to her legs and Julia made a very unfeminine adjustment to her inside seam to keep it from riding up further. She definitely didn't look or feel her best; even her sweat seemed to smell like the lingering aftermath of vomit and, what body parts weren't covered by sweat, were covered by a thin film of recycled air mixed with road dust and a generous helping of self-disgust. She grabbed her purse and made her way down the sidewalk back the way she had just come, glancing into each store window as she walked by.

Julia reached the end of the block to decide where to turn next, the two gentlemen on the bench now aware of her presence across the street. She waved to them and one waved back, his friend taking his pipe out of his mouth long enough to give her a small nod.

Noticing that she was standing in front of a small corner grocery store, Julia walked in, relieved to feel a steady stream of air conditioning hit her from a vent directly above the front door. She stood there, face up, letting the cool air wash over her and dry the beads of sweat on her forehead. It wasn't until someone opened the door behind her and a small bell chimed in welcome that she realized everyone in the store was staring at her.

Everyone constituted a twenty-something bleach blonde woman behind the counter, a man in overalls with a handful of individually-wrapped beef jerky, and an elderly woman with a scarf tied over her head to keep rollers in place, who was peeking at Julia from around the corner of one of the store's two aisles.

Julia moved to the side to let a young boy, about twelve years old, walk by her. He was the only one who didn't look surprised to see her, his attention more focused on the display of Little Debbie snack cakes than on the woman in the entryway who was acting like she had never felt air conditioning before. His mission clear, the boy grabbed a lemon snack pack and threw the exact change on the counter before breezing by Julia and causing the doorbell to chime wildly as he walked out. Had he sensed anything out of the ordinary, his love of creamy yellow icing over white cake apparently trumped his need to investigate.

"Hi," Julia said softly. The silence in response made her feel awkward and, as much as her inner voice advised her against it, she felt compelled to fill the silence.

"I just got into town," she continued, stating the obvious. "Sure does feel good in here."

Silence.

The man opened one of the beef jerky packages and began gnawing on it, the cylinder-shaped meat sticking out of his mouth like a cigar. The old woman patted the scarf around her head lightly to make sure her rollers were all still there, and then grabbed the handle of her purse with both hands.

"I'm just going to get a cold drink," Julia said, pointing to the refrigerated coolers in the back of the store. Why she felt the need to broadcast her next move, she wasn't sure, but she felt like it was a good call for this particular situation.

The little old woman moved out of Julia's way as she surveyed the selection of soft drinks in the cooler and selected one the color of fluorescent orange. Although she wasn't typically a soda drinker, Julia felt a strong need for fizz and caffeine.

Grabbing a bag of pretzels on her way to the counter, Julia smiled at the man ahead of her in line, his purchase of ten beef jerky sticks an interesting choice when twenty-count boxes of the same thing were available in front of them. The beef jerky stick that he had started eating was disappearing without his use of hands, an impressive move that she assumed he had mastered through practice over the years.

When it was her turn to check out, the woman looked at Julia cautiously before typing the amount of her two items into the old register. Grabbing a crumpled handful of bills from her shorts pocket, Julia handed her two and gestured for her to keep the few pennies in change. She opened the bag of pretzels with the soda under one arm and stopped short of the door.

"Is there a hotel in town?" Julia asked, looking first at the woman behind the counter, and then at the old woman who had taken a few steps up the aisle. Beef jerky guy had already left. "Anything's fine," she said. "Doesn't have to be fancy."

Checking her rollers again, the woman looked at the blonde

behind the counter before answering, almost like she was weighing whether to give Julia information.

"There's no hotel here," she said, waving away the idea of accommodations as ridiculous. Taking a step closer to Julia and looking her up and down, the woman moved her handbag over to the other arm and sighed heavily. "There's a bed and breakfast at the old Shanley place, though." She then looked away, as if ashamed that she had shared the town's secret.

"Oh, that's fine," Julia responded, ignoring the less-than-pleased look of her informant. "That sounds lovely. Where is the bed and breakfast?"

"Avenue E," the blonde said, shrugging her shoulders toward the old woman like there was no choice but to let Julia know.

"Avenue E," Julia repeated. "Okay, thanks again."

She left the small store and could feel the women's eyes follow her as she opened the orange soda and chugged it sloppily on the sidewalk. A few drops fell onto her white T-shirt and she didn't even try to wipe them off, although the fluorescent color was guaranteed to stain anything on contact. With the sun setting quickly, Julia had trouble reading the street sign a block away.

Avenue B.

"Well, this shouldn't be too difficult to figure out," Julia whispered, loading a handful of pretzels into her mouth and washing them down with soda. She raised her soda bottle in mock toast toward the men still sitting on the bench, which seemed to confuse them because they just stared at her as she walked back toward her car.

"Avenue E, Avenue E," Julia sang in the spirit of a kindergarten song as she climbed inside and started the engine. "We've found you B, but we need to find E."

It took her approximately forty seconds to find Avenues C,

D, and eventually E, exactly where she had expected to find them among the cross streets. With the sun now almost set completely, Julia drove slowly down the tree-lined street and looked for some sign that any of the old Victorian-style homes were used for something other than a traditional family residence. Most of the homes towered over the store fronts on Main Street and their large yards and tailored landscaped sidewalks were beautiful in their perfection.

A particularly large gray home with white trim caught her eye, its shrubbery so meticulous that it looked like someone had taken hair scissors to its edges. Julia stopped in front of it. A large stained-glass window extended from the top of the front door to well into its second level, and even its house numbers shone so brightly that they might have been spit-shined. A brass holder secured to one of the home's porch columns displayed an American flag, its perfect folds lying at rest until the next wind and call of duty.

Julia was about to put her vehicle back in drive when she noticed the wrought-iron sign in the yard with *B&B* engraved in gold, the tiny sign out of proportion with the stately size of its surroundings. Julia grabbed her overnight bag from the back seat and made her way up the manicured path. Small red flowers lined her way along a sidewalk that had tiny hand prints and glass pebbles embedded in its cement. She set her bag down in front of a large wooden door with frosted glass inlay and narrow windows lined with lace curtains on either side.

The brass doorbell, when she rung it, started as a traditional chime but then launched into a melody. Over it, Julia heard a careful and quick little pitter-patter of feet making their way to the front door.

Given the cool reception that she had received in town, she was surprised to be greeted by a plump, gray-haired woman who swung the door open with a wide smile. "Oh, dear, you must be *so* tired," she began, gesturing for Julia to grab her bag and quickly come inside. "Oh, you poor, poor thing."

It only took Julia a moment to realize that the woman had been given the heads-up as to her arrival. Either the store clerk or roller-wearing patron had called her before Julia had finished her orange-soda toast to the old men on the bench. She couldn't help but smile; even the most high-tech of social media was no competition for small-town efficiency when it came to spreading gossip.

Julia stood in the foyer and tried to look around, but a sudden hug from the woman caught her off guard. "Oh, sweetie, you must be starving," she said, taking a step back to look at Julia as if the details of her last meal were displayed somewhere along her waistline. "I can fix you something. What would you like?"

"Oh, that's so kind of you," Julia said. "But I grabbed something in town and would really just love a shower and good night's sleep." She smiled so as not to offend the woman, but guessed from her demeanor that that wasn't a serious risk.

"Oh, of course," she said. "We're just going to get you settled in and down for the night." She shuffled her way over to a large roll top desk.

"I'm Julia," she said. "It's so nice of you to give me a room tonight." Julia peeked into the room next door, which had a twelve-person dining room table set for an elaborate dinner party. A chandelier hung from a scalloped centerpiece in the ceiling and a green velvet couch straight from the 1880s sat in front of the bay window. Everywhere Julia looked, there was a porcelain figurine, clock with swinging pendulum, or fringed lamp shade. She had to resist touching the wallpaper in the foyer, a series of floral arrangements tied with ribbons.

"Well, hello there, Julia," the woman said, putting a hand to her forehead as if embarrassed that she hadn't introduced herself earlier. "I'm Opal, Opal Shanley."

Of course you are, Julia thought. The name couldn't have fit this bundle of grandmotherly energy any better. Opal looked like a woman who loved her afternoon coffee chats with friends; someone who could whip up a batch of award-winning cookies to entice you to stay a bit longer and talk about the goings-on of a small town where everyone's business was everyone's business. "Well, Opal, you have a beautiful home."

"Oh, aren't you *sweet*," she said, stopping what she was writing in her guest registry to look up and give Julia a wink. "I'm just happy as a peach to have you!"

There was something about Opal and the ornately decorated house that made Julia feel instantly relaxed, like the weight of the world wasn't allowed inside, like an altered reality could be created among the pendulum clocks and fringed lampshades based on the unique needs of its guests. Julia smiled, not to be polite, but because she couldn't stop. She was pretty sure that she had been smiling since ringing the doorbell.

"Oh, here we are," Opal said, losing her place in the registry and trying to find it again with her finger. "Here we are. I'm going to set you up so nice, you'll get the best sleep you've ever had."

Still smiling, Julia believed her.

"Follow *me,* chick*adee*," Opal said, climbing the curving staircase carefully with help of the banister. She led Julia to a room at the top of the stairs and opened it with an old skeleton key, exposing the exact room that Julia had imagined she would have.

Everything was floral—the heavy fabric of the drapes, bedspread, wallpaper, and embroidered pillow on a chair covered in pink satin. Silk flowers hung over the bed and stood in vases throughout the room. There was even a pillow on the bed in the shape of a flower, its ruffles fanning out like the petals of a rose.

An old cedar chest sat at the end of the brass bed, a quilt folded neatly over it in case guests got a chill. A white stone fireplace was on the wall opposite the bed, its mantle home to a porcelain figurine of a woman dancing in a ballgown and man's top hat. Cross-stitched Bible verses were framed and hung around the room on any wall that had space, and an antique dressing table with a silver brush and mirror set and a cloudy looking glass sat next to the door going into the bathroom.

"Oh, this is perfect," Julia said, more happy than she could have imagined in a room that was anything but ordinary. "This is absolutely perfect."

Opal stood there, her hands crossed across her plump belly, looking proud as can be by the feedback. "I call this the Rose Room," she said, rearranging a few silk flowers in a vase on a table next to the door. "There's just something about these flowers that make me happy." Opal looked like she didn't want to leave, but realized that she had to eventually. She put her hands on her hips, perhaps to keep from fluffing a pillow or starting another cross-stitch project right then and there.

"Well, now you just run yourself a hot bath and get a good night's sleep," Opal said, turning to leave. "I'll have a big hot breakfast waiting for you tomorrow morning, with plenty of good coffee." She said the last part with a wink and Julia wondered if, indeed, the house was some sort of spiritual wormhole that could sense what guests' souls needed the most. In her case, good coffee and a hot bath topped her list of things required for mind, body, and soul rejuvenation.

"You read my mind," Julia said with an appreciative laugh. All she needed was a wand and bit of fairy dust and Opal would be a true-life fairy godmother.

Opal closed the door with a small wave and Julia walked into the bathroom, excited to see a claw-foot tub underneath a small stained-glass window that was high enough to still maintain privacy. One-inch black and white tiles covered the entire floor and half of the walls, the remaining walls painted a pale yellow.

Julia had never taken a bath in a tub like this and couldn't wait to try it out, twisting the faucet as far as its hot water handle would go. Steam quickly filled the small room and Julia searched for her travel shower gel, emptying its entire contents into the tub to create lavender-smelling bubbles that floated around the room.

She heard the knock on the door as soon as she walked back into the bedroom and opened it, assuming that Opal had forgotten to tell her something about the room. She must have been knocking for some time because Opal looked a little relieved, standing there smiling, holding a crystal glass that was filled almost to its rim with champagne.

"Thought maybe you'd like a little something for the tub," she said. "I always say, bath bubbles deserve drink bubbles."

Completely out of character, Julia took the glass and hugged Opal, a virtual stranger in a wonderfully strange house in a town she couldn't point to on a map. Opal squeezed her back, looking happy that her bubbly surprise had been so well-received.

"Thank you," Julia said, finally pulling away. "I'll enjoy this." She raised the glass toward Opal, her second mock toast to strangers within the last hour, and shut the door as Opal made her way back downstairs. Forgetting the water running, Julia rushed back to the bathroom and shut it off just in time before bubbles starting flooding the tiled floor.

Peeling off her clothes and leaving them in a pile in the middle of the floor, Julia sunk into the bath, wincing at the sting of the hot water on her skin. Although not very long, the claw-foot tub was deep, so the water came up to Julia's chin as she rested her head against its side. She took a sip of the sparkling wine, a sweeter white than she was used to, and let her taste buds adjust to the shock as her body adjusted to hot water.

She closed her eyes and listened to Opal busying herself with something downstairs. A few pots and pans crashed to the floor in what Julia assumed was her early prep for breakfast.

It was only then that Julia realized it. Since entering this sleepy little town, she hadn't given one thought to the memories that had made her run away. It was as if her thoughts about what occurred earlier that day, the past few weeks, and entire last year, had been left by the road to collect dust somewhere beyond the town's limits.

Those thoughts and memories weren't welcome here; the town of Friendly wouldn't let them in.

Chapter 19

This Old House

Julia felt like she should go jogging or at least attempt some sort of physical activity to keep her arteries from clogging completely, but she was pretty sure she couldn't move.

When Opal had promised her a big hot breakfast, she had no idea that meant three kinds of breakfast meat, marmalade toast, and a thick gravy poured over eggs.

It was delicious at the time, but the meal now sat like a huge gravy meatball in Julia's stomach that made her feel both incredibly satisfied and gluttonous. The need to unbutton her shorts suggested that she should have more strongly resisted the last few sausage links "that would have been a shame to waste."

The two cups of coffee with heavy cream probably didn't help, but Opal hadn't lied. The coffee was good and there was plenty of it.

Julia now sat at the edge of town, a green sign reading "You've Made a Friend in Friendly" bidding her farewell with its ghostly figures' arms raised in goodbye. She didn't know what to do with her time, but was sure that she wasn't ready to go. Her reluctance to drive past the town limits sign was a pretty

161

good indication that she wasn't ready to climb out of its spiritual wormhole quite yet.

Julia had had the best sleep of her life in the Rose Room, the heavy comforter and thick drapes burying her in a blissful darkness that blocked out everything except for the smell of bacon and fresh ground coffee that, when combined, were strong enough to finally entice her out of bed a few hours ago.

It had taken her a minute to remember where she was. At first she had felt like had traveled back in time to her grandparents' house: the lace doily under the alarm clock was almost identical to the one that lay between the nightstand and clock in the guest room that she slept in on their farm. Once a few roses came into view, however, Julia remembered where she was. Opal loved roses; her grandmother preferred lilies.

Julia and her sisters had spent many a happy weekend exploring the forty acres of Georgia countryside owned by Evelyn's parents. Half of it was transformed into farmland and the other half left to grow in the wild and unruly manner that her mother detested.

Liv, Georgia and Julia would spend hours playing in the shallow creek that ran through their grandparents' property, arranging rocks into natural beach homes for their Barbie dolls who sunbathed and took an occasional dip to swim alongside the water spiders.

Even at a young age, Julia was aware of the tension between her mother and grandmother, Mabel. Accusations of snobbish behavior by a daughter who thought herself too good for her humble upbringing were passively tossed around during family dinners.

Julia remembered asking Liv what *snob* meant and not really getting an answer. Her oldest sister instead distracted her with a promise to look for the new litter of kittens tucked away safely somewhere in their grandparents' hay loft.

As a child, Julia was too busy pretending to be a princess in her grandmother's canopy bed to give much thought to the friction between the two primary female role models in her life. She only knew that her grandmother made the best sugar cookies in the world, but her mother preferred oatmeal raisin, a complex relationship broken down into sugar and spice in the mind of a child.

It was only as she grew and Evelyn started making comparisons between Julia and Mabel that she grasped the extent of the resentment. Any similarity that she had with her grandmother was an unwelcome reminder to Evelyn that there was a part of her daughter that she couldn't relate to.

Julia tried to understand, and even tried to talk to her mother about mending her relationship with Mabel, but grew tired of the hollow resistance that was based solely on pride. In time, she stopped trying and simply prayed that the women would see the light on their own. And, if they couldn't reach a point of understanding, she prayed that they would simply grow up and accept each other for who they were—different from one another and, yet, completely the same.

Julia had insisted on sitting with Opal in the kitchen for breakfast. She felt the large table in the formal dining room was more suitable for guests who hadn't ran out of soap to shower because they decided to use all of theirs to create bath bubbles the night before.

Julia sat at the tiny kitchen table and ate everything Opal put in front of her. Her dinner of pretzels and orange soda had made her wake up famished.

As she busied herself around the kitchen, Opal told Julia about what it was like to grow up in Friendly. Her description of the "old days" were not that different than what Julia had seen of the "new days" in the town so far.

Opal talked about her husband, a Paul Bunyan-type of

man with a gentle laugh who had died of cancer eight years ago. Julia could picture him, a burly man with a bushy mustache who volunteered at the fire department and made elaborate bird houses as gifts for the town's oldest residents. Because he had dreamed about opening a bed and breakfast when they retired, Opal used the life insurance money to make her husband's dream come true, but then laughed because he had also joked about opening a kiosk on a beach somewhere and she wondered if that might have been a better use of the money.

Julia felt both sympathy and jealousy toward the sweet widow. Her tale of high-school sweethearts who couldn't have kids and so became the world to one another was the kind of love story that Julia had chosen to believe didn't exist. She thought it safer to think of things as *impossible*, rather than *unattainable*.

Hearing Opal describe burying a part of herself with her husband, however, was something that Julia couldn't imagine surviving and it took everything in her not to leap up from her chair and give Opal another hug when she described taking picnics to his grave.

Although Vivian briefly flashed across her mind during the conversation, imagining what she must have felt losing a daughter, Julia refilled her coffee cup and drank the memory away with a scalding sip.

"Oh, I'll tell him about *you*," Opal had said, rinsing out the frying pan and scraping grease off its bottom. "My Henry would have *loved* you, a sweet girl on the cusp of something wonderful who ventured into our little corner of the world. He would have thought you were just the bee's knees!"

Julia smiled. She wondered why Opal thought she was on the cusp of something wonderful, but was afraid to ask. If she considered her worthy of a graveside conversation with her beloved Henry, Julia didn't think there could be a higher compliment and decided to just leave it at that.

She now sat staring at the fake people on the sign waving goodbye and wondered how many people had driven through this tiny town without really seeing it; without appreciating the flowers that hung from the lights on Main Street, the architecture of the homes along Avenue E, or the trees that still stood at attention as they had during the Civil War.

Julia wondered how many people drove through without noticing the fire hydrants that had just gotten a new coat of glossy red, the sign for *Soda Fountain* in the drug store window, or the perfectly manicured cemetery where Henry now lay. When many, if not most, sailed through this town without seeing any of it, Julia felt compelled to drive as slowly as possible to see it all.

She told Opal not to count on her for lunch—the thought of eating anything in the next twelve hours unimaginable—but asked if she could keep her Rose Room for the time being. Opal smiled and clapped excitedly, happy to have the company as long as Julia was willing to stay. There was something about that big house on Avenue E that made Julia excited to return to it at the end of the day; it was like a giant Victorian-style hug full of champagne bubbles and the sound of pendulums marking time.

Julia checked her rear-view mirror before cranking the steering wheel to the left and turning a sharp U-turn to drive back toward town. As she made her way down Main Street, she met a truck on the road and waved with a single finger and head nod before taking a right onto Avenue C. Although she had passed it the night before on her way to the bed and breakfast, she had caught a glimpse of a park on that street that she wanted to explore further.

As soon as she turned, however, she found the traffic was at a stand-still; a small brick church with a white steeple had apparently just let out its Sunday morning service and women in white and pastel-colored hats were walking arm in arm with their counterparts, a few of whom stopped to talk to drivers passing by. Nobody seemed in a hurry or bothered by the blocked street. A group of children took turns jumping up the church steps and swinging barefoot from the railings, their Sunday shoes abandoned in the grass nearby.

Julia sat with her elbow out the open window and rested her chin in her hand as she watched a young woman chase a toddler who was faster than he looked, dodging in and out of the church's shrubbery in a seersucker suit. Finally catching him, the woman lifted him up and planted a huge kiss on his cheek, which made the little guy squirm playfully and wipe the kiss off.

Julia didn't notice when traffic started to move again, but the car behind waited patiently for her to move without honking. She moved past the church and imagined the Sunday dinners that awaited these families, pineapple slices covering baked ham filling their homes with the smell of tangy honey.

The bellowing laughter of four old men was the last sound Julia heard before pulling away, the scene of a perfect Sunday fading from her mirror like a snapshot of life gone by.

Seeing the park emerge on her left, Julia decided not to stop when she spotted a family spreading tablecloths over picnic tables and unpacking Tupperware containers. A gazebo stood in the middle of the park, a few girls jumping between its benches like Liesl did in the *Sound of Music* as one of the women, presumably their mom, gestured for them to come and help.

Julia didn't want to intrude, but made a mental note to come back to the park later, maybe to try a few bench-leaps herself. She remembered those days; there was a time when Julia and her sisters were too busy pretending to be Charlie's Angels to help their mother unpack the picnic lunch that she insisted include real plates, cloth napkins, and silverware. Julia wished that she could send these girls in the gazebo a telepathic message urging them to lock these days away in a memory jar somewhere for safe keeping because Liesl eventually grew up, and so would they.

As she approached the edge of town, the houses in Friendly became more contemporary in design. At the property line of the last house, the town came to an abrupt stop; Avenue C turned to gravel and residential lots were replaced with fields of green waves rising and falling with the wind. Julia continued to drive, having nothing but time to explore an area that she had committed to staying in for at least another day.

The road grew narrower and the gravel larger as she drove further out of town, a few getting tossed up by her tires and hitting the underside of her vehicle like machine gun fire. The fields surrounding her were as active as the town itself, a bushy brown tail disappearing into the thick of roadside weeds as Julia turned a corner, a yellow-bellied bird sitting atop a fence post watching her drive by.

Julia traveled about a mile until the road forked off. The sudden need to make a decision gave her pause, but she veered right and then thought that she should probably turn around. The fields in front of her looked no different than the ones she had already passed; they were just further away.

Julia looked for a pasture opening to turn into and then noticed a mailbox at the end of a drive, its black finish as faded as the American flag that once decorated it. She pulled into the drive, but a chain link fence drawn across two posts blocked entry and she maneuvered the SUV into an angled position to keep out of the road even though she hadn't met another car since leaving town.

Julia hopped out of the SUV and shut the door. The midday heat wasn't helping her need for a nap: the full belly and warm sun making Julia feel like a content dog who needed to curl up somewhere and sleep away the remainder of the lazy day.

She leaned on a fence post and squinted to see the farmhouse at the end of the drive. The noonday sun was so bright that she needed to shield her eyes to see.

The house stood about a quarter mile up the drive, its chimney rising slightly above the roof line and casting a shadow across the top of the wrap-around porch. A trellis painted white to match the house covered the open area bottom of the porch and ground, a bush with bright yellow flowers threatening to overtake the porch from one side.

The house was perfectly symmetrical, a solid square with windows mirroring each other on each side and two columns at the top of the front steps leading up to the porch. The outside had seen better days, deep crevasses in its paint like wrinkles on an aged face. A thick strip of grass grew along the dirt driveway's center, tire tracks on both sides well-worn by years of regular travel.

Two red barns, one quite a bit larger than the other, were a backdrop to the house that looked like it should belong to one of the families now making their way home from church for their Sunday ham.

FOR RENT

The red and white sign had been nailed to the post that Julia was leaning on, a telephone number scrawled with thick black marker in the space provided. In contrast to everything else, the sign looked new: neither the black lettering nor numbers had been faded by a sun that was harsh enough to fade even the most permanent of ink within days.

She looked at the sign, and then back at the house, wondering if its interior was as inviting as the porch swing that sat empty and the barn with its doors slightly open, just waiting for someone to come in. The house needed a little help, but didn't look abandoned. Even the weeds along the driveway had been trimmed by a recent mow and a single newspaper waited in a small orange mailbox designated for *The Friendly Dispatch.*

Julia looked down the road both ways, the only sign of life a few sparrows playing tag in the sky, the loser nosediving into a group of trees that appeared out of place among the largely empty landscape. Another farmhouse sat on top of the next hill, its brick facade like an ugly stepsister to the bright white siding and black shutters of its neighbor. Julia looked around the quiet country land that surrounded her and felt like the FOR RENT sign was meant for her, like a treasure map visible only to the person meant to find the gold.

She grabbed her cell phone from the passenger seat, relieved to see that she still hadn't received any text messages. With the signal at one bar, she held the phone over her head and searched the airwaves for another bar or two, afraid to allow common sense the opportunity to talk her out of what her inner bench-leaping Liesl was telling her to do.

She typed in the first three numbers, observed the natural pause that comes in the seven-number break, and then typed in the last four numbers, putting her ear to the phone to wait for someone to answer.

"Hi, this is Kennedy. Leave me a message and I'll get back to you as soon as I can. Have a good day."

Julia bit her bottom lip, realizing that she had a decision to make before the little beep demanded that she either talk or hang up.

Beep.

"Hi, my name's Julia. I'm standing in front of a house on," she said, looking around for some sort of street marker. "A gravel road. A gravel road not far outside Friendly." She paused for a moment and watched the sparrows start a new game of tag, the leader flying high into the sky before taking a sharp turn to the right to fake out his friends.

"I'd like to talk to you about renting the house."

Julia repeated her cell phone number twice and tossed the phone through the open window of her SUV, hoping it would land on the soft seat.

She walked over to a group of wildflowers growing in a ditch and started picking them, arranging a small bouquet to bring Opal. The purple clusters of petals with thick stems weren't roses—they might even be weeds—but they were pretty. If they did turn out to be weeds, Julia would love them even more; unexpected beauty from a surprising source more respectable somehow than the predictable cheerfulness of daisies or tulips that didn't have to try to be noticed.

Julia tore off a long blade of grass, careful not to get a cut along her fingers, and wrapped it around the stems of the purple unknowns, tying it in a knot to secure the bouquet. She looked at them proudly, anticipating an over-the-top reaction from Opal when she walked in with a gesture from the great outdoors.

Julia opened the car door in time to hear the familiar sound of her wind chime ring tone alerting her to an incoming call. She recognized the number as the one she just called.

On the cusp of something wonderful.

Chapter 20

Stamps and Lemonade

"It's been in our family for over a century," said Kennedy Blackwell, keeping one hand on the porch railing as she walked across it. "My dad grew up here, my brothers and I grew up here, and I can't tell you how many summer nights we spent out on this front porch. I swear, I wouldn't be surprised if the wood knows our names." She sat on the railing, letting her feet dangle in a way that made Julia think she had done it a thousand times before.

Kennedy looked a bit older than Julia, maybe early forties, and had been happy to meet her at the farmhouse the next day. If anything, she sounded surprised to hear that someone was interested in renting it, and an outsider to the area at that.

"We lost dad a few months back," Kennedy said, wrapping her arm around the porch column and leaning her head against it. "And Mom's been gone for about three years now. When you lose so much so quickly, you just can't bear to lose anything else." She smiled affectionately at the old house, like it could hear her and would know if she was following through on her promise to not let it go. "Even though we've all moved at least a few hours away, my brothers and I just hate to part with it. We can't bring ourselves to sell. We figured it makes more sense to rent it out until we figure out what to do."

Julia smiled sympathetically as she walked to the chair, retracing years of steps walked by the Blackwells as they made their way over the uneven porch floorboards. She settled into the rocking chair and let it extend backwards, the cracked wood stretching its muscles under her as it tried to remember how to move.

"Everything here stays," Kennedy said. "We've taken some personal items out, but besides that, this is exactly how my dad left it." She leaned back, checking out a wasp nest that had formed under the lip of the porch roof. "You might like having a move-in ready place, but then again, my dad was a bit of a hoarder when it came to some stuff. You'll probably find spray paint dating back to the early eighties in the basement and a few dozen cans of spray grease. There's not a drawer in this house that sticks, I can tell you that."

Julia rested her arms on the rocking chair's and let it determine the rocking pace.

Kennedy looked lost in her memories and she didn't want to intrude, happy to spend this time looking out to the end of the drive where she had stood, staring at this very porch just twenty-four hours before.

Neither woman had an agenda; Kennedy would have probably been fine if nobody moved into a house that she wanted to shrink and wear like a charm around her neck, close to her heart. And, before she had reached the top of the well-worn drive, Julia had a feeling that the house was special. As soon as she walked up the steps to its quirky front porch with uneven railing, she knew she was right. Because Kennedy couldn't live here herself, Julia hoped that it would bring her some peace of mind to know that the place that held so many memories for her was being well cared for. Julia wouldn't be renting the house as much as she would be adopting it.

"Whatcha lookin' for, hon?"

Julia got the sense that the woman behind the counter, a different one than during her first trip to the grocery store, was more curious than interested in helping.

She studied Julia up and down, her thick eyeglasses stopping when she came to the package of miniature chocolate chip cookies that she was holding to her chest like a prize.

"Oh, um, I'm not really sure what I need quite yet," Julia responded. Her bubble of hope that the store would carry anything other than instant coffee popped as soon as she spotted a single brand on the shelf.

"Lemonade," she suddenly said, raising a single finger in the air like a light bulb had gone off.

"Aisle one," the woman responded, watching Julia like she was about to shoplift.

"Great, thanks."

Julia grabbed a plastic shopping basket at the end of the aisle and dumped her cookies into it, followed by a jar of spaghetti sauce, packet of noodles, and a loaf of bread. Finding the small corner of the store devoted to dry drinks, she marveled at the absurdity of having more options of lemonade than coffee before choosing a large-sized container and tossing it on top of the bread. Desperately looking for anything else appealing, but finding nothing, she plopped her basket on the counter and smiled at the woman staring back.

"Is there any other place that sells coffee around here?" she asked, trying not to sound judgmental as to the store's selection. "And stamps. I need some stamps."

"Post Office is two blocks up," she responded, nodding in a non-specific direction. "Lots of folks go to Kreanley to get fancier stuff than what we have here. You might want to try there." She loaded Julia's items into a brown paper bag and gave her the handles. "Welcome to town," she said, this time smiling. Both middle bottom teeth were missing.

"Thanks," Julia said, taking the bag and making a mental note to ask Opal where she got her coffee and what, or where, Kreanley was.

She hoisted the bag onto her hip and decided to carry it to the post office, considering it qualifying as both a work-out in cardio and weights. She hoped she was walking the right way: the general head nod by the cashier had provided little guidance.

She walked past a hardware store, women's boutique, and a small store that looked like it sold home furnishings from the 1950s. Unlike those stores back home that labeled themselves shabby chic, however, the inventory of this store had simply stayed on its shelves for decades.

A set of green depression glass plates and goblets was displayed in the front window of the store, a mock table setting with folded cloth napkins creating the illusion of dinner ready to be served. Julia had seen a glass set like this one at a flea market recently. Retro chic enthusiasts from the suburbs had engaged in a bidding war to see who could take it home. Julia knew that the flea market bidders were looking for a way to distinguish their lives; they lived in cookie cutter homes with living rooms painted the same shade of light beige as their neighbors and were eager to pick up something that they could point to as proof that they were unique.

In contrast, Julia suspected that this type of glassware stood proudly in china cabinets all over Friendly, sets handed down within families and appreciated for their timeless style. Like everything else in this sleepy town, the glassware in the window had nothing to do with trends and everything to do with quality.

Spotting the familiar blue eagle symbol in a window one block further down, Julia repositioned her shopping bag and walked in, bells on the post office door alerting everyone to her arrival. There was a small line waiting for the postal worker behind the counter and Julia looked around the room, surprised at how contemporary it was with its colorful displays of padded packaging envelopes and printed boxes for every occasion. There was a small display of stationery and matching envelopes, the selection limited to either mint green with a pink flower border or pale blue with a cartoon sun wearing sunglasses shining on top of the page. Julia grabbed the mint green stationery set and took her place in line behind a man with apparent seasonal confusion—he was wearing shorts, sandals, a flannel shirt, and hat with furry ear flaps.

"Howd-ya," he said, twisting around. Julia couldn't understand what he said exactly, but assumed it was intended as a friendly greeting.

"Mailin' sometin'?" He scratched his gray beard stubble, working his fingers into his skin so hard that it left red marks. The man clutched a single stamped envelope and Julia wondered if he knew that he could simply drop it in the mailbox.

"Buying stamps," she responded, now getting the attention of the three people in front of the man. They said nothing, but looked at her intently.

"Yep, just buying some stamps," Julia repeated, happy to move forward in line when a young mother at the counter grabbed hold of her package and maneuvered a stroller toward the door. She smiled at Julia as she walked by, rolling her eyes at her toddler who was trying to unbuckle himself and squealing with frustration at his failed efforts. He tossed a Cheerio at Julia before his mom managed to get him out the door, driving the stroller with one arm and balancing the package under the other.

The hat-wearing man stared at Julia as he made his way toward the counter, shifting his weight from one foot to the other as he struggled to find something to say. Although the gray in his beard was deceptive, Julia guessed he wasn't older than forty, the deep lines next to his eyes suggesting either a lifetime of laughter or squinting against the sun. Just as he was going to say something, it was his turn in line.

He handed the envelope to the man behind the counter and watched as he tossed it in the outgoing mail bin. The scene appeared to Julia like a routine that everyone there was used to.

"See ya, George," the postal worker said, waving to the man who was adjusting his hat to make sure it covered his ears before stepping out into the eighty-plus-degree weather.

"Make sure you take care of this one," George said, pointing at Julia, who had stepped up to the counter. "She needs stamps, so you need to get her some stamps."

"Will do, George," the man said, with a look on his face that showed he was taking his command seriously. "I'll set her up with our best."

The bells on the door chimed as George walked out; he paused briefly to look up at the sun like he was surprised to see it there, before crossing the street and disappearing behind a bread delivery truck.

"George's harmless," the man said with a smile, in case Julia was concerned. "He comes in here every day to send a letter to his nephew who lives in California. Says he doesn't trust the mailboxes to get it to the right place."

"He seems really nice," Julia said. "Everyone here does."

"So, you want a book of stamps, huh? We got a few flowery options, some fireworks left over from the July fourth holiday, and the good ole' American flag." He pushed his glasses further up his nose and smiled, the smell of coffee on his breath reaching her across the counter.

"The American flag ones are fine." Flowery stationery with matching stamps was just too much.

Julia paid for her items and put the stamps in her purse, and the stationery on top of her groceries. She held the door open for a middle-aged woman coming in, her perfume coating Julia in a musky scent as she walked by.

She timed the drive back to the house—seven minutes. She stopped at the entrance to the drive and got out of her vehicle and tore the plastic FOR RENT sign off the post and tossed it onto the seat next to her.

She had checked her bank account balance that morning and her transfer had cleared, so it was official. She had adopted the farmhouse and every rusted, slanted, aging, splintered morsel that came along with it. She drove up to the house and parked in the shade of a huge tree out front, not yet feeling comfortable parking in the barn-turned-garage. She would have to let that level of familiarity develop on its own.

Julia had spent the better part of the morning walking around the house and getting to know its bones. There were creaks in certain floorboards, banister spindles that were loose and spun around if touched, and a hole in the wall next to an electrical outlet that was waiting for someone to come back and finish the job.

Wallpaper in traditional floral and stripe patterns covered each wall and she sensed that layers of wallpaper from years gone by provided insulation underneath, different colors and patterns peeking through where seams had come unglued. Perfect squares of unfaded wallpaper showed where pictures used to hang.

An oak hat rack stood in the corner by the front door, a

single gray wool hat dangling from one of its hooks like it had been forgotten.

Julia had felt uncomfortable walking around, feeling like a voyeur with every door opened and room explored. She couldn't bring herself to open the closets, the possibility that another person's clothing might be hanging there a level of personal intrusion that she felt was beyond the parameters of her rental agreement.

The house was larger than she had initially thought. A brass and crystal chandelier hung over an eight-person table in the dining room, a lace runner spread across the table like an airstrip waiting for a plane to land. And on the table's matching sideboard was a silver tray holding decanters with dark liquors. A large oak china hutch stood proudly against one wall keeping a watchful eye over the room, a layer of dust covering its interior glass shelves except for clean circles where glasses had been removed.

From the bright yellow and white wallpaper in the kitchen with spice and herb border to the cross-stitched hunting duck on a couch pillow, not a thing in the house was Julia's taste. And, yet, the house felt safe and comfortable, like the T-shirt that you live in at home, but won't wear in public. Every square inch of the house hadn't just been inhabited, it had been *lived* in; Julia couldn't help but feel that the house was happiest this way— happiest with life inside.

She put her keys onto the small china plate on the entryway table, assuming that was its intended purpose, then took the bag of groceries into the kitchen and unpacked what little she had bought, setting it out on the countertop.

Getting comfortable filling the cupboards with her own stuff was, too, going to take time. With no choice but to look through them to find a pitcher for the lemonade, Julia opened the cabinets one by one.

She finally found a pitcher in the dining room sideboard, a frosted glass design wrapping itself around its center like a ribbon. She rinsed out the dust from its bottom and dumped a healthy cup of the lemonade mix inside, opening drawers in search of a wooden spoon with one hand while holding the pitcher under the faucet with the other. The sugary granules settled on the bottom, floating upward like yellow stars into space. Julia grabbed a rubber spatula, the only large utensil she could find, and started a lemonade whirlpool to dissolve the mixture.

She opened the only cabinet she hadn't yet explored and smiled at what she found. All three shelves were filled with green depression glassware, elaborate goblets in two sizes lining two shelves, plates stacked neatly on the third. Julia took one of the glasses down and blew dust off its rim, rinsing it out and filling it with room-temperature lemonade.

She picked up the stationery, took a pen from her purse and made her way out to the front porch, moving the rocking chair closer to the railing. Bringing her feet up to rest on it, she pushed off the railing with her legs and rocked steadily, trying to find the motivation to write letters that she wished could write themselves.

Although all three letters contained the same basic information, Julia altered the recitation of current events based on the receiving party.

To her parents, she kept the details to a minimum, describing her departure from the Southern Sunset Center as more of an administrative decision based on the weighing of objective factors that she found no need to identify. She wished them well, assured them that she was "on the road to getting back to herself" and promised to be in touch again soon.

Her letter to Genevieve took a slightly different approach, a few expletive-ridden sentences describing her true impressions of clinical therapy and the Bebes of the world among references to firemen in birthday cards and cocktails waiting to be consumed.

To Gwen, Julia started her letter off with an apology, a wish that she could share more, but the explanation was too long and complicated for the limited pages of stationery that came with the small-town gift set. She wrote that her sudden departure was in no way reflective of how she felt about their friendship, her appreciation at having such a strong and trustworthy confidante in the center one of the few bright spots of her time there.

It was only while writing her letter to Gwen that Julia realized the impact that her leaving might have had on her friend. A wave of guilt washed over her for leaving without saying goodbye. She had left Gwen alone to answer questions that she shouldn't have had to ask; she deserved better than that and there wasn't a word Julia could write on this floral stationery that was going to change it.

To each—her parents, Genevieve, and Gwen—Julia provided an overview as to the little town that she was staying in, providing enough facts to let them know she was safe, but not enough to share the experiences that she was still trying to process.

In each letter, Julia left her friends and family with the same parting words to comfort them should they have any lingering concerns.

Seriously, don't worry. I'm okay.

And, although the same words had been spoken many times over the last year, this time Julia actually meant them. This was the first time she had said, "I'm okay" in as long as she could remember and actually believed it to be true.

Chapter 21

Burt

"You could die out here, you know."

Startled, Julia peeked around the corner. An old man stood just outside the screen door. He wasn't looking inside the house, but rather standing with his hands deep inside the pockets of work overalls, staring off into the distance with his back to the door. He turned his head as he talked to make sure the words reached her.

"Got some damn copperheads round here that'll eat ya whole. Copperheads don't get ya, there's plenty animals waitin' in line." He breathed in deeply through his nose and then spat off to the side, a wad of something or other sure to form a pool on the front porch.

Julia didn't move; she was still holding on to the butter knife that she had been using to spread jelly on her toast. She now regretted choosing it and not one of its sharper neighbors from the drawer.

"Whatcha know 'bout wells, huh?" he asked, turning his head to talk through the screen door and showing Julia his full profile. His silver hair was worn longer than most men in the area and his bulbous nose was twitching up and down, perhaps getting ready for its next deep inhale. Seventy years old, maybe, but then again, perhaps younger. Years in the harsh Georgia sun seemed to age people in different ways, this particular man seemingly a textbook example of "weathered and worn," a term she had heard to describe men who had spent their lives developing a harsh outer layer that prevented them from baking completely from the elements.

He still stood there, his head turned to the side, as if waiting for Julia to respond. She didn't; instead, she wiped the sweat from her palm and gripped the butter knife tighter, wondering if she was strong enough to deliver a blow with enough force to drive the dull blade into skin.

"Yeah, you probably don't even know 'bout that well, do ya?" the man asked, shaking his head to show how disgusted he was by such ill-preparedness on her part. "You don't know where that hole is, you'll probably just be walking along some day and fall right in, trapped down there with those spiders that are bigger than my hand." He spat again and wiped his mouth on his sleeve, sucking in what seemed like an abnormal amount of snot as he worked on another Olympic-sized loogie.

"Those damn spiders killed my cat, God damn it!" He seemed agitated by the memory, taking a few paces forward before returning to his spot in front of the screen door. "You want to see something inhuman, you shoulda seen what those goddamn shit eight-legged freaks did to my cat. Holy Mother of God, I thought there was some goddamn devil worship going on in my barn the way that poor animal had been massacred."

Julia looked toward the back door, weighing her odds of running for it before the man could get inside. Even if she made it out, she'd have to outrun him to her vehicle, which even at his age and condition, she guessed wouldn't be easy because it was parked less than ten feet from the front porch that he was standing on. Not to mention, her keys were lying in the tiny bowl next to the front door.

"Now listen, I don't know much, but I sure as hell know that you got no business on this property, I tell ya that." He turned again, this time further so he could look inside the house. Julia backed up to hide behind the corner, waiting for the squeak of the screen door as the signal that she needed to make her move. "I've known the Blackwells for decades, kindest souls on Earth those folks, and I don't know how Hank would feel 'bout you livin' here. Clara liked her kitchen a certain way, you see, and I just have to believe she's lookin' down and dying all over again to see you rustle round in her stuff."

Julia lowered the knife to her side, watching the man look into the sky like he was trying to catch sight of Hank and Clara, perhaps looking for some sign that they approved of his handling of this stranger who had squatted on their land. He may very well have come to murder her and drop her in the well with cat-killing spiders, but Julia was pretty sure he was just trying to protect friends who were gone and who he missed in his own rough way.

The screen door was unlocked; in fact, it barely even closed, the wood so warped along its bottom that it curved outward, and couldn't keep flies away, much less a man intent on coming in. Had he wanted to enter, he would have, which is what convinced Julia that she should just go outside and talk to him. Just in case, she grabbed the keys from the bowl as she passed and stuffed them into her pocket.

"Hi," she said, opening the screen door and walking onto the porch. The man moved over to give her room to get by. She sat down in the rocking chair and gestured for him to do the same on the two-person bench with its seat upholstered in a white and yellow sunflower pattern.

He reluctantly did so, avoiding eye contact with Julia and

folding his hands, resting them between his legs. Heavy bags hung under each of his eyes and a few coarse hairs were so long they curled upward and made it look like his eyebrows had legs. His skin was leathery and smooth as if the sun had burnt off the layers, leaving behind only those like a weather tarp with no elasticity. Whatever bravado he exuded with the screen door between them was lost now that Julia had actually come outside. He sat silently and fixed his gaze on the driveway like he was waiting for someone to come home.

"I can tell you were close with the Blackwells," Julia started, rocking softly and following his stare. "I talked with Kennedy quite a bit and she shared some stories about growing up here. It's truly a special place." At the mention of Kennedy, Julia thought she saw the man's eyes shift slightly and his brow soften, so she continued.

"I'm Julia, by the way," she said, turning toward the man and holding her hand out to shake. He looked surprised at the gesture and stared at her hand like he didn't know what to do with it before taking it and pumping it like you would in a business meeting with an adversary across the table.

"I'm Burt. Burt McGallagher." He looked down the driveway again, and then further up the road. "I live 'bout half a mile that way," he said, pointing at the brick house on the hill that Julia had seen from the road. "I've lived in these parts my whole life, and so have the Blackwells. Spent almost every Christmas Eve in this house and Easter Sundays, too." He sniffed, but this time it didn't look like a loogie-working sniff, but rather an effort to keep his emotions pushed down and his mind distracted.

Julia got it. Burt McGallagher and Hank Blackwell had been close friends and raised their families together on neighboring farms in one of Georgia's most tucked away corners. With Hank's passing a few months ago, Burt was now alone. He had nothing except the memories of his friend and the realization that, as his friend saw it was time to go, so soon would he. Julia could only imagine how difficult it was to see someone else—a stranger to the town—move into the house and cast a shadow across the memories that he had made there. Although she was cautious of this man ten minutes before, her heart broke for him now.

"You know," she started. "I admired your house when I was out driving and found this one. These two houses are the only ones that you can see from the road and there's something so beautiful about them; it's almost like I could tell that there was something really special between these two."

Still not looking at her, Burt smiled, nodding in agreement, if not appreciation. He allowed himself to relax against the back of the bench, his tense shoulders now lowered and his hands falling naturally on his knees.

"Can I get you some lemonade?" Julia asked. "I'd love to hear some of your stories about this area. Maybe some memories of this house and spending time with the Blackwells."

Burt looked at her, first with surprise, and then with a small smile.

"I mean, if you have time to spend with me because I know you must be busy," Julia added, not wanting to appear like her gesture was simply charitable.

"Tell ya what," Burt said, sitting up and pulling something out of his back pocket. "You go get yourself some lemonade and I'll just sip on this." He jiggled the flask around to make sure it had something in it before taking off its lid and taking a swig, a slow and steady burn evident from his pursed lips and rapid eye blink. Julia smiled as she stood, the broken capillaries on Burt's nose fanning out like a red veined road map. "Gin blossoms" she had heard this condition called, the flowery pattern relatively common on the faces of old men like Burt who preferred homemade hooch over lemonade or sun tea—men who preferred homemade hooch to just about everything.

"Sounds good," Julia said, leaving Burt on the front porch as she made her way into the kitchen and poured herself a glass. She was actually relieved he had declined a drink, the only acceptable lemonade in these parts likely batches made from fresh squeezed lemons and recipes passed along from generation-to-generation guarded like any time-honored secret. Julia assumed that her store-bought lemon-flavored crystals wouldn't go over well with a man who seemed to pride himself on not taking the easy road in life.

As hesitant as he was to give her a chance, she didn't want to sour his impression further by exposing herself as someone too lazy to squeeze a piece of fruit to make a drink.

By the time Julia got back to the porch, Burt had lit a cigar and had his legs stretched out, feet crossed at his ankles. She smiled as she stepped over them, settling herself back down into the chair and rocking with her head resting on its tall back.

"This is God's country," Burt said, taking in a long puff of the cigar and blowing it so the smoke wouldn't hit Julia in the face. She found the gesture sweet, albeit surprising coming from someone who had found no problem spitting phlegm into pools on the front porch.

"Yeah, I know that everyone says it, but it's true bout this part of the country. So much left untouched. It's like God protects it, keeps dirty hands off of it cause it's more special than the rest." Burt took another sip from the flask and puffed a few puffs, this time forgetting to blow it away from Julia. Her eyes burned from the smoke and she coughed, wondering if the earlier gesture had been an unintentional act of kindness.

For the next hour, Burt told Julia stories about his youth and memories of Hank, the two of them inseparable since birth, their mothers best friends.

He talked about a simpler kind of life, a life that he wished society would get back to, when families gathered around the radio and snowstorms meant a cup of cocoa and peppermint stick that were appreciated because they were given maybe twice a year.

Burt talked about enlisting in the army together and marrying their high-school sweethearts, settling into their childhood homes and vowing to raise their children together. And, they did. Hank's three children approximately the same age as Burt's oldest three. Beau came a few years later, a surprise fourth child for Burt and Annie who had settled into their family of five and had to adjust to such an unexpected arrival. Burt spoke of all his children with pride, but the glimmer in his eye and smirk when describing his youngest suggested that he and Beau had a special bond.

Julia got the sense that Burt considered those years the best —the years spent as young families figuring out their paths in life and just happy to walk them together. When his wife, Annie, died almost ten years ago from cancer, Burt essentially moved in with the Blackwells, spending every waking minute with them at their insistence.

When Clara later got sick, Burt got Hank through it the only way he knew how, with long talks on this very porch and a jug of hooch that he carted all the way from his barn. These last few years had been bittersweet, the widowers alone, but not lonely, their presence in each other's lives the one thing they could rely on as their children moved away and seasons changed at a more frenzied and hurried pace.

With Hank now gone, Burt spent his days in his old brick house alone, staring at this one from the rocking chair on his front porch and finding it difficult not to want to do it all over again. He knew these were supposed to be his days of rest, but he would gladly give them up for one more day with his wife and closest friends, shucking corn on the front porch and listening to Johnny Cash on the radio while their kids played in the sprinkler on the front lawn. What he wouldn't give for another one of his wife's cherries jubilee, the sound of his friend's laughter and Bing Crosby serenading them from the record player with thoughts of glistening treetops.

Julia's heart broke for Burt, his life reading like a fantastic book that you know is nearing its end. She could picture it all—the family picnics and his wife's potato salad that had won a blue ribbon at the county fair, the hard days in the field and cold beers at night, and knowing that every tear shed and smile earned was shared equally among these two families.

She understood why he considered her an intruder; she had waltzed into this home like it was simply a house that served a purpose, when it was so much more. To Burt, it was all that he had left of a chapter in his book that he didn't want to close. Julia suddenly didn't feel worthy of living here; she didn't feel like she had lived enough, grown enough, or seen enough to fill the space left by these people who had loved with their whole hearts and accomplished more living on this property than she was ever capable of.

In a world of *doing* and *succeeding* and *excelling*, the Blackwells and McGallaghers did something that people value very little these days—they simply *lived*—and their hearts were full from enjoying every minute of it together.

As much as Julia wanted to get up, pack her bags, and leave with a heartfelt apology, she couldn't do it. Burt had confided in her, a perfect stranger, and trusted her with a glimpse into a life that had been shared with very few. She wished she had known all of this when she spoke to Kennedy, wondering now if she was as deferential as she should have been to her family and the pain that she must have felt handing over keys that unlocked as many memories as they did doors.

Julia thought of Kennedy sitting on the railing of the front porch and staring off at something only she could see, now realizing that she was probably watching the ghostly footsteps of those who had once danced in the grass and blew the feathery seeds off dandelions to chase them in the wind.

Julia wedged her sandals into the floorboards of the porch to stop the chair from rocking. Burt was done talking, the look on his face one of exhaustion at having relived years within a matter of minutes, his breath slow and steady as he watched a wasp make its way toward the nest that Kennedy had spotted a few days before.

Julia took a sip of lemonade, the ice cubes long gone and diluting the drink into nothing more than lemon-flavored water. She thought about her next words carefully, concerned that saying too much might scare the poor guy off and make him retreat to his own porch. She didn't want that; she wanted Burt to stay and turn her into the type of person that would have made Annie and Clara proud, the type of person who shucks corn when the going gets tough and blares 'Folsom Prison' from the barn radio to drown out a bad day.

"I wish I would have known them," Julia said, realizing how silly it sounded given the circumstances. If Hank and Clara weren't gone, she wouldn't have had any reason to sit on this front porch and drink from their green depression glassware. Then again, maybe she would have run into them in town, a few friendly faces among the deeply skeptical in the grocery store or a smile greeting her with the door held open as she entered the post office.

"Hearing your stories, memories about what you all accomplished and the lives you lead makes me feel like I've been wasting mine," Julia said.

This caught Burt off guard. His brow furrowed as he took a

long puff on the nub of cigar, shaking his head like he was about to correct her.

"No, no," Julia said, before he had the chance. "I mean that in the best possible way. Sometimes you have to be reminded of what it's all about, this whole life thing." She sat for a moment, watching Burt's face as he took in her words and tried to make sense of them.

"I've been lost," Julia said, looking away so he wouldn't see the tears in her eyes. "I've been really, really lost."

And, with that, the floodgates opened. Julia told Burt everything, starting with her place as the youngest in a proper Southern family and continuing with her decision to leave the Southern Sunset Center and ending with her decision to stop for a while in Friendly.

If there was any judgment cast in Burt's mind throughout her tales of a closeted lesbian sister, married lover, miscarried baby, and time in rehab with women who cut themselves and inject their lips with illegal products from Mexico, he showed none; just casually lit another cigar during a break in her story when she went inside for a refill of lemonade.

Julia told Burt things that she hadn't told anyone; she confided in him that she felt like God had punished her by taking away her baby, discussed the friction between her mother and grandmother, and admitted feeling less-than in Evelyn's eyes when compared to her sisters. She also shared things that had nothing to do with her current state of mind, including her deep resentment of women who didn't have cellulite, irrational fear of bubble wrap, and the fact that she had pretended to like her mom's bread pudding for years, but actually thought it was disgusting and resembled baby food.

There was something about talking to someone without a clipboard that made the words flow freely. The lack of analysis or clinical diagnosis was liberating when it came to sharing information with no risk of consequence or scribbled comment in her file.

"You need to tell your family where you are," Burt said gently, uncrossing his ankles and stretching his legs out in front of him before recrossing them again the other way. "They'll worry bout you."

"Oh, I have," Julia said, telling him about the letters that had been mailed the day before that were safely in transit. "I'm not hiding," she said, afraid that his mental wheels were spinning furiously to decide if she was being honest.

"You say it like that's a bad thing," Burt said, picking a small piece of tobacco from his bottom lip and flicking it onto the porch. "Nothing wrong with hiding from the world as long as the life you're livin' is real. You don't owe the world an appearance; you just owe yourself an honest life at the end of the day."

"I guess I never thought about it that way," Julia said, leaning as far back as she could in the chair and letting it stretch its rocking legs.

"Sounds to me like your plate's been piled high with some shitty things to deal with," Burt continued, digging for another piece of tobacco that had become stuck under his lip. "Some shit's heavier than others and you've got yourself a heavy plate." Finding the piece, he flicked it angrily toward the floor and then looked at his cigar like it had done it on purpose.

"Don't be so hard on yourself. There's no hard and fast rule to living life. If we end the race smarter than we began, I think we're in pretty good shape."

Julia smiled and watched the sun lower itself on the horizon. The two of them had talked the afternoon hours away like they didn't have a care in the world. And, at that moment, Julia felt like she didn't. At that moment, she felt like the weight welded to her shoulders had been lightened somehow by being told that it was okay she was here—it was okay to hide a little as long as she kept on living.

"I best be goin'," Burt said, rising from the bench slowly, resting his hands on his knees to allow them time to remember how to bend. Arching his back to stretch slightly backwards, he put the flask back into his pocket and walked toward the porch's front steps, Julia following him. Easing his way down the steps, Burt made his way toward an old 1950s Chevy truck that had as much rust as paint on its frame.

"Burt," Julia called, waiting for him to turn around. "Were you just kidding about those copperhead snakes?"

He smiled wickedly, spitting a wad of something onto a flat rock along the driveway. Julia waited for him to admit that he had been trying to scare her with tales of otherworldly snakes and wells that funneled into the center of the Earth with spiders that mutilate cats for fun. He looked into the tall grass that grew alongside the driveway and stepped closer to the truck.

"Yeah, welcome to copperhead central," he said with a wink. "Those damn things will eat ya whole."

Chapter 22

Weeds

Julia loved feeling the cool dirt between her fingers, a few slippery worms writhing in anxiety at having their dark hideaway disturbed.

She scooped up the dark soil and let it fall between her fingers back to the ground, watching it crumble as its dehydrated layer gave way to moist ground beneath. She had seen a pair of gardening gloves in the shed, a bright yellow pair with tulips, but they looked brand new and never worn. Julia wondered if Clara had been like her—preferring the feel of the cool dirt over clean fingernails—or perhaps it was Julia who was like Clara. It seemed appropriate under these circumstances to give deference to the first who tilled this ground.

Julia thought back to the garden at the Southern Sunset Center and the women digging for their lives in soil that grew almost nothing. She thought of them as she took another handful of dirt and let it fall from between her fingers.

Julia had slept in that morning. The bedroom she had chosen to call her own faced west, protected from the harsh sunlight. It had its own bathroom, one of the few rooms in the house that looked recently remodeled, with a ceramic tile shower and plenty of counter space. The bedroom was one of the largest, a king-sized bed with matching mahogany wardrobe filling the space, with a small writing desk and antique chair in the corner. Julia had always wanted a wardrobe instead of an actual closet. The story of *The Lion, The Witch and The Wardrobe* had made a huge impression on her as a child; the thought of opening one of those doors and being transported into another realm was worth more to her than the modern-day storage solutions provided by walk-in closets that catered to women who wanted to see their shoes displayed by color.

The bedroom also had a window seat that overlooked much of the backyard, a cushioned seat from which to explore the land around the house in private and from a bird's eye view. It was from that window seat that Julia discovered the garden, or at least the silhouette of an old garden, its belly now so full of weeds that only careful eyes could still see the life that it once held.

She had made herself a big cup of coffee that morning—a bag of fresh grounds generously provided by Opal during her last visit—and ventured out into the backyard to explore her most recent discovery.

The garden wasn't huge, maybe ten feet square, and it was tucked away in one of the backyard corners. Julia tried to pull some of the weeds, but they had roots like miniature trees with narrow trunks for stems. She grabbed hold of the larger ones with both hands, balancing on her heels to hoist them from their turf and fling them into a pile. Hidden under some tall grass, she found three garden stones, hand prints tattooed into their dark cement and colorful pebbles sprinkled along the edges. The names Kennedy, Seth, and Theo were written with tiny fingers along the top of each stone, a small heart alongside Kennedy's name.

Julia felt bad that these stones had been left behind by the family, not so much forgotten as disguised. She couldn't leave them there like this. It was like seeing a cemetery that everyone had abandoned, grave markers left to decay like the bodies laid to rest six feet beneath them. She couldn't live here and let the stones stay tucked away. Energized by a cup of good coffee and with more brewing in the kitchen, Julia ventured out into the back shed to see what she could find to help bring the garden back to life.

Evelyn had never wanted her girls to get dirty. She claimed she wanted to raise "refined children" whenever their grandmother suggested that they be allowed to get as dirty as their imaginations allowed.

If her mother dressed Julia and her sisters in white dresses during a visit, Mabel was sure to hand them an old baking tin with instructions to make her a mud pie. Try as Evelyn might to deny her upbringing, Julia relished knowing that her mother had been raised on a farm; the manure and manual labor was an indelible part of Evelyn, regardless of the efforts she made to cover it up with fine china and flowery perfume.

Julia could never understand why her mother resisted it all. The sunsets and smell of lilacs on the farm were more of a spiritual experience than any church sermon Evelyn had made her sit through. Julia's focus always more on tearing off the pit-stained dress that she had been stuffed into than sermons or hymns sung off-key.

She could close her eyes now and still smell those lilacs, even though they hadn't visited her grandparents' farm since she was twelve years old.

After a particularly bad argument between Evelyn and Mabel, her mother had insisted that her parents needed to travel to the city if they wanted to see the girls.

The shed was really more like a small barn, its heavy doors locked only by a metal bar that could be swung out of place.

Julia had assumed garden tools might be stored inside and was surprised to slide the doors open and discover a picker's dream: vintage oil cans and metal signs displayed on a shelf that spanned one entire side and wrapped around to the wall on the other end. She had seen enough *Antiques Roadshow* episodes to know that the signs and cans were worth something.

On the wall opposite the display was a giant pegboard, tools hung on hooks according to size and utility. The lack of human disturbance for the last few months had turned the space into an amusement park for barn spiders, elaborate webs extending from the highest rafter to the lowest point on Hank's work bench; only Charlotte herself was missing. Julia found herself waiting for the benevolent webmaster with a sultry voice to welcome her into their fray.

Seeing a rack of tools in the far corner, Julia walked past the riding lawn mower, its distinctive green and yellow colors at odds with the rest of the shed that had been aged with a sepia filter. She selected a hoe and pointed shovel, pretty sure that neither were up for the task of breaking through soil that had been taken over by a small forest.

She made her way back to the garden and realized that her hot cup of coffee no longer sounded like a good idea under the hot sun.

Pulling as many weeds as she could, Julia started murdering the ones left with blows of the hoe, severing their stalks and digging into the dirt for any roots that remained. Within minutes, she was an absolute mess, her hands blistered and becoming more raw with every swing of the handle. She wiped her hands on her shirt, leaving smears of dirt, weed remnants and sweat.

After an hour, she had cleared the edges of the garden, carefully removing the handprint stones so they didn't become collateral damage.

She didn't hear him approach and the sound of a male voice behind her startled her so badly that she squealed and brought the hoe up like a sword.

"Whoa, there," he said, putting his hands up in surrender. "After seeing what you did to those rhubarb plants, I sure don't want to get in your way."

"Oh shit," Julia said, looking toward the pile he was staring at. "That was *rhubarb?* I thought they were weeds."

"Not a huge fan anyway," he said, smiling sympathetically. "I'm Beau. My dad said that I might want to stop by to check on the city girl who's bound to kill herself on the Blackwell's farm."

"Ah, you're Beau," she said, leaning on the handle's end of the hoe. "Your dad told me about you. The youngest in the clan, right?"

"That's me," he said, studying the garden and trying to hide a smile.

Beau looked about her age and, although his facial structure was that of his dad, Julia wouldn't have guessed that her hooch-drinking neighbor would have a son like this. Beau's hair was worn long and shaggy, a chocolate brown with hints of red natural in the sun, curling over the collar of his gray shirt. At over six feet tall, he towered over his dad, and the tattoos along both arms suggested that he was true to his birth order's tendency toward rebellion, a trait that she couldn't imagine going over well with Burt. Then again, maybe by the time Beau came along, Burt and his wife were too tired with the three older kids to really care.

"Not real sure what you plan on planting this time of year," he offered.

"Oh, nothing," Julia quickly responded, not wanting to appear dumb. "I just wanted to clean it up a bit. I found those stones in here and thought they deserved a nice home." She gestured toward the three stones that lay in a row at the garden's edge.

"Oh wow," Beau said, walking over to them. "I remember these. The Blackwell kids were more my siblings' age, but I spent quite a bit of time in this backyard, following them all around trying to convince them that I was cool for my age. Whatever age that happened to be at the time."

"It's tough being the youngest sometimes," Julia said, shrugging.

"It can be," Beau responded. "Then again, I wouldn't have wanted to trade places with my older sisters and brother. Standards were too high." He smiled and knelt down to take a closer look at the garden stones, the memories that they brought back written across his face as he touched the tiny handprints.

"So, what *are* you doing here exactly?" he asked, more curious than accusatory. Julia had the impression that Burt had filled him in, but he wanted to hear her version of the story.

"I needed gas and it seemed like a good place to stop," she lied, proud of herself for flirting so effortlessly.

Beau laughed, revealing beautiful white teeth.

"How'd you get here?" she asked. "I didn't hear a car. Did you walk?"

"Rode my bike," he said, looking toward the front of the house, although it was blocked from view.

"I found a great old bike in the shed," Julia said. "Thought I might put some air in the tires and take it for a spin one of these days."

Beau smiled and looked away, embarrassed. Julia didn't yet realize that he was embarrassed for *her*.

"It's a Harley," he said. "Different kind of bike."

Rather than try to save face, she laughed. And so did he. Julia was embarrassed, both by the silly assumption and the fact that she was so focused on the garden that she had effectively tuned out the roar of a Harley making its way up the drive.

"Do you want some help?" he asked, picking up the shovel without waiting for her to respond. "We can do the work in half as much time. Maybe even less if we stop digging up actual plants." Beau gave her a wink and Julia could feel herself blush.

"Touché," she said, picking up the hoe and bringing it down hard on a weed that had been causing her problems all morning, its roots like talons gripping something below the surface.

Beau was right; between the two of them, an all-day project for one turned into a two-hour project for both of them. Julia started on one end and Beau the other, clearing out the overgrown plants and weeds that had infiltrated the space.

As they worked, they talked, Beau sharing his journey from rural farmboy to freelance photographer with a regional lifestyle website. His work kept him on the road for much of the time, but he had an apartment in Kreanley, the elusive town rumored to have good coffee. Beau confirmed the rumors, describing the town of 15,000 as popular among the locals for its Quik Trip, Pizza Hut, and chain grocery store. Come Fridays, you could apparently spend your entire night waiting with the rest of your neighbors from Friendly for a large pepperoni or deep dish of extra cheese.

After carting away two wheelbarrows full of weeds, plants, and an occasional mummified carrot, Beau and Julia placed the three garden stones back in their original location and stepped back to look at their work.

"Clara loved this garden," Beau said, leaning on the handle of this shovel. "When she passed away, I think Hank just found it too hard to come out here."

Something started to ring, softly, like the sound of miniature bells used for holiday projects being brought together like cymbals. They both looked for where the sound was coming from, zeroing-in on the open door to the shed where she had found the garden tools.

They walked in and spotted a wind chime hanging from one of the rafters, not far above the top of the pegboard tool bench. It looked like a child's project, various colored stones and bells woven together with pieces of colorful string and attached to a colander. Tiny pieces of string had been tied into bows above some of the bells and the late morning sunlight used the glass beads to cast a rainbow across the floor. Although the small windows in the shed were shut and there wasn't a breeze to be felt, the wind chime continued to rock slowly side to side, its song playing like a prayer sent out into the universe.

Julia walked over to the wind chime and stood on her tiptoes to draw it off its hook. "Can you help me hang this on the front porch?" she asked. She felt like this must be a Father's Day gift from the same timeframe as the stones. Clara had brought a piece of her children into the garden to keep her company and Hank was reminded of them by a soft chime as he puttered around the shed.

"Sure," Beau said. Julia couldn't tell from his expression if he thought the gesture was sweet or strange. She didn't want to appear strange; she didn't want to appear like the strange girl who decided to rent an old farmhouse and till a garden months too late for planting. She didn't want to appear like a lost thirty-something who secretly longed to live the life of strangers. She didn't want to appear to be those things, but realized the descriptions would be accurate.

Julia walked up to the front of the house next to Beau in silence, wondering what his dad had told him about her, yet realizing it might be best not to know. If there was one thing she had learned over this past year, it was that others' impressions were meaningless; in the canvass of life, she should never allow someone to stand before her painting and tell her what it meant. How could they really know?

Julia held the wind chime shoulder level as she walked, careful not to let the string strands twist and get knotted. She handed it to Beau on the front porch and told him that she would get them something to drink, anxious for a minute alone.

The screen door eased closed behind her, its hinges letting out a sorrowful moan as they were forced to open. On her way to the kitchen, she stopped to take a look at herself in the hallway mirror, an oval antique blemished in places by tarnish so her reflection looked like she had some horrible skin condition. In reality, her appearance didn't fare much better. She had large pit stains and a line of sweat directly under her boobs and there were dirty handprints along the bottom of her shorts and smeared across her belly from when she tried to wipe the sweat off. There was mud on her cheek and ear from when she swatted a bug away only to realize it was just a weed fragment. And the dirt added just enough texture to her hair that it held a few strands suspended outright. She noticed something in her front teeth and pried it loose, a tiny piece of red apple skin set free.

"Lovely," she said. The damage was too extensive to actually remedy at this point.

She walked back onto the front porch with two glasses of lemonade and saw Beau balancing on the railing, hanging on to the edge of the porch roof with one hand as he leaned as far as he could to secure the wind chime loop onto a hook that had once been used to hang plants. After a few misses, he finally connected the two and jumped off the railing onto the grass below.

"There you go," he said, standing back to admire his work. "One grade school art project hung successfully."

"It's perfect," Julia said, handing him his drink. He looked at it curiously for a minute, before taking a sip and coughing jokingly.

"Wow, what is this exactly?"

"What do you mean," she asked, pretending to be offended. "It's the finest powdered lemonade that money can buy in Friendly."

Beau shook his head and took her glass, disappearing inside the house and returning empty-handed.

"Let's go," he said, walking toward his motorcycle, a black and silver Harley that defied all laws of gravity by standing upright. The cautious city girl inside Julia would have never even considered riding off on two-wheels with a stranger; the new-found country girl walked toward the bike wondering how fast it could go.

"Where are we going?" she asked, wishing she had the opportunity to at least throw some water on her face and tie her hair back. Then again, maybe first impressions were overrated because her appearance could only go up from here.

"We're going to get you some good ole' fashioned sweet tea," Beau said, swinging one leg over the motorcycle and waiting for her to do the same. "My dad makes the best sweet tea this side of the state," he said with an exaggerated Southern accent.

As she got within ten feet of the motorcycle, a swishing sound from the tall grass next to the driveway got her attention, two black eyes emerging as its body followed. The biggest snake that Julia had ever seen outside the confines of a zoo slithered its way across the gravel, unaffected by their presence. Its body kept going and going, the black and gray scales looking almost fake in their pattern's perfection. Julia jumped back and cupped her hands over her mouth to stop from screaming, taking a few steps away from the snake, but worried about getting too close to the grass from which it came.

It finally disappeared into the tall grass on the other side and

Julia tried to compose herself, new pit sweat stains forming from fear.

"Jesus!" she said, looking to Beau for his reaction. "What the hell? That thing was as long as I am! What do snakes eat down here?"

"Yeah, you've got to watch out for those copperheads," he said, putting his sunglasses on with one hand and revving the bike's engine with the other. His grin was as playfully wicked as his dad's. "Those damn things will eat ya whole."

Chapter 23

Fireflies

Julia had gotten used to hearing the old truck make its way up the drive, whipping up small whirlwinds of dust behind it as Burt hit the brakes too late and skidded into the gravel patch that was his designated parking spot. Even in the back shed she could hear the tires roll their way toward the house. Another entertaining visit from her sweet and eccentric neighbor was on the afternoon's schedule.

Burt had stopped by regularly since their initial visit, always to "check in," but really just for an excuse to sit on the porch and visit for a while.

Julia loved the company: each chat with Burt was like a trip back in time when the fields were worked by multiple generations of family farmers and evenings were spent talking instead of texting. He usually arrived with a jug of sweet tea under his arm, always with a few words of dismay that Julia had reached her thirties without a clue how to brew proper tea.

Topics ranged from his family's gatherings with the Blackwells to the new owners of the local hardware store, alleged cheapskates who caused quite a town tizzy when they recently took away the "leave a penny, take a penny" cup by the register. Every now and then Beau was mentioned, but only if Burt discussed his latest photography assignment and "where in the great state of Georgia those website people sent him this time."

Julia was busy moving old gasoline cans out of the way so she could wheel the bicycle out of the shed. Its dark shade of blue was lighter than it had appeared inside, and a thick layer of dust covered its frame and leather seat. A small silver bell was fastened to the handlebars, a high-pitched *ting* echoing throughout the shed each time Julia accidentally bumped it.

Weaving her way through the tools and cans toward the door, she walked the bicycle toward the front of the house, anxious to greet Burt with her latest find and hear any stories that he might have had about Old Blue, a name that fitted a bike that had seen a sunny trail or two.

She rounded the corner of the house and rang the bicycle's bell repeatedly to mark her arrival. Expecting to see his truck, she was surprised to find a white sedan in its place, its mystery driver no longer behind the wheel.

A bit more hesitant, Julia walked the bicycle around to the steps by the front porch, leaning it against the railing as she looked around for some clue as to who had arrived.

Hearing footsteps on the porch, she mounted the stairs and paused at the top when she spotted a person at the far end, leaning over the railing in search of something, or someone.

It took only a second for Julia to realize who it was. "Gwen?" she asked, hoping she was right.

Her friend spun around, her beautiful white smile greeting her.

"Gwen!" Julia ran and met her halfway across the porch. The women wrapped their arms around each other and laughed as they swayed side to side.

"Oh my God!" Julia said, still not ready to let go. "I can't believe you're here."

Gwen was the first to release her grip and step back to take a long look at her friend who had fled rehab without so much as a goodbye or wave in her direction. "Girl, I've never been both so pissed off and happy to see someone," she said, laughing. "How could you?! You left me there to deal with all of the crazy alone!" Gwen shook her jokingly to show her frustration.

"I know, I know," Julia pleaded, grabbing her friend again and pulling her in, so thankful for having someone to hug right now. She thought she was okay being alone, but realized at that moment the true magic of the human touch.

"I can't believe you found me. You got some tracking skills or what?" Julia said, motioning for her friend to sit down on the rocking chair while she hopped onto the railing.

"Well, gee, let's see," Gwen started sarcastically. "In your letter, you said that you had rented an old farmhouse by a town called Friendly. Wasn't too difficult. Once I got into town, a few people in a tiny grocery store were all too eager to point me in your direction." She rested her head on the back of the chair and rocked rhythmically, its wooden bones skilled at lulling sitters into a sedated state.

"People are a little odd," Gwen said, wrinkling up her nose. "Guy in that store was buying a year's supply of beef jerky and they kept referring to farms like I knew the people."

"Yeah, there are some characters here," Julia responded, glancing briefly at the brick farmhouse up the road. "I can't really explain it, though. Some inner voice just told me to stay here and lay low for a while."

Gwen looked at Julia with a bit of suspicion, one eye squinting to watch for any sign that Julia's body language belied what she claimed. "Got to watch those inner voices," Gwen said. "Dr. Rayborn would want you to explore those further." She laughed quietly, rubbing her hands up and down the smooth wooden chair arms. "Dr. Rayborn would be concerned, but Barkle would hope that the voices in your head wouldn't want to talk longer than your allotted session time."

"Shit, Gwen," Julia said, shaking her head with shame. "I'm so sorry I left like that. I wish I could have told you why."

"No, worries. I'm actually sorry, too. I was a total bitch those last few days you were there. I guess that place got to me. The whole forced confessional in front of everyone isn't my thing." Gwen looked down, searching the porch's warped floorboards for the right words. "It felt like a public shaming in a way." She shrugged and looked to Julia for some sign of understanding, which she got with a sympathetic smile and nod. "But, I'm here now." Gwen threw her hands up in celebration. "I've got a few days before I head back to the outside world. Thought I'd stay for a bit, if you're up for some company."

"Are you serious!?" Julia jumped off the railing and started shaking her hips in a poorly executed dance move that was intended to convey her excitement. She pumped her arms in the air like the party was about to get started. "Want something to drink?" she asked excitedly. "Burt brought me some sweet tea yesterday."

Gwen cocked her head to one side. "Who's Burt? Do tell."

"Oh Lord, don't get any ideas," Julia said with a laugh. "He's my neighbor. A sweet older guy who lives all alone and just likes the company." Any mention of his son who Julia couldn't seem to get off her mind was better left out for the time being.

"Sweet tea sounds nice," Gwen said. "And it definitely has its place. But I was thinking maybe we could wet our whistles with something even sweeter." Before she had even finished the sentence, Gwen was halfway to her white car. She rummaged around in the passenger seat then turned around victorious and held up a bottle of pink wine.

"Oh, why the hell not?" Julia said. "From what I can tell, time doesn't move too quickly around here, so might as well not wait for happy hour. I'll get some glasses."

"Save 'em," Gwen said, making her way back onto the porch. "We're sitting our asses on the porch of a farmhouse that looks old enough to have seen some Confederate soldiers, let's do away with civility, shall we?" With that, Gwen twisted the cap off the bottle of wine and chugged from the bottle, then wincing from the sappy sweetness.

"Where'd you even get this?" Julia asked, taking a swig and making the same face as Gwen.

"From some roadside stand on my way here," Gwen said. "There was a big sign advertising wine, pecans, and fireworks."

Julia remembered seeing the sign. She also remembered wondering what kind of person stopped by a roadside stand to buy liquor, nuts, and dynamite.

"Why'd you stop with this?" Julia asked, laughing and taking another swig. "Why didn't you load up on pecans and Fourth of July shit while you were there?"

Gwen sat up in the chair as if offended, placing one hand on her chest. "For your information, I've got a bucketful of nuts on the passenger side floor and a few sparklers in the trunk. You never know when you might want to light one of those babies up."

The women giggled, the wine already warming their stomachs and clouding their minds. Julia looked at the bottle before passing it back to Gwen. The label spoke nothing of alcohol content. In fuzzy font that had been printed off an old laser jet printer, the label simply read *Pink Berry Wine*, with a poor quality image of a giant raspberry floating underneath the name.

Because the munchies set in quickly, Julia put a pizza that she had picked up during her latest trip to Kreanley, where the pizza parlor that made pies ready-to-bake was a welcome change, in the oven.

When the sun started to set, the heat index dropped significantly, and the pink sky made a beautiful backdrop for a dinner of pepperoni and cheap wine. Julia now sat on the bench where Burt had stretched his legs, the smell of cigar smoke still lingering in the upholstered seat.

"So, how is everyone?" Julia asked, grabbing another slice off the baking sheet and wrapping the melted cheese around her finger to keep it from falling.

"Oh, you know," Gwen started. "Pretty much the same. Rose went home a few days ago."

"She did?" Julia was surprised. The grieving woman had not yet even begun to face the reality of losing her mother when she had left. "I hope she's okay."

"That place wasn't right for her," Gwen said. "The forced interaction and scheduled sharing sessions, those aren't right for her. She needs to grieve her own way." She grabbed another slice, folding it in half and taking a bite out of its end. "I'm glad she left," she said with her mouth full.

Julia nodded silently. Rose was a sweet and kind woman who would shed a tear for anyone not yet ready to do so themselves; Julia hoped she could find the peace that she was looking for outside that place.

"Her kids seemed really nice," Gwen continued, still chewing. "Her son and daughter came with her husband to drive her home. Sweet kids, looked about fourteen and sixteen. Husband seemed nice, too."

Julia leaned back, resting her head against the side of the house. The pizza and wine combination created a comforting heaviness in her belly, a tipsy fog dulling some senses and bringing others into greater focus. She was glad to hear that Rose had a great family to go home to, but was saddened by it all. She wasn't struggling with personal demons or a questionable past; Rose was dealing with the effects of loving someone too much and not being willing to let them go. Tragic as it was, Julia found something beautiful in the torment, a life full of love was so much better than one closed to experiencing true loss.

"Oh, Lord!" Gwen said, suddenly sitting upright like she had forgotten something. "Speaking of kids, Bebe's came for a visit." She took another bite of the pizza and stared at Julia, pausing effectively to build the anticipation.

"Let's just say, a lot was explained," Gwen finally continued. "Her two daughters came. They're knock-outs. Beautiful girls. Clearly, mama bear is trying to compete with baby bears and not holding up so well." She sat back again, rocking with more force now that a topic had come to mind. "It was sad, really. The whole thing."

"Why?" Julia asked, not surprised to hear that Bebe's home life was anything but ordinary.

"They were mortified. Her girls look like they're in high school, maybe college. Not sure. They looked so embarrassed to be there and didn't really want anything to do with their mom. Bebe was even more manic than usual, running around to everyone trying to introduce the girls, but they didn't engage with anyone." Gwen shook her head at the thought, the pink light from the setting sun making her silhouette glow.

"That's sad," Julia said, not sure of what else to add. She did find the entire thing sad, but not because of the display of insecurities that Bebe exhibited and everyone focused on.

She found it sad that her life had detoured somewhere and she probably had no idea how to re-route it. Beneath the Botox and bad fillers, Julia could still see the outline of a woman who was once beautiful. She had looked at Bebe once or twice at the center and caught a glimpse of who she once was, a classic beauty with perfect bone structure who most likely wore a crown or two at homecoming or her high-school prom. Julia found it incredibly sad to think that, once upon a time, Bebe might have been happy and secure. Once upon a time, she might have sat around drinking wine straight from a bottle with good friends, talking about what her life would look like someday and the figurative doors that she would walk through.

Julia bet that she hadn't even considered lopsided lips, alienated children, and a stint in rehab as possibilities.

"Yeah, after they left, she kind of took another nosedive," Gwen said, interrupting Julia's thoughts. "She got in trouble for stealing lemons."

Sure that she must have heard her wrong, Julia raised her eyebrows and couldn't hide a smile. "Come again?"

"She stole the lemons from the kitchen that were supposed to be used for tea," Gwen said, describing the lemon-stealing incident as casually as she would the weather forecast. "Apparently, she read about some do-it-yourself facial peel that she wanted to try with lemons. They found an entire hoard under her bed."

Julia and Gwen stared at each for a second before bursting into giggles again.

"Shit, we shouldn't laugh," Julia said, trying to stop herself by shaking her hands in the air. "It's sad really."

The giggles kept coming, however, exacerbated by her belly warmth and the natural high that she got from eating gooey food.

"Oh my God, stop," Julia said, clutching her stomach, the wooziness brought on by questionable wine now making her second guess her decision to chug it freely. "I seriously think I pulled something from laughing."

Gwen's giggles had stopped, but she still had a wide smile on her face as she looked off into the distance. "Wow, well isn't this a sight," she said, staring off at the horizon that had now turned a majestic purple along its pink and yellow edges. "Absolutely gorgeous sunset."

Julia looked at the sunset proudly, like she owned it somehow and was responsible for her little corner of the world that offered them such a glorious view.

"How's Cate?" she asked, not taking her eyes off the horizon.

Gwen laughed, reaching for another piece of pizza, but then thinking better of it.

"Cate's good," she said. "She took it hard when you left and wasn't too happy when I took off, either. But she's good. Doesn't have too much time left there herself."

A high-pitched bark sounded off somewhere in the distance. Julia was now used to the distinctive call of hyenas at nightfall.

"Oh, she and Sylvia got into it again on movie night," Gwen added, still looking to where the creepy barking sound had come from. "Dr. Rayborn got tired of hearing them bitch at one another. She boxed up all of the Richard Gere movies and hauled them away. Sylvia completely freaked out and threw the *Alien* movie at Cate. She actually hit her in the head and gave her a nice little gash across her temple. We called it *Gere Gate*."

"Lord, why doesn't that surprise me," Julia said. "I bet there's a *Pretty Woman* movie poster hung somewhere in Sylvia's house."

"Probably over her bed," Gwen added, launching them both into giggles again.

"Hey, don't fault a woman her fantasy," Julia said, trying to get her laugh under control.

"I tell you, Vivian took your leaving really hard," Gwen said.

The mention of her name was enough to sober Julia up quickly. She reached for the bottle of wine on the porch floor and was disappointed to find that not a drop was left.

"I think you were the only friend she had there," Gwen added. She must have seen the look on Julia's face because she immediately tried to back-pedal, not wanting her friend to feel worse than she already did for leaving so suddenly. Little did she know that Julia's guilt had nothing to do with a quick departure.

"I didn't mean it that way," Gwen said. "You had to do what you had to do, I get it. I'm sure Vivian will be fine." She started to rock again, eager to change the mood, but not realizing that she was making it worse.

"Some guy came to see her," she said. "I assume it's that deadbeat husband. Good-looking, but you could tell there was something there. Something slimy hiding underneath."

Julia put a hand on her stomach, trying to avoid eye contact with Gwen and keep the pizza from coming back up. She had vomited all over the place the last time she saw her friend and wasn't about to go there again. Gwen must have sensed something because she suddenly jumped up and started pacing the porch, a physical diversion to a very physical reaction that Julia was having to their conversation.

"What the hell are those things?" Gwen asked, peering off into the distance at the symphony of barks that responded to one another in synchronized timing. "Girl, you got werewolves around here? Am I going to go to bed tonight and wake up to some yellow eyes out my window?" She smiled at Julia, a look of concern on her face when the smile wasn't returned.

"Hey, you okay?" Gwen asked, pulling herself onto the porch railing. Her yoga pants, tank top, and flipflops providing

213

very little protection against the mosquitoes. She swatted a few away and murdered one on her knee.

"Yeah, I'm okay," Julia said with a sigh. She thought about it; she thought about telling Gwen everything, but didn't have the energy to launch into a tale that would take them well into the wee hours of the morning. She felt guilty that she had shared more with Burt than she had shared with Gwen, but it felt safer confessing something to a third party who didn't really know anyone involved.

Gwen knew the other side of the story—she had sat in a room while a blonde-haired beauty cried at the memory of losing her daughter, her marriage, and a life that had been shattered into a million pieces by an avoidable accident and a heartless whore. Vivian hadn't described the "other woman" that way—she hadn't actually mentioned the "other woman" at all—but Julia felt like she wore the badge like a scarlet letter for all the world to see. Hester Prynne, the courageous protagonist from Hawthorne's *The Scarlet Letter,* crossed her mind briefly. Julia envied her; at least Hester got the opportunity to raise her daughter in love, secrets and all.

It was clear that Gwen didn't believe Julia, but she didn't push, deciding instead to get her cell phone from her purse and flip through its screens in search of something.

A soulful voice then began to ooze from the phone's speaker, a guitar its only backdrop as lyrics about the long days of summer echoed off the porch ceiling and house walls. Gwen gave Julia a wink as she settled back into the rocking chair. Only a sliver of pink was still on the horizon: the sun had decided to call it a day and hand the stage over to fireflies that lit up the darkness with their twinkling bulbs. Her eyes and mind heavy, Julia focused on the blinking lights, the fireflies dancing along to music that felt like it had been written for moments like this. The tension left her shoulders and her mind returned to the foggy slumber that it had been floating in and out of that evening.

She didn't feel like going back there, back to the memories that sucked years from her life each time she relived them. For now, she wanted to sit next to her friend, appreciate the moment, and watch the best of nature's light display.

Dance, little fireflies, dance.

Chapter 24

Training Wheels

Julia was embarrassed to reveal just how difficult it was for her to keep up with Gwen. Her friend took the hills effortlessly, standing up slightly as she pedaled, causing her calf muscles to tighten and bulge out like firm pillows on the back of her legs. She kicked up gravel as she went, flinging a few small rocks back at Julia as she rounded a corner and slid unexpectedly, a particularly worn area of road as smooth as glass under the bicycle tires.

The red bicycle had been hidden behind a giant metal gasoline sign that still had a few rusty screws along it edges from where it had been ripped off the side of a building. The tires looked a bit worse for the wear, but Julia found a hand-held pump and hoped that any air holes would be small enough to buy them the time for a quick ride along the country road.

Gwen hadn't missed a beat when her bicycle slipped on the gravel, putting one foot down for a split second to steady herself before giving a quick "whoa!" as she stood back up and continued to pedal.

Julia knew her friend was in shape, but she had no idea that Gwen's version of a leisurely bike ride would cause side-splitting pains and gasps for air as she struggled to stay within a respectable distance and not collapse on the side of the road. Julia didn't even know where they were at this point. Gwen's ability to navigate new terrain was as impressive as her ability to ride it.

Without looking back, Gwen pointed to something in the distance. Julia didn't see what she was pointing to at first, but then noticed the small tornado that was spinning along the rows of an empty field, a brown whirring mass floating above the ground. It seemed surreal in a way, like a baby tornado who had lost its mom somewhere in the wide-open space where all dirt and dust look the same. Julia risked crashing her bicycle to watch the mini tornado as it touched down briefly and kicked up again, turning slightly before whirling down a row of dirt and traveling away from them.

Julia realized that she had fallen behind and raced to catch up with Gwen, who was now riding without hands and looking down both lanes that met in a fork in the road in front of them. She then put both hands back on the handlebars and leaned left, traveling through a mud puddle from an unexpected rain shower the night before.

Julia followed, avoiding the puddle, and used her energy reserves to pedal fast enough to catch up to Gwen so they could ride side-by-side.

Relieved that she now knew where they were, Julia settled back and enjoyed the ride toward town. A farmer with a large golden retriever was busying himself in a field, studying a piece of machinery that had either broken down or been abandoned.

Julia started ringing her bicycle bell to get his attention, both she and Gwen waving to him like he was a long-lost friend that they had been trying to find. A look of concern on his face, the farmer stood there for a minute, taking in the two girls in garden hats riding down a country road acting like they knew him. As his dog barked in greeting, its tail waving like a propeller ready for lift off, the farmer took off his hat, wiped his brow and waved back a bit reluctantly.

The Friendly city limits sign followed soon after. Julia was relieved once the bicycle tires hit pavement and the ride became a smooth one. The old seat lacked in padding, and her butt had started to go numb, the tension building in her muscles now that they were more relaxed and fully aware of what they had just gone through. Not wanting to think about the ride home, Julia focused on providing Gwen a tour of the town, gliding along the streets as she pointed out the charming park and church scene that greeted her arrival just a few weeks before.

Another family was unpacking their picnic basket. This time a group of boys was tossing a football around, the instruction to "Go long!" echoing behind them as Gwen and Julia made their way past the park and toward Main Street.

Gwen's time in Friendly had been limited to her visit to the grocery store. So a man with an armful of beef jerky and cashier with bleach blonde roots was her only impression of a town that Julia had developed a soft spot for.

Eager to erase the beef jerky visual and introduce her to its charming side, Julia sped along the street and in front of Gwen. She steered wide of a line of parked cars that had gathered in front of corner bar, a deer head decorated with Christmas lights in an otherwise dark room visible from the street.

As they rode past, the heavy wooden front door opened and a few alcohol-fueled shouts of congratulations spilled out onto the street. "Just Married" was written sloppily in soap on the back of a car window at the front of the line. Although the days tended to run into one another, Julia realized that it was Saturday afternoon. The parking spaces usually empty were now filled with poorly-parked cars and the streets were busy with shoppers jaywalking because there was no reason not to.

Pointing so Gwen knew they were heading right, Julia led the two-person bicycle caravan up onto the sidewalk of Main Street, the barber pole spinning just a block away. Pulling over, Julia hopped off her bike and leaned it against a brick store front, waiting for Gwen to do the same.

"They're okay if we just leave them here?" Gwen asked, leaning her bicycle next to Julia's. "These things are probably considered antiques. Someone might try to steal them."

Julia looked at her friend, trying to determine if she was kidding or just naive. Sensing the latter, she laughed and patted Gwen on the arm. *"Everything* in this town is an antique," she whispered. *"We're* the things that stand out, not the bikes."

As they walked toward a small café that she had discovered her last time through town, Julia pointed out the depression-style glassware in the window of the home furnishing store and told Gwen about how she discovered the green set in the farmhouse kitchen.

Gwen stared at her, a small confused smile forming. "Not really my thing, but I can tell that you like it," she said, leaning in closer toward the window to examine the detail of the glass that Julia claimed was there. "It's like we've taken a step back in time here." Gwen waved at a little girl walking toward them with her mom, her tiny hands helping to push the stroller of her baby brother who was asleep, his face shielded from the sun.

"I'll give it to you," Gwen said. "You seem to have stumbled upon the one place that is in no hurry to keep up with the rest of the world."

They continued down the sidewalk toward the bright orange awning that marked the entrance to the café. Julia remarked, "I don't usually want to hide from the hustle and bustle of life, but it's tempting to curl up in this place and hide for a while."

There it was again. That reference to *hiding*. Before her

219

Tiffany Killoren

conversation with Burt, Julia would have resisted any suggestion that she was hiding from life; now, she wished she had done it sooner.

A few wooden crates of tomatoes stood side by side in front of the café, their skin stretched so thin that they looked ready to burst, threatening to spray juice and seeds across the front window that read Sonny's Café in gold lettering.

Julia adjusted her bra straps to make sure they were hidden as she walked inside, suddenly aware that the purple bra's polka dot pattern could probably be easily seen through her gray tank top.

Taking out her hair band and retying her ponytail, she motioned to a small table by the window, knowing that all eyes were on the beautiful black girl and her friend with the see-through shirt making their way to the two-person table decorated with a single sunflower in a glass vase.

"I'm going to guess they're not used to strangers round these parts," Gwen said out of the side of her mouth, holding up the plastic-covered menu with someone's morning eggs crusted onto its front.

A waitress walked over with two small glasses of water in one hand, nodding to the table next to them that she heard their request for a coffee refill.

"How ya'll doin', loves?" she asked, smiling brightly at Julia and Gwen, the smell of coleslaw and flowery perfume filling the air as she sat the glasses down in front of them. Sandy, the name engraved in white on her black name tag, hung almost sideways as it stretched the thin fabric of her sundress. "What can I get ya'll today?" Her smile widened even further, showing a front tooth slightly discolored and stained with her pink lipstick.

Julia and Gwen ordered club sandwiches—the menu's "house specialty"—and bottles of root beer from a local brewer. Others in the small café soon lost interest in the two of them,

220

turning back to their mid-afternoon meals when they realized that there was really nothing to see.

"So, how's everything with you?" Julia asked, moving the sunflower vase over to one side so it wasn't in her line of vision. "What are the plans when you get home?"

Gwen looked out the window, the wedding celebrators now making their way down the opposite side of the street toward another bar. The groom's bow tie was dangling from the corners of his collar; another tux-clad man in his twenties walked with his arm around his shoulder, holding a bottle of beer to the sky and singing something off-key as others followed. There was not a bride to be seen. Julia wondered if she was celebrating in another bar with her bridesmaids, the two groups eventually meeting up and sharing pitchers of beer as some small-town marital rite of passage.

"Well, I have some great things planned," Gwen said, still staring out the window. "I just don't happen to have a clue as to what any of those are right now." She tried to smile, but failed, genuine concern flashing across her face as she made eye contact with Julia and then quickly looked away.

"I lost everything," she continued. "I lost my temper and the rest followed. My career, my law license, my reputation. My little brother's staying at my place until I figure things out, so at least I don't lose my apartment." She took the sunflower out of the vase, bringing it to her nose and breathing in deeply before putting it back in the water and pushing the vase further aside.

"The thing that gets me is, I'm *not* an overly angry person," she said. "I worked my ass off to prove myself in a profession where men are still provided more opportunities than women. The glass ceiling is still very much there and there's more than one partner in a corner office who thinks that women don't have what it takes to cut it in the legal profession. What did I do? I lost my cool one day and proved them right." Gwen glanced around the restaurant, not so much to see if people were listening, but to avoid having to look Julia in the eyes. "They say that we aren't the mistakes we make, but it doesn't seem like it. I made one idiotic mistake and it's now defining everything. I lost everything."

Julia watched Gwen shift in her seat, trying to find a safe place for her eyes to land. She wasn't used to seeing her like this, without the strength and resiliency that Julia had come to rely on during her short stay at the center. To now see her vulnerable and afraid shook Julia's world in that moment. She felt like a child who realizes that a parent needs comfort, a child who realizes that she needs to step up to the plate, pull her own shit together, and be the rock instead of the person always leaning on it.

"I don't know much," Julia said, looking out the window so Gwen wouldn't feel pressured to look at her. "Lord knows, I've made mistakes and carry those with me like we all do. People talk about reinventing themselves and I think that means different things to different people. To me, it means that we're always supposed to be moving forward, looking for ways to improve ourselves."

She paused as their sandwiches arrived, a colorful mix of meat, vegetables and cheese between toasted bread with a giant pickle on the side. They came on those plates that look ceramic, but could probably withstand a drop from a ten-story building. They were patterned with a circle of the smallest of red roses.

"Maybe you were meant to make that mistake to find the life that you're actually supposed to live," Julia continued, opening the top of her sandwich to inspect what lay inside as Gwen did the same. "If you hadn't made that *mistake*, maybe you would have lived out the rest of your life in a lie. Maybe that *mistake* wasn't a *mistake* after all." She dove into the sandwich, a few pieces of tomato torn off and hanging from the side of her mouth, mayonnaise dropping onto her chin.

"You're a class act, Julia," Gwen said, laughing as mayonnaise fell and hit Julia's plate. They both laughed, the wine-induced giggles from the day before were now back, but with less of a mental fog and more of a root beer high.

Gwen tackled her sandwich in a more respectable way, cutting it in half and taking small bites that left nothing dangling from her mouth. She looked like she was going to ask Julia something, but thought better of it, instead taking a bite of her pickle and commenting that its taste didn't go well with home-brewed soda. Julia appreciated that Gwen hadn't pushed her to tell her own story; the only thing she knew at that point was that Julia had gone to rehab with a diagnosis that could apply to ninety percent of the population. And probably the other ten percent are simply better at disguising that they, too, suffer from stress, anxiety or exhaustion. Gwen never asked for specifics and Julia had never offered them, afraid that her friend wouldn't look at her the same if she knew too much.

Gwen's *mistake* could be explained by cosmic serendipity. Julia's story read like a book that you wished you hadn't pulled from the shelf: too many lives swept up in a series of events that left nothing good behind—like the tiny tornado in the field, just kicking up dirt and looking for a place to land.

The friends finished their sandwiches and left a larger tip than was called for on a twelve-dollar and fifty-cent tab, waving to Sandy as they walked out, hearing "See ya'll soon" in return.

The afternoon sun seemed hotter than ever, their skin's tolerance weakened from the café's air conditioning.

"I guess nobody wanted our antique bikes," Gwen said with a smile, turning her bicycle around and facing the way they'd come.

"Everybody in town's probably got a similar model," Julia

said, hopping onto Old Blue, her butt cheeks stinging from the repeated assault brought on by poor padding and a seat shape that didn't favor female anatomy.

Rising a few inches from the seat, she pedaled down Main Street, feeling her gluteus muscles resist the sudden strain. As she prepared to turn onto a side street toward the old stone church, she heard the rev of an engine. Her eyes were drawn to a motorcycle making its way down the street. She caught Beau's eye as she was making the turn. His smile and small wave spread goose bumps like wildfire along her arms and neck, and the afternoon heat was no match for the wave of adrenaline that washed over her.

Julia pedaled faster. This time Gwen found it difficult to keep up as they passed the church where a few paper lanterns left over from the wedding flew erratically from strings trapping them to the railing on the front steps. Just as Julia rode past, one broke free, the white lantern flying alongside their bicycles for half a block before riding a wind wave up to the sky. Julia watched until it disappeared above the trees, playfully diving in and out of the leaves until the wind lured it away like a feather in flight.

Gwen raced to catch up with Julia, pretending to steer her bicycle toward hers and run her off the road. Once they hit the town limits, cars became of little concern. They were the only transportation on the road, other than a slow-moving tractor driven by a boy who looked ten years old, at most. He nodded to them in adult acknowledgment as they passed.

Familiar with this stretch of road, Julia took the last corner and smiled when she saw the top of the farmhouse welcome her in the distance, its black roof clean from the rain shower the night before.

About a quarter of a mile from the driveway, Julia pulled over, startling Gwen with the sudden stop so she shot past her and skidded to a halt herself. Julia laid the bicycle down in the tall grass and made her way into the ditch toward a cluster of black-eyed Susans. She plucked a handful of flowers and carefully arranged them in one hand, creating a large bouquet of golden petals with billowy black eyes staring back from their centers.

Jumping back on Old Blue, she winked at Gwen as she rode past, holding the bouquet in her right hand while she steered with her left and made her way toward the mailbox with the faded American flag. Gwen used her two-hand advantage to race Julia the last stretch of road and beat her to the driveway, laughing like a mad woman as she pumped her hands victoriously and sailed down the dirt road that was as smooth as pavement from years of the Blackwells comings and goings.

They saw the car at the same time, a black four-door sedan parked next to Gwen's vehicle in what little shade was provided by the tree in front of the house.

Gwen glanced back, questioning, but Julia just shrugged. She had no idea whose car it was or what they were doing there. Jumping off their bicycles and leaning them against the trellised bottom of the porch, they walked around the front of the house together, glancing around for any sign of a visitor waiting for their return. Finding none, they walked up the front porch stairs and opened the screen door. The inside door with its diamond-shaped windows fanned out in a half-circle was already open.

"Did you leave that open?" Gwen whispered, pointing to the wooden door.

Julia shook her head, twisting her mouth into a concerned grimace to show that she didn't know if they should go in. She looked for some sign from Gwen, but her friend looked just as confused, gesturing for Julia to walk in first as she held the screen door open for her. Still clinging to the bouquet of black-eyed Susans, Julia entered, careful not to open the screen door wide enough to squeak.

Hearing nothing at first, the women tiptoed into the entryway, Julia glancing quickly at the small ceramic dish that held her keys. She was relieved to see they were still there, but didn't want to grab them, afraid that the jingle-jangle would alert someone to their arrival. Gwen peeked inside the dining room and followed Julia toward the kitchen. A loud *bang* filling the air as cabinets were emptied and pots and pans tossed onto the floor. Gwen grabbed Julia's arm and clung to her, the two women walking as one as they synchronized their steps and made their way silently down the small hallway. As they reached the entryway, another pan fell to the floor, a cuss word in a familiar voice following it.

Gwen and Julia looked at each other puzzled, Gwen's grip loosening on her arm. They knew that voice.

Julia walked around the corner, followed closely by Gwen, both of them staring at the scene. The cabinets had, in fact, been cleared and an old frying pan now rested on the stove with butter splattering from the heat. A woman with her back turned to them was humming as she cracked an egg into a bowl. She must have sensed the shift in energy behind her because she spun around.

"There you are!" Cate said, smiling, trying to catch a string of yolk that was dripping from the eggshell. "Got these eggs at a roadside stand. Want some?"

Chapter 25

Purge

"Uh, yeah, it wasn't hard," Cate said, mimicking Gwen's response when Julia asked how she had managed to find her in the meandering thick of Georgia countryside.

"When Gwen got your letter, she told me that you had decided to stay for a while in a town called Friendly," Cate continued. "Seriously, I thought she was kidding with the name. Like it was some euphemism or sarcastic twist on your current state of mind." She laughed at the thought, piling a mound of scrambled eggs onto her fork and losing half of them on their trip to her mouth.

"Once I got here, I went into a diner on Main Street and asked if they knew where the brooding stranger and her black friend were staying." She smiled, putting her fork down on the porch railing and tossing what was left of the eggs toward a bird that was on the losing end of a battle with a worm wedged safely under a rock in the driveway. "It was actually pretty funny how quickly they responded. Safe to say you two have made an impression on this tiny little town."

"We've tried," Gwen said, settling onto the bench and reaching for her toes in a deep yoga stretch.

"I figured Gwen was here," Cate said, gesturing toward her and answering the question they were just about to ask. "When you left, you said that you had a stop to make for a few days, so I assumed you were going to try to find the escapee." She winked at Gwen and then smiled at Julia, not willing to let her completely off the hook for the abrupt manner in which she had left. "I'm just glad you're okay. At least you made a memorable departure."

Julia looked at Cate, studying her as she pried off a few pieces of egg stuck to the plate and flicked them toward the bird that looked more terrified than appreciative. She couldn't believe Cate was here—that either of them were here—the thought of Gwen and Cate putting their lives on hold to track her down and make sure everything was okay seemed like a love story all of its own. The last year had dealt her the full deck of emotions, but this was a feeling she hadn't experienced in a while. At this moment, watching one new friend do yoga and the other make faces at a bird that rejected an egg offering, she felt incredibly lucky.

"Thanks, I'm okay," Julia said. "And, I don't care how you found us. I'm just glad you're here." She smiled and tossed Cate an ear of corn to unhusk. She then ripped the husk off the ear in her own hand, its hairs cascading down the corn like a silky white wig.

Gwen grabbed an ear of corn and spent approximately ten seconds tearing it apart before tossing it into the second bin and reaching for another.

"What are you doing?" Julia asked. "Look at all of those hairs left on it. You suck at corn husking, Gwen."

"It's impossible to get them all off!" Gwen responded. "They stick to everything. You'd need tweezers to pry those things off completely."

"Well, I don't want to eat any of yours," Julia said. "It'd be like flossing your teeth during dinner."

Gwen grabbed another ear of corn from the bin and scratched her temple with her middle finger to flip Julia off.

Although it was early evening, the sun showed little sign of retiring for the night. Its glow from the western sky was just as bright, if not as harsh, as the light at midday. The only sign that the Earth's internal clock had made its rounds was the burping of a bullfrog nearby, its croaks growing more intense as day finally showed a willingness to succumb to nature's nightlife.

Julia rocked slowly in her favorite chair as she worked on the corn, Gwen on the bench, and Cate sitting cross-legged on the porch's wooden floor. She looked thinner than Julia had remembered her, the muscles and veins protruding from her arms a drastic departure from the extra layer of softness that seemed to envelop Friendly residents. Based on Opal's cooking and the plates she saw piled high with buttery grits and starchy goodness at the diner, Julia wasn't surprised that living here meant developing a little padding—a little extra something that made everyone here squeezable like a baby with ankle creases and chubby cheeks.

"So, how are *you*?" Julia asked Cate, plucking Gwen's ear of corn from the bin and taking the hairs off one by one. Gwen didn't notice; she was too busy prying corn hairs off her yoga pants.

Julia didn't know why Cate had been admitted to the Southern Sunset Center and, although she suspected that Gwen did, she never asked. Cate wasn't usually in Julia and Gwen's group therapy sessions so she didn't know how much of her story she shared with others. And it was not really any of Julia's business. That didn't stop her from wondering, however; she couldn't help but be curious as to what brought other residents there. She figured it was probably a lot like prison, women sizing each other up and assigning crimes according to appearance and street smarts, looking for some sign as to whether they were bunk mates with a murderer or the mastermind of a diamond heist.

With Cate, Julia was at a complete loss. Their time at the center largely revolved around games of Jenga, and refereeing movie night. The level of familiarity with which Cate had approached Julia her first morning there had set the stage for a natural friendship to form, but there was little talk between them about anything personal; although Julia assumed Cate was married based on the delicate silver and diamond band on her ring finger, she couldn't have told you her spouse's name, their hometown, or how Cate filled her days before entering the doors of rehab.

Julia only knew that she liked strawberry cream cheese on her bagels and hated Richard Gere. And, if she didn't before entering rehab, she certainly did now.

Julia had expected Cate to respond by not responding, an ambiguous "fine" or "same shit, different day" comment, which had been her usual answer to this question when Julia asked it every day at breakfast.

Julia asked Cate how she was as a form of cultural greeting, never anticipating a substantive response to the hollow question. Toward the end of her stay, she had asked more discreetly, taking rare opportunities when they were alone to ask Cate how she was doing so she would know that she cared. Even then, however, the answers were always the same. *Fine. Same shit, different day.* Sometimes she would shake it up: *I'm living the dream* was her go-to response on days when there was a public showdown with Sylvia or when Dr. Barkle assigned her another diary entry that she had no intention of writing.

Julia expected Cate to respond similarly this time. The

sound of husks being torn off provided a steady beat to the frog burpings that had now escalated as others joined in.

It amazed Julia how quickly evenings set in around here, a sentence started when the sun was still high in the sky could end with a fuzzy glow behind the horizon before your thought was completed. This was her favorite time of day. The temperature drop brought new life to the tiny creatures that stay hidden for hours, their songs waking sleepy friends to let them know that it's now time to play.

Cate was focused intently on the husk that she had just torn off, feeling its edges and slowly tearing it in half. She looked tired; her cheekbones were pronounced, but not in a good way. There was a hollowness beneath them, the shadows that ran along her cheeks mirroring those under her eyes. Her curls were held back in a colorful fabric headband, an inch or two of growth betraying the golden highlights that had been carefully brushed on, pieces left untouched to create the illusion of being sun-kissed. She sat a bit slumped over, like a weight had been sewn into her shoulders and drew her toward the ground. Always quick with a response or funny comment, Cate said nothing this time, ripping the corn husk along its beveled seam and wrapping one of the pieces around her finger.

"Hell if I know," she finally said, unwinding and re-wrapping the husk around her middle finger. "I did my time at the center and they claim that I'm cured. They signed these papers and handed them to me like it's all I need to start over, like they're my passport to a new life."

Although Julia was tempted to put down her corn and focus on Cate, she decided not to, the mindless task was perhaps enough distraction to make it easier for her friend to talk. Clearly thinking the same thing, Gwen tossed an ear of corn into the bin, half of its husk still on, and reached for a new one.

She glanced at Cate, then at Julia, before ripping off the ear's protective sheaf like she was skinning an animal.

"I don't know," Cate said. "They have to be pretty strong pieces of paper if they're going to keep me from..." She unwrapped the small piece of corn husk from her finger and played with the curl that it made, bobbing it up and down in the air to watch it bounce.

Julia didn't want to be curious, but she was, like she had been given the first sentence of a book's plot and now wanted to know the rest.

"Yeah, not sure if those papers are going to keep me from eating my weight in, well, pretty much anything," Cate continued, stretching the husk smooth and starting all over again. "Not sure how those papers or what the doctors told me are going to keep me from throwing everything up before my kids get home from school and still getting my son to baseball practice on time."

The pieces were slowly coming together for Julia. She was surprised that the idea of Cate suffering from an eating disorder had never crossed her mind.

Oreos. Julia remembered Cate's comment her first day about not writing a diary entry about her love of Oreos. She felt stupid that she hadn't put it together, that she hadn't figured out that Cate's battle was with food, her way of picking off Julia's breakfast plate and never eating more than half a slice of pizza at movie night. Even the eggs that Cate made when they arrived that afternoon had been tossed to the birds. She had taken a few bites then thrown the rest over the railing.

"I don't have a good relationship with food," Cate said, using air quotes to show that these words had been spoken by someone else. "No shit, Sherlock." She bent her neck to her left shoulder, a crack signaling that the source of any tightness had been found. Cate then did the same on the other side, twisting her neck this time to find the sweet spot until she heard a crack and massaged her neck back into place.

Julia winced, the sound of someone cracking their knuckles always enough to make her queasy.

"My kids didn't deserve this," Cate said, looking agitated. She jumped to her feet and batted at the stray corn hairs that had stuck to her bare legs. Cate hopped onto the railing and stretched her legs out, leaning against one of the columns and watching the sun set lower in the sky.

A faint pink glow had started to form around it, the first stage of the sun's symphony of colors that accompanied its fall to slumber each night. The first stage was pink, and the next a deep purple haze; Julia thought the sunsets here resembled a candle that was fighting for the chance to burn being slowly snuffed out. Although Cate was staring at it, Julia could tell that her mind was elsewhere.

"Hardest thing that I ever did was send Libby and Pete to live with their dad," Cate said, shaking her head at the thought of it. "We separated about six months ago. He couldn't deal with it. He couldn't have a wife in a little black dress and pearls excuse herself at the dinner table with his clients so she could throw up in the restaurant bathroom."

Gwen glanced at Julia, who had given up trying to pretend that this was a casual conversation and abandoned her corn. Feeling justified doing the same, Gwen tossed hers to the floor and stood up, taking a few steps closer to Cate who was now wiping a few tears off from her cheek.

"Ironic, don't you think?" Cate asked, laughing nervously through her tears and looking briefly at Julia and Gwen. "I wanted to stay thin because that's what all the executive wives looked like. They'd walk into these dinners looking so glamorous and put together, their makeup perfect and their tiny waists barely even able to fill out a size two dress. I started purging to just start the process, you know? I wanted to just get down to a good weight and then I was going to keep it there the right way." Cate took out her headband and ran her fingers through her hair, the stress wearing on its texture with visible split ends and frayed edges.

"Yeah, pretty damn ironic," Cate continued, watching the frantic pattern of a few bats flying overhead, the first to leave their daytime roost to hunt. "He left me because of something that I started doing to make myself perfect for him."

Gwen and Julia exchanged concerned glances, Julia got up from the rocking chair and sat down opposite Cate on the railing. She brought her knees up to her chin and leaned against the other column, wanting Cate to know that she was there for her if she wanted to look her way. Cate didn't; she focused her gaze on the bats, a few now taking nosedives toward the grass. The burping sound of bullfrogs had stopped completely.

"It was Libby's tenth birthday," Cate said. "We had a mad hatter tea party at the house, complete with this great little makeshift room with a miniature door for the girls to crawl through like they were Alice." She smiled at the memory, a few more tears falling that she didn't care to wipe away.

"She was so happy, all her friends were there and I bought her this gorgeous dress that was way too expensive for a ten-year-old, but she just *had* to have it." Cate started picking at her nails, a cuticle bleeding as she tore it off and flicked it toward the yard. She sucked on her finger to get the bleeding to stop, the tears now falling more steadily and making it difficult for her to talk.

"The cake was exactly what you'd think of for an Alice in Wonderland party. It was three off-center tiers, in pink and green fondant icing with little squares, triangles, and circles of white icing decorating it." Cate outlined the shapes with her fingers, showing Julia and Gwen how tall the cake stood.

"Seriously, that thing cost more than most people's wedding cakes."

Gwen caught Julia's eye, the look of concern on her face suggesting that she didn't know this story either, that they had both been in the dark about what had brought Cate to the center.

"Yeah, that should have been a great day," Cate continued. "And it was, right up until Libby walked in on me throwing up her birthday cake. Her *birthday* cake." Cate looked at Julia, the sobs that she had kept behind an emotional dam now freely flowing, her body heaving from the sudden release of it all.

"I can't even describe her little face," Cate said between sobs, covering her face with her hands and clawing at her mouth like she was trying to keep the words from coming. "I couldn't even stop, I knew she was at the door, but it kept coming up. I couldn't even stop her from seeing that."

Julia rubbed one of Cate's legs and Gwen walked over to her, wrapping an arm around her and pulling her in close. The dark shadows under her eyes and cheekbones now looked more reflective of the demon that formed them, a disease devouring Cate from the inside out that vowed to never let her feel full again—or *whole.*

"I can't fail them again," Cate said, leaning into Gwen. Julia kept a hand on her leg, not wanting to focus on its feel, but alarmed by how easily she could fit her hand around it. To most, Cate would look exactly like what she had wanted to project—a healthy, vibrant, fit woman without an ounce of cellulite and arms so toned they would complement even the most daring of dress cuts. In reality, she had been wasting away, unable to savor any bite of food going down without thought as to when it could come back up. And, Julia would bet that she wasn't the only woman in a little black dress and pearls at the executives' table that had that problem.

"You won't," Julia said, forcing her friend to look her in the eyes. "You won't fail them *again*, because you didn't fail them *before*. You're human and you have a disease that you needed some help with. Being a mother doesn't make you infallible, it just makes you less forgiving of yourself. I can tell that you love your kids with your whole heart and I guarantee you that they know that, too."

Cate searched Julia for some sign that she was telling her the truth, that she hadn't completely broken her children or damaged them in some irreparable way.

"I'm not a mom," Julia continued. "But I'd love to be someday. I imagine that the hardest part about being one is feeling solely responsible for their view of the world and wanting to protect them from the ugliness in it. You know what? The world's not pretty and it's not easy. The best thing for your kids to know is that people need help sometimes in life and only the truly strong ones ask for it." She jumped off the railing and wrapped her arms around Gwen and Cate, squeezing them tightly.

"I'm so proud of you," she whispered to Cate, giving her a kiss on the top of her head before letting her go. "Honestly, I'm so proud of both of you."

"Are you proud of my corn-shucking skills?" Gwen asked.

"Not in the least. You suck at that."

"Are you proud of my bike-riding skills?"

"And then some." Julia turned to Cate and wiped a few tears from her cheeks. "You should see this girl on an old bike from the shed out back. She owns these country roads. She's a wild bike-ridin' woman."

Cate smiled and patted her face, the color that had drained from it was now coming back with a rosiness to her cheeks.

"Can you stay a little while?" Julia asked, hopping back up on the railing and returning to her perch-position. "Gwen's going to stay a few days. We can consider this the last stage of our treatment." She walked over to the metal bin holding the sweet corn still waiting to be shucked. "Who's going to help me with all of this if you leave?" she asked, laughing.

"Honestly, girls, if I had known that an evening with you two would be better than a month in therapy, I'd have suggested this a long time ago." Cate smiled, pulling the headband back into place and taking in a deep breath. Her eyes were a bit brighter now; they had been cleansed, one of the many benefits to a good cry that falls out of nowhere like a rainstorm with the sun still shining.

"Anyone need a drink?" Julia asked. She was already on her way to the front door because, even if nobody else wanted one, she was going to pour herself a glass of whatever grape concoction Gwen had secured most recently from a roadside stand.

"Yes," Gwen simply said, hand raised in the air.

"Pour me a smidge," Cate said, measuring out a small amount with her fingers. She turned suddenly and hopped off the railing, looking toward a sound that came from the middle of the yard.

"What was that? Did you hear it?" she looked nervously at Gwen, who still had her hand raised.

"Probably a copperhead," Julia said casually as she opened the screen door. "Watch out. Those things will eat ya whole." She laughed as she walked inside the house, proud at how authentic she sounded when passing along the warning.

Proud, and surprised at how natural it felt.

Chapter 26

No Reservations Needed

Julia woke up to hair in her face, a few strands stuck up her nose and creating the uncomfortable sensation of a sneeze coming on that goes nowhere. She sat up quickly and rubbed her nose, pushing Cate's head off her shoulder in the process with a shove that sent her halfway over the side of the bed.

"What the hell?" Cate whined, pushing against the floor with one arm to keep from falling out entirely. "Julia, you suck." She hoisted herself back up onto the queen-sized mattress and buried her head under the pillow. "You suck," she said again, her voice now so muffled that it sounded more like *oo sook*.

Julia sat there, her head foggy from the bottle of wine the night before that turned into two, and then a few shots of something they found in the kitchen cupboard. The evening before was largely a gray area, with snippets of color coming back as she surveyed the room and looked around for Gwen.

She now recalled the bottle of whiskey, a dark golden brew in a dusty bottle tucked away behind the spice rack, a conversation about whether whiskey expires as they poured a few shots in orange juice glasses and decided to assume the risk. Somebody got sick; the distinctive sound of a body rejecting alcohol still rang clear in Julia's ears, but she couldn't remember whose ass she was visualizing leaning over the railing and hurling into the bushes.

"Well, shit," she said, rubbing her nose again because the tickling sensation remained. Her tongue felt like it was twice as thick as it should have been, a feathery coat covering where taste buds used to be.

"Gwen?" Julia asked, a vague recollection of them all crashing in the same room suddenly coming back to her. The pillows had been tossed off the window seat, the vision of Gwen using it as a dance party platform now forming, a tribute to 80s classic dance tunes something that they thought was a good idea around one in the morning.

"Gwen?" Julia asked again. "Did you walk like an Egyptian last night?"

"Damn straight," a voice came from somewhere near the end of the bed, an arm raised to signal that she was alive and camping out on the floor. "I'm pretty sure I was also a karma chameleon."

Julia made her way to the sound of the voice and hung her head over the end of the bed, discovering Gwen flat on her back with a sweatshirt pulled over her face to block out the harsh morning light. She was wearing hot pink leg warmers.

"Where did you get the leg warmers?" Julia asked, not as surprised to see the relic fashion statement as she really should have been.

"What leg warmers?"

"The leg warmers that you're wearing."

"I've never worn leg warmers."

"I guess there's a first time for everything."

Without removing the sweatshirt from her face, Gwen brought one of her legs up to feel what she was wearing.

"I guess I'm wearing leg warmers," she said, putting her leg back down. "I'm pretty sure we found a box marked *eighties party* in the basement."

Julia brought her head back up, but the sudden rush of blood was too much to take in her condition, so she lay back down and tried to put the pieces together.

"I actually have no recollection of going into the basement." The thought of invading the privacy of the Blackwells by going through their leftover stuff made her feel guilty, like she was having fun in a situation caused by loss. She hoped an eighties party box was the only one they opened; she could live with their borrowing of leg warmers, but hoped that, even in a drunken state, she would have stopped before sifting through anything more personal.

"So, I confide in you two about binging and purging and then end up throwing up half my weight from alcohol that you made me drink," Cate said, now peeking out from under the pillow. "Maybe you're not the great influences that I thought you were."

Cate's ass was the one leaning over the railing.

"Admittedly, my mind isn't as sharp as it usually is," Gwen said, still lying down. "But, I have no recollection of making you drink anything."

"Peer pressure," Cate said. "I never want to feel left out."

"I'm not feeling great," Julia said, a wave of nausea now adding to the layer of fuzz that seemed to cloud her mind and every inch of her body.

"I am," Cate said, burying herself under the pillow again. "I fee gwape," she muffled.

Julia jumped off the bed and ran toward the bathroom, kicking the door shut behind her as she reached the toilet and tried not to look at the regurgitated remnants of their eighties party from the night before. Her eyes closed tightly and she let her body do what it had to, punishing her for poor judgment in the mixing of alcohol that she had known not to since her early twenties.

"Liquor before beer, never fear. Beer before liquor, never sicker," Gwen shouted.

"We didn't drink *beer*!" Julia responded, annoyed. She threw up again and tried to remember if there was any drinking rule for when not to combine homemade wine and whiskey. She decided there was no need for any such rule: most people were smart enough to figure it out on their own.

When she emerged from the bathroom, she found Gwen snuggled up with her blanket on the bed and Cate still hidden somewhere under a cotton pillowcase with sunflowers stitched along its edges.

Julia leaned against the door frame, feeling physically better, but now just wading through the fog left behind from too much booze. Julia looked at her friends in the bed, finding it hard to believe that a month ago she didn't know either of them. A little over a month ago, she had been chasing after toilet paper rolls in a grocery store parking lot, her emotional state as stable as the tampons that she left floating in the puddles alongside her car. If someone had told her then that she would now be in a farmhouse in southern Georgia, a bulimic and woman with anger management issues in her bedroom, she would have thought them insane. As odd as it all seemed, an old house, bulimic, and woman with anger management problems appeared to be exactly what she needed. Her old life, once the memories that defined her, were starting to feel like snapshots from her past.

Instead of feeling overwhelmed by the memories of pain and loss, she was starting to feel like the experiences were simply part of a larger whole—like fabric squares in a quilt of many shapes, styles, and colors, some more dark than others, but all of them necessary to make the quilt whole.

"I. Need. Coffee." Gwen was staring at the ceiling now, the blanket pulled up to her face like she was watching a scary movie.

Julia suddenly felt a pit in her stomach again, this time completely unrelated to the alcohol that she had filled it with the night before. She was out of coffee, the last of the grounds brewed the day before when she and Gwen decided to drink the energy needed for the bicycle ride.

"Guys, I'm out of coffee," she whispered.

Cate pulled the pillow off her head and both she and Gwen stared at Julia, waiting for the punchline.

"I'm sorry," she said. "Don't panic. I know where we can get some, but we need to get off our butts."

As the doorbell played its extended melody, Julia could hear the familiar fast-paced footsteps make their way toward the front door. She had anticipated an excited reaction, but didn't gauge the effect on her throbbing head of the high-pitched voice that greeted them.

"Oh, my word!" Opal exclaimed, bringing both hands to her cheeks. "Julia!" Opal shrieked like she hadn't seen her in ages, although it had been just a few days. She hugged her and stood back, waiting for an introduction to the two women who were with her. Opal looked all three of them up and down, even her cheerful smile not enough to mask the concern that she had with their disheveled appearance.

"Opal, this is Gwen and Cate, friends of mine," Julia said, gesturing to each respectively. "I'm not going to lie. We had a bit too much fun last night." Spotting herself in the hallway mirror, Julia tried to smooth down a few flyaway hairs, but it was no use. They had become unruly with dehydration and sweat, so she just let them fly.

"Well, my, my," Opal said, shaking hands with the girls and standing back with a mischievous grin. "You girls look a bit worse for the wear," she said with a laugh.

"We probably look better than we feel," Cate offered, smiling and taking a look around the foyer. "What a beautiful home."

"Thank you, dear," Opal said, beaming with pride. She loved taking care of people—young or old, healthy or sick, sober or hungover. "You girls follow me," she said, walking toward the kitchen. "I'll make sure the pot's extra strong."

"You're a lifesaver, Opal," Gwen said, seeing herself in the same mirror and wincing from the reflection.

"I've been called that from time to time," Opal said, already disappearing around the corner into the kitchen.

The girls sat around the wooden kitchen table, Cate needing to rest her chin on her hand to keep it upright. Even with a hangover and her stomach contents somewhere in the shrubbery in front of the farmhouse, she looked healthier than when she had arrived. Dark circles had been replaced by pale splotches of skin that simply needed to recover from the pink wine and golden whiskey that had infiltrated her blood cells and made them off-color for a while.

"So, were you girls all by yourselves last night?" Opal's tone had turned playful, her words dancing along with her floating footsteps around the kitchen, as she opened and closed cabinets that stored coffee and sugar in colorful containers.

"Just us," Julia responded, taking a stack of freshly cleaned plates off the island and putting them back on the exposed shelf above the counter. "We managed to do enough damage on our own."

"Oh," Opal said, gliding over to the coffee maker and shrugging her shoulders. "I thought maybe Beau McGallagher had stopped by."

Julia felt herself blush, both at the mention of his name and the manner in which Opal had said it, teasing her like a schoolgirl who had a crush on the cute boy in the back of the bus. She could feel Gwen and Cate sit up a little straighter, their attention momentarily diverted from their throbbing heads to a potential juicy topic of conversation.

"Who's Beau McGaaaaallagher?" Cate asked, stretching the vowel out like it held secrets of its own. "I *knew* there was some sweet spot to this place other than the tea!" She pounded the table with one hand, startling Opal as she poured grounds into the coffee maker so she spilled half of them onto the counter. Opal scooped up what had fallen with her hands, smiling and avoiding eye contact with Julia.

"Are you serious?" Gwen asked, laughing. "You've got some guy here and he's from the *Dukes of Hazzard*?" She and Cate giggled together, their hangovers suddenly gone and replaced by bright and curious eyes.

"Oh, honey, no. He spells it like Beau Bridges." Opal was having fun with all of this, turning on the coffee maker and swinging her hips like the brewing process had a tune of its own.

"Whoa," Julia said, hopping up and walking over to Opal. "I'm not real sure where you got an idea like that, but there's nothing going on between me and Beau."

"Is he good-looking?" Gwen asked.

"Well, yeah, I guess," Julia offered reluctantly, trying to pretend like she had to think about it before giving her response.

"Nice?"

"Yeah, he seems like a nice guy," Julia said. "But it's not like I know him that well."

"Single?" Cate chimed in.

"I think so."

"Then why *isn't* there anything going on between you and Beau Bridges?" Gwen asked coyly, batting her eyelashes and tilting back onto two legs of the kitchen chair.

"Mm-hmm," Opal hummed, pointing into the air like Gwen had just hit onto something important. She continued to dance while the coffee brewed: girl talk is sweeter than any sugar high to a Southern lady.

"Oh, whatever," Julia said, waving them both off. She got four mugs down from the shelf and lined them up on the counter, using every ounce of brain power to will the last few drops of coffee to hurry up and fall into the pot.

She could feel Gwen and Cate's eyes burrowing holes into the back of her skull. If she so much as sensed a whisper being exchanged between the two, she was going to toss the crocheted trivet nearest her at their heads. The counter seemed full of them; multiple red, white, and blue trivets left over from some Fourth of July event were within arm's length and ready for launch.

"We're just giving you a hard time," Gwen said, still leaning backward. "I'm just saying, a little roll in the hay never hurt anyone."

"Well," said Opal, "one of those Hardin boys down off the old Sidewinder Road actually was fooling around with his gal last summer and rolled right onto a pitchfork hidden by the hay. Rumor has it that he had to have fifty stitches to his backside and sit on a donut for week!" Opal made a circular motion around her butt in case they didn't understand the delicate nature of the injury.

Cate and Gwen nearly fell off their chairs laughing, and

Julia held her head to stop it from throbbing from the sound. Opal just stood there, coffee pot in hand, proud that she could add such an entertaining twist to their conversation.

"Now, who takes cream?" she asked, lifting the coffee pot to show that it was ready.

"Opal," Cate said, wiping a few laughter tears from her eyes. "You're awesome."

"Oh, honey," Opal said with a wink. "You have no idea."

Julia gathered the mugs and brought them over to the table. A plate of freshly-baked cookies appeared like they were made for the occasion. She was curious as to why Opal mentioned Beau, but also, afraid to ask, not wanting to look too eager or interested.

How, though, did Opal know that Julia had even met Beau, and that he was of interest to her? The thought that maybe he had mentioned her during Friendly conversation was enough to brighten up Julia's eyes and wash away the sluggishness that she wore like a cape—that thought, and the first sip of amazing coffee, a gentle roast blend that burned as it went down.

"So, here's what we're going to do, love bugs," Opal started. "The three of you are going to go with me on my ladies' afternoon."

Julia exchanged looks with the others. Nobody wanted to ask what a ladies' afternoon actually entailed. Lucky for them, they didn't have to.

"Once a week, I wander on down to Petunia's, the beauty parlor right off Avenue B," she continued. "You know, right in between the flower shop and that place that wanted women to come inside and work out on those machines in a circle? That place that went out of business last year." She gestured to Julia like she knew what she was talking about, the location of a beauty parlor beside a store she had never seen and one that had left a year before her arrival.

But Julia nodded like she understood, shrugging to Cate and Gwen when Opal looked away.

"They'd just love for you girls to come with me," Opal said, sipping her coffee and feeling the curls in her hair that were in need of adjustment. "Oh, my, they'd just *love* it if you'd come."

Opal's mention of *they* in this context made Julia a bit uneasy, like there was a group of women who somehow already knew too much about them and were ready to pounce if they walked in the door.

"You know, Cate was just mentioning that she wanted a bit of a makeover," Julia said, taking this opportunity to pay her friends back for the fun that they had had at the earlier Beau reference. "Yeah, and Gwen, weren't you mentioning something about getting some new makeup tips or your nails done?"

Opal looked as pleased as could be and Cate and Gwen smiled sweetly in return, a sharp kick delivered to Julia's shin under the table.

"Or, wait," Julia continued. "Gwen, you mentioned you need a wax."

"Well, that settles it," Opal said, pouring a little more coffee into her cup and adding two heaped spoonfuls of sugar. "We're going to wrap up our girl talk here and finish it over at Petunia's. They'll be fine with you just walking in, we don't need any appointment or fancy reservations."

Julia tried to hide her smile, burying her face in the steam rising from her coffee mug. Truth be told, a spa would register at the top of her list of favorite places at this moment, but she had a feeling that Petunia's wasn't the kind of place that covered your face with a warm towel to open your pores. She gathered that it wasn't as much a place to relax as it was a place you went to get in-the-know.

"I can help you girls on the inside," Opal said, raising her coffee cup. "But those girls over there, they can help add a little spit-shine to your outside."

"I could use a little spit-shine," Julia said, raising her mug in *cheers*.

Opal put another spoonful of sugar into her mug, shaking her head like ladies do when someone in her presence has spoken gospel.

"Darlin', can't we all."

Chapter 27

Shades of Blue

It took them over an hour to decide. The three opinions migrating toward different shades on the color wheel were enough to drive the hardware store owner, Jerry, into his storeroom with an instruction to "Call me when you figure it out."

Gwen thought the traditional woodwork and heavily upholstered furniture in the house called for a shade of navy to look right. Cate thought just the opposite, the warmth of the accessories and trim needed a lighter shade of blue to keep the room from looking old and dated. Julia didn't really know what she thought. She just knew that Kennedy Blackwell loved the idea of her painting the living room and giving it a fresh look, so she had enlisted her friends to help with the job. She was beginning to wonder if she should have limited their involvement to manual labor.

"Sorry, Gwen, but I don't really like the navy," Julia said, tossing that color swatch aside. "Too dark. It seems counterproductive. I'm trying to lighten the feel of the space."

"I swear, I just saw them transform a living room in an old house with this color on HGTV. It's beautiful," Gwen said, grabbing the swatch again and pleading her case. "It's classic. Don't go trendy."

"I don't want to go trendy," Julia said, wrinkling her nose at the shade of baby blue that Cate was showing her. "I don't want to go trendy. I want to go *Julia.*"

"What's *Julia*, exactly?" Cate asked, sifting through the pile of colors that Julia had already rejected and pulling a few back out.

"I'm not sure," she said. "But I think I'll know it when I see it."

Julia grabbed another swatch of colors, this one from the blue-green row with a photo of a sunroom with a view of the beach as its visual marker. She flipped through the options and stopped on one, a creamy mix of blue, green, and gray that was so subdued it could not commit to membership in any of the color families. Its name—*Tranquility.*

"Hey, Jerry!" Julia called. "I figured it out!"

"For the love of all that's good in this world, what did they put in my hair!" Cate had one hand on the steps of the ladder she was trying to balance, and the other hand in her hair.

"I don't think it's so much the product, as the amount of back-combing," Julia offered, opening a paint can with the small screwdriver that Jerry threw in with their purchase. Based on the way he looked at the three of them in the hardware store, he must have suspected that any help he could provide would be a good thing. When he was checking them out, he sent them back three times for a drop cloth, extra rollers, and trim brush. Even though he rolled his eyes, Julia caught him smiling as the women got into an argument about who was more inept at painting preparation. When it came time to leave, he told them to wait by the door as he selected the small screwdriver and a can of paint remover "just in case."

"Oh, is it called back-combing down here?" Cate asked, shaking the ladder in anger. "Back-combing. Teasing. Hair torture. They all seem to fit."

At the salon the day before, the beautician had been particularly harsh with Cate, dividing her hair into segments and teasing them until her hair stood on its own. Smoothing down just the top layer, she had emptied half a can of hairspray to make sure it held, congratulating Cate on now having a "hair do" instead of a "hair don't." As the beautician cackled at how clever she was, Cate stared daggers at Julia in the mirror, the diameter of her head quadrupled by the hair ball that had turned harder than cement around her head.

"Mine's not much better," Julia said, pulling at her ponytail. "She did the same thing to me."

"Son of a…" Cate shook the ladder until the hinges fell into place. "There," she said satisfied. "That's a lie, by the way. Your hair didn't even remotely meet rat's nest level. Mine did. And then there's Ms. Gwen, who got by with a manicure and eyebrow wax."

"Hey, I'm not exactly excited about having the American flag painted on my fingernails," Gwen chimed in, moving the lamp that had been on the end table to a safer location. "I can't help it that my black hair saved me your fate. They didn't know what to do with it."

"It meant a lot to Opal that we went," Julia said, pouring too much paint into the roller pan and dripping a sizable glob onto the plastic drop cloth. "Geez, thank God for Jerry," she said, walking around the paint splatter and tripping over the unopened package of painter's tape.

"Are we going to use this?" she asked, grabbing the tape.

"Nah," Cate answered, climbing the ladder and positioning

herself on the second-to-top step. "I'm meticulous. And too much prep work cuts back on the instant gratification process. Now, hand me some paint."

"Cate, you haven't even taken off the curtains," Gwen said.

"I'll figure it out when I get to them."

"You're kind of a train wreck waiting to happen."

"All aboard!"

With that, Cate took the tray that Julia handed her and balanced it delicately on the ladder's shelf. Concerning safety issues aside, her approach to the project violated essentially every do-it-yourself rule for adequate preparation and proper execution. Because Cate was a fly-by-your-seat kind of girl, the tension between her personality and Gwen's perfectionism had resulted in more than one colorful exchange that Julia had to referee, including a tense moment in the backyard when Cate came close to eating a flower that she thought was edible, but wasn't quite sure.

"Well, anything's better than this mauve," Julia said, wrinkling her nose at the shade on the walls.

"Pretty sure it's called *Dusty Rose* in these parts," Cate said with a sharp twang and primp of her big hair.

"Whatever it is, it needs to go," Julia said. "And I hope Jerry's right about not needing primer with this paint. If this goes wrong, the room's going to look purple."

"Here goes nothing," Cate said, rolling on the first stripe of wet paint. "Goodbye Dusty Rose, hello Tranquility."

Oh, if only it was that easy, Julia thought. How great it would be if you could just paint over the ugliness in life, erasing the scuffs, dings, and scratches in your energy field with a color that sings to you in a high gloss finish. How great it would be if tranquility came in a gallon-sized can with a complimentary screwdriver. For now, the color on the walls would have to do and, even with the Dusty Rose still shining through, Julia loved the beginning of the transformation.

It took them a half an hour to get into the groove, each responsible for painting a different part of the room. Because Cate loved standing on ladders—a strange thrill that she jokingly attributed to her need to look down on people—she assumed responsibility for everything above Julia and Gwen's heads. Gwen and Cate divided up the rest, each taking two walls and moving the furniture into the middle of the room or out into the foyer where it wouldn't be damaged by the hundreds of tiny beads of paint that Cate sent out into the room every time she overloaded her paint roller and didn't bother to blot some of it off before slapping it on the wall.

Maybe it was the monotonous—yet soothing—motion of the roller brush against the wall that lulled Julia into a relaxed state. Then again, it might have just been the paint fumes. Regardless of what got her there, Julia lost herself in the project, enjoying adding new life to a room that had witnessed so much living.

She didn't intend to use this as an opportunity to share her story, but it came out on its own, the words flowing as freely as the paint that settled into the cracks and crevasses of the walls and made them look new again. It would have made sense to start at the beginning, but that's not how the words wanted to flow.

"I ruined Vivian's life," Julia began, bending over to roll her brush through the puddle of paint in the tray that she had poured too thick.

"What?" Gwen asked from behind her.

"Shit," Cate muttered as she painted over a spider web in the corner that she had failed to notice, clearly not paying attention to what Julia said.

"I ruined her life," she repeated, taking in a deep breath to assess if she really wanted to go through with this. The first few words had been spoken, the proverbial door opened to a vault that she had kept under lock and key for too long. These were her friends; they wouldn't judge her for the things that she had kept from them. If they did, she probably deserved it and that was okay too.

"I fell in love with Vivian's husband, got pregnant, lost a baby that I wanted more than anything, and then went to rehab to find out that I had actually become friends with my boyfriend's wife." Julia let the words fly, refusing to give them wiggle room to make a U-turn and retreat.

"I became friends with the one person who I had never wanted to think about, the one person who I never allowed myself to imagine. I never allowed myself to consider how *her* life had been affected. And, then I sat there that day and listened to the tragedy that they went through to get to the point in their marriage where he steps out on her with some stupid single girl in the city."

Julia kept painting, making sweeping strokes in the shape of a W to provide the most coverage, like she had seen on home improvement shows. She was the only one painting, the sound of other brushes in the room had stopped, but Julia didn't look behind her.

"When Vivian started to tell her story, I got suspicious," she continued. "But I didn't even let myself imagine that the guy that screwed me over was her husband. I mean, what are the odds. That's about as far-fetched as it gets."

She stood back to stare at the wall. Small patches of Dusty Rose were showing through. If she didn't look around, it was like sharing her story with an empty room, the wall casting no judgment on her past or the winding road that she had taken to get here.

"That note," she said, shaking her in disbelief. "That note

that she wrote about the anniversary dress. That's when I knew. I found that note."

Julia could hear Cate and Gwen breathing. It was like they were in a time warp, the world completely silent except for the sound of their heavy breathing. Julia still couldn't turn around, afraid that if she did, she wouldn't be able to continue. And, she wanted to. She wanted to share her secrets in this room, with these women, just like they shared their stories over roadside wine and sweet corn on the front porch. She owed them that level of honesty and trust. She owed herself that.

Julia led with the worst and worked her way backward, slowly sharing the details that formed the flesh around the story's hard pit. All the while, she kept staring at the wall, viciously attacking any Dusty Rose peeking through with a layer of Tranquility.

The Dusty Rose began to represent details of her story; as she spotted the old paint shining through, she'd remember another fact that she had forgotten to share. The color of Matthew's eyes. The way he pursued her and made her feel like the most beautiful woman in the room, even when surrounded by younger and more beautiful girls who would have gladly elbowed her out of the way to be his next competitor at darts. The way he would cradle her after sex and whisper in her ear, sometimes describing how happy she made him and other times making her laugh by whispering how hungry he was and what he would pay for a double cheeseburger delivery.

As the Dusty Rose disappeared, so did Julia's secrets; she stood back one more time and stared at the wall, realizing that there was nothing left of either. That's when she finally turned around to find Cate and Gwen standing there, paintbrushes still grasped in their hands, a shared look of shock on their faces.

"*Julia,*" Cate whispered softly. She wiped her nose, leaving a streak of turquoise across her cheek. "Why didn't you tell us?"

"I couldn't. I could barely admit it to myself."

"I can't believe this," Gwen said, taking a step toward her. "Like you said, what are the odds? I mean, seriously. What are the odds that *she* would go where *you* are?"

She and me. Gwen had hit on the divide that Julia felt since leaving the center, the invisible barrier between her life and the one that she had helped ruin. *She, deserving of a hug, and me, deserving of public vomiting.*

"Julia," Cate said, dropping her paintbrush and ignoring the splatter marks that it left on the freshly painted wall. "Julia, you can't blame yourself for this, you realize that, right? This isn't your fault. You didn't know." Her look was one of both concern and confusion, the wheels still clearly spinning as she processed the story that Julia just told.

"Is that the standard?" Julia asked. "Am I absolved if I didn't *know* he was married?"

"Well, yes!" Gwen said. "Of course, you are! *He's* the asshole, Julia. *He's* the one to blame for all of this."

"It was easier to think that way," Julia said. "When I went to the center, it was really just an I-got-involved-with-an-asshole situation that I needed to work through. Since leaving, I realize the situation was anything but simple. My heart broke for Vivian. My heart broke for *him*. Losing a child the way that they did? And, then, I felt guilty for feeling anything but contempt for him. I lost a baby and thought I would die from the pain that I felt. Then I thought, what would a baby have done to Vivian? Here's this woman who's sweet, and considerate, and forgiving. She doesn't deserve anything that's happened to her. I left the center more messed up than when I went. There was no way that I could stay and see her, knowing the role that I played in her sadness."

"Oh my God, that was *him*," Cate said, looking at Gwen as the memory came back. "We saw him that time he came to visit her. Holy shit, can you imagine if you had still been there?" She covered her mouth with her hand at the thought, experiencing just a taste of what Julia had had to process over the last few weeks.

"Well, I guess you guys now know why I threw up during group time. It wasn't a bad bagel."

Gwen sat down on one of the chairs they had moved into the center of the room, throwing her arm around the back of the chair and holding onto it for support. She took a deep breath, still shaking her head in disbelief.

"I just can't imagine what you must have felt when you left," she said. "I know you didn't feel like you could, but I wish you would have told me, just so you didn't feel like you were going through this alone."

"I *am* going through this alone," Julia said. "Sharing it with other people doesn't change that. At the end of the day, when I'm lying there at night unable to sleep, I am the only one going through this." Julia meant it; nobody else could truly understand what it meant to wade through the ugliness alone. Just as she couldn't fully understand Cate or Gwen's issues, they couldn't really ever understand hers, and there was a painful loneliness in that realization. At the end of the day, they were each left to battle their own demons that came in the dark and quiet hours.

"I know it sounds crazy, but this place has helped." Julia looked around the room with affection, noticing for the first time how beautiful it looked with its new color transformation. "There's something about this place," she said. "Sitting on the front porch, I feel like I'm living a different life than the one before, like the ugly is left at the end of the driveway and only the good stuff is welcome."

"Well, I can see that," Cate said. "Within hours of arriving, I told you guys stuff that I haven't told anyone. It's everything.

Tiffany Killoren

The house, view, little critters in the grass. It's like it all just wants you to share stuff. It's safe here."

Cate smiled as she looked around the room, wrinkling her nose suddenly when she noticed the paint that she had gotten on the white ceiling.

"I'll fix that," she said, pointing overhead.

Julia smiled, exhaustion from both the home renovation and purging of secrets now settling into her muscles like she had run a marathon. With just one wall left to paint, she poured more paint into her tray and repositioned herself, aware that too long of a break would make finishing the project harder, just like she knew that stopping mid-story would make it impossible to keep talking. She had found the courage to tell her story, so she wasn't about to let a painting project get the best of her.

"You sure that you want to keep painting today?" Gwen asked, moving her painting tray next to Julia's. "We can finish tomorrow if you just want to go chill for a while."

"Better yet, we'll finish up here," Cate offered, moving the ladder over to the wall that was covered with wood paneling instead of paint. "Why don't you go take a nap or pour yourself a cocktail."

"I appreciate the gesture," Julia said. "But I want to see this through. We're on the home stretch."

Julia wouldn't have been able to sit still had she tried, her skin tingling like it had been cleansed with an antiseptic, individual arm hairs standing at attention as she shivered periodically despite the lack of air conditioning. Something had been awakened in her and she wasn't interested in putting it to sleep again; rest was the farthest thing from her mind and she didn't want alcohol to dull her senses. For the first time in as long as she could remember, there wasn't a need.

"You heard the girl," Cate said playfully. "Let's get rid of this horrible paneling."

Cate and Gwen looked at Julia who, in turn, was looking at the wall.

"Yes," she said, rolling a thick stripe of gray blue across the paneling's edges and stretching as far as her tiptoes allowed.

"Time to get rid of the old."

Chapter 28

The C Wing

Julia gave up on getting the marshmallow to stay on the stick. She tossed it into the fire and went to work scraping the gooey residue off her fingers.

"Do you need me to make you one?" Gwen asked with fake sympathy, rotating her marshmallow in the fire so the heat would be evenly distributed. "Apparently, I'm a pretty good s'more maker."

"Ah, you're a woman of many talents," Julia said, grabbing the plastic bag next to her and popping a giant marshmallow into her mouth, followed by a bite of chocolate and piece of graham cracker. "It's not pretty, but it tastes the same," she said with her mouth full.

Cate sat on a lawn chair with her arms crossed on her chest and her feet perched up onto the brick border of the fire pit. The flames shifted in her direction and she wiggled her toes from the wave of heat.

They had finished the living room mid-afternoon, and, after an hour of clean-up and rearranging of furniture, all three women had taken a nap. Julia laid down on her bed, Gwen fell asleep on the couch, and Cate dozed off on a blanket in the backyard; although the last to fall asleep, she had been the first to wake up thanks to a surprise visit from an army of ants and a particularly loud bird that tormented her from its position on a fence post.

"I lost a baby, too."

Julia and Gwen looked at Cate, who was rubbing her arms like she was cold and staring directly into the fire. They exchanged a quick glance before waiting for her to continue.

"I've never told anyone that," she said. "I mean, of course my husband knew, but nobody else. I think that's what made him stop loving me. It was about a year ago. I was pretty bad at the time, with the purging, and I didn't know that I was pregnant right away. I stopped as soon as I found out, but I lost the baby about a week after. The doctor told me not to blame myself, but how couldn't I? My husband certainly did."

Cate gestured toward the bag of marshmallows and Julia tossed them to her. She grabbed a few and pried them onto the stick next to her, creating a snowman from three large billowy clouds of sugar before sealing its fate in the fire.

"I just wanted you to know that I understand," she said, rotating the marshmallows and looking unconcerned that they had actually caught on fire. "I understand what it feels like to lose a baby."

"I'm so sorry," Julia said, regretting that she had just stuffed her mouth with another round of cold s'more ingredients because it made her sound less than sincere. She hurried to swallow, chewing the marshmallow as quickly as the gooey paste allowed.

"Oh, Cate," Gwen said. "You've been through so much. You can't take responsibility for this, too. You have to listen to what the doctor said. This isn't your fault."

"It's not," Julia said, now ready to talk. "I'm sure your doctor told you the same thing that mine did. This *happens*. Call it nature, God's way, or unfortunate circumstance of science, this just *happens* sometimes and there's nothing that women can do about it. Letting yourself think differently doesn't help or change anything. You'll just drive yourself crazy."

Fully aware that she was a walking and talking contradiction, a hypocrite in the worst possible way, Julia let her own words sink in. Since her miscarriage, she had buried herself alive under *what if* scenarios, a flurry of thoughts and regrets that slowly suffocated her. Despite grounding her spiritual beliefs around a benevolent God, Julia had convinced herself during the darkest of times that she was being punished; punished for playing a salacious role in marital infidelity and hurting innocent people. Or, perhaps punished for her primal urges and inability to resist premarital sex. There were even moments when she felt like she was being dealt the consequences of not being a good enough daughter, a wholesome and consummate reflection of what her mother had wanted and felt she deserved.

Julia eventually realized that, if you wanted to believe that the bad things in life are brought on by mistakes and regrettable decisions, you'll find the evidence to support it. And, if you want to believe that it's all just part of life's growing pains and a lesson in resilience—absent retribution—you'll find plenty of evidence to support that, too. Because it was up to her to decide which way to believe: she didn't want to waste any more time with the weight of guilt crushing her chest. She wanted to breathe.

"I know that's easy to say," Julia continued, watching bugs fly suicide missions into the flames. "It's so easy to tell someone not to worry, that it's not their fault and they need to move on with life. Believe me, I know how it feels to be on the receiving end of those words and want to shove them down the throat of the person saying them, desperate to make them understand, to make them feel a fraction of what you're going through. *It'll be okay* have to be the most hollow words in the human language because there's really no way to know. As horribly flawed people trying to make sense of it all, we just have to figure out for ourselves if we have enough faith to believe that it's true."

"Do you have faith?" Gwen asked, reaching for a beer from the twelve-pack box that she had been using to balance her s'more tools.

Julia thought for a moment before responding. "You know, I think I do," she said. "I've seen both sides and I don't like what life looks like without it."

She gestured for Gwen to toss her a beer and caught it with one hand. She opened it with her head turned, prepared for the frothy geyser that sprayed from the shaken can.

"I didn't think you liked beer," Cate said, settling back into her chair and repositioning her feet by the fire.

"I don't," Julia said, taking a sip. "I think too many quarter draw nights during college spoiled my taste for it. I can't drink beer without traveling back to those bars with their sticky floors and sweaty guys desperate for someone to go home with." She shuddered, trying to shake the memory off.

"Here's to sticky floors and sweaty guys," Gwen said, raising her beer in toast.

"Here's to new beginnings," Julia said, raising hers.

"Here's to forgiving ourselves and having a little faith," Cate said, raising an empty hand cupped around an imaginary glass.

Another bug circled the fire before diving into the flames, a small crackling noise signaling its demise.

"Why do they *do* that?" Julia asked, watching another bug follow its flight pattern. "What a way to go."

"Maybe they're told, like us, to follow the light if you see it," Cate said, laughing.

"Maybe they're just sick of flying," Gwen offered, taking a

swig of her beer. She studied the can, her mind wandering off somewhere.

"So, you know that day during group that I shared what brought me to the center," she asked.

"I remember," Julia said.

"I wasn't in your group session, but you told me about it," Cate said.

"Well, that wasn't the whole story." Gwen paused to take another drink, this time chugging the beer like she was looking for courage hidden in the bottom of the can.

"What do you mean?" Julia asked.

"What I said is true," Gwen answered. "It's just a part of the story, though. I *did* vandalize my boss's car after he threw me under the bus with the client. I *did* agree to go to the center as part of a diversion deal that I made when he pressed charges. I *did* get fired and lose my law license. That's all true."

Cate and Julia sat in silence, waiting for her to continue. A bat that swooped down a bit too close to the fire caused them to panic for a minute, but they quickly regrouped.

"Let's be honest, throwing colleagues under the bus to deflect responsibility is pretty much a daily occurrence in the world. It's just the price of working with people whose entire identity is based on how others perceive them." Gwen shrugged like what she said wasn't much of a secret, not in her professional world anyway.

"I wouldn't have keyed someone's car over that," she continued.

Julia and Cate exchanged glances, curious as to where the story was heading, but not wanting to ask too many questions.

"I had been fooling around with him for a while," Gwen said. "My boss. Mick, Mick Jeffries." She said the name like it hurt her tongue.

"Stupid, I know. He wasn't that much older than me, maybe

five or six years, but he was a partner, my boss, and I knew it was wrong. The firm wouldn't have approved, but it's happened before. They usually quietly separate the love birds without creating a scene, transferring attorneys to different divisions, and sometimes offices, to create a barrier between work and personal lives. We kept it pretty quiet, maybe too quiet, because nobody really understood why I acted out the way that I did when everything happened."

"So, you were sleeping with this guy and he tossed you to the wolves when push came to shove on a case?" Cate asked. "Asshole."

"Was he married?" Julia asked.

"No," Gwen said. "Longtime girlfriend, though. She's a lawyer in another firm. I didn't know that at first. Even when I found out, he told me that they were one of those on-again off-again relationships and neither took it real seriously. I'm sure he lied about that. He lied about everything else.

"To other people, it seemed like I lost my shit because he was a misogynistic pig who sacrificed the female attorney to make himself look better. It was so much easier pretending that the situation was a glass-ceiling type of thing, it was so much more respectable than admitting that I was a stereotype, too. He felt me up in the elevator that morning, and threw me under the bus that afternoon. And both times, I let him."

"The fact you had a relationship with this guy doesn't change the fact that he screwed you over at work," Julia said. "You didn't do anything wrong. Well, I mean, you probably shouldn't have keyed his car, but it doesn't sound like you did anything wrong on the case to deserve that. It sounds like he told you what he needed to tell you to get his way both professionally and personally. You can't take responsibility for that."

"Here's to forgiving ourselves," Cate said. "Remember?"

"Yeah, well, you can imagine why I didn't feel comfortable telling Dr. Barkle about all of this," Gwen said. "It's not like he comes across as a real open-minded soul."

"*Open*-minded?" Cate laughed. "He doesn't come across as *minded*!"

"Did you love him?" Julia asked.

"No," Gwen said, without taking even a second to think about it. "It was never about finding my soul mate or being blinded by passion. I wish it was, I wish that I could explain it away by some emotional trigger that I couldn't control. That wasn't it, though." She rubbed her eyes and blinked rapidly, tiny embers and smoke from the fire shifting in the wind and blowing directly toward her.

"I'm embarrassed to even admit it," she continued. "It made work more interesting." She shrugged and looked ashamed, the fire shifting again and sending a flurry of sparkling embers toward Julia.

"I never enjoyed being a lawyer. I was good at it, but I never enjoyed it. Having something hot and heavy in the office made it easier to get out of bed in the morning." She shifted in her seat and avoided looking Cate and Julia in the eyes. "It sounds so stupid, but it was like having a crush on some guy in high school. It made geometry class more tolerable if you could look forward to seeing him and pass notes when the teacher wasn't looking."

"Well, aren't we a bunch of losers," Julia said, surprised to find that her beer can was already empty. "We're like a Lifetime movie."

"Speak for yourself," Cate said, tossing a marshmallow at her. "I'd like to think that my story deserves at least a mini-series."

"Oh, shit!" Gwen said, opening another beer and inspecting her finger. "I chipped my nail. Damn it, there go the little stars she painted." Taking a drink, she sat back down and leaned back as far as the chair allowed, the cloudless night providing a twinkling canopy of eternity to stare into.

"Seriously," Gwen said, sitting back upright. "What's up with this place? I've now officially told you two more than I shared with my mom, best friend, lawyer, and the anger management specialist that the firm insisted that I see before firing me. What is it about this place that just, I don't know, *makes* you talk."

"I really don't know," Julia said. "I've wondered that myself. Honestly, I think there's something about how old everything is here. The house, soil, garden, shed, all of it. From the minute you enter the driveway, there's something so strong and steady about everything here. It's all seen so much, weathered so many literal and figurative storms, and yet it's still here. It's all still standing. That's kind of hard to find these days."

"I think you should live here forever," Cate offered. "There's something special about this place. You need to live here so I can come and visit if I ever need to get it together again. A few days here is better than a year in therapy."

"I second that," Gwen said, raising her beer can to show her support. "I want my own room, though. I'm not sleeping with you two anymore."

Cate got up and walked over to the beer, taking out the cans and setting them down next to Gwen's chair.

"Let's be honest," she said. "You're probably the one who's going to drink these anyway," she whispered. "I'll be back!" With that, Cate took the empty cardboard box and disappeared around the front of the house, returning after a minute with a black marker. She tore off the front of the box along its seams and turned it over, writing something with the marker that Julia couldn't make out in the darkness.

"The three of us are alumni of the B-Wing, the place they

267

put Richard Gere freaks, mistresses, professionals who make bad choices, and balloon-lip enthusiasts who don't know when to quit with the injectables."

"Whoo-hoo!" Julia said, laughing and raising her arms with pride.

"Well, because this place helped me a hell of a lot more than the center did, I propose that we name it something special. Ladies, let me introduce you to The C-Wing, the only place that you'll ever need to go to get whole again." She held the cardboard sign up, *The C-Wing* written in thick font across its front.

"I love it," Julia said with a smile. She looked lovingly at the farmhouse, the light from a few lamps in the living room shining out from one of the windows and onto the lawn, a warm glow welcoming them back inside whenever their time around the fire was done. Thinking back to her diagnosis—an *SEA* classification—Julia found the double entendre of a C-wing designation all the more appropriate.

"Yeah, I wish I had known about this place before I wasted precious moments of my life watching a therapist pick wax out of his ear with a pen cap," Gwen said, laughing. "I might have actually seen some things at the center that took me a step or two *back*, rather than forward."

"Bebe." All three women said her name at the same time, laughing that their minds had taken them to the same place; the image of a woman who was a poster child for adult insecurities the first to come to mind in the string of things they'd like to forget.

"Oh, poor Bebe," Cate said, suddenly serious. "Girl's messed up, but I hope she finds her way, too."

"I know," Julia said, feeling a little bad at the laugh they had at her expense. "But I think it's going to take a little more than sweet corn and a s'more or two to get her back on track. It would take at least six months for the fillers alone to work their way out of her system."

"To Bebe," Gwen said, raising her can as they joined her. "May she find her true self."

"To Bebe," Cate and Julia responded, Julia taking a sip of her beer and Cate making a peace sign in the air.

"Well, I'm heading inside," Gwen said, standing slowly and bracing her knees. "Painting wiped me out and every muscle hurts."

"Me, too," Julia said, shifting the seared wood in the fire pit around to make its small embers safe to leave unattended.

Julia, Cate, and Gwen made their way toward the front of the house, the crickets serenading their way. When they reached the porch, Cate grabbed Julia by the shirt sleeve and handed her the cardboard sign.

"I think you should have the honor," she said, gesturing toward the house.

Gwen turned around to look at them and smiled. "Me too," she said.

Julia took the beer box sign and smiled, tracing the words *The C-Wing* with her fingers and looking up at the house. She walked up the steps to the front porch and, dragging a chair over to the front door, stood and balanced on it for a moment.

"Thank you," she whispered, propping the sign up on the ledge above the door. *The C-Wing* now stared down proudly on all who entered. "Thank you for everything."

Chapter 29

The Bee's Knees

"I'm truly sorry, but I'm taking this hat with me when I go. I have no choice. It was made for me." Cate adjusted the wide brim of the floppy gardening hat that she found in the shed, twisting it on her head to find the perfect position like she was trying to screw on the cap of a bottle.

"My head was made for wearing hats," she said. "My mom has always told me so." Cate adjusted the hat one final time and looked at herself in the hallway mirror before taking the cup of coffee that Julia offered her and walking out the front door, allowing the screen door to bang shut behind her.

Julia smiled at Cate's self-assuredness; she was anything but simple. Her life appeared to be a contrast in insecurities tempered by the occasional flash of self-absorption. None of it bothered Julia. In fact, she found her friend's complexities oddly comforting.

Cate was for nobody to "figure out." She was who she was and simply aspired to be the best version of her flawed self. And, with her words, stories, and observations, Julia drew nuggets of profound wisdom. Cate was even right about the hat—it looked good on her—and she wasn't going to apologize for saying it.

Julia refilled her coffee mug and followed Cate out the front door, intending to stop the screen door from slamming. But she was too late, and it banged anyway. Gwen was still asleep and, although she and Cate had tried to stay quiet during breakfast, a particularly funny story involving German chocolate cake and a projectile sneeze had left Julia gasping for air at the table. Sleeping was next to impossible if anyone else was up in the house; those who were awake acted like toddlers trying to stay quiet while a parent slept. Noise somehow found them, making the dullest of moments entertaining and the quietest of moments loud.

Julia and Cate loved working in the garden, tilling the soil for no reason other than the fact that they enjoyed turning it over and making it new again. Now that the entire garden had been tilled, the exercise was virtually effortless. The fine soil provided no resistance to the hoe's blades as they rotated their way through the garden.

Julia had pinned her hair on top of her head and kept strands out of her eyes with a bright pink sun visor, a picture of a flamingo holding a cocktail and *Tropicana Resort* stitched in cursive across its front. She had found the visor hanging in the bedroom closet, a pair of matching fluorescent sandals displayed on a shelf like the prized vacation souvenir that they likely were.

Julia rolled the short sleeves of her T-shirt up above her shoulders, waterfalls of sweat dripping down her back and into the waistband of her shorts. She felt gross, but in a wonderful way; sweating in the southern sun was like a natural cleansing that her body needed to feel pure again.

They hadn't been outside a half hour when they heard the screen door slam and saw Gwen appear from around the corner. She didn't look happy, coffee splashing out of a black mug as she walked toward them. A black mug that Julia was pretty sure she hadn't washed since using the day before.

"What the hell is wrong with you two?" she shouted as she got closer. "All I asked is for one day to sleep in, but I woke up to pans being thrown in the sink, doors slamming, and this one howling like she's a seal." She gestured to Julia, sending more coffee splashing to the ground. "I mean, seriously. It's like you're children." Gwen took a sip of her coffee and seemed surprised to find hardly any left in the mug.

Cate pulled the brim of the hat over her face to hide, her shoulders shaking up and down from laughter.

Julia bit her bottom lip and rested her chin on the end of the hoe handle, trying desperately not to laugh and make Gwen's mood worse.

"We tried to be quiet," Julia lied. "I mean, *I* tried, but I don't think Cate's capable of using an inside voice." She whispered the last part of the sentence like there was a chance Cate wouldn't hear.

"You're a bitch," Gwen said, tossing the last few droplets of coffee onto the ground. "You too," she said, pointing angrily at Cate who had pulled her hat down so low that it looked like she was a headless gardener.

"We love you!" Julia yelled, laughing as Gwen made her way back to the house. "You're our hero!"

"Oh, shut the hell up!" Gwen yelled without turning around, tripping over a piece of the garden hose that Julia had used the day before to water the lilac bushes alongside the house. Just as Gwen looked ready to launch into a tirade against the hose, the sound of gravel turned all of their attention toward the driveway and the cloud of dust that was making its way toward them.

"Expecting someone?" Cate asked, pulling the brim of the hat up so she could see.

"Not that I know of," Julia responded. "Unless you think I should make up another room for someone from the center who found out where we're hiding." She squinted as the car made its way toward them, and then realized quickly that it wasn't a car. It was a motorcycle.

Beau disappeared around the front of the house, but Julia could hear him skid to a familiar firm halt beside the tree.

Gwen was closer to the house than Julia and Cate and got there before they did, gesturing with a wicked smile toward the man who was covered in dust.

When she was a teenager, Julia had a black and white poster of a man on a motorcycle above her bed; he wore aviator sunglasses, three days' worth of stubble, and a sexy smirk. To her at the time, he represented the ideal man.

She now stood there with sweat running between her boobs, wearing a flamingo sun visor and three days' worth of leg hair stubble, and realized that a pretty accurate version of that poster man was walking towards her.

"Well, good mornin'," Beau said, wiping off the dust from his hands onto his jeans. He extended a hand toward Gwen. "I'm Beau."

Gwen, mouth slightly open, looked at Julia before taking his hand and pumping it firmly. "Well, hello to *you*," she said coyly, adjusting her yoga top to make sure that all of her assets were tucked firmly inside.

Beau then walked over to Cate, running his hand through his dark hair before shaking her hand. Cate smiled widely and Julia could see questions that she couldn't wait to ask spinning like a hamster wheel in her head.

"Been a crazy few days," Beau said to Julia. "I've been out of town on a few assignments, but saw you the other day in Friendly. Thought I'd stop by to say hello and see how everything's going. Looks like you have some company now, so that's good. This is a big house to stay alone in."

Julia could feel Gwen and Cate staring at her, their smiles like reflectors in the late morning sun.

"All's good here," Julia said, realizing that her voice had cracked nervously. She felt like she had been approached by the cute guy at the school dance and her friends were waiting anxiously to see how she'd react. Julia couldn't tell if her nerves were from seeing Beau again or from being in the spotlight when it happened. Regardless, the butterflies of a schoolgirl crush were flittering in her stomach and she decided that, when approached by the cute guy, you might as well take a spin on the dance floor.

"Beau grew up in that great brick house up the road," she said, trying to act as normal as possible and pointing to Burt's house. "He knew the family who lived here really well and was nice enough to stop by to check in on me." Julia regretted leaving her sunglasses inside, now unable to avoid eye contact by any of the three people staring at her.

"Cate and Gwen are my friends from..." she started, but stopped herself, not wanting to violate their privacy by disclosing that they were also seeking treatment at the center.

"We were her rehab peeps," Gwen offered with a grin. "No shame, here. The first step toward self-improvement is realizing that we all could use some."

Beau smiled at her, taking his sunglasses off and cleaning them with a corner of his T-shirt.

"Well said," he responded. "I have no doubt that you three are far more well-adjusted than most of the people wandering around. Good for you for doing what you need to do to live honestly."

"Don't be too impressed," Cate said. "We're pretty messed up." She laughed and leaned on the handle of the hoe that she was still holding. "Except for Julia, though. I think she's probably more pulled together than the people at the center who were trying to help us." Cate winked at Julia, her attempt to build her up in front of Beau not subtle in the least.

"Don't tell me you're still messing around in the garden," Beau said, putting his sunglasses back on and walking toward the corner of the house to take a look. "Seriously, it's going to be the best-tilled soil in the south."

"Have you ever heard of sand therapy?" Julia asked. Judging from his reaction, she assumed not. "Well, this is our farm version. It's garden therapy."

"Interesting," he said, shooting her a shy smile and running his hand through his hair again. "Whatever works, I guess. I'm sure my dad would let you work in his garden if you run out of challenges here."

Gwen moved closer to Julia and stabbed her in the ribs with her elbow.

"So, Beau, what do you do?" Cate asked, turning her head sideways and leaning against the hoe handle like an intrigued child. "You mentioned being out of town on assignment. What kind of assignment?"

"I'm a photographer," he said, shrugging like he was reluctant to admit it. "I guess I'm trying to find my way in life, too, capturing moments one still shot at a time." A phone then started ringing and Beau realized that it was his, jogging back quickly to his motorcycle to get it.

"It's very *Bridges of Madison County*," Cate whispered, keeping her eyes on Beau as she skipped over to Julia. "A sexy photographer who glides in and out of town on assignment. You, a pretty farm girl looking for an adventure. I love it."

"You're ridiculous," Julia said, brushing Cate's hand off her arm and gesturing for her to keep quiet.

"What's *Bridges of Madison County*?" Gwen asked, looking confused.

"Tell me you're kidding," Cate said.

"No, I don't know what those bridges are. Are they around here?"

"Seriously, Gwen. We need to get you in touch with your girly girl side. It's an amazing movie with Meryl Streep and Clint Eastwood. Based in Iowa. She lives on a farm and is longing for something exciting in life. He's in town on an assignment and has a gypsy soul. They fall in love and have a few hot days before her family comes back from the fair with their prize-winning cows."

Gwen looked at Cate like she had grown a second head, but then realized that her description of the movie was anything but a joke.

"Don't forget about the necklace," Julia whispered. "He takes the necklace and wraps it around the rear-view mirror, just waiting for her to run to him in the rain. It's so amazing."

"Oh, the *necklace*," Cate whispers, clutching Julia's arm like she had forgotten the most important part. "The *necklace*. I always want her to pull that door handle and run, just run to him."

"You two are pathetic," Gwen said, laughing. "I'm embarrassed to be your friend."

"You love us," Julia said, patting Cate's hand to break her free from the daydream that she had fallen into involving Clint Eastwood and his dangling necklace. "You need a little Madison Bridges in your life, Gwen. I saw a VCR inside. Maybe we can find a tape of the movie to rent in town." She laughed and watched Beau as he talked on his cell phone, the sun overhead highlighting strands of red in his hair and the metal tips of his riding boots. It surprised even her, this feeling that she had when she saw him—a tattooed-antithesis of the man who had broken her heart and brought her to this place—a man who seemed to relate to being lost in his own wonderful way.

Julia suddenly thought back to the late nights eating sushi

with Matthew and the times that she had convinced herself she was leading the perfect life.

A wave of emotion washed over her; unlike the stifling grief that she had long lost herself in, however, this wave consisted of nothing but regret and a pinch of shame. Julia had now turned another corner; she no longer pined for the life she had with Matthew, but regretted the time wasted spinning a life web that wasn't real. Or, as Beau had said, living a life that wasn't honest. Watching him nod to something said on the phone and tuck in his dirty T-shirt, she had a feeling that Beau put a great deal of value in living honestly and according to his own playbook. Like the purple flowering weeds that grew wild along the driveway, he seemed quite perfect in his imperfections. Whether weed or flower, Julia realized that it doesn't really care what it's called as long as it makes you happy.

"I should probably run," Beau said, putting his cell phone in his back pocket and walking toward them. "My editor needs a few more touch-ups on some photos that I submitted yesterday." He rolled his eyes, signaling that he found the request unnecessary.

"Sure was nice meeting you two," he said, smiling at Gwen and Cate. "I hope we have a chance to talk again. Take care of this one." He nodded toward Julia and smiled in a way that made her knees buckle, the image of the poster above her bed like a glossy billboard in her mind.

"Will do," Cate said with a sly smile. "We can't stay forever, though. You should probably stop by again soon to check on her."

Beau smiled as he walked away, shaking his head at Cate's poor attempt at subtlety. "No worries," he shouted out behind him, straddling the motorcycle and giving them a small wave goodbye.

Beau actually spotted it first, another plume of dust creating a small tornado up the long driveway. The car was driving too fast, kicking up rocks and skidding off the road like its tires objected to the feel of gravel underneath.

"Well, isn't this the place to be," Cate said. "Who now? You got another good-lookin' guy stopping by for a visit?"

"Not that I know of," Julia said softly, suddenly realizing that she recognized the car. It was a gray BMW sedan owned by someone who swore she would never drive it on anything except the smooth streets of the city. She couldn't believe what she was seeing, a film of thick dust covering a car that was professionally washed and detailed often and smelled of the rainforest, compliments of a stash of air fresheners kept stored in the glove compartment and changed regularly.

"I can't believe it," Julia said, taking a few steps toward the car that had come to an abrupt stop. Beau sat ready on his motorcycle, but made no move to leave, balancing the five-hundred-pound metal goliath with both feet firmly on the ground.

"I can't believe it!" Julia shouted, running over to the car and getting there just as Genevieve stepped out. She grabbed her friend and almost knocked her over from the force of her hug, wrapping her arms around her so tightly that there was nothing for Genevieve to do but laugh and wrap her arms around Julia just as tightly. Overwhelmed by the surprise of seeing her, Julia started crying, now too embarrassed to let go because everyone would see.

"You're crazy," Julia said through her tears, not aware until that moment how much she had missed her best friend. "I can't believe you're here."

Genevieve slowly pried herself away and looked at Julia a bit concerned, a few tears running down her face now, too.

"Well, let's see. My best friend doesn't call me, but rather writes me a letter, telling me that she's ran away from rehab, rented a farmhouse, isn't coming back anytime soon, and is staying in a town with no coffee, but claims she's *fine*. Yeah, you get a letter like that, you track your friend down." Genevieve started laughing, wiping the tears away from Julia's face and looking her up and down. "Girl, though, you look good! Nice hat."

"I *am* good!" Julia said, laughing. "Get over here and meet my friends." She started walking toward Cate and Gwen, but a familiar voice stopped her in her tracks.

"Hey, wait a minute. I came all this way and don't even get a hug?"

Julia whipped around to see her standing on the other side of the car, an arm perched on the passenger side door that she had emerged from.

Georgia.

Chapter 30

Georgia Lights

The box was marked HOLIDAY and, unlike the cardboard boxes stacked dangerously high in her storage unit back home, this one actually contained what it claimed to.

Julia maneuvered the box to the end of the shelf, cradling it as she lifted to protect the side that had turned brown and weak from water damage.

"Let's see what's in here," she said, balancing the box on one shoulder as she gently lowered it to Georgia.

"Let me just get this out there," Georgia said. "I object to the use of any plastic Santas. I'm all about throwing a party, but let's be reasonable. The leaves haven't even started to change yet."

Since Genevieve and Georgia's surprise arrival that morning, the house had been electrified, words spoken over one another at a dizzying pace that left Beau shaking his head and pleading for mercy. He had taken off shortly after introductions were made, the curiously raised eyebrows of her sister and best friend rivaling the dramatic arched brows of Cate and Gwen when they caught sight of him for the first time.

Within ten minutes of meeting, Cate and Gwen had been

brought into the close circle of Julia, her sister, and Genevieve—
an immediate bond formed among the women.

Little time was spent discussing *why* Georgia and
Genevieve were there; their initial looks of concern all but gone
by the time they had toured the farmhouse and met the women
who had cushioned Julia's departure from rehab. They were
there because they loved her; some of the most complicated
decisions in life can be explained as simply as that.

"No Santas," Julia promised, standing on tiptoe to check out
the labels on the boxes stored near the back of the shelf. "I'm
pretty sure that I saw the plastic North Pole scene in the other
corner."

As cheery as the rest of the farmhouse was, the basement
was anything but. The air hung heavy with the dampness from
cinderblock walls, a small window providing the only light other
than the naked bulbs suspended from overhead beams and
turned on with a tug of their dangling strings.

Some items had been recently removed, the edges of
vanished boxes still chiseled in the floor dust like chalk outlines.
The Blackwell children must have taken what they wanted and
left the rest for another day, the box marked HOLIDAY among
those left behind, including a few marked HIGH SCHOOL
and another generically labeled WIRES AND STUFF.

Julia was about to start down the ladder when a shoebox
caught her eye. It was bigger than most shoeboxes, the kind that
held boots, and was tucked away from the rest as if it had fallen
from the top of a pile and had been forgotten. She reached for it
and pulled it closer, wiping the thick dust off its side so she
could read the words written on the brittle piece of masking
tape.

Wedding dress. The box had been taped shut, so she
couldn't peek inside.

"Heads up," Julia said, tossing the box down to Georgia.

Tiffany Killoren

"What's this?" Dust flew as soon as the box was airborne and Georgia wiped her hands on her shorts, blinking rapidly to keep the particles from stinging her eyes. She didn't take the time to read the label, turning her attention to the string of colorful Christmas lights that she had found in the box earlier handed to her.

"I think we're good," she said as Julia made her way down the ladder. "You just wanted to find some lights for the trees, right?" She held up multiple strings of lights, all of which had been meticulously wound around small wooden boards to keep them from getting tangled in storage. "These people must have been pretty neat and organized."

Grabbing the dusty shoebox in which was stuffed a dress that represented one of the most special days in a woman's life, Julia just smiled.

"Maybe," she said. "Let's get out of here."

Julia swatted at an imaginary cobweb and made her way toward the stairs, tugging a light pull along her way and encasing them in darkness. Following Georgia up the stairs, she tucked the shoebox under her arm and decided to keep its existence to herself for the time being, placing it in the corner of the kitchen counter with the label facing the wall.

Gwen, Cate, and Genevieve were making a mess, pulling pots and pans out of the lower cupboards in search of something particular.

"We're going to need a bigger pot," Cate said, trying to fit a small rectangular baking dish into a round saucepan. "I refuse to believe that this family lived here as long as they did without owning a proper pot for boiling crawfish."

"Maybe that cutie on the motorcycle has one we can borrow," Genevieve said, looking up at Julia and giving her an exaggerated wink. "I bet that boy knows how to heat things up."

The corny comment brought giggles from the rest of the

282

women and a sharp elbow to the rib from Georgia, who might
have felt a little out of place contributing to any discussion
about the hotness of some guy on a bike.

"I'll ask Opal," Julia said, ignoring them all. "She's coming
early to help us with prep stuff, and I bet she has something we
can use."

With five women now staying under one roof, throwing a
party simply provided a formal setting for the energy that was
already whirling its way through the house. A party seemed
logical, a gathering to introduce the cast of characters from
Julia's past and present a natural way to connect her life's dots.
Burt, Beau, and Opal were all coming, with Burt immediately
assuming responsibility for boiling crawfish as part of a recipe
that he claimed had stood the test of time over decades. Opal
volunteered to bring side dishes, which left the five women in
the house with all cocktail responsibilities, and decoration
duties.

"Think we can string those lights from the trees?" Julia
asked.

"Just need a ladder," Georgia said. "And an extension cord."

"Back shed."

"I'll go get a start on this," Georgia said, looking at the pile of
pots and pans like she would volunteer for anything that didn't
involve her cleaning up the mess in the kitchen. "What are we
doing for drinks?"

"Poor man's sangria," Gwen said. "I'm coming up with a
mixture of roadside red wine, club soda, and fruit that we have
left over from our last trip to town."

"Sounds dangerous," Cate said.

"The good stuff usually is," Gwen added, pulling up the
sleeve of Genevieve's T-shirt to check out one of her tattoos.
The two of them quickly emerged as kindred souls, friendly jabs
exchanged within minutes of meeting, their shared wit an

understood and appreciated trait that too often went over the heads of others.

Julia leaned against the door frame and smiled, taking in a scene that she wouldn't have been able to imagine a month ago. A room of strong and beautifully flawed women playing like a symphony in front of her of all that was right in the world. In *her* world.

Let's get this party started, she thought.

The drinks were strong, the tiny orange wedges doing nothing to soften the mix of red wine and "dash of bourbon" that Gwen decided to toss in at the last minute for no reason other than she found a bottle in the kitchen cupboard.

The crawfish boil was a similar smorgasbord, potatoes, corn, and onions tossed in with the shellfish, along with some sausage that Burt had left over from a meal earlier that week. The menu was not unlike the group of people eating it, an eclectic mix of personalities and backgrounds that somehow came together to simmer into something wonderful.

For Julia, the night was bittersweet; her friends and family were leaving the next day to return to whatever new version of "normal" awaited them. The fact that Georgia had made this trip with only thirty-six hours off from her hospital shift made her visit all the more poignant. She had spent the little time that she had off on unforgiving country roads instead of curled up under her covers where she belonged. And, just a few hours before when Julia spotted both Gwen and Cate's packed bags resting by the doors of their bedrooms, she felt the familiar rise of panic in her chest at the thought of being left here to figure it all out on her own.

She then remembered taking that first step onto the front

porch, however, and realized that that was the way it was meant to be. Julia could take comfort in being surrounded by people who loved her, but in the end, the journey was hers to make alone.

Cate, Gwen, Genevieve, and Georgia were all huddled under the tree talking, heads whipping backward in laughter as Genevieve worked the proverbial room and talked wildly with her hands. Julia smiled, certain that she knew the story being retold from their many nights at happy hour. Then again, she had been gone awhile and Genevieve may have had recent adventures that Julia didn't yet know about. That thought made her sad—the feeling of missing out was difficult for her to process—but Julia had her own stories to share and looked forward to the time when they could sit down somewhere and make up for lost time, Genevieve snapping her fingers at a waiter to refill their drinks as they lost themselves in conversation. There would be time for that; there would time for all of it.

Although Julia had been talking to Burt and Opal, their shared lifetimes in Friendly resulted in a language that only they could understand. Stores that closed decades ago were described by the characters who owned them. Families were referred to by a single name or nugget of gossip that made them easily identifiable. Significant events of the past six decades were discussed as if no time had gone by, the details surrounding the "Schaefer barn fire," "summer of red ants," and "food poisoning at the church picnic" flowing in a way that made it impossible for Julia to decipher when, where, or how each occurred.

Burt and Opal talked in a way that outsiders would never understand, their shared history with the town as impenetrable as handprints in the sidewalk. Visitors could place their hands on the hardened cement, but they would never fit the same way as the fingers that made the imprint so many years before.

Julia watched Opal as she placed fingertips to her lips to stifle a giggle that shook her entire body. Apparently, there was a salacious part of the story that Burt was now telling about "the night the streetlights went out" that struck Opal as particularly funny, her fingertips lingering over her lips to stop any laugh that threatened to break through.

That's when Julia saw it, the glistening twinkle in Opal's eyes that suggested a reaction fueled by something other than a shared memory. Julia leaned slightly over to catch a glimpse of Burt's face. There was a glow in his cheeks caused by something other than a swig from his flask.

Opal and Burt were flirting. The thought of it made Julia's heart skip a beat as she rested her head back on her lawn chair; she hadn't even thought of it, this unexpected love connection between the two people who first reached out to her and welcomed her to the town in their own way. She hadn't thought of it, but now questioned how she had ever missed the possibility.

Some of the holiday lights in the trees were small, white and twinkling. Others were strings of large multi-colored bulbs that glowed steadily where they were lit, a few broken or missing bulbs like an ellipsis among the trees between areas of light. She stared at the sky, a twinkling mix of fireflies, stars, and Christmas décor.

At that moment, with the laughter of her friends and family echoing in the night sky, Julia felt blessed beyond measure and knew that this feeling—this memory—would see her through.

"I'm going to go inside to get the pies," Julia said, pretending not to notice that Opal and Burt had completely cut her out of their conversation and had moved on to some story about their high school and the theft of a neighboring school's goat mascot.

Opal took a moment to wave acknowledgment, but Julia could tell that she didn't want to take her attention away from Burt, perhaps concerned that a break in the conversation would sever their connection. Julia didn't think that she had anything to worry about, Burt's face a rosy-cheeked signal that he was enjoying the conversation as much as she was.

Julia walked around the small bonfire, catching Gwen's eye and signaling that she would be back in a minute. She stepped over a box of fireworks on her way toward the house. Burt's contribution of sparklers and bottle rockets from a Fourth of July years ago a sweet gesture that resulted in more than one reference to a celebration of Julia's "independence day." And Gwen's roadside sparkler purchase added a feel of serendipity to the moment.

She made her way around the side of the house, the voices left behind now blurred into a hum by the walls of the house between them. It was dark where she walked, a soft glow of the lights out back serving like a nightlight just bright enough to make out shapes and objects in front of her. Dark enough for her eyes to play tricks on her, Julia darted out of the way as a snake made its way across the grass, only to realize that it was the handle of a shovel that she had forgotten to put back in the shed after cleaning out the bonfire pit that afternoon.

"Be careful," she heard him say. "Those tools are dangerous."

Julia spotted the figure of a man walking toward her, arms carrying something to his side like he was a trapeze artist walking a tight rope. She and Beau had talked briefly that night, but he had been too busy with the crawfish boil to sit down and relax.

She was thankful for that; she had rather they keep busy than lose themselves in conversation, her eyes glistening like Opal's in a way that would have made it impossible to deny her feelings when she was inevitably confronted by her friends. She didn't like to feel on display and, if she had to guess, Beau didn't either.

"Well, fancy meeting you here," Julia said, immediately regretting how stupid she sounded. According to Genevieve's menu of pick-up-lines, this one would have been classified as a double burger with extra cheese.

"A girl can never be too careful," Julia followed-up quickly. "The one time that I let my guard down out here, I'll step on one of those snakes that you claimed will eat me whole or fall into the well that your dad is sure I'm going to die in."

As Beau approached, she saw that he was smiling. She squinted to make out what he was holding.

"What do you have there?" she asked, realizing then that he was carrying two pies.

"Oh, thanks, I was just ready to go inside to get those," she said with a smile. "I'll go get the plates and forks."

"Here, why don't you take these," Beau said, handing the pies off to her. She balanced each one on her palms like he did, the bottoms of the pans still warm. Opal had made an apple and blueberry pie from scratch that afternoon and brought them over for the girls to put in the oven, insisting that pies taste better when they're eaten where they were baked. Another life lesson in Southern charm—go figure.

Julia stood there and waited for Beau to say something, but he didn't. The lights from the back of the house shone just brightly enough for her to see that he was staring at her. Just as she turned to walk back to the party, Beau touched her arm and turned her around. He brought her closer, cradling her face in his hands and tilting it upward, and then kissed her. His kiss was soft, yet firm; gentle, yet passionate. Beau was strong and confident as he guided Julia's body, the two of them in their own dance under the stars. Julia, still balancing two pies and unable to move, felt vulnerable in the most wonderful of ways. She loved the feel of his whiskers, a few days' growth removing any roughness and turning them into a soft bristle brush across her cheek. He smelled simply of the outdoors, no cologne or aftershave needed; it would have only masked what nature had created perfectly.

This was all Beau; he was in charge, pulling away briefly like he was going to stop, but then kissing her again, more deeply this time and less restrained. Julia's ears pounded with the beat of her pulse when he eventually pulled away, the steady rhythm racing like a blood rush from her heart to extremities, her hands going numb from the heat of the pies and effort not to drop them.

"It just seemed like the right time," Beau said, taking a step backward toward the house, his wicked smile shining brightly in the night sky. His smile, a crooked grin that had warned her about copperheads; a mischievous smile that accompanied a head shake when he met her friends and became dizzy from the relentless banter. That smile, as unique and charming as the person who wore it. Julia didn't know what to do, so she just smiled and held the pies up like a waitress balancing trays.

"I'd have to agree," she said softly, smiling as he turned around and made his way toward the front of the house.

Julia heard a crackling sound, an electrified energy that spat a few times and then settled into a warm sizzle.

"Do sparklers have expiration dates?" she heard someone ask, followed by another round of spit and crackle as a second sparkler was lit.

With pies raised, Julia headed back to the party, shivering slightly despite the hot temperature. The air had become energized, little rockets of light launching around the corner and flying like shooting stars across the shadows.

Sparks were indeed flying.

Chapter 31

Write What You Know

She laid it on the bed, the long sleeves and skirt resisting Julia's efforts to release them from their wrinkled cocoon inside the shoebox. She gently pressed the sleeves into the comforter, forcing the satin fabric to remember how it once laid, how it once was worn. The dress was tiny. You would have to have a petite frame to fit into the champagne-colored gown. It was a relatively fitted and streamlined design that Julia assumed dated back to the early 1900s, or even earlier. Unlike the plunging necklines and strapless selections of today, Julia was struck by the elegant modesty of this gown's design, an elaborate lace collar and matching bodice reminiscent of a day when beautiful garments were defined, not by what they revealed, but by how they were worn.

The house was empty, a fact that she was all too aware of as her isolated footsteps echoed on the wooden stairs. Cate and Gwen had left right after breakfast, neither wanting to launch into extended goodbyes. They preferred to leave at the same time, which Julia assumed was so they could avoid the sinking feeling that comes with not knowing when you'll see a friend again, choosing instead to simply wave as they parted ways at the interstate.

Goodbyes were never easy; Julia had slept little the night before, anticipating the opening of the door that her friends would have to walk through and then close, leaving her on the other side.

The party had gone on much later than any of them had planned, miniature groups chatting and disbanding, different groups then forming so each partygoer had talked to every other partygoer in as many combinations as was mathematically possible. Julia felt guilty, trying to focus on the conversations that surrounded her, but her mind kept flittering back to the kiss, a memory as sweet and succulent as the pies she was holding and every bit as habit forming.

When Beau winked at her from across the bonfire, she felt a renewed sense of confidence, like the two of them shared an intimate secret that nobody else would understand.

And, when he lit a sparkler from the bonfire and handed it to her, she thought she might join the weightless embers as they made their way upward.

Julia had cried saying goodbye to Gwen and Cate, the exact reaction that they were hoping to avoid when they nonchalantly tossed their bags into their trunks and mentioned seeing everyone soon. There were no such plans; Julia knew that once everyone got settled back into their normal lives, the opportunities to see one another would disappear as calendars became filled with color-coded entries and the day-to-day challenges that came with merely existing in the world weighed them down once again.

These last few days had been a gift, a perfectly wrapped package from the universe that came but once in a lifetime; they had all been allowed to hit the "reset" button on their lives and live in the moment of pause, experiencing a pocket of pure presence before the filmstrip starts to roll again and expectations build. Julia knew that she would see her friends again, but they all knew that it would never be quite the same. Yes, she would miss Gwen and Cate, but she knew that they had to move on; her tears stemmed more from appreciation than they did from loss.

Georgia and Genevieve left after lunch, the three of them lingering on the front porch in an antithesis of the quick goodbye from earlier that day. The air wasn't heavy with doubt about seeing each other again: her sister and best friend were her foundation, the sturdy core of all that she was and ever will be. The question was not one of *if*, but only of *when*. Both Georgia and Genevieve were well-aware that Julia had planted roots in a farmhouse hours from where life awaited their return. They were happy for her, but sad for themselves.

Neither of them encouraged her to come back to her old life; because they loved her, they couldn't ask her to return to a colorless existence when she was living life with a painter's palette here. They wouldn't do that to her, and she appreciated that they didn't even try.

Julia made her way down the wooden staircase, her hand gliding over the banister railing that had been worn smooth from journeys downward such as this. She tried not to focus on the silence that surrounded her, concerned that she would fall victim to a cycle of unproductive thoughts and memories that seemed to emerge when nobody else was around.

Appreciative of a loud kaw-kaw cry of a bird passing by, Julia reminded herself that there was really no such thing as silence; it was simply a matter of where life's volume dial was turned in that particular moment. Coming off a few days of that dial turned all the way up, there was simply going to be an adjustment period to being alone in the house again.

Julia stood in the doorway of the living room and took in

what still remained of the fresh paint smell. It had been coined The Tranquility Room for obvious reasons, its color changing with the sunlight throughout the day. Now, with a late afternoon glow shining through its east-facing windows, the room's mood was one of a renewed and calming energy.

Julia went over to a box in the corner that she had put aside during the painting project, a box that she had assumed was mistakenly left behind when the Blackwell children packed up the most cherished of items and took them to their new homes.

She opened it and made her way through old framed photographs, black-and-white images of people she didn't know staring back at her, their serious looks piercing the glass. Julia removed the photos and stacked them carefully beside the box, eager to find the one that had caught her eye the first time she had gone through them after moving in.

There, at the bottom of the box, was a wedding photograph, the bride with brunette ringlets and a bouquet of wildflowers. She stared at Julia from her seat on an upholstered chair, her new husband with a hand resting on the back of the chair and look of pride on his mustached face. The bride was smiling playfully, the corners of her lips turned slightly upward like she thought the entire process of posing for a formal photograph a bit silly and uncomfortable. Her eyes told a story, a life that she was eager to live waiting for her across the marital threshold, the photograph the first page of a chapter that she was anxious to write. There was no mistaking the elaborate lace collar and intricate detailing—the bride was wearing the wedding dress spread out carefully on the bed upstairs.

Julia took the photograph with her as she tracked down her phone, forgetting where she had plugged it in overnight to charge. Finding it on the kitchen counter, she hunted through the pile of papers that she had accumulated looking for Kennedy Blackwell's email address.

Opening her email seemed strange; she had barely looked at it since leaving for the center, not really interested in responding to emails from friends who, unaware of her situation, were touching base regarding a new bar opening or band playing on Friday night.

She wanted to let Kennedy know about the dress, however, and was willing to put a toe briefly back into the water of electronic communication in order to do so.

Julia scanned her inbox quickly, looking for signs of emergency or heightened alert in the subject line that would warrant her actually reading any of them. She skipped over it the first time, only noticing the name of the sender when she was scrolling back up to the top and was fairly confident that life was continuing unfazed in her absence. When she noticed the email, however, that feeling changed.

C_Jones@TWestPublishing.com

Cecily Jones. Julia's heart dropped; the Editor-in-Chief of *Georgia Now*, the magazine that she worked for back home, had sent her an email. Although not unexpected, seeing her email address in the inbox was still alarming, the message sent late the night before. Julia had written to Cecily Jones shortly after she decided to rent the farmhouse, guilt-ridden that her employer would think she was still on personal leave when, in fact, she was spending her time flirting with her neighbor's son and tilling a garden with no intention on planting seeds.

She didn't want to receive a paycheck dishonestly; her employer had been nothing but accommodating and understanding throughout this entire ordeal, so she owed her an explanation.

Julia had sat at the kitchen table one morning, energized by a cup of good coffee and the realization that she had nothing to lose, and dictated an email to Cecily Jones that provided as much detail as to her situation as she was comfortable sharing with her boss. Emboldened by her new surroundings, Julia had pitched the idea of writing for the magazine remotely, creating a column that focused on rural living in the state of Georgia—everything from recipes, landmarks, history, and places to see to anthropological essays on the families who had worked the land for generations.

When she had hit "send" on that email, Julia didn't let herself think about a response; she was just relieved that it had been sent and the truth told. The flip side of her email now sat bolded in her inbox, the boomerang returned.

Julia could pretend that she didn't care either way, but that would be a lie. It is natural to care what other people think. The thought of her stint in rehab making the rounds at the office and what people might say caused her cheeks to grow flushed, the heat of embarrassment felt even hundreds of miles away from its source. She shouldn't care, but she *did*. She shouldn't be afraid to open the email, but she *was*.

Not only was she concerned about Cecily Jones' reaction to a rather unfiltered disclosure of her personal saga, but receiving confirmation that she no longer had a job would add a financial stressor to a pot that she had steadily stirred to a simmer. Figuring out a Plan B for financial survival would turn up the heat and get that pot boiling again.

Julia went over to the refrigerator and took out the generous single slice of Opal's apple pie—all that remained from the pies that had been served warm and washed down with a dangerous alcohol mix that tasted more of bourbon than wine as the night wore on.

She took a clean fork and carried the pie out onto the front porch, sitting down on the top step and carving out a giant bite as a few black birds parachuted to the ground to watch for crumbs. She felt like she was waiting for exam results for a test she knew she failed, the small flicker of hope that she had guessed right to a few questions all but snuffed out by the practical side of her brain that knew she had answered wrong. The magazine was a business, and a successful one at that, made profitable by decisions that could not be swayed by emotional ties or personal connections.

The thought of turning her situation into an opportunity to write her own column seemed far-fetched at best. Julia took another bite of pie, realizing that her glorious little bubble floating in the Georgia countryside was about to get popped.

Julia looked toward the road, willing a cloud of dust to form behind a motorcycle traveling up the driveway. Beau had left the night before with a cryptic "see you soon" goodbye, leaving her to analyze gender differences in the definition of "soon." Sure, she would like to see him, but her sights on the road now were in search of a distraction, a playful intermission to delay reading an email that lay in wait like a letter unopened.

Julia squinted down the driveway and then searched the intersecting gravel road in both directions, disappointed that there wasn't even a tractor in sight to justify a moment of diversion. Because the birds were hopping on their tiny claws annoyed, Julia tossed them pieces of pie crust and watched them battle it out, the first beak to the pie earning a beak to the head by its bitter competitor.

Julia put the pie pan down and picked up her phone, hitting the email message twice to open before she could find another reason not to. She looked down the driveway one last time before shielding her eyes from the sun to read the small screen.

Julia,

Courage comes in all forms, but I consider honesty with oneself and others to be among the most rare. Thank you for your message and willingness to confide in me. I'm sure it wasn't easy, and I commend your honesty on both a professional and personal level.

A few things of note. First, rest assured that your leave of absence has not been the talk of the office. Your issues are yours alone to deal with and we informed anyone who asked that you were out of the office on a work-based matter. I am nothing, if not discreet. Second, I couldn't help but sense embarrassment in your email; hold your head high for seeking out what makes you happy in life. I, too, traveled a winding road to get where I am today—a failed marriage and string of personal and professional carnage lining a path that I had always envisioned paved with gold. If there is one thing that I've learned in life, it's that we're only accountable to ourselves at the end of the proverbial day. Damn the rest and those who judge us to avoid looking at themselves.

Regarding your pitch for a remotely-written column, I'm not sure that we're in the position to move forward with that at the moment. That being said, I'm intrigued. When you emerge from your haven in the countryside and need a taste for city cuisine, schedule a lunch through my assistant and we'll talk. In the meantime, we can assign you some starter articles that you can work on from there to find your groove.

Take Care,

Cecily

P.S. Her name was Susan—she was an amazing mentor when I was starting out in the publishing world. She opened doors for me when nobody else would and I always vowed to do the same when I met someone like me—someone whose spirit might outshine their experience level right now —but who has the heart to go the distance. If that garden makes you happy, keep tilling it.

Julia read the email two more times. She felt many things at that moment, relief at the top of the list, followed closely by pride. She respected Cecily Jones; to not only be supported, but encouraged, by her to pursue this alternative lifestyle made Julia even more confident that her judgment was sound and based in something real. Cecily Jones was known for her sharp wit and savvy business sense—if she saw something special in Julia, who was she to argue.

She picked up the pie and ate what was left on the fork, the birds looking offended that she had held out on them. Taking the pie pan back into the kitchen, she resumed looking for Kennedy's email address, finding it scratched on the back of a yellow flyer with a picture of a ferris wheel on its front.

The county fair was now apparently in full swing, 4-H barns full of award-winning livestock and quilts on display in what the flyer boasted as "the newest air-conditioned convention building" at the fairgrounds. Julia wanted to go, a sudden urge to celebrate Cecily Jones' email rising like champagne bubbles in her belly, giddiness and relief making her want to jump onto a carousel horse and eat her weight in funnel cakes.

First things first: Julia drafted an email to Kennedy about the dress and accompanying photograph, excited both at the opportunity to share her find and the resulting visit that might occur because of it. Julia would love to hear more about the house and the years of memories that filled it. She wished that she would have asked more questions when she had the chance, but like so many things in life, the questions only emerged with time and a level of comfort that welcomed them.

Julia re-read her email, hoping that it didn't sound like she had made the dress discovery by rooting around where there was no need for her to be in the basement. She felt a bit guilty, knowing in her heart that she had rooted around more than was necessary to locate holiday lights, she and Georgia intrigued by the number of empty Tupperware containers and hoard of canned goods that one family felt it needed. Choosing to forgive herself for harmless voyeurism, Julia turned her attention back to the reason for her email.

Hi Kennedy!

I hope all is well with you. I wanted to drop you a line to let you know how much I've enjoyed my time so far in this amazing house—I felt at home immediately, no doubt due to the love that filled its walls for so many years. Thank you for being so open to some minor changes; I'd love for you to see the new living room color!

So, now for the second reason for my email. I had a few friends over the other night, and we used some lights that we found in the basement to decorate the trees outside (hope you don't mind). I stumbled upon a box that had fallen behind one of the shelves labeled "wedding dress." I couldn't leave it in the basement—the dress is exquisite, and matches one worn in a photo I found in a box left in the living room. I will keep the dress safe until I see you again.

~Julia

After her second read-through, Julia hit send and launched the email message into the electronic universe. She stood in the kitchen, trying to figure out her next move for the day. Julia was used to spending the late afternoon hours sitting on the front porch talking to her friends, details of their lives confessed in verbal diary entries, the farmhouse driveway like a lock and key to secrets shared within. She was used to spending the twilight hours rocking on the porch and watching the bats engage in air combat maneuvers as they stretched their wings from a long day's slumber.

Julia had gotten into a routine these past few days and was now faced with the task of creating a new one, so she did the only thing she could think of. She poured a giant glass of sweet tea and waited for inspiration.

Wandering into the living room, Julia scanned the book titles stacked on the dusty built-in shelves surrounding the fireplace. The gold lettering was difficult to read, scratches in the soft font erasing parts of words or dulling them to the point that they were illegible. She ran her fingertips over the bindings, newer titles disguised as antiques by being disrobed of their glossy cover jackets. She came upon a thick book cloaked in dark red, bold silver lettering still pristine and identified a title that she was familiar with from her college literature days. *Anna Karenina*—a story of a conflicted woman penned by a conflicted Russian author—seemed just the type of book she could lose herself in as the sun set and nightlife came out to play.

Letting the screen door slam behind her, Julia moved the rocking chair over to the end of the porch and rested her feet on the railing, opening the dusty pages and taking in their sweet decrepit smell. And lose herself she quickly did. The pages were read and turned quickly as Julia was transported to Russia during the 19th century, a woman's societal expectations at odds with her heart's calling. An hour flew by, and then another, her trip to another land so real and intense that she didn't hear the humming in the distance.

A cloud of dust finally awakened her from her literary trance as the motorcycle came to a stop in its regular spot under the tree.

Beau didn't turn off the engine, instead holding up a second helmet and yelling to her from the bike. "Want to go for a ride?"

Julia put *Anna Karenina* down and was surprised to see the sun well on its way to setting in the western sky. She had been reading for hours, her mind now on its way back from the journey that Tolstoy's words had taken her on, a re-emergence into present-day Georgia and its fireflies that came out before the sun was even set. Julia slipped on her shoes and ran down the front steps, catching a firefly mid-air and making a wish before setting it free.

Chapter 32

Belated Gifts

It took a second or two to remember where she was, the texture of the ceiling and its Rorschach water stain still slightly unfamiliar in the early morning mental fog. Focusing her eyes on the stain, Julia saw an angel with its wings outstretched, face turned toward the heavens as if waiting to be carried upward. If people saw Jesus's face in toast, she didn't know why she couldn't see an angel emerge from mildew.

Julia rolled over on her other side and tucked her hands under the pillow, careful not to disturb the comforter's folds that covered a still-sleeping chest. She synchronized her breathing with Beau's, the rise and fall of his chest and soft nose whistle a backdrop to the sliver of light that was cutting through the curtains like a shiny knife of gold across the floor. Julia had always thought there was something intriguing about watching someone sleep, their vulnerability never more evident than in the unconscious eye flutters and finger twitches that accompany emergence from another night's rest.

She fixed the strap of her tank top and rolled onto her back. Although Beau had crawled under the covers at some point, she had laid on top, wanting to soak up every little wisp of crisp air that had flown through the window overnight. Her head was a little foggy, but that was to be expected, a dinner of deep-friend Oreos, funnel cake, and lukewarm beer at the fairgrounds appealing more to her sense of adventure than judgment. The octopus ride that repeatedly tossed their spinning car into the air like wild tentacles was also to blame, but she would have ridden it again and again, just to hear Beau shriek like a schoolgirl afraid of a spider. Kissing on top of the ferris wheel was fun because it was so cheesy, the whoops and hollers of teenage boys in the car behind them making Julia blush and feel sixteen again.

And kiss they did, but that's all. Talking into the early morning hours about family, regrets, and dreams not yet pursued reminded her of a simpler time, a time when she wasn't afraid to talk about the life that she wanted because it hadn't disappointed her yet. Lying there next to Beau, watching him fall peacefully to sleep, she realized that there was still time to sit at that pottery wheel and spin her clay into something wonderful.

Julia slid off the bed and tiptoed out of the room, closing it slowly behind her so as not to wake him. She walked down the stairs, careful to avoid the third one from the top because it was loose and squeaked loudly if stepped on. The light from the sun rising on the other side of the house had just begun to reach the front, the view out the front door like a haze from a dream state. Julia went into the kitchen and turned on the coffee pot, thankful that she had ground beans the day before; she would do what she could to let Beau sleep, but if coffee was at stake, she would have ground those coffee beans and apologized after.

As soon as the first drop hit the pot, the smell filled the entire room. Julia loved the smell of coffee as much as the taste, the heavy aroma reminding her of walking into her grandparents' kitchen on the farm and being greeted by a delicacy that she wasn't allowed. She loved to watch her grandmother drink from a small china cup, placing it gently on a matching saucer between sips; the entire practice seemed so refined and civilized, even when the coffee drinkers were wearing overalls and still had mud from the field on their boots.

Julia filled the biggest mug that she could find and walked toward the front of the house, taking something out of a kitchen drawer on her way. Squeezing through the screen door so its hinges wouldn't have to stretch, she sat on the top step of the porch stairs and took her first sip of coffee, letting the mug linger under her nose so the smell would fill her head with all that was fresh ground and lovely. She finally sat it down on the porch and picked up what she had brought out, a mint green envelope with pink flower border; it was addressed and stamped, waiting for a drop onto the postal highway.

The name on the envelope made Julia's heart rate quicken— Vivian Harris.

She hadn't spent time at Matthew's apartment, a flag that waved bright red in hindsight, but had his address in her phone and could only assume that Vivian had since relocated there from Chicago. The envelope in front of her was thick, thicker than the others she had sent to family and friends; this envelope contained pages of admissions, explanations, and apologies that Julia felt like she owed the woman whose life had been a seesaw of highs and lows. Julia tapped the envelope against her knee and looked toward the road, spotting a truck traveling too quickly around a corner and losing its traction for a moment, back wheels spinning out from behind and creating an impressive dust cloud before regaining control.

In her heart, Julia knew what the right thing to do was. Sending this letter might make her feel better, but it would do nothing to lessen the pain of the woman on the other side, ripping open wounds that were too fresh for anyone to touch.

Julia had written the letter out of guilt and the need to confess, but realized that involving Vivian would be her most selfish act yet. It was like pulling someone off the dock because she didn't want to drown alone.

At first, Julia had thought that there needed to be resolution and, without truth, that wouldn't be possible. She had since realized, however, that it's not about making things whole again. Sometimes, there are loose ends in life that can't be tied, and it takes a strong person to just let them fly.

"What are you doing up so early?" Beau was either better at sneaking out the screen door than she was, or Julia was so wrapped up in memories that she had tuned the world around her out for a moment.

"Thoughts of funnel cakes and stale beer kept dancing in my head," Julia said, scooting over on the step to give him room to sit down, but he didn't move toward her. Instead, he leaned against the porch railing and yawned.

"Coffee's on," she said. "Want some?"

"Nah," Beau said, looking around the yard like he didn't recognize it this early in the morning. "You got plans for the day? I have to run to the house quick, but I'll be right back."

Julia wished that he would stay and sit with her, but he was already looking toward the old brick house on the hill like he wished he was there. She put the envelope down on the side opposite Beau, not wanting to invite questions. Although she had already told him a generalized version of events—and had no doubt that Burt had filled him in on the rest—she really didn't feel like explaining her thought process as to whether to send her ex-boyfriend's wife a letter outlining her participation in the downfall of their marriage. Julia figured such conversations—if they ever occurred—were probably better over wine than coffee that was still struggling to waken her.

Beau was already halfway to his bike, spinning around and

giving her a little wave before jumping on the motorcycle and revving its engine. The loud noise in the quiet countryside was startling, a flock of birds slumbering in the trees shot into the sky like a rocket from the rude awakening. Julia watched as Beau made his way down the driveway, rocks and pebbles shooting into the tall grass and scaring more birds hiding out on his way to the road.

She grabbed the letter in one hand and her coffee in the other, traveling around the side of the house toward the back shed. As soon as she turned the corner, the direct sunlight made it difficult to see, a harsh contrast from the shaded porch that felt at least ten degrees cooler.

Passing by the fire pit, Julia walked over to the ashes left behind from the party and buried the mint green envelope deeply within them, burrowing the paper into an ash grave to await its own cremation. She didn't stop until the entire envelope had disappeared, a charred piece of wood moved slightly to secure its place and serve as a marker. At some point —be it today, tomorrow, or a week from now—she would light the fire and watch the embers reach for the sky, the words on the pages transforming into tiny orbs extending toward the stars as a sign of self-forgiveness and peace.

Julia pulled open the heavy sliding doors of the shed and walked inside, her eyes needing a moment to adjust once again to a dramatic change in light. Walking along the work bench, she looked for a box that she had spotted during an earlier visit, a small shoebox marked with a thick black marker and left for safe keeping on one of the floating shelves. Finally spotting it, Julia stood on tiptoe to knock it down, catching it as the top fell to the floor and a few packages of seeds fell with it.

A single word was written on the box. *Flowers.*

Julia leafed through the extensive selection. There were tiny white packages with brightly colored wildflowers on their front, the seeds inside just waiting for the opportunity to touch soil and see what they were capable of. Julia had been tilling the garden since she arrived, working the soil in preparation for something that she couldn't quite visualize or fully understand.

With the envelope now buried in the ashes outside, Julia realized how she wanted to pay tribute to all that was left unsaid. When the time and season was right, she would plant a flower garden; she would drop seeds into the soil representing memories released and a new life embraced.

She would plant seeds for a baby that she didn't get a chance to hold and a little girl who she never met. With every seed dropped into the garden and covered with dirt, Julia would cherish a memory and experience gained, watering and caring for it until the moment came when it would burst from the soil anew, bright, and alive.

Julia cradled the box of seeds in her arms, unaware that she was crying until tears dropped onto a tiny package with a bright purple flower on its front. The color and shape of its leaves made her think of her grandmother, a lover of lilacs and anything that brought Julia joy. She knew exactly where she'd put it, an empty space next to the garden perfect for a lilac bush. Or maybe two.

She had just finished picking up the flower seed packages from the floor when she heard Beau's motorcycle. The sound surprised her as it approached the house. He wasn't kidding; he promised to come right back and couldn't have been gone fifteen minutes.

Any unacknowledged worry stemming from his quick departure was now gone as Julia swung the heavy wooden doors of the shed closed and walked quickly toward the front of the house with the box of seeds still cradled close to her chest.

Julia rounded the front of the house to see Beau on the

porch looking for her, something hidden behind his back with one hand.

"What are you up to?" he asked with a smile, glancing at the box that she was holding.

"I found some flower seeds in the shed," Julia explained. "I think I know what to do with the garden come spring."

"Well, it's nice to know that you plan on sticking around here that long," Beau said, shifting nervously from foot to foot. There was something about seeing him uncomfortable that made Julia smile, his tough exterior a hardened shell to the same uncertainties, feelings, and emotions as everyone else.

It emboldened her, because she found her own insecurities not as scary because of the realization that she wasn't special; everyone has their tics; everyone shifts nervously from side to side every now and then.

"What do you have there?" she asked, trying to see what he was hiding behind his back. She walked up the porch stairs and smiled at Beau's attempt to keep something hidden, turning slightly every time she tried to get a glimpse of what had caused him to rush home so early that morning.

"I made you something," he finally said. "You mentioned that it was your birthday recently and it doesn't sound like you spent it in a very fun place. I thought maybe we could make up for it."

He brought me a birthday present, Julia thought. *He didn't just bring me a birthday present, he* made *me one.*

Julia thought back to the day she had spent at the center, the birthday cards that she read in Dr. Rayborn's office like snapshots from a different life. Sitting there that day, sinking into a smelly chair with dreams of stealing it and adding it to her collection back home, Julia couldn't have imagined that now, weeks later, she would be given a re-do. In her wildest of daydreams, she couldn't have imagined standing on the porch of a farmhouse, clutching a box of flower seeds, waiting to be given a homemade gift from a motorcycle-riding photographer who had kissed her on top of the ferris wheel the night before.

"Can I see it?" Julia asked, almost in a whisper. She could tell that Beau was nervous to give it to her for some reason, but couldn't imagine why. The gesture itself was so sweet that he could have handed her a box of rocks—she would have loved it.

Beau paused for a moment and then brought a piece of wood out from behind his back. It was about a foot long and five inches tall, the edges sanded smooth, and the wood finished with a shiny glaze that brought out its red and golden tones. He tilted it so she could read something engraved across its front, words burned into the wood in a cursive font.

The C-Wing.

Julia just stared at it, taking her eyes from its words only briefly to meet Beau's, and then turning again toward the sign. There were no words; she couldn't speak and wouldn't know what to say if she did.

"I don't know the story," Beau started. "That piece of cardboard above the door is obviously really important to you, though. You and your friends mentioned it during the party, and I could tell that it was something special." He paused, searching Julia's face for some signal as to her reaction.

"I just figured that something that important deserved a nicer display." Beau shrugged, his hands shaking slightly.

Julia walked over to him, touching the words etched along the front of the sign with her fingertips. She smiled and looked up at him, a tear running down her face for the second time that morning.

"This is the nicest gift you could have ever given me," she said, now laughing through her tears. "This might be the nicest gift in the history of all birthdays."

His shoulders relaxing with relief, Beau smiled back,

handing the sign to Julia and revealing a chain on the back to hang it from.

Julia took the sign and, opening the screen door, pulled closed the heavy wooden door inside. A small hook rested just below the tiny fanlight windows, a rusted hook that Julia assumed had held wreaths and welcome signs for family and friends that no longer came. She took the chain on the back of the sign and hung it carefully, allowing the sign to fall where it chose to land across the door.

Taking a step back, Julia wrapped an arm around Beau's waist and leaned her head on his shoulder, comforted by the hug that she got in return. She looked at the sign on the faded wooden door, surrounded by a door frame with chipping paint, on a porch that leaned slightly and was home to at least a few wasp nests, and felt her entire body relax. She had never felt so at home. She had never before been in such a perfect and beautiful place.

Yes, she would definitely stay.

Epilogue

She looked beautiful in her dress, a cocktail-length vintage gown with petticoat and lace trim. The sweet scent of her rose bouquet attracted a few bees, but they were dismissed quickly by the swift and steady hand of her groom. He looked dashing as well, a black suit and matching tie with sequined detail adding a level of formality that would have otherwise been missing in the suit alone. Julia had talked him into it, telling him that "a little bling's never a bad thing" when it came to weddings.

The flowers were in full bloom, the garden transformed into a wonderland of colors, scents, and textures with blooms of different shapes and sizes rising toward the sky. Julia tended to the garden daily, even when there was no need, cutting a few blooms to arrange into one of the many vases that she had around the house.

Julia didn't want to cry, but she didn't even try to stop herself, the beauty of the day calling for a release of any emotion that saw fit to make an appearance.

As Opal and Burt exchanged their vows under the tree in her backyard, Julia looked into the small group seated on folding white chairs and met Gwen's eyes first, and then Cate's, their smiles beaming in the late afternoon sun at the display of love before them.

Genevieve and Georgia sat behind them, laughing quietly about something shared behind the privacy of a paper fan that did nothing to hide their girlish giggles.

Julia held her bouquet of lilacs tightly and looked across at Beau, the handsome best man, standing proudly next to his dad. Catching his eye, Julia winked and smiled. Beau, hands clasped behind his back as he rocked back and forth on his heels, raised an eyebrow and gave her a wicked smile.

THE END

Acknowledgments

Therapy is a big word. *Uncharted* Therapy is an emotion. Moving to an old farmhouse in a town lost in time appeals to me greatly, some days more than others. I like to think that I moved there for a while when writing this book, the rocking chair on the porch calling to me like an old friend. Thank you to Alan, Max and Finn for understanding that I was lost somewhere in the countryside when tucked away in my office. And my parents would be the first to help me move into an old farmhouse if that was my dream because they're dream makers. I love you all. Thank you to Stephanie, my fearless agent, for advice and emoji texts when I need them. The team at Bloodhound Books has been amazing on this journey, specifically Betsy and Tara's guidance, Clare's editing expertise and the design team's ability to make me tear up over a cover. And, for my friends - laughing with you as we share this incredible journey of life is the best therapy there is.

About the Author

Tiffany Killoren is an author, former attorney, magazine editor and freelance writer. Her novel, *Good Will*, was released in 2020, followed by *Uncharted Therapy* with Bloodhound Books in August 2024, and debut mystery, *Pretty Dead Things*, under the pen name Lilian West in late 2024.

Tiffany's writing about film directors, celebrity bodyguards, artists, and national musical performers has been featured in multiple magazines, as well as her work focusing on community programs and area entrepreneurs. She is a contributing writer to a lifestyle magazine, authored a monthly *Bookish* column and is a regular speaker at writing seminars and other events.

She currently resides with her husband, two sons and an incorrigible pup in a Kansas City suburb.

www.tiffanykilloren.com

Instagram (@TiffanyKilloren_Author / @LilianWest_Author)
Twitter (@TiffanyKilloren)
Facebook (Tiffany W. Killoren, Author Page)
TikTok (@TiffanyKilloren)

A note from the publisher

Thank you for reading this book. If you enjoyed it please do consider leaving a review on Amazon to help others find it too.

We hate typos. All of our books have been rigorously edited and proofread, but sometimes mistakes do slip through. If you have spotted a typo, please do let us know and we can get it amended within hours.

info@bloodhoundbooks.com

Printed in Great Britain
by Amazon

46440290R00182